Christmas with the Ops Room Girls

Vicki Beeby writes historical fiction about the friendships and loves of service women brought together by the Second World War. Her first job was as a civil engineer on a sewage treatment project, so things could only improve from there. Since then, she has worked as a maths teacher and education consultant before turning freelance to give herself more time to write. In her free time, when she can drag herself away from reading, she enjoys walking and travelling to far-off places by train. She lives in Shropshire in a house that doesn't contain nearly enough bookshelves.

Also by Vicki Beeby

The Women's Auxiliary Air Force

The Ops Room Girls
Christmas with the Ops Room Girls
Victory for the Ops Room Girls

VICKI BEEBY

Christmas
with the
Ops Room
Girls

1 CANELO

First published in the United Kingdom in 2020 by

Canelo
31 Helen Road
Oxford OX2 0DF
United Kingdom

A CIP catalogue record for this book is available from the British Library.

Print ISBN 978 1 80032 092 5
Ebook ISBN 978 1 80032 089 5

Look for more great books at www.canelo.co

Printed and bound in Great Britain by Clays Ltd, Elcograf S.p.A.

3

To my nieces, Emma and Elena.

Here's hoping you prefer it to 'Makeup on Mars'.

Chapter One

Aircraftwoman May Lidford found a strange sight as she drove her truck through the village of Amberton. A large bus was parked outside the village hall, blocking May's route to the RAF station, and a crowd of children was clustered around the doorway. They huddled together, hands on hats to secure them against the brisk autumn breeze, and all had large labels pinned to their jackets. Suitcases and canvas bags in varying degrees of repair stood at their feet.

'Oh, the poor things!' May hardly realised she had spoken aloud. These must be evacuees, sent away from their homes and families to keep them safe from the Blitz. May's attention was caught by one girl in particular who looked to be about ten years old. She stood at the edge of the group, clutching the hand of a little boy. Judging from the way she hovered over him, she was shielding him from being jostled by the older children. Her mousy brown hair might have been in a neat ponytail at the start of the day, but now straggly locks had come free and hung around a pale, thin face. She looked like she had outgrown her skirt a good six months ago, for the hem didn't quite reach her knees, and May could see it had been let down at least twice. It had been carefully sewn, though, and her clothes were clean and pressed. Clearly she came from a caring family, even if it was a poor one.

It was clear that it would be some time before the bus moved to allow her past, so she pulled up by the kerb. As she was returning from delivering spare Hurricane parts to a forward station near the coast and was now officially off duty, she felt no rush to get back. She propped her elbow on the steering wheel and watched as a tall, middle-aged woman with immaculately coiffed blonde hair marched around the boys and girls. May vaguely recognised her as Miss Foster, the headmistress of the village school. The woman read the labels pinned to each child's chest and referred to her clipboard. Then she would beckon to one of the waiting men or women who would lead the child away. May's heart went out to these poor children, who must be desperately missing their homes and families, and were now being housed by complete strangers.

'Not that some of them won't be better off away from their families,' May muttered, remembering her own Birmingham childhood. Leaving her father and brothers to fend for themselves while she joined the WAAF was the best decision she had ever made. Especially now she had such good friends in Jess and Evie. And Peter. As ever, her heart ached when she thought of kind, handsome Peter Travis. She had met him while he was stationed in the Amberton Operations Room, but now he had transferred to active duty at another fighter station. From what she had heard, his squadron was regularly sent to intercept bombing raids. She couldn't hear of an air raid without picturing Peter doing battle in the night skies, never able to relax until she got another letter from him. Only now could she truly appreciate how her friend Evie had suffered, working in Ops during the Battle of Britain, knowing exactly how much danger her young man was facing.

May was jolted from her reverie when Miss Foster approached the girl and her brother. She beckoned to one of the women still awaiting her charge. May recognised her as Mrs Evans, who ran the village haberdashery store. She was in her early forties and ran the business and household alone while her husband was away in the Navy. She was also an active member of the Women's Royal Voluntary Service and the parish council. Whenever May had bought anything from the haberdashery, she had always felt as though Mrs Evans was looking down at her, although whether that was because of her Birmingham accent or the fact that the WAAFs had a reputation of being 'fast', she couldn't tell.

Mrs Evans took the girl by the hand and moved to lead her away. When the little boy, who could be no more than five, clung to his sister and followed, she shook her head, lips pursed. Then she spoke to Miss Foster. May couldn't hear what was said, but from the body language it was clear she didn't want to take the boy as well. Miss Foster crouched down beside the boy and tried to prise him away from his sister. He clung all the more tightly. His round face crumpled.

Almost without realising it, May flung open her door and was halfway to the boy and girl before she hesitated. What could she do? She was a lowly WAAF, looked down upon by many of the so-called respectable village housewives. What influence did she have here?

The girl was now clinging to her brother, and May could hear what she was saying. 'Please, Miss, we've got to stay together. I promised!'

There was something in the girl's face – a weight of responsibility – that struck a chord with May, who remembered her own childhood, taking care of her frail mother and doing all the cooking and cleaning for her father and brothers. This was a girl with worries and responsibilities beyond her years. Even though she still had no idea how she could help, she knew she had to do what she could.

She hurried up to the children and crouched down. 'What are your names?' she asked.

The girl, whose label proclaimed her to be Margaret Hardy, looked up. A flare of hope lit her eyes. 'Are you a police lady? Please don't let them take my brother away from me. I promised I'd look after him.'

May's heart sank. 'No, I'm—'

But Mrs Evans cut across her. 'This is nothing to do with you.' She tugged the girl's arm. 'Say goodbye to your brother, Margaret, and come with me.'

The girl wrenched her arm free. 'No one calls me Margaret. I'm Peggy. And I'm not going anywhere without Davey.' She turned large brown eyes upon May in mute appeal.

May now regretted getting involved and giving Peggy false hope. She turned to Miss Foster. 'Isn't there some way they can be kept together?'

The headmistress shook her head. 'I can't force someone to take more children than they've been allocated.'

'Couldn't you take Davey, too, Mrs Evans?' May asked.

'Certainly not.' Mrs Evans fumbled in her pocket and pulled out an official-looking letter. She thrust it in May's face. 'I've been told to billet one child, and that's bad enough. Lord knows, it will be a struggle enough to feed one, the way things are going. I haven't got room for more.'

Peggy looked at May. 'What about you? Can't you take us?'

For a wild moment, May had a vision of arriving back at the Waafery with two children in tow and had to bite back a smile at the thought of Flight Officer Ellerby's reaction. She opened her mouth, but Mrs Evans got in first. 'Lord's sake, child. You can't go with her. She's a WAAF.' Judging from the expression on her face, she might have said 'hussy'. May shouldn't have been surprised by Mrs Evans' reaction, given that a vocal section of the villagers – mostly the more well-to-do women – had a poor opinion of the WAAFs. She'd heard the whispers when she'd been to the village: *consorting with men in the pub, of all places; I dread to think what they get up to; don't want them mixing with my daughters.* For the most part, May ignored them – they'd not been trapped in a shelter while bombs rained down. They'd not seen dead colleagues pulled from rubble mere feet from them. They didn't have to watch men who were their friends fly into danger four or five times a day, never knowing if they would come back. No. They just complained about the noise of the Hurricanes and the rowdiness of the men and women of RAF Amberton when they celebrated the fact that they had survived another day.

A hand fell on May's shoulder, making her jump. 'It's young May Lidford, isn't it?' came a booming voice that sounded familiar.

May twisted around to see the kind farmer who had helped her and Peter when their car had been strafed. His wife stood beside him with two boys. 'Mr and Mrs Bowes,' she said with a smile. 'It's good to see you.'

'Gathering up a few waifs and strays,' Mr Bowes said, indicating the boys with a jerk of his head.

Mrs Bowes stepped forward. 'Do you need any help, dear? We couldn't help noticing there seemed to be a bit of an argument.'

'Oh, it's just these children want to stay together.'

'Oh dear.' Mrs Bowes took in the scene, and a tiny frown puckered her brow when she glanced down at Mrs Evans' hand tight on Peggy's arm. 'I see.' She bent down to address Peggy. 'My dear, I wish we could take you both, but we've only got the one attic room for the children. It wouldn't be suitable.' Something about the way Mrs Bowes regarded Mrs Evans told May the two weren't friends, and May could sense real regret that Mrs Bowes was unable to billet Peggy. 'But we've got room for your brother, and we promise to take good care of him.' She turned to Davey. 'What's your name?'

A label with 'David Hardy' was pinned to Davey's chest, but Evie admired how Mrs Bowes addressed the boy with a smile to put him at his ease.

Loosening his grip on Peggy's hand, he said, 'Davey, Miss.'

'Well, then, Davey, do you know these two young lads here?' She pointed to the boys standing with Mr Bowes. One looked to be about Davey's age and the other a couple of years older. Both had fair, tufty hair, jackets buttoned up to the chin and shorts revealing knobbly knees and goose pimpled stick-like legs.

He nodded. 'Joe and Harry Black, Miss. Joe's my friend.'

'That's good, then. Now, Davey, my name is Mrs Bowes, and Mr Bowes and I have a farmhouse with a lovely attic room our own boys used to sleep in before they left home. There are plenty of toys and books. You can share it with Joe and Harry, and you'll still see your sister at school. If Mrs Evans agrees, Mr Bowes can even bring her to the farm after church on Sundays. How does that sound?'

'Don't think you'll be able to take the girl's rations,' Mrs Evans snapped, while Davey glanced between Peggy and the Blacks, clearly torn.

'I wouldn't dream of it,' Mrs Bowes replied, with an expression of distaste. 'It's cruel to separate the pair, so we should both do our bit to make them feel at home.' She addressed Davey. 'What do you think? Would you like to stay with us?'

Davey gave one last look at Peggy then let go of her hand and nodded. It was Peggy whose eyes welled with tears while Davey scampered to the Bowes' cart, chattering to Joe and admiring the handsome white shire horse in its harness.

'Come on, then, girl,' snapped Mrs Evans. 'I haven't got all day.'

May watched, feeling helpless as Peggy clutched her bag and the food parcel, craning her neck to peer over the top of her burden as she trotted after Mrs Evans. She was sure the girl would be miserable with Mrs Evans. She wished she could speak out, demand that Peggy live with someone else, but who would listen to a WAAF who had no right to be there? After a last glance at Peggy, she returned to the truck.

–

'You should have seen them, Jess. They looked so lost and frightened.' May stirred the milk in the saucepan too vigorously, slopping some upon the stove top. The smell of burning milk filled the kitchen. When she had returned to High Chalk House that evening, the manor requisitioned to house the WAAFs of RAF Amberton, she had raced straight to the room she now shared with Jess since their other friend, Evie, had left. To her relief, Jess was already there, having been given the night off from her duties in the Operations Room, and she was polishing the buttons on her tunic to a bright shine. May hadn't been able to get Peggy and Davey out of her mind, and the story had burst out of her before she'd even removed her greatcoat. She had been so worked up that in the end Jess had suggested making cocoa.

Jess Halloway waved May away. 'Better let me make the cocoa. If you spill any more there won't be enough to fill a thimble.'

The mention of thimbles reminded May of Mrs Evans and her haberdashery shop. She handed her friend the wooden spoon with a scowl then sat at the large wooden table and fiddled with a teaspoon. 'And I pity that poor girl who's got to live with Mrs Evans.'

Jess turned to face her, eyebrows raised. 'Mrs Evans who runs the haberdashery shop?' When May nodded, Jess's pretty face clouded. 'I 'ate to think of any evacuee in 'er care.' If May hadn't been so upset, she would have smiled at the way Jess's accent had slipped back into her native East End. Jess, who had been an actress before the war, usually spoke in the polished English heard on the BBC. 'I was in 'er shop the other day, buying a new darning needle,' Jess went on. 'She served two people before me, even though I'd got there first, and then she 'ad the cheek to talk to Mrs Stevens in a loud voice about all the WAAFs lowering the tone of the village.' Jess levered the lid off the tin beside her and spooned cocoa into the steaming milk with a heavy hand. Then she flung the spoon onto the counter with a clatter. 'The bloody cheek of the woman. We're the ones keeping her business going. I've 'alf a mind to use another 'aberdashery. Even if it does mean trailing all the way to Chichester.'

'You're lucky,' May said. 'You only have to see her in the shop. At least you're excused church parade.'

Jess poured the cocoa into two chipped enamel mugs, wrinkling her nose. While Jess stirred carefully measured amounts of sugar into each mug, May rose and quickly washed the milk pan and spoons. 'I can imagine 'er, though,' Jess muttered, moving to May's side to rinse the teaspoon. 'I bet she looks down that long nose at you all and talks to 'er neighbour in a stage whisper about painted Jezebels.' She glided across the kitchen with a snooty expression, her mouth turned down in such an uncanny impersonation of Mrs Evans that May smiled in spite of herself.

'You could be Mrs Evans herself if you weren't wearing such a bright shade of lipstick.'

Jess clapped her hands to her face, her scarlet lips stretched into a wide 'O' in mock horror. 'What? Sully herself with face paint like a cheap actress?'

'Anyway, last week she was even worse. After the service she said to the vicar's wife in a voice loud enough to be heard in Southampton that she was surprised at the dear vicar for welcoming sinners into the church.'

Jess snorted. 'I bet Mrs Grey gave her short shrift.'

'She did. She said that the vicar had to welcome sinners or the church would be standing empty every Sunday.' May smiled, remembering Mrs Evans' outraged expression at the implication that she, too, was a sinner.

However, the laughter faded in May's heart as she followed Jess up the steep staircase to the former school-room – now a cosy sitting room at the top of the house. Her thoughts returned to Peggy and how she was faring in Mrs Evans' care.

'I should have done something,' she said once they were curled in their armchairs, cradling their mugs. The WAAFs weren't supplied enough coal to light a fire in the schoolroom so the grate was empty. Instead the girls were wrapped in blankets they'd taken from their beds in the old nursery next door. 'It seems so cruel to separate a small boy from his sister.'

'But what could you have done? Mrs Evans was told she had to billet someone, so if she hadn't taken Peggy it would have been some other unfortunate child. There was nothing you could have done.'

'I know. It was none of my business.' Mrs Evans' words still rankled. Surely it was everyone's business if a child was suffering. Despite Jess's words, she couldn't help feeling she should have done something. If only she was confident like Jess, she could have persisted. Found another family able to take two children. Let Mrs Evans take one of the older girls.

Jess shook her head. 'I didn't say it was none of your business. Look, I don't get out and about as often as you, but I'll keep an eye out for the girl. Maybe there will be something we can do later on.'

Jess drew a letter from her pocket. 'Here's something to cheer you up.'

May brightened. 'A letter from Evie?'

'Not Evie. Peter. It's for you.' She handed the envelope to May. 'You'd already left when the post arrived, so I picked it up for you.'

May tore open the envelope, feeling a swell of gratitude at this sign that Peter was still alive and well. She'd been so afraid for him when he had left the relative safety of his job as senior controller in the Ops Room to retrain for operational flying. The last letter she had received told her he had passed and was being posted to Oldbourne near Chichester. It was a comfort to know he was nearby but it meant she now studied the casualty lists with growing dread. When Peter had asked if he could write to her, she had hesitated, not wanting to give him hope that she could ever accept his courtship. Although she couldn't imagine loving anyone else as deeply as she loved Peter, she didn't feel able to commit to him. Not when the only example she had of married life was her father's treatment of her mother.

Still, she was glad she had agreed they could write to each other. Although she couldn't commit to him, she couldn't face breaking off their relationship altogether. She always took great comfort from his letters and enjoyed sharing any simple news that would get past the censor. She quickly scanned the letter now, planning to study every word more thoroughly when she was alone. She'd hardly got past the opening lines when her heart gave a lurch.

'He's got a 48-hour pass,' she said to Jess, who had walked over to the mirror on the chimney breast and was tidying her hair. 'He wants to see me.'

'Well that's good, isn't it?' Jess's reflection stared at her, one perfectly pencilled eyebrow arched in enquiry.

'I… yes, of course.' She *did* look forward to seeing him. In fact, she felt quite jittery at the thought.

Jess clearly sensed her hesitation. She abandoned her hair, leaving one golden lock dangling over her cheek and knelt on the rug beside May's feet. 'May, I know you're afraid of ending up like your mother.' She took May's hand between both of her own. 'But Peter would never treat you badly. Trust me if you don't trust yourself – he's one of the good ones.'

May wished she could be more like Jess, who radiated confidence. Had she been born so sure of herself or was it something she had learned? 'I wish I could. Trust myself, I mean.'

'Course you can,' Jess said. 'It's obvious. Of all the WAAFs at Amberton, you picked me and Evie to be your friends. What better proof could you need that your instincts are spot-on?'

May gave a reluctant smile. 'It's not just that. I mean, I know Peter is the best man alive.' She felt a rush of giddiness as she remembered all the acts of kindness Peter had shown her – treating her to tea and cakes when she had been his driver; the way he had taken care of her after she'd been dug out of the bomb shelter when Amberton had been bombed; shielding her, putting himself between her and harm when they had been strafed by an enemy aircraft on his last day at Amberton. He was nothing like her father, who would have had no hesitation in using her mother as a human shield, May was sure.

'Then what is it?'

May swallowed. She had never put this into words before; it was something she *felt* but didn't know how to explain. 'My mother,' she said finally. 'My father treated her like dirt, but she never once said no to him. Never told him to make his own tea or pick up the clothes he'd just flung on the floor. He treated her like dirt,' May repeated, 'but she let him.'

The teasing expression had faded from Jess's face to be replaced by one of deep concern. 'You think... what – your mother *made* him be cruel to her?'

'Yes... no... oh, I don't know.' This was why she'd never tried explaining it before. In her heart she understood perfectly what she meant but that certainty crumbled to ashes the moment she tried to put it into words.

Then Jess's eyes widened. 'You think you're too much like your mother. That you can't stand up for yourself.'

May nodded. It wasn't the whole of it – it didn't fully explain her deep unease, but it was the closest she could get.

'It's not true,' Jess said. 'You're stronger than that.'

Hope flared. 'How do you know?'

'You escaped. Your father and brothers expected you to stay home forever, to wait on them hand and foot, but you left.'

May forced a smile. 'Perhaps.' But Jess was wrong. May had run away. She hadn't been strong enough to stand up for herself so she had run to the WAAF and hidden behind the uniform.

It was time she changed. She might not have been able to help the evacuees today, but it had shown her one thing: she needed to learn to speak up for herself.

'Jess, can you help me be more like you?'

'Why would you want to be like me?' To May's surprise, Jess looked faintly uneasy. 'You're lovely as you are.'

'But you're so confident. You can speak up for yourself. I need to be more like that.' She looked at her friend in hope.

Jess's face cleared. 'I know what might help.'

'What?' At this point, if Jess declared she should eat slugs every day, she would do it.

'Acting lessons. When I was an actress, I knew plenty of others who were so shy they wouldn't say boo to a goose in everyday life, but tell them they had to play Joan of Arc and suddenly they were transformed into a bold warrior-maid.'

'Joan of Arc,' May sighed. Now there was a woman who had spoken up. Then her heart quailed. 'But acting? You want me to stand up on stage in front of loads of people?'

'You could do it if you wanted.' Jess must have seen the terror in May's face. 'Don't worry, I didn't mean that. But you can learn techniques that would really help. Confidence is about how you feel inside, of course, but you'd be amazed how just changing the way you stand and breathe – *looking* like a confident person – can make you *feel* like one.'

'How?' May was sceptical.

Jess tilted her head to one side. 'I suppose it's the way other people react to you. Here. I'll show you.'

She stood up, turning her body half away from May. With hunched shoulders and arms hugged across her chest, she darted sideways glances at May, never meeting her gaze. 'May,' she said in a quavering voice, 'I think, maybe, acting lessons would help. I mean… only if you want to.'

May laughed despite herself. She could see where Jess was going, painful as it was to see this extreme caricature of herself. 'I'm not that bad. Am I?'

Jess unhunched herself. 'Course not. I was just making a point. Now watch.' She drew her body straight, her shoulders back and raised her chin. She turned so her body was facing May and met May's gaze with an unwavering look. She looked, in fact, more like Jess. 'Which person would you have more confidence in?'

'You, obviously.' May could see what Jess was getting at.

'Try it then.' Jess gestured to May to rise. 'Stand straight. No, not like that.' May had pulled herself to stand to attention as though on parade. 'I want to speak to you like a normal person and I can't do it while you're staring over the top of my head. Relax a bit more. Meet my gaze.'

'How can I stand straight and *not* look over your head?'

Jess laughed. 'May, you're tall but you're not a giant. Picture Alex talking to Evie. He's not all hunched up, is he?'

May thought about it for a moment and found that by relaxing her stance she could still meet Jess's gaze without slumping.

'I don't know what to do with my hands, though.' The trouble with having to concentrate on how she was holding her body was that she became painfully aware of her arms and hands. Her arms felt at least six feet long, all awkward angles and clumsy positioning.

Jess nodded. 'It's very hard to learn to use your hands and arms so the gestures look natural when you're acting. Just try holding them loosely by your sides. If you really don't know what to do with them, clasp your hands lightly in front of you.'

It was a while before Jess was satisfied. May kept hunching her shoulders or twisting her hands. 'That'll do for a start,' she said in the end. 'You look more confident when you stand like that, even if you don't feel it. You'll find people treat you differently, pay you more attention, if you're not trying to fade into the background.'

May wasn't sure she wanted people to pay her more attention; being head and shoulders taller than all the other women at RAF Amberton garnered her quite enough attention already. She held her tongue, though; Jess had a light of battle in her eyes that brooked no argument.

'What do you say?' Jess asked. 'Do you want me to give you acting lessons? Help you be more confident?'

'There's more?' May had thought this was it.

'Course there is. There's tons more to acting than learning how to stand.' Jess strode up and down as she spoke, as though delivering a lecture. 'There's movement, breathing, learning about different characters and how they react. And that's before you start learning how to speak, how to project your voice, how to get into another character's head and make people believe you're not May from Birmingham but Joan of Arc or Lady Bracknell or Juliet.'

May sank into her chair, her head spinning. When she'd first met Evie and Jess, she'd thought Evie the intelligent one, with her quick ability with maths. Now she thought Jess must be a genius if she'd learnt to do everything on that list. It seemed there was more to acting than learning lines and repeating them. 'But that would take years,' she said.

'It will take some work but it won't take as long as that. You can do it – I wouldn't suggest it otherwise.'

'And you won't make me perform in front of others?'

'Not unless you want to, though I think you could be good if you tried.'

May opened her mouth to protest, and Jess held up her hand. 'But no,' she said in reassuring tones, 'I won't make you do anything you don't want. This is just between you and me to give you a way of dealing with the Mrs Evanses of this world.'

May glanced at Peter's letter, lying on the rug beside the chair. Then she thought of Mrs Evans with her 'It's none of your business' and May promised herself that was the last time she would let anyone ignore her opinion. 'You're on,' she said. Although she dreaded to think what she was letting herself in for. Still, whatever Jess made her do, it would be worth it if she could finally learn to stand up to people like Mrs Evans.

'Excellent,' said Jess, flinging herself into her armchair with a sigh. 'Now, your first homework—'

'Homework?' The word burst out in a wail. May thought of Evie, poring over her maths textbooks. 'I didn't agree to homework.'

'It's nothing difficult.' Jess tucked her feet under her. 'Your homework is in two parts. First I want you to make the conscious effort to stand tall. The more you practise, the more natural it'll feel.'

May nodded, relaxing. She would have done that anyway.

'And secondly, I want you to watch people.'

'Just watch them? I do that anyway.' Whenever they were in a large group – in the pub, for example – she never felt able to speak up but she always enjoyed watching people and listening.

'That's why I think you'll be good at this. All I want you to do is study people – their posture, their gestures, that sort of thing – and think about what that tells you about how they're feeling.'

'I can do that.' It actually sounded quite fun.

'I know. You're going to be brilliant.' Jess nodded at the letter. 'Now, what are you going to do about Peter? Are you going to have that date?'

Chapter Two

It wasn't a date, May told herself as she inspected her face in the mirror two days later. Peter had been at pains to stress in his letter that he didn't want to put any pressure on her. They would just meet as friends. It was that reassurance that had encouraged her to agree.

She glanced at her watch. Quarter to ten. She'd have to leave in ten minutes if she was going to make it to the station in time. She blew out a breath to calm the butterflies in her stomach and tried to arrange her hair. She wished Jess was there; she could work magic with hair, styling May's chestnut locks into elegant, gleaming waves. But Jess was still on duty, having made May swear to tell her all about the date – no, May corrected herself, just two friends meeting – when she got back. Feeling very daring, she picked up the lipstick Jess had persuaded her to buy in Brighton what felt like a lifetime ago. Until now, she had only worn it at Jess's urging, but she felt she ought to make an effort for Peter. She applied it then examined the effect in the mirror. She had to admit Jess had chosen the perfect shade for her: a deep garnet that seemed to make her pale face glow.

A sudden wave of panic washed over her. Was this too much? She and Peter were only meeting as friends. Would he read too much into the meeting if she wore lipstick and – she glanced at the tiny cut-glass bottle beside her

– perfume? Then she remembered Mrs Evans and her low opinion of the WAAFs. Well, she would show the likes of Mrs Evans. She picked up the perfume and dabbed a drop behind each ear, enjoying the light floral scent. She wasn't going to be cowed into Mrs Evans' idea of so-called respectable behaviour. The shopkeeper looked down her nose at the WAAFs who wore make-up and went to the pub, but at least those WAAFs had a good heart and were serving their country. May had half a mind to raid Jess's supply of cosmetics and really go to town, then cycle past Mrs Evans' shop made up with face powder, blusher and mascara. She gave a half-laugh. Don't be silly, Lidford. You've got no idea how to apply it. You'll look like a three-year-old who's got into her mother's make-up. After one last look in the mirror, she grabbed her gas mask and left.

They had arranged to meet at the railway station at Chichester. As her branch-line train rolled into the station, she peered through the grimy window, searching for signs of Peter. Her hands trembled and she fumbled with the door latch before she finally got the door open and jumped down. Crowds of people lined the platform but it was hard to make out faces through the rolling clouds of steam. The anxiety that she had managed to suppress during the short journey now resurfaced. What if he had changed? What if she couldn't think of anything to say?

A light touch on her elbow made her jump and she turned to find herself gazing into Peter's smiling face. His dark red hair was ruffled from the chill wind that whipped up the dust along the platform, but May didn't feel the cold of it. She experienced the same feelings of warmth and homecoming she always associated with Peter, and some of her fears subsided.

'May,' he said. Heat crept up her face at the tone of pleasure, almost wonder, that he managed to put into that single syllable. 'It's wonderful to see you.'

There was an awkward moment when he leaned forward as though to kiss her cheek but lurched back. Then they were shaking hands as though this was a formal meeting. May examined his features carefully, looking for signs of injury or strain and was relieved to see he appeared to be in good health.

'Thanks for inviting me.' She cringed inwardly. She'd never been awkward in Peter's company before. Just as when Jess had shown her how to stand straight, her arms felt longer than usual and they seemed to have developed at least two extra elbows. Her right palm still burned from Peter's clasp. Part of her wished she could put her hand in his again, but that wasn't what friends did. And this was definitely not a date. However, when they walked out of the station and turned towards the town centre, Peter offered her his arm. Friends could walk arm in arm. She slipped her hand into the warm gap between his elbow and body feeling giddy.

If only she could think of something to say. Why did she feel so awkward? She had never been stuck for words around him before. Of course, most of the time they had spent together at Amberton had been in the course of duty, when she had driven him to the station or meetings at other RAF stations. Sometimes, when there had been time to spare, he had treated her to tea at a cafe. They had also met at the pub and even danced together at the Midsummer dance, but they had always been with other friends. This felt different. This time the only purpose of their meeting was to spend time together. She could almost hear Jess saying, 'Sounds like a date to me.'

Her inability to utter any more than banal observations on the weather and her journey continued until they happened to walk past a tea room. Its windows were steamed up, but she could glimpse a cosy interior with pretty teacups and an inviting display of cakes and buns on the counter.

'Would you like to go in?' Peter asked. 'It's getting parky out here, and I could do with a cuppa to warm me up.' He grinned suddenly. 'And I have to admit, I've missed watching you enjoy a Chelsea bun.'

It was as though the weeks had rolled back to the ease she had felt with him before, when he had teased her over her enjoyment of the sticky buns. May relaxed. 'I'd like that,' she said.

They sat at a table in the window and a stout middle-aged woman in a smart black dress and starched apron arrived to take their order. 'We've no coffee, I'm afraid,' she began with no preamble.

'Tea would be fine,' Peter said, with an enquiring look at May, who nodded. 'And I'd like a rock cake. What would you like, May – a Chelsea bun?' There was a twinkle in his eye that elicited another smile from May, and she nodded again.

May looked around the tearoom at the other customers while they waited for their order. Most were older women – housewives taking a break from the stress of queuing for much-needed food, May guessed. There was a younger couple in a corner, sitting with their heads close together. The man wore the uniform of a naval officer.

May watched them for a while then said, 'Jess is giving me acting lessons.'

Peter's brows shot up. 'Practising for a career on the stage after the war?'

May giggled and explained a little of what had led her to ask for Jess's help. She described her encounter with Peggy and Mrs Evans while carefully avoiding any mention of Peter. 'Jess thought acting lessons would help with my confidence,' she finished.

Peter frowned. 'You've always seemed confident in your job,' he said.

The waitress returned with their tea and cakes, and May thanked her before replying, 'That's because I know what I'm doing. I could drive before I joined the WAAF. Once I'd learned my way around the area, it was easy.'

'I never knew you could drive before you joined up. When did you learn?'

'My father made sure I could drive.' May didn't want to spoil her precious few hours with Peter with thoughts of her father, so she hurried on. 'Anyway, the reason I mentioned the acting lessons was because Jess gave me homework.' She picked up the pot and began to pour.

'Please tell me you're not going to stand on the table and give one of Lady Macbeth's speeches.'

May slopped tea into her saucer and hastily put down the pot. 'No fear. My acting lessons are just between me and Jess.' She poured the tea from the saucer into the cup then kept that for herself and poured a fresh cup for Peter. 'No. Jess told me to study other people's body language to work out what they're feeling.'

Peter's face cleared. 'So that's why you were staring at the couple in the corner.' He shot them a glance then returned his attention to May and lowered his voice, meaning May had to lean closer to hear. So close she caught the scent of soap and saw the light catch the reddish glint of stubble along his jaw. She had a sudden, shocking image of pressing her lips to it. She clapped her fingers to her mouth and shot Peter an uneasy glance. The image had been so vivid, she could swear her lips burned from the scrape of stubble. She half-expected Peter to raise a hand to his jaw and look round to see who had kissed him.

'I was trying to work out if they are happy to be reunited after a time apart, or if this is their last day before he goes to sea,' May said, more in an attempt to get Peter to look away from her. She was sure her face must be scarlet.

Peter, annoyingly, didn't look away. 'It's their last day together,' he said.

'How do you know?'

'The way he's looking at her, like he's trying to photograph every inch of her face, memorise every smile and gesture.'

May studied them surreptitiously, but soon realised she could have produced a pair of binoculars and given Peter a loud commentary on their appearance for all the notice they would have taken. There was none of the lightness she had seen in Peter's face when they had met at the station. The woman was smiling, but there was a brittleness to her expression, perhaps in the way her brows were drawn together, that indicated she was trying to put on a brave face for her companion but was on the brink of breaking down. And Peter was right: there was an intensity in the way the man was looking at the woman as though he was storing up memories against the coming famine.

It struck her then that this could be the last time she saw Peter. Her gaze snapped back to him.

Peter must have read her expression, for he gave a crooked smile. 'Don't,' he said. 'You won't get rid of me that easily. Let's just enjoy the day and not let the war intrude. Tell me more about the wicked Mrs Evans.'

May launched into the full tale, grateful for an excuse to change the subject. 'She made me feel like a piece of dirt,' she concluded.

Peter nodded. 'I don't blame you for worrying about the poor girl,' he said.

'I know. Isn't it bad enough they have to be separated from their parents without having to be torn away from their siblings as well?'

She cut a piece of her Chelsea bun and popped it in her mouth, but it was flavourless and stuck to the roof of her mouth. The baker must have scrimped on the ingredients.

'How does it taste?' Peter asked, cutting his own rock cake in half.

She forced a smile. 'Lovely.'

Peter added a sugar lump into his cup and stirred, regarding her thoughtfully. 'I know how worried you must be for the girl – Peggy, is that her name?' When May nodded he continued. 'But there really is nothing you can do about it. The housing of evacuees is nothing to do with the WAAF, or any of the services. You'll get yourself into trouble if you try to interfere in village affairs.'

May forced herself to swallow another piece of the tasteless bun then took a sip of tea to wash it down. The dough seemed to stick in her throat no matter how much tea she drank. She knew Peter was right, and couldn't blame him for warning her to stay out of trouble, but she'd hoped he would have an idea of a way to resolve the problem.

She pushed aside her disappointment and asked how he was finding his new squadron.

Peter's face brightened and they passed the rest of the time in the tearoom discussing the various personalities at Oldbourne and Amberton. But although it was good to be with Peter again, his warning against interference had tarnished her enjoyment.

—

Their day out was not going well. As they wandered around the outside of the cathedral, Peter watched May while she craned her neck to admire the spire. It was always difficult to get May to talk about herself, so her quietness wasn't surprising. Still, she seemed particularly withdrawn.

A whole day alone together had been a mistake. It was too much. She must be worried he would try persuading her to a commitment she wasn't ready for. He should have arranged to meet her in the Horse and Groom, somewhere familiar in the company of their friends. She would have been more relaxed then.

Before he had left Amberton, he had made no secret of his feelings for her. He was sure that deep down she did love him in return, but for some reason she believed herself to be unlovable. From oblique references she had let him know it was to do with the life she'd had before joining the WAAF. One day he would find out, and then woe betide the person who had made the most beautiful woman in the world believe she was graceless and ugly. He'd watched her blossom in the WAAF, become more confident in her abilities, had seen how Jess and Evie's friendship had encouraged her to believe she wasn't entirely worthless, but there was still a long way to go. He hadn't pressured her when it had been clear she wasn't able to return his feelings. All he could do was keep telling her how much he admired and valued her and prayed she would one day believe him.

Once they had completed a circuit of the cathedral's exterior, May faced him, her dark brown eyes serious. 'Can we go inside? I... I'd like to light a candle.'

They went in and walked down the aisle, breathing the mingled scent of candle wax, incense and old books. Their footsteps echoed in the empty vastness. Around them he could hear soft whispers from people hunched in the pews. He guessed they were offering up prayers for absent loved ones in a scene that must be repeated in every church across Britain and the whole of Europe.

They found the votive candles at the shrine of Saint Richard. Tier upon tier of flickering flames, fragile as the hopes they represented, cast a golden glow upon May's face as she dropped a coin into the box and lit a candle from the flame of another. She placed it in the pricket stand and then stepped back, head bowed as she contemplated the candle flame. Peter hadn't intended to light a candle himself, but as he watched, he realised how so many of his own hopes for the future centred around her. If he could have just one prayer granted it would be for her to be freed from whatever it was in her past that had stripped her of her confidence. He fumbled in his pocket and pulled out a ten bob note, stuffing it awkwardly in the slot intended for coins. Then he lit his own candle and left it there, adding it to the hundreds of prayers already offered.

Whether it was an answer to prayer or just the damp chilly air clearing his mind, he didn't know, but he realised his mistake the moment they left the cathedral. He shouldn't have discouraged May from talking about the evacuees. It was important to her and he had told her it was none of her business. It had come out more abruptly than he'd intended, but he knew the risks of sticking one's neck out in the RAF and presumed it was the same in the WAAF. He had done well and come a long way from the days when he'd been a sergeant pilot before the war. When he'd gained his commission, it had been a struggle to fit in with the mysterious, unspoken rules of conduct an officer was expected to follow. He'd learned to keep his head down and not offer opinions that might be unpopular. May was set for a successful career in the WAAF. He didn't want her falling foul of the senior officers. The very people who could make or break her.

They walked towards the cross and Peter groped for a way to undo his earlier error. 'I've been thinking about those evacuee children you were telling me about,' he said, pleased when May's face brightened. 'What happened to the boy – Peggy's brother?'

May tightened her grip on Peter's arm. 'That's the only good thing that came out of it all,' she said. 'Mr and Mrs Bowes took him in, with two other boys.'

Bowes. The name sounded familiar, although he couldn't remember where from at first. Then he recalled the kind farmer and his wife who had helped them when their car had been destroyed in an enemy attack. 'Well he'll be happy there,' he said. 'He'll have a fine time with all that space to run around in.'

'I know. And Mr and Mrs Bowes are lovely. I know they'll take good care of him.'

And then Peter saw how he could make up for his earlier blunder. 'Do you have any time off tomorrow?' he asked.

'I actually have a 48-hour pass,' May replied. Her cheeks turned pink. 'When I requested a 24-hour pass, my flight officer said I was overdue for leave and gave me an extra day.' She was starting to gabble so Peter rescued her.

'Well that's fine. It occurred to me that I should visit the Bowes to thank them for their help. Would you like to come with me? It's Saturday tomorrow, so that evacuee lad of yours will be there. You can check up on him, maybe offer to take a message to his sister. Then we can have lunch somewhere before I have to get back to Oldbourne.'

May's glowing face told him it was exactly the right thing to do. 'That would be wonderful. It would help Peggy to hear news of Davey. I mean, they go to the same school, but I don't know how much they see of each other.' Then she frowned. 'But how would we get there? I won't be able to get a car.'

'Leave it to me. I'll sort something out. I'll pick you up from the Waafery at ten.' Even if he had to call in all the favours he'd ever been owed, he would do whatever it took to undo the mess he'd made of today and make tomorrow a success.

—

At five to ten the next morning, Jess came flying into the schoolroom, where May was arranging her hair at the mirror. 'Hurry up, he's here. And guess what he's driving?'

'He has a car?' May turned from the mirror, the right half of her hair neatly pinned, an unpinned lock still dangling upon her left shoulder.

'Not a car. A motorbike.' Jess gave May a broad grin. 'The perfect excuse to snuggle up to him.' She took the hairbrush from May and expertly finished May's hairstyle. 'There. You'll knock him dead. Now go on. Don't keep him waiting.'

May snatched up her cap and greatcoat and was about to leave when Jess called her back. 'I nearly forgot. I've had the best idea. Meet me at the Horse and Groom this evening. There's loads to discuss.' Then she shooed May out, refusing to be drawn into an explanation.

The moment she stepped outside, the sight of Peter beside a shiny red motorbike drove all other thoughts from her mind. 'Where did you get that?'

'Isn't it a beauty? It's a Triumph Speed Twin. Only borrowed, I'm afraid. A friend of mine at Oldbourne owed me a favour.'

May eyed it with trepidation. Thankfully it wasn't raining; she didn't want to turn up at the Bowes' farm looking like a drowned rat. She could only hope her new uniform greatcoat would keep out the cold. Would there be enough room for them both? The saddle didn't look very large. It was going to be exactly as Jess had said: she would have to sit very close behind Peter.

Peter must have seen her nervousness because he gave a reassuring smile. 'Don't worry. I'll get us there safe and sound. It's only a couple of miles, and I'll keep the speed down.'

There was no getting out of this if she wanted to check on Davey. The memory of the boy's tear-streaked face made up her mind. After tying her scarf around her head to keep her hair in place, then tucking her cap in her pocket to avoid it being blown away, she climbed into the saddle behind Peter.

Peter glanced over his shoulder, his eyes bright. 'This makes a change from you being the one to drive me around the countryside. Hold on, and lean into the corners.' He kicked the starter, balancing on his prosthetic leg a little awkwardly, and then they were off.

May started the journey holding on to the back of the saddle but the moment they took the first bend, she forgot her reservations and wrapped her arms around Peter's waist, resting her cheek against his shoulder. There was something solid and reassuring about the breadth of his shoulders; her fear melted away and she was left with a feeling of exhilaration, watching the hedgerows whiz by at a far faster speed than she'd ever achieved on a bicycle. The wind rushed in her ears, whipping her cheeks and bringing tears to her eyes. The howl of the engine ripped into the peaceful air, scattering flocks of starlings from the bushes, chattering their alarm. May glanced at the speed dial over Peter's shoulder and was surprised to see they were only going at twenty miles per hour. She had been convinced they had been flying along at racing speeds. Peter had been true to his word and taken great care. Yet again it made her wonder why she was so reluctant to agree to start courting. He had shown her time and again he would take care of her, could always be trusted. What was making her hesitate?

Before long they had reached the humpbacked bridge that had been the scene of the attack a few weeks ago. The only sign of it now was a patch of darker tarmac where the bomb crater had been filled in and fresh stonework on one of the walls where the moss hadn't yet had time to take hold. May could only wish that other scars from the war could be so easily mended. She shuddered, remembering reports of the bombings in London, with scores of lives lost. As awful as it must be for Peggy and Davey and others like them to be separated from their families, at least they were somewhere relatively safe, where they weren't facing nightly bomb attacks.

As if summoned by her thoughts, Davey himself dashed into sight in the orchard they were passing. He was giggling, his unbuttoned coat billowing behind him as he ran, accompanied by two other boys. They seemed to be chasing falling leaves. All were dishevelled, muddy and glowing with happiness.

Peter swung into the yard beside the farmhouse and held the bike steady for May to dismount. Immediately she missed the warmth of his body.

'I take it one of those scamps is the lad we've come to see?' he said, propping the bike on its stand. 'They look happy enough.'

'They do.' May immediately made up her mind to find an excuse to visit the haberdashery later that afternoon to see if she could see Peggy. The girl would be glad of news from her brother, she was sure.

'Well, if that isn't a turn-up for the books,' Mrs Bowes said when she opened the door to them a moment later. 'I was only saying to Mr Bowes the other day: *I wonder how that nice young pilot is getting on*, I says. And here you are. And Miss Lidford, too. Come in, come in.'

The last time they had been there they had been taken to the kitchen, which seemed to be the centre of life in the farmhouse. This time Mrs Bowes led them to a large but cosy parlour. A collection of armchairs in varying states of wear was arranged around the fireplace. A distinct smell of applewood drifted from the crackling log fire. The large windows offered a view of the apple trees, glowing bronze under the autumn sunlight. The boys were still there, darting from tree to tree.

'What a wonderful playground,' Peter said with a nod at the orchard. 'I see your household has expanded since I was last here.'

'And we would have taken more if we could,' Mrs Bowes replied. 'Miss Lidford knows what I mean. A crying shame it is, to separate siblings. But we've already got land girls billeted in our other two bedrooms, so there's only the attic room left for the boys. You'll stay for lunch, won't you?'

May hesitated, with a glance at Peter. 'Well, we wouldn't want to impose. You must be finding it hard to stretch your provisions to feed three hungry boys.' She wished she'd thought to bring a gift with her. With food rationing in place, unexpected visitors couldn't be easy to cater for.

Mrs Bowes waved her objections away. 'Don't you be worrying about that. We can't offer you the spread we would have given you before the war, but there's plenty to go round.'

Peter was fumbling in the canvas bag he carried. He'd had it slung across his shoulders on the motorbike. 'Then we'd love to accept, Mrs Bowes. I brought you a couple of gifts as a thank-you for taking care of us so well last time.' He produced a cake tin. 'This is one of my mother's famous fruit cakes. She insisted on baking it when she heard I was coming here. And this is from me.' He pulled out four bars of chocolate. 'I'm sure the boys will enjoy these.'

'There was no need to bring anything, but thank you.'

After a while, Mrs Bowes excused herself to fetch some tea. May looked at Peter curiously. 'Does your mother live near here?' She'd thought she knew Peter so well, but she realised they usually only spoke of their life in the service. May had never spoken of her family and as Peter hadn't spoken of his, she'd assumed his parents had died. The only thing she knew of his past, apart from the accident that had cost him his leg, was that he, too, had come from a working-class family. She hadn't asked him about his background because talk of Peter's family would inevitably turn to questions about her own. She really didn't want to think about them, let alone talk about them. The only people she'd spoken to about her family were Jess and Evie. Even then, she'd shared the bare minimum.

'My parents live in Portsmouth,' Peter replied. 'Have I never told you?' When she shook her head, he went on, 'My father works at the docks. I stayed with them last night. I don't get to see them much, and I wanted to reassure myself they were coping with the air raids.'

'Has it been bad there?'

'They've escaped the worst, thank God.'

Mrs Bowes came back then, so May was forced to quell her curiosity. They chatted for a while until the boys came running in from the orchard. Mrs Bowes ordered them to wash and change before lunch. By the time they trooped into the kitchen, where lunch was laid, they looked clean and tidy, as though they didn't know the meaning of the word 'mud'.

When Davey recognised May, and learned she was from RAF Amberton, his face lit up. 'My sister lives in Amberton,' he said.

'I know. I thought I could take a message to her from you if you'd like.'

'Yes please!' He bounced on his chair, making it creak ominously. 'Auntie Marge, can I fetch the picture I made for Peggy?'

Mrs Bowes looked around from where she had been inspecting something in the oven. 'Go on with you then. This pie could do with another five minutes.' She turned to one of the other boys. 'Run out into the barn and tell Uncle Ned lunch is ready.' She saw May's look of surprise and laughed. 'We couldn't have the lads calling us Mr and Mrs Bowes. Hardly the way to make them feel at home.'

Davey dashed away and there came the sound of thundering feet on the stairs. A minute later he was back, bearing a creased square of paper. On it was a drawing of a house with four windows and a door. A corkscrew of smoke coiled out of the chimney.

'That's lovely,' said May, taking the paper. 'What are those in the garden – cows?'

'Chickens.'

'Oh, of course. I can see their beaks.' She turned the paper over and saw the words, 'Scotch Oatmeal' printed in bold letters. Beside the label, pencilled in large, carefully formed letters was: *Too Peggy. Wiv love throm Davey.* 'Did you write that all by yourself? You're very clever.' The little boy glowed as she slipped the paper in her pocket. 'I have to visit Mrs Evans' shop this afternoon, so I'll make sure Peggy gets it. It's going to make her so happy.'

After a delicious lunch of chicken and vegetable pie – more vegetable than chicken but nonetheless delicious for it – with potatoes and yet more vegetables, Peter announced regretfully that they must be off.

Mrs Bowes took May aside as she helped her on with her coat, out of earshot of Davey and the other boys. 'I'm so glad you're going to see Davey's sister. I don't like to tell tales, but Mrs Evans is a hard woman. I wasn't happy when I saw she was taking in an evacuee. Not happy at all.'

There wasn't time for her to explain, but May's uneasiness increased. She and Jess were going to pay a visit to Mrs Evans, and she was going to do her utmost to see Peggy.

Chapter Three

Jess was still on duty when May got back to High Chalk House. May paced the schoolroom, waiting for her return. She hoped Jess wouldn't mind being dragged to the haberdashery after a long stretch in the Operations Room, because she needed her friend's moral support.

Jess breezed in soon after, humming a happy song under her breath. There was a glow around her that made May wonder if she had been with Milan, the Czech pilot who was clearly smitten with Jess. Jess had frequently declared herself to be enjoying nothing but a harmless flirtation, but May had occasionally caught a yearning expression on her face when she looked at Milan that said otherwise.

'I've got the best news,' Jess began. 'I'll tell you all about it at the pub. Are you ready?'

May never ceased to be amazed at Jess's boundless energy. She followed Jess into their shared bedroom to collect her cap and coat, while Jess applied a fresh coat of scarlet lipstick. 'Do you mind if we go to the haberdashery on the way?'

'Why, so you can enjoy being called a painted Jezebel?' Jess blotted her lipstick then adjusted the seams on her definitely non-regulation stockings. But she frowned when May explained about Davey's picture and what Mrs Bowes had said at the end of the visit. 'This calls for full make-up.' She picked up her compact. 'If I'm going to be called a scarlet woman, I may as well look the part.'

Watching Jess apply powder and full eye make-up that enhanced rather than hid her bright blue eyes, May couldn't help admiring Jess's spirit. She had worn lipstick to the Bowes' farm but had wiped her face clean after getting back, not wanting to give Mrs Evans any reason for criticism. Part of her wished she could display some of Jess's defiance but she knew she would never dare.

Once Jess was satisfied, they collected their bicycles and set off for the village at a sedate pace so as not to mess up their hair. Jess was still fuming at Mrs Evans. 'Honestly, you'd think she'd be grateful for the work we do, putting our lives on hold for the war effort. If she'd had to go through half of what we have in the past few months, she'd be changing her tune.' Jess broke off as they navigated a series of water-filled pot holes. Ahead, the flint tower of All Saints Church could be seen above the hedgerows, marking the centre of Amberton. May's stomach tightened at the prospect of having to face Mrs Evans. At least Jess was with her. For Peggy's sake, she liked to think she would have faced Mrs Evans alone if necessary, but it was so much easier with company.

All too soon they arrived at the centre of the village. May usually enjoyed visiting the pretty village with its thatched cottages, flint walls and winding lanes with quaint shops, however this time she would be glad to escape to the snug of the Horse and Groom to learn Jess's mysterious good news. They propped their bikes outside Evans' Haberdashery. Jess peered into the diamond-paned bay window, ignoring the display of needlepoint cushions and embroidery threads, using the glass as a mirror while she smoothed an errant lock of golden hair into place.

'Let me do the talking at first,' she told May. 'By the time I've finished, you'll look so pure and innocent in comparison, she'll do anything you ask. Now, remember our first lesson: stand tall and look confident even if you don't feel it.'

May privately thought that Mrs Evans would look down on the Virgin Mary herself if she walked into the shop in a WAAF's uniform, but she kept her mouth shut and followed Jess. Despite Jess's instructions, she could feel her shoulders hunching; her lifelong habit of trying to look invisible was too hard to break after just one lesson.

The vicar's wife was being served when they walked in, the bell above the door jingling to announce their arrival. They hovered by the door, examining a display of thimbles while Mrs Evans fawned over Mrs Grey in an ingratiating tone. When Mrs Grey had finished, choosing a length of woollen cloth to make skirts for the two evacuee girls in her care, she turned and smiled at May and Jess. 'How wonderful to see you both,' she said. 'It really brightens up the place to see the WAAFs in their smart uniforms, don't you think, Mrs Evans?'

Mrs Evans muttered something unintelligible.

Mrs Grey turned to May. 'I know I've seen you in church.' She paused. 'May Lidford, am I right?'

'That's right.' May was stunned how Mrs Grey could remember her name from the ranks of WAAFs who attended church parade most Sundays. Though, on reflection, she realised she must stand out, being taller than most of the congregation.

Then Mrs Grey frowned at Jess. 'I think I've seen you once or twice, but I'm afraid I can't remember your name.'

'Jess Halloway.' Jess shook Mrs Grey's proffered hand. May couldn't resist shooting a glance at Mrs Evans, who looked furious that the vicar's wife should be paying notice to two WAAFs. 'I can't attend church often because I'm usually on duty.'

'I do understand. I do so admire you girls for all you're doing.' Mrs Grey graced them with a genuine smile. 'Well, I must be off.' She departed to the accompaniment of the jingling bell.

The moment the door closed behind Mrs Grey, Jess strode up to the counter. 'I'd like some strong cotton to match my uniform, please.' She twitched aside her coat and pointed to her skirt. 'I want to shorten the hemline. At the moment I'm not showing nearly enough leg.'

May had to imagine she was on parade with Flight Officer Ellerby glaring at her to stop her laughing out loud at Mrs Evans' outraged expression.

'Well, really,' was the only thing the shopkeeper said. Shaking her head, she picked out a reel of cotton that was a good match for the RAF blue worn by the WAAFs. Although Mrs Evans didn't approve of WAAFs, it didn't seem to stop her from stocking plenty of thread the right colour for their uniforms. 'Is there anything else I can get you?'

When Jess said with a sweet smile that that was all, Mrs Evans wrapped the cotton in brown paper and rang the amount up on the till. Jess handed over the money then stepped aside for May. May approached the counter full of trepidation. She knew Jess's plan had been to make May seem saint-like in comparison, but as far as May could see, all it had achieved was to confirm Mrs Evans' worst suspicions of WAAFs.

'Can I see Peggy, please, Mrs Evans?' May asked. She made a conscious effort to keep her back straight as Jess had shown her.

Mrs Evans didn't look impressed. 'What for?'

'I've got a letter from her brother. He asked me to deliver it.'

Mrs Evans stuck out a bony arm. The electric light glinted upon a thin gold chain around her wrist. 'Give it to me. I'll take it.'

May hesitated. This hadn't been her plan at all. Mrs Evans lived above the shop, and May had hoped she would let her into her flat to see Peggy. She certainly didn't want to hand the tatty piece of paper to Mrs Evans, as she suspected it would end up in the waste paper basket and not find its way into Peggy's hands at all.

If Jess hadn't been there, lending her silent support, May would probably have handed over the message and fled, but taking courage from Jess, she said, 'He wanted me to give it to her in person.' She wished her voice didn't tremble so badly. Jess would have looked her in the eye and made her request in confident tones that expected no refusal, not squeaked like an apologetic mouse. She would definitely have to continue with her acting lessons. Half of her wished Jess would speak up on her behalf, but after her performance with the skirt, she doubted that would help matters.

'Please,' she said. 'It won't take long.'

'Oh, very well,' said Mrs Evans. She turned to the door behind the counter that must lead into the stock room and the living area. May went to follow her when Mrs Evans turned on her. She had to crane her neck to look May in the eye, yet still managed to give the impression she was looking down on her. 'Wait here, if you please. I won't have the likes of you in my flat.' She disappeared through the door, closing it firmly behind her.

'Cow,' Jess muttered. 'Probably worried you'll see her pointed hat and broomstick.'

Before May could beg her to keep her voice down, the door opened again and Mrs Evans appeared, ushering Peggy into the shop. When May had last seen her, Peggy had worn her hair in a messy pony tail. Now it was arranged in two plaits dangling down to her shoulders, braided so tightly May was sure they must pull her scalp painfully. Her hair was parted in the centre in a line that had been combed with engineering precision. She came to stand before May, the corners of her mouth pulled down in a scowl. The only flaw in her mask of rebellion was a slight reddening around the eyes.

'I don't know if you remember me, but—'

'You're the lady who wouldn't take me and my brother.'

'Quiet. It's rude to interrupt,' Mrs Evans snapped. Then she put her hands on her hips and glared at May. 'Well, hand it over. I've got work to do.'

May exchanged a helpless glance with Jess. With Mrs Evans hovering behind them, listening to every word, there was no chance of encouraging Peggy to reveal how she truly fared.

Even if she did, it would make no difference, a tiny voice said in the back of her mind. *If Peggy says Mrs Evans is treating her badly, what can you do?*

She forced a smile and pulled the paper from her pocket. 'I saw your brother this morning,' she said. 'He did this for you and I promised to give it to you.'

Peggy's face brightened and she took the drawing, the corners of her mouth tilting upwards when she read the message on the back.

'Well, girl, where are your manners?'

The light faded from Peggy's face. 'Sorry, Mrs Evans.' She craned her neck to speak to May. 'Thank you, Miss.'

Before May could say anything else, Mrs Evans clamped a hand on Peggy's shoulder and steered her towards the back of the shop. However, when she reached the door, Peggy wriggled free and peered back at May. 'How is he, Miss?'

'He's really happy, Peggy. Mr and Mrs Bowes are very kind.' It was all she had time for before Mrs Evans had pushed the girl through the door and slammed it shut.

–

'What an evil woman,' Jess growled as they wheeled their bikes to the Horse and Groom. 'I knew I didn't like 'er, but I never dreamt she could be so nasty to a child.'

'I can't bear to think what life is like for her,' May said. 'Did you hear how Mrs Evans spoke to her? Like she was a piece of dirt?' Her indignation made her unusually talkative. 'And Peggy has to call her Mrs Evans! Davey and the other boys called Mrs Bowes Auntie. I mean, it's sad that they have to be separated from their mothers, but at least Mrs Bowes is treating them with love and kindness, and letting them treat her house like their home.'

'Anyway,' said Jess as they parked their bikes outside the Horse and Groom, 'let's forget about Mrs Evans. We can't do anything about her, and I've been dying to tell you my news all day.'

When they were seated at a table in the snug, half pints of shandy beside them, May made an effort to take an interest in Jess's news. After all, Jess was right: there was nothing she could do about Peggy at the moment. However, she made a mental promise to look out for her whenever she was out and about in the village and see if she could snatch a chance to talk to her privately and find out how she was being treated.

'Tell me this amazing news, then.' Probably to do with which girl in the Ops Room was engaged to which pilot.

Jess leaned across the table, her eyes shining. 'What with us all facing Christmas away from our families, I thought we could all do with cheering up.'

'Speak for yourself. This Christmas is going to be the best one I've ever had. Even if we have another bomb raid.' All her previous Christmases had been spent cooking and cleaning. No different from any other day in the year.

Jess waved away her objection. 'You know what I mean. We've all been working flat out for months and the news is getting worse, not better.'

May couldn't deny it. Day after day, news of the bomb raids on London and other towns and cities had spread alarm among the servicemen and women of RAF Amberton.

'I think I preferred it when they were bombing us,' Jess went on. 'I mean, getting trapped in that shelter...' She shuddered, paling under her face powder. May knew how she felt. She still had nightmares of being trapped in the air raid shelter, clawing at the rubble to free their comrades who had been buried when a bomb struck near the entrance. 'Thank God my Auntie Vera has gone with Hannah to stay with a cousin in Wales. They're all alone now Uncle Jack is in the Navy, and I'd have been frantic if they'd still been in London, facing the blitz all alone.'

'Who's Hannah?' Jess didn't speak much about her family but May gathered that Jess had been more or less brought up by her aunt. She hadn't liked to pry, as her own family life was something she preferred to forget.

'My little cousin. A sweet kid.' A faraway look came into Jess's eyes. 'I miss her.'

'At least she's safely out of harm's way. And your aunt.'

'True enough. Although I get terrified every time I—' She bit her lip. 'Well, let's just say Ops can be a frightening place to work. There are times I wish I knew less about what was going on. It's bad enough worrying about Mil— our pilots.'

May was sure Jess had just stopped herself from saying 'Milan'.

'I'm glad I don't know what Peter's doing when he's flying. It must have been awful for Evie knowing every time Alex was on patrol.' May didn't know exactly what the mysterious 'special duties' were that Jess and Evie had carried out in the Operations Room, but she could make a good guess that it involved tracking the movements of Amberton's four fighter squadrons. 'No wonder Evie decided she had to be transferred. I wonder how she's getting on?' Evie had been transferred to Bawdsey Manor in Suffolk to train as a Filterer Officer.

Jess's face brightened. 'I got a letter from her today. *We* got a letter, in fact. It was addressed to both of us. She's really enjoying her course by the sounds of it.'

'No chance of her coming back, then?' Happy as May was for Evie's success, she missed her terribly.

'No such luck, but she's promised to visit when her course is over. She'll get some leave before she starts officer training.'

May brightened. 'Is that the news you wanted to tell me?'

Jess shook her head. 'It's even better. As I was saying, I thought everyone on the station could do with cheering up and I had a wonderful idea. I thought Hellerby would never go for it, but I asked her this morning, and she thinks it a great plan. Asked me to organise it. What do you think?'

'I don't know. You still haven't told me what your idea is.'

'Oh yeah.' Jess laughed. 'Got a bit carried away.' She leaned forward, shining eyes fixed on May's face. 'We're going to do a pantomime for Christmas.'

'Really?' May had to restrain herself from clapping her hands like a child. She'd always longed to go to the pantomime when she younger, but her father would never take her. 'That's a wonderful idea. When's it going to be? Who's going to be in it?'

'Well, Hellerby thought Christmas Day would be the best day, what with everyone missing their families. What do you think?'

'Sounds perfect. We could do with something to put us in the Christmas spirit.'

'I know.' The eager light faded from Jess's eyes, and May knew she was thinking of all the victims of the Blitz. Her thoughts drifted to the evacuees, separated from their families.

Then Jess gave a shake of the head. 'Anyway, I thought we should do *Cinderella*.'

'I love *Cinderella*.' It had been her favourite story as a child. She'd often wished she had her own fairy godmother to help her escape her life of drudgery. Instead it had taken a war. At least this year she could watch it, enjoying the knowledge that she'd managed to escape her life of drudgery all by herself.

'It's the best one for us, considering it's going to be an all-female cast.' Jess chewed her lower lip for a moment. 'It would be better if we could get a couple of men to play the ugly sisters, though. I'm sure some of the Czechs would be up for it – Jiří or... or Milan, maybe.' Jess's cheeks turned pink. 'But that would depend on them getting a 24-hour pass and... well asking them to commit to a date two months away feels like... like tempting fate.'

There was a brief silence. May thought of Peter. Where was he now? Safe in the Officers' Mess? Or was he this moment fighting for his life in the air? Jess was seemingly absorbed in studying her fingernails but May guessed she was thinking of Milan.

'I think you should ask them,' she said. 'They could do with some fun, especially after everything that happened with Karol.' In September one of the Czech pilots of Brimstone squadron had turned out to be a Nazi spy, part of a plot to get enemy parachutists into the country. The RAF had tried to hush it up, but the secret had got out. Despite the fact that Milan had had a hand in Karol's capture, some of the locals now eyed the Czechs with suspicion. May was aware of the mutterings in the village, which infuriated her, considering they were putting themselves at risk day after day for a country that wasn't their own.

Jess looked up and smiled. 'It would be better to have men playing the ugly sisters.' She snorted. 'I wasn't looking forward to asking Hellerby to take on the role.' Hellerby was, in fact, Flight Officer Jean Ellerby. She had given Jess a hard time at first, but had eventually been won over.

'I take it you'll be playing Cinderella,' May said.

'Of course. The advantage of being the organiser is that I get to pick the plum role.'

'What about Prince Charming?' May was surprised Jess wanted to cast Milan as one of the ugly sisters. She'd have thought Jess would want him to play opposite her.

47

'Haven't you guessed?'

'No. Well, I thought you were going to ask Milan to play one of the ugly sisters.'

'The principal boy is traditionally played by a woman in pantomime.'

'You're going to ask Jean Ellerby?'

Jess flung back her head and laughed. 'May, you kill me. You really do. Things might have improved between me and old Hellerby, but not to the point where I could face playing Cinders to her Prince Charming.' She tilted her head. 'Although it might explain why Cinderella did a runner from the ball and went into hiding. No,' she went on, fixing May with a significant look that sent a trickle of unease down her spine. 'We need someone taller than her. Someone elegant, who could carry off wearing tights with panache.'

'I can't think who would agree to that.'

'Can't you? Because I've got the ideal girl in mind. She's the perfect height, has a good singing voice, although she'd never admit it, and she could command the stage if only she believed in herself and let herself try. Plus, she'd look amazing in tights.'

'Who?'

'You, of course, idiot. I want you to play Prince Charming.'

Chapter Four

'You're joking.' Then, when Jess didn't show any sign of laughter, May added, 'Aren't you?' She looked at Jess anxiously, all her enjoyment at the prospect of a pantomime draining away.

'Course not. You'll be brilliant.'

'But I can't go on stage in front of loads of people.' May had a flashback to her school days, to when she'd been called upon to answer a question in front of the whole class or, worst of all, recite a poem or read aloud from a book. Some children had enjoyed the attention but not May. Right now, she felt the same clamminess on the palms of her hands, the same rapid heartbeat she'd always felt when the teacher was looking around the class, deciding who should read next.

'It won't be loads of people,' Jess said in the soothing tones someone would use to calm a frightened puppy. 'Just those of us at the station who are off duty at the time.'

'That *is* loads of people. And I'll know them. That makes it worse.'

'How?'

'I… it just does. Everyone will laugh at me, and I'll have to face them every day after that knowing they've seen me make an idiot of myself.'

'You won't make an idiot of yourself. No one will laugh at you. Except in places where they're supposed to laugh. You'll be great. Everyone will love you.'

All May could do was shake her head. Too many times in class she'd frozen, unable to speak. The same would happen to her in the pantomime, she just knew it.

'Please say you'll do it,' Jess said. 'It won't be half as much fun without you.'

'I...' She couldn't do it. She should just say no. Explain how the prospect of performing terrified her. Jess was her friend. She wouldn't force May to do it once she understood.

'And it would be brilliant for your confidence,' Jess went on, oblivious to May's inner battle. 'Prince Charming knows exactly what he wants and he's not afraid to go after it. By teaching you how to act his part, I can teach you to look and behave more like a confident person.'

No. I can't do it. Please don't make me. But the words stuck in her throat. Instead, she said, 'Let me think about it.'

Jess gave her a beaming smile. 'I knew you wouldn't let me down. This is going to be great.'

'What is?' This was said by a man just behind May. Even if May hadn't recognised the voice with its slight accent, she would have known from the glow that suddenly seemed to envelop Jess that it was Milan Mašek speaking, one of the Czech pilots from Brimstone squadron. He stepped into view and May saw that his friend Jiří was with him.

'May is going to play Prince Charming in our pantomime.'

May drew breath, about to protest that she hadn't actually agreed to do it, but Milan spoke first. 'What is a pantomime?'

'Buy us a drink and I'll tell you all about it.'

And the moment when May could have corrected Jess had passed. May contented herself by deciding she would explain to Jess later on that she couldn't possibly play Prince Charming while Jess decided what drink she would like. It would be easier when they were alone back at High Chalk House.

She drained the dregs of her current half pint and watched Milan and Jiří as they went to the bar. Milan was just leaning over the bar to catch the landlady's attention when a portly middle-aged man in tweeds shoved him aside. 'A pint of bitter please, Joan,' he said.

May heard Jess take a sharp breath. 'Gawd 'elp us,' she whispered, echoing May's silent prayer. May couldn't see Milan's face, but she could tell from the stiffening of his shoulders that Milan wasn't going to quietly step aside.

'I was here first,' he said.

The man ignored him and addressed the barmaid. 'You shouldn't be serving the likes of that lot.' He jerked his head in Milan's direction. 'Who's to say there isn't another spy amongst them?'

May felt a cold chill wash over her. The locals might have been more distrustful of the Czechs since the incident with the parachutists, but she had never seen anyone be quite so confrontational.

The barmaid, however, folded her arms and glared at the man. 'Don't you tell me who I can and can't serve in my pub, Arnold Walker. If you can't keep a civil tongue in your head, you can go elsewhere. When we were being bombed last summer, Flight Lieutenant Mašek here was up in the air, fighting the enemy while I have it on good authority you were cowering in your shelter, crying for your mother.' She turned to Milan. 'Now, what can I get you, love?'

Arnold Walker's face turned puce but he said nothing more. A short while later, Milan and Jiří returned to the table carrying the drinks.

'Blinkin' cheek,' Jess said, scowling at Arnold Walker. Much to May's relief, the man had his back to their table so didn't see. 'I've 'alf a mind to give 'im what for.'

She pushed back her chair, but May clutched her arm. 'Please don't make a scene,' she said. 'I think he's drunk.' She'd seen enough of her father and brothers on pay day to know how easily tempers could flare when drink was involved.

'May's right,' said Milan. 'I do not care what he thinks. Anyone who matters knows we are good eggs.'

May stifled a grin. Milan had already spoken good English when he'd arrived, but he'd picked up some phrases from his fellow officers which sounded incongruous when spoken in a Czech accent.

Jiří took a drink from his pint glass, leaving a line of white froth on his upper lip. 'Tell us about this... penty-mome?'

'Pantomime,' Jess corrected. 'Panto for short.' She took a sip from her glass of lemonade. 'It's a kind of play we do at Christmas. Very light-hearted. Usually the story is a fairy tale like *Cinderella* or *Sleeping Beauty*. We're doing *Cinderella*.'

Milan's brow wrinkled. 'I do not know *Cinderella*.'

Jess summarised the story and Milan's brow cleared. 'Ah, we have that story, but she is called Popelka. Popelka is more spirited than your Cinderella. She makes the prince work to win her.' He gave Jess a significant look. 'You are more like Popelka, I think.'

To May's surprise, Jess didn't seem to be able to meet Milan's gaze but studied her drink and didn't reply.

Jiří, clearly oblivious to the atmosphere, still seemed fixated on the differences between versions. 'Popelka only has one stepsister,' he said.

Jess seemed to grasp at the change of subject. 'In pantomime, Cinderella's ugly sisters are traditionally played by men.' She leaned across the table, her eyes lighting up, nearly knocking over her drink in her eagerness. May shot out a hand to steady the glass before it fell. 'I've had a wonderful idea,' Jess said. 'You two should play the ugly sisters. You'd be brilliant.'

Milan didn't seem to want to let Jess escape so easily. 'What part are you playing?' he asked her.

'Cinderella.'

'Then I would rather play the prince.' May felt quite uncomfortable on Jess's behalf. Milan's gaze was locked on Jess's face. 'I think I would be good at running after Cinderella.'

Jess was actually blushing, which was most unlike her. 'May's playing Prince Charming. In panto, the leading man is played by a woman.'

May felt too sorry for Jess to contradict her. She would wait until they were alone before telling her she couldn't do it. Jess seemed to need rescuing, though, so she laughed and said, 'Although I would make a more convincing ugly sister. No one would be surprised that my feet were too big to fit Cinderella's glass slipper.'

Jess gave her a grateful smile. 'You're far too beautiful to play an ugly sister. Anyway—' she switched her attention to Milan and Jiří, seemingly in charge of her emotions again '—I think it would be good for you to take part. When the locals hear about it, they might think better of you.'

Milan shrugged. 'I told you, I do not care what the locals think.'

'I think you do. Besides, I care. I hate to see you and Jiří... all of you... being snubbed when they should be thanking you. If it weren't for all of you, Amberton would likely be no more than a smoking crater by now.'

Jess raised her drink to her mouth but then gave a little squeal and banged her glass back onto the table. 'No, wait. I've had an even better idea. Listen.' She leaned forward, eyes shining. 'What if we held it at the village hall? We could invite the whole village, spread some much-needed cheer at Christmas when plenty of folks will be missing their loved ones. And if people see you being funny as the ugly sisters, maybe they'll start treating you better again.'

Milan clearly saw Jess wouldn't take no for an answer. He threw up his hands. '*Ano*. I will do it.'

'What about you, Jiří?'

Jiří's eyes were dancing. 'Why not? It will be fun, I think.'

—

The next day being Sunday meant church parade for May. The WAAFs formed up outside the Admin block and marched out of the gate and down the lane towards the village. May used the time to fret about her involvement in Jess's pantomime. The news had been met with shrieks of delight when the girls had returned to High Chalk House after the pub. Enough girls had offered to take part to fill the available roles, and more had volunteered to help with scenery, props and costumes.

Everyone said how brave May was to play Prince Charming and how glad they were she had offered to take the role. No one else wanted to play a man. That made it impossible for May to take Jess aside and admit that she didn't want to play Prince Charming, that the thought of appearing on stage terrified her. Especially now the venue had changed from High Chalk House to the village hall. Flight Officer Jean Ellerby had surprised Jess by first saying what a good idea it was to involve the village and offering to speak to members of the Parish Council to ask permission to use the village hall. But that surprise had been nothing compared to the shock when she'd asked to play another role none of the others wanted – Cinderella's wicked stepmother.

'There's a turn-up for the books,' Jess had said, yawning, as they'd trudged up the stairs to their bedroom much later. 'Who'd have thought old Hellerby would want to help? And I've got to direct her! I'm so glad you're playing Prince Charming, May. I'm going to need all the moral support I can get if I'm going to have to tell Hellerby what to do.'

Tramp, tramp, tramp went the WAAFs' feet in time to May's pounding thoughts. There had been no way she could tell Jess she didn't want to take the role after that. May had lain awake late into the night, racking her brains for a way out, but still hadn't come up with a solution before she eventually drifted off. By the time she woke up, Jess had already gone, so there was no chance to talk it over. May could only hope she would find some inspiration during the service.

They arrived at the church just in time to see Mrs Evans, wrapped in a smart navy coat with matching hat, march Peggy towards the church hall, where the Sunday school was held. Peggy dragged her feet, scowling at everyone they passed. May's heart went out to her; her worries over the pantomime were trivial when compared with Peggy's problems.

The clip-clop of a horse's hooves announced the arrival of a cart. May looked up to see Mr and Mrs Bowes arrive sitting high up on the front seat, a rug over their knees against the chill. Davey was sitting in the back with the other two boys, also wrapped up warm. As May filed in to the back of the church with the other WAAFs, she comforted herself with the thought that Peggy would be able to see Davey in Sunday school.

As the service progressed, it seemed as though all May's worries were lined up at the front of the church, jostling for first position. In addition to Peggy and the pantomime, Peter was there, always near the forefront of her mind. Evie was never far from her thoughts, either, even though she was no longer at Amberton. How was she getting on with her training? May missed Evie. If she was honest, much as she loved Jess, she felt more akin to quiet, studious Evie. Evie would have understood her fears about the pantomime, whereas outgoing Jess could never under-stand how hard it was for May to even hold conversation with more than one person, let alone stand up on stage in front of the whole village.

Evie wouldn't have done nothing about Peggy, either. She might be quiet but she wasn't timid. She had a confi-dence in her abilities and her opinions that May lacked. May wished Evie was here now. She would know what to do.

May still hadn't come to any conclusions by the end of the service. As she filed towards the door, she saw Jean Ellerby talking to the vicar's wife. She was surprised when

Mrs Grey called her name before she could go through the door.

'May, Flight Officer Ellerby was just talking about you.'

May's heart lurched but Mrs Grey must have seen her expression, for she laughed. 'Oh, it was highly complimentary, I assure you. She was telling me all about your wonderful idea of holding a pantomime on Christmas Day.'

'It's not my idea. It was Jess's.'

'I know, but you're playing Prince Charming, aren't you? How marvellous and brave.'

Brave. There was that word again. May was anything but brave and she wished people would stop telling her she was. And it was clear there was no way she could get out of playing Prince Charming now. Not when the vicar's wife was expecting her to do it. But Mrs Grey was still talking, so all May had to do was smile and nod.

'I've told Flight Officer Ellerby I'm sure there won't be any difficulty with using the village hall,' Mrs Grey was saying. 'And, of course, with evacuees in the village it will be lovely for the children to have something to look forward to. Poor dears, they must miss their families so much.'

And then an idea clicked into place that would at least help Peggy and help May reconcile herself to the thought of performing. 'Mrs Grey, do you think any of the evacuees would like to take part? I'm sure we could find them roles, and it might be fun for them, don't you think?'

'That's a wonderful idea. I'll speak to Miss Foster, their headmistress.'

'And—' May drew a gulping breath '—do you think you could ask especially for Peggy? I... I think she would be perfect for one of the parts Jess has in mind.' May willed Mrs Grey to understand her meaning, as she didn't want to give voice to her misgiving in front of Flight Officer Ellerby. Mrs Grey, she was sure, was also worried for Peggy. Having Peggy involved with the pantomime would be a chance to befriend the girl, persuade her to let them know if she was unhappy.

Mrs Grey's gaze flicked to Mrs Evans, who was speaking to Arnold Walker in a nearby pew. As she watched, Mrs Evans handed him a book. 'For your dear wife,' she said in a carrying voice. 'I do hope she enjoys it.' Then she trilled a laugh that set May's teeth on edge.

A grim expression appeared on Mrs Grey's face. 'Leave it with me,' she said.

As they marched back to the base, May's stomach was in knots. She hadn't resolved any of her existing problems, and now she had a new one: how to tell Jess they needed to include children in the pantomime. What if Jess hated the idea? With a sinking feeling, May realised there was no getting out of the pantomime now. She couldn't ask Jess to involve the children as a favour to her, then back out of playing a role that no one else wanted. Besides, May needed to take part or she wouldn't have the chance to befriend Peggy. No matter how much the prospect terrified her, May was playing Prince Charming.

–

May found Jess in the NAAFI at lunchtime. They took their meals to a table by the window and May toyed with her eating irons as she tried to think of a good way of telling Jess what she'd done.

Jess peered at the slice of pie on her plate, levering up the pastry with her fork, and wrinkled her nose. 'The woman at the counter swore it was beef and potato pie, but I'm not convinced that's beef.' Then she shrugged and started eating. 'Ah, well. What doesn't kill me will make me stronger.'

The roar of several Hurricanes flying overhead set cups and plates rattling throughout the canteen. Used to the noise, May automatically held onto her mug to stop the vibrations tipping it over.

'Jess,' she began, once the noise had died down, 'what do you think about having children in the pantomime?'

'Never work with animals or children,' Jess said without a pause. 'I don't know who said it, but they were right.' Then her gaze sharpened. 'Why?'

May related her conversation with Mrs Grey. 'So you see, I thought it would be an ideal opportunity to befriend Peggy,' she concluded. 'Give her a chance to tell us if Mrs Evans is treating her badly.'

Jess looked at May thoughtfully. 'What is it about Peggy that's taken your interest?'

'She's all alone, with no one to turn to.' Just like she had been after her mother had died.

'You do know that even if Peggy did tell us something was wrong, there might not be anything we can do about it?' Jess's voice was gentle. 'We don't have any influence in the village.'

'But I have to try. Please tell me you'll let the children join in.'

Jess pursed her lips and pushed her remaining piece of pie around her plate with her fork. May waited, sure Jess would agree once she'd got over her initial reluctance.

Finally, Jess's shoulders slumped. 'Very well. I suppose I owe you a favour for playing Prince Charming. You can have your way.'

May gave her first genuine smile of the day. 'Thank you. You won't regret it.'

'I already do.' Jess finished her last mouthful then flung down her eating irons. 'I don't know. Between you and Evie, you've had me chasing saboteurs across the fields and saving evacuees. It's a miracle my hair hasn't turned white.'

May grinned, eyeing Jess's beautifully waved blonde hair. 'I think you're safe for now.'

'Well, I'd better get back to Ops.' Jess picked up her tray. 'Meet me in the schoolroom tonight and bring some paper. We have a script to write, and you're helping now you've made me include a bunch of children.'

–

Several hours later, May and Jess were sitting at the rickety table in the schoolroom, bent over an old exercise book, pencils in hand. A brass table lamp lit the table in an amber glow while a squally wind rattled the window panes behind the blackout curtains.

'The characters so far are: Cinderella, Prince Charming, the ugly sisters, the wicked stepmother, Buttons and the fairy godmother.' Jess wrote the names down, adding the name of the person playing them beside each one. 'We'll also need extras for the ballroom scene, Prince Charming's retinue, and so on. People can double-up with those sorts of roles. But what shall we do with the children?'

May chewed the end of her pencil. 'We don't want anything with too many lines to learn.' She gazed at the page in front of her. The exercise book had belonged to Evie and the top of the page had something – May had no idea what it meant – written across it in Evie's precise handwriting. The strange squiggles must be something mathematical, but it looked like a magical incantation. She gazed at it as if the symbols would resolve themselves into the perfect answer.

'I think they should have a fairly simple song and dance routine near the start,' Jess said, 'then they can sit at the side of the stage for the rest of the performance and enjoy the play. Maybe join in with the song at the end.'

'Songs.' May had forgotten pantomimes involved songs. 'I won't have to sing a solo, will I?'

'You've got a good voice.'

May looked at Jess in horror. 'I haven't. I couldn't sing in front of all those people.' She didn't know how she was even going to speak in front of an audience, let alone sing, though if it meant helping Peggy she would do it. But sing? She thought she would die of fright.

'Don't worry. This is the advantage of writing the script ourselves. We can write it how we want. Any songs for Prince Charming will be with other people.'

May relaxed. She traced a symbol on the paper like an elongated 'S'. 'I've been thinking about what Milan said about Cinderella.'

'You mean about how Prince Charming has to earn Cinderella in the Czech version?'

May nodded. 'I've always thought...' She hesitated, but then ploughed on in a rush, 'I mean, how do Cinderella and Prince Charming know they'll be happy together? They only dance together once. How can they learn all they need to know about each other from one dance?' She had danced with Peter at the Midsummer dance. Being in his arms, swaying in time to the music, had been one of the most intoxicating experiences of her life. But that was because she already knew him, knew, deep down, that she loved him. If they had danced at the start of their acquaintance, she wouldn't have felt that way.

She knew she wasn't explaining herself very well and expected Jess to laugh off her objections, but to her surprise, Jess was nodding. 'You're right. We're WAAFs, after all. We shouldn't be doing a pantomime that shows a woman waiting to be saved. She needs to take destiny in her own hands.'

Flashes of the story appeared in May's head. 'We could have Cinderella escaping from the house at the start of the play, going into the forest to play with the other children – played by the evacuees.'

Jess picked it up. 'Yes, and Prince Charming appears. Hunting deer or something.'

'Only Cinderella hides the deer because she likes animals.'

Jess looked thoughtful. 'A pantomime deer? That could work.' She scribbled something on her page and her lips curved into a slow smile. 'Yes! How about this? We get Milan and Jiří to play the deer – because we don't see their faces, they can be made up as the ugly sisters inside the costume. The deer limps into the glade and Cinderella hears the hunting horns and knows she has to hide it.'

'How does she hide a deer?'

'This is panto, remember, it's supposed to be funny. Cinderella wraps the deer's antlers in ivy and leaves and pretends it's a tree. It can do a funny dance behind the prince's back and stand still every time he turns around.' Jess scribbled something else. 'We can work out the details later. But the point is, it gives them a scene together where they can take a fancy to each other.'

'Cinderella and the deer?' May said, laughing.

'It would almost be worth it, to see Mrs Evans' expression. No. Cinderella and Prince Charming. You don't escape that easily.'

'Oh! I've had another idea.'

'Go on.'

'Well, what if the fairy godmother isn't just Cinderella's fairy godmother, but a sort of guardian spirit of the forest? After the prince has gone, she can appear and thank Cinderella for saving the deer. Tell her if she ever needs help, to call for her and she'll appear.'

'I like it!' Jess was writing down the ideas so fast, May thought the pencil would set fire to the page. 'And we can also have a scene between Prince Charming and the king – no, wait, we'd need another man for that. Better make it a queen.' She made another note. 'The queen tells the prince she's invited princesses from all the neighbouring kingdoms to a ball because it's time the prince chose a wife, and the prince persuades her to invite all the girls from the village as well because he wants to meet Cinderella again.'

'And that's why Cinderella wants to go to the ball so badly,' May said. 'Because she wants to see him one last time. Although she knows she can never be his.'

Amazed at how quickly the story was evolving, the girls worked late into the night, only pausing every now and again to creep down to the kitchen to make more drinks.

Eventually, Jess glanced at her watch and gasped. 'I've got to be on duty in four hours. I'll have to turn in, or I'll be useless tomorrow.'

She rose and stretched, then grinned at May. 'You know, it was a good idea of yours to involve the children. We're going to make this a Christmas to remember.'

Chapter Five

The two days that followed were so busy, May hardly got a chance to even speak to Jess, let alone find time for them to work on the script. On Monday May had to drive the station commander to a meeting in London and got back so late she fell into bed as soon as she reached her bedroom. She had taken to carrying around the exercise book with her notes on the script, and while she was waiting for the station commander to finish the meeting, she scribbled down some more ideas.

The next day she had to drive a pilot from Catseye squadron to the hospital. He'd been forced to do a 'pancake' landing on the field when his Hurricane's undercarriage had been damaged and wouldn't lower. Although he'd avoided serious injury, the MO wanted him to have his head X-rayed. Again, it had been late by the time she returned to the Waafery.

But she perked up when she found a letter from Mrs Grey waiting for her.

I've spoken to the children's headmistress, Mrs Grey wrote. *She thinks it would be a splendid idea for some of the evacuees to be involved in the pantomime. There are five children living in the village who would like to take part, including Peggy. The others would love to come and watch the performance itself. Can you and your friend come to the vicarage at 7.30 on Wednesday evening? If so, I'll introduce you to Miss Foster so you can make the arrangements.*

Thankfully Jess was free the next evening, so they had gone to the vicarage and met Mrs Grey and Miss Foster. Mrs Grey gave the welcome news that the parish council had agreed to let them use the village hall for the performance and the rehearsals.

'I hope you won't be taking up too much of my pupils' time,' Miss Foster said with a small frown after listening to Jess's description of the children's scenes. She didn't seem to share Jess's enthusiasm, making Jess wonder if Mrs Grey had stretched the truth in her letter when saying Miss Foster had thought the pantomime a 'splendid idea'. May suspected Mrs Grey had used all her powers of persuasion to get the headmistress to agree. 'If their school work suffers, I will have to withdraw them from the cast.'

'Oh, they won't have much to learn,' Jess said. 'I can assure you it won't interfere with their schooling.'

'What if...' May began, then hesitated when all eyes turned to her. But Jess's encouraging smile gave her the confidence to speak up. 'Why don't we hold separate rehearsals for the children? To start with, I mean.' Heartened that no one immediately disagreed, she went on, 'That way they won't need to attend rehearsals so often, and they won't have to sit around when we're doing a scene they're not involved in.'

'Excellent idea,' Mrs Grey said.

'Perfect,' said Jess. 'That way we can hold rehearsals for the adult cast members up at High Chalk House in the ballroom. It will save us trailing down to the village each time.'

Even Miss Foster gave the idea a grudging nod and May felt a swell of mingled pride and relief that she'd found the courage to give voice to her idea. She rewarded herself with a slice of fruitcake while Jess and Mrs Grey decided upon the rehearsal dates. They settled upon the following Tuesday for the first children's rehearsal, which was Jess's next full night off.

The best news of all came when Mrs Grey revealed she had been involved in a local amateur dramatic society before the war. She offered to let them use the costumes and props, which were still stored in the village hall. It also turned out that she was an able musician, and volunteered to play the piano during the performance and write music for any songs.

'I can't wait to look through the costumes,' said Jess as they cycled through the pitch-black lanes back to High Chalk House. 'It will save us a load of work if we can find suitable ones ready-made.' She swerved to avoid a pothole that their shielded headlamps only revealed at the last moment. 'And your idea was brilliant, May. I was worried Miss Foster wouldn't allow her pupils to join the cast, but you won her round.'

She chatted all the way back to High Chalk House, her enthusiasm contagious. For the first time, May felt flutterings of excitement over the pantomime. Maybe Jess was right, and playing Prince Charming was exactly what she needed to boost her confidence. Only half listening to Jess, she allowed herself to dream of a day when she would have the self-assurance to admit to Peter that she loved him.

–

'Gather round the front, children.' The five children – three girls and two boys – had arrived for the first rehearsal, their coats, hats and gas masks placed on chairs at the back of the village hall.

Straight away, Jess got each one to say their name, their favourite animal and favourite food. How Jess could speak with such composure to a group of giggling, fidgeting children, May would never know. She supposed that after teaching English to the Czech pilots last summer, five schoolchildren couldn't be much of a challenge. But to May they were as terrifying and unpredictable as unexploded bombs.

At least, four of the children giggled and fidgeted. Peggy stood a little apart from the others, scuffing the floorboards with the toe of one shoe.

'Today, we're going to learn the opening song,' Jess said, handing out sheets of paper that had been torn from the back of Evie's exercise book. 'We haven't got a pianist today, but I can teach you the tune.' Sadly, Mrs Grey had caught a cold and sent her apologies, but she promised to attend the next rehearsal. 'The song lyrics are written down here, but we'd like you to learn the words before we meet next week.' Jess went on to describe the scene the children would take part in at the start of the pantomime.

One little boy listened, wide-eyed. When Jess got to the part about the deer, he craned his neck to look around the hall. Then his hand shot up. 'Can we see the deer, Miss?'

Jess laughed. 'You won't see it tonight. It's played by two of our pilots, and—'

She broke off when the squeak of the door behind the heavy blackout curtain heralded a newcomer. Milan pushed through the curtains and approached the front. 'I thought you might want someone to play the piano,' he said. He gave a brief smile to May and the children, but the whole of his attention was fixed on Jess. May was reminded of the intense look he had given Jess when he had explained how Popelka made the prince work hard to win her. It seemed he was set on showing Jess that he was intent on winning her.

Jess looked uncharacteristically flustered. 'I didn't know you—' She stopped. 'Thank you. That would help.' She handed him the sheet of music Miss Grey had sent. 'Can you sight-read?'

Milan gave a crooked smile. 'I haven't played for some time but I'll manage.'

An upright piano stood at the side of the stage. Milan took his seat and arranged the music on the stand. Then he opened the lid and ran through a series of scales. It was immediately apparent that Milan was a pianist of considerable talent. Despite the protestation that he hadn't played in a long time, his fingers flowed across the keys, turning even this most basic of exercises into a thing of beauty.

Jess stared at him, eyes wide. May had to smother a laugh. She had never seen Jess at a loss for words before. When Jess showed no sign of emerging from her trance, May gave her a small nudge.

Jess snapped out of her reverie with a start. 'Well.' She gave the children a bright smile. 'First of all, I'm going to ask Milan to play the tune through a couple of times. Then I'll sing the song. Try following the words while I'm singing them. Finally, we'll all give it a go.'

By the time Milan had played the simple, lively tune through twice, Jess had fully regained her composure. The children listened, entranced, while Jess sang Cinderella's song, listing all the chores her stepmother made her do. The chorus was for Cinderella and the children, with the children urging her to put down the basket she was using to collect berries and come and play with them instead.

The children picked it up easily, helped by Milan's expert playing. They were just starting the third run-through when the wail of the air raid siren split the air.

'Quick, gather up your coats and gas masks,' Jess ordered the children, picking up her own greatcoat from where she had draped it on the front of the stage. Then she turned frightened eyes on May. 'I don't know where the nearest shelter is. I didn't think to check.'

Now May had reason to be thankful that her duties had led her to drive through the village so often. 'Follow me. There's one just behind the hall.' She snatched up her own coat and flung it on while Jess raised her voice to be heard over the siren.

'Follow May. Don't worry, everyone. It's bound to be a false alarm, but we're going to the shelter to be safe.'

They filed out and May led them onto the village green behind the hall. Most of it had been turned over to vegetable plots, but there was a large communal shelter in one corner. Milan made a game of it, making the children pretend they were rabbits, hurrying for their warren. When the smallest boy tripped and fell and started to cry, Milan picked him up and hoisted him on his shoulders. 'Now you ride on the pantomime deer.' The boy giggled as Milan trotted for the shelter.

They met Miss Foster at the entrance. 'Thanks goodness,' she said, doing a swift count to make sure all the children were accounted for. 'I was just coming to find you.'

They bundled inside and saw by the lantern light that a few other villagers were there. May's heart sank when she saw Arnold Walker – the unpleasant man who had been in the snug at the Horse and Groom on Saturday. He scowled when he saw Milan, but said nothing. Perhaps the presence of the children prevented him from repeating his accusations of the other day. Whatever the reason, May could only hope he didn't start up again.

May took care to sit beside Peggy. Now was as good an opportunity as any to try befriending the girl, although May didn't want to bring up the subject of Mrs Evans in a shelter full of people who were bound to know her.

Peggy was shaking, hugging her arms across her chest. 'Davey will be so frightened,' she said. 'I hope he's alright.'

'He'll be fine,' May said. 'Mr and Mrs Bowes live right out in the country, well away from any raids. Anyway, they've got a good, strong cellar.'

The boy Milan had picked up was now sitting between Milan and Jess. He seemed to have recovered from his fright and was staring at Milan in fascination. He pointed to the wings on the chest of Milan's tunic. 'What are these for?' he asked.

'They mean I'm a pilot.'

'Why aren't you up there, then?' Arnold Walker demanded. 'You should be fighting them.'

Jess shot him a glare. 'Because his plane's still being repaired from the last time 'e was up there.'

May could tell she wanted to say more, but Milan put a hand on her arm and gave a small shake of the head. Jess ignored him. 'You've changed your tune since Saturday,' she said to Mr Walker. 'Before, you accused him of being a spy. Now you want to know why he's not up there saving your neck. Make up your mind.'

Even in the dim lantern light, May could see Mr Walker's face was turning a mottled shade of red. He started forward but the gentleman sat beside him held him back. 'Now, now, Arnold. This is neither the time nor place.' Mr Walker subsided, though he continued to shoot glowering looks at Jess and Milan. All in all, it was a relief when the all-clear sounded a few minutes later.

'There you go,' said Jess with an encouraging smile at the children. 'What did I tell you? A false alarm. We're nice and safe in Amberton.'

'Until the Jerries decide to bomb the RAF station again,' Mr Walker muttered under his breath.

Fortunately, Peggy didn't seem to hear. She gave May a shaky smile. 'That was scary. Have you been in an air raid before?'

May nodded. 'A couple of times, but it wasn't so bad.' There was no way she was going to describe to the frightened child the terror of being buried when her shelter had been hit, or running for her life to get off the road when her car had been strafed.

'We had raids where I live,' Peggy said. Possibly her reaction to fear had made her more talkative, made her want to reach out for comfort. 'That's why we had to come here.'

'Where are you from?' May asked, slinging her gas mask over her shoulder.

'Coventry. My mum still lives there.' Peggy shivered. 'I hope she's all right.'

'I'm sure she'll be fine.' May ducked out of the entrance and into the chill night air. The sky was clear, and a scattering of stars glinted overhead, lending the slightest silvery light to the scene. The perfect conditions for bombers. She shivered. The air raid at Amberton might have been a false alarm, but bombs would be falling somewhere, she was sure.

'It's pointless carrying on with the rehearsal now,' Jess said to the children as she emerged from the shelter. 'We'll walk you all back home.'

However, by the time they'd gathered everyone together, most of the children's foster parents had arrived to collect them. Only Mrs Evans was missing. The group dispersed, leaving Peggy with May, Jess and Milan. May didn't often get angry, but a flare of rage burned at this further evidence of Mrs Evans' lack of care for a child all alone and far from her family. Was she so heartless that she didn't care for Peggy's safety? Was she so lacking in imagination that she couldn't put herself in the girl's shoes and understand how it must feel to walk home all alone in the blackout, through a strange village?

'Come on,' May said, holding out her hand to Peggy. 'We'll walk you home.'

'It's not home,' Peggy said, 'and I'm too old to hold hands. I can find my own way.'

May let her hand drop. 'I know you can, but no one should be out alone in the blackout.' She struggled to think of a way to reach the girl. When she had been Peggy's age, she could never have spoken her mind to an adult. She still found it hard, if she was honest with herself. She glanced back at Jess hoping for help, but Jess was speaking to Milan in a low voice and clearly hadn't heard. 'What would your mother say?' she asked finally, praying that Peggy's mother was more caring than Mrs Evans. 'Would she want you to be out alone after dark?'

She could just make out Peggy's shape in the darkness. Her head was bowed as though studying her feet. 'No,' she muttered eventually.

'There you go then,' said May. 'I wouldn't want your mother to learn I'd sent you ho— back to Mrs Evans in the blackout on your own.'

Peggy nodded and fell into step with May without further protest. Jess and Milan followed.

This should be the perfect opportunity to encourage Peggy to talk about life with Mrs Evans, if only the girl didn't radiate standoffishness. Perhaps Jess would have known how to talk to her, but Jess was engrossed in conversation with Milan. Still, May had to try.

'How are you getting on with Mrs Evans?' she asked. The moment the words were out of her mouth she knew she had been too abrupt.

'All right,' Peggy said, hunching further down. Although she didn't move any further away from May, she managed to give the impression of creating distance between them.

May could have kicked herself. She should have known Peggy would be reluctant to talk. Hadn't May always brushed off questions about her home life when her teacher had gently tried to ask if all was well? She should have known Peggy would react the same way. It was going to take more than a quick chat to uncover how Mrs Evans was treating Peggy. She was going to have to work at making friends with the girl over the next few weeks. Suddenly playing Prince Charming didn't seem so bad if it meant she had another chance to make things right for Peggy.

'You mentioned your mother,' she said as her opener in the campaign. 'What does she do?' She instantly hoped it wasn't a tricky subject. She knew she wouldn't like to talk about *her* family.

Thankfully, this seemed to be the right thing to ask. Peggy straightened and closed the gap between them. 'She works in a shoe shop. And my dad, he used to work in the Post Office. But—' her voice dropped '—he's in the army now.'

'You must miss him.'

'I really do.'

They had turned into the High Street by this time and were drawing close to the haberdashery. Peggy slowed. 'I... I can carry on alone from here.'

'Nonsense. We'll see you to the door.'

Peggy turned to May. May could just see her face as a round, pale blur against the darkness. 'I don't think... it's not a good idea.'

'Why not?'

'Mrs Evans, she... I don't think she approves of WAAFs.'

They were only about ten paces from the haberdashery, so May decided not to argue. Anyway, it was pointless disagreeing, when both she and Jess had experienced Mrs Evans' dislike. 'Go on, then. We'll see you inside from here.'

Peggy hesitated, then said in a rush, 'Thank you for letting me have a part in the panto. See you next week.' She sped off before May could reply.

Chapter Six

'Red Leader, this is Acorn. Vector zero six fife at angels two zero.'

'Acorn, Red Leader. Received and understood.' Peter kept his eyes on his compass as he banked his Hurricane, climbing steadily. He hated night flying. With the blackout, there were no lights to be seen, no features on the ground to fix on. He had to trust his instruments completely. The worst thing was not having a visual check on his height. Horror stories abounded of pilots who had ended up ploughing their aeroplanes into the ground, convinced they were still well above ground-level.

However, with enemy bombers making nightly raids across England, targeting factories and homes alike, they had no option but to try and intercept them before more civilians lost their lives. His stomach tightened as he realised the vector Oldbourne Ops had sent would take his patrol through Surrey. No doubt it was an attempt to intercept bombers heading for London. He shuddered to think of bombs flattening more houses. How many people would die tonight if he didn't intercept and stop the raid? Everyone had seen the newsreels showing houses reduced to matchwood and people scavenging in the ruins for the remnants of their possessions, but to him the images were personal. A sign of his failure.

He shut his mind to the horrific images. He needed all his concentration to find and destroy this latest wave of bombers. The trouble was, finding a Staffel of bombers before they could release their payload was next to impossible in the dark. The Chain Home network was directed out to sea. It could track enemy aircraft until they reached the coast; after that the RAF depended upon observers on the ground. This worked well in daylight – and had proved their salvation during the Battle of Britain – but at night the observers couldn't see what was in the sky. It usually needed a piece of luck such as a searchlight beam catching a wing tip to give away a bomber's location.

He glanced at his instrument panel again. According to his readings, he should be approaching the target. He leaned over to peer through his canopy, twisting his neck to look behind then scanning the blackness for any sign of enemy bombers. A crescent moon came out from behind a cloud, and Peter glimpsed a silvery glow far below. It must be the moonlight reflecting on water – probably a river – but it was impossible to make out any landmarks to pinpoint his location.

Dark shadows blotted out the light. Instantly Peter was tense and alert. More clouds or enemy aircraft? He craned his neck and squinted up at the moon, but whatever had briefly blocked the moonlight had gone past. Where were the searchlights?

Then he caught another glimpse of movement below and slightly to the right.

He toggled on his radio and spoke to the rest of his flight. 'Bogey at one o'clock. Below us. Move to intercept.'

He sideslipped, craning his neck to search for another glimpse of the unidentified aircraft. It had to be the enemy; surely Ops would tell him if there were friendly aircraft in the area. If they could only keep the element of surprise, it gave them a chance to stop the bombers before they reached their target. After days of failing to find the aircraft they'd been sent to intercept, the whole squadron was desperate for a win. Although he told his men every day that the nightly bombings weren't their fault, it was impossible not to feel crushed by guilt when news of each night's atrocities filtered through. If only they'd tried harder, looked in the right place, maybe the women and children being pulled dead from the wreckage would still be alive. He'd never thought he could miss the exhausting days of the Battle of Britain, when he'd been senior controller in the Ops Room at Amberton, but now he was almost nostalgic for that phase of the war. Then it had been pilot against pilot. A clean fight. Then the Luftwaffe had been intent upon destroying the RAF. Now they had moved their attention to civilian targets, and no one in Britain was under any illusions about the ugliness of war.

A beam of white light stabbed the air, closely followed by another and another. Searchlights. Peter jumped as an explosion to starboard rocked his machine. The anti-aircraft gunners had started up. Another hazard of night flying was having to dodge the ack-ack from your own gunners.

One of the silvery rays struck a wing maybe a hundred feet below. Immediately more beams homed in and finally captured their prey: a Heinkel. Peter dived, his thumb twitching over the firing button.

'Wait for it,' he muttered. Despite the temptation to fire, he resisted, knowing the bullets would fly wild until he was closer. 'Hold your fire.' Even focused wholly as he was upon his prey, he was aware of ribbons of tracer from the other Hurricanes, their gun ports spitting fire. He was on the point of firing when another explosion shook his Hurricane, and something smashed through his canopy, forcing him to perform a tight roll and bank away. Planes flew in and out of sight as they were picked out by the searchlights. Then came the sight he dreaded: orange and crimson flames bursting up from the ground as German bombs hit their target. Peter's Hurricane rocked as the force from the blasts struck. With alarm he saw that he had lost height from his last attack. He pulled back the control column. For a horrible moment he thought his engine would stall. From this height, he doubted there would be time to recover. He had a brief flash of May's face and a deep sense of sorrow at the thought that he would leave the world without winning her heart. Then the Merlin engine surged into life and he was clear.

He toggled on his radio. 'Aim for bombers that haven't dropped their load.' But it was futile. There was no way of telling. By now the light from the fires revealed a group of bombers heading back out to sea. He let them go; it was more important to stop any Heinkels that still had bombs to drop. He climbed, scanning the skies for a glimpse of any more bombers swooping on their target, but he could see nothing. A glance at his fuel gauge told him it was time to return to base. The end of yet another patrol where they had failed to stop the enemy. He gave the signal to his squadron and headed back to Oldbourne.

Already he was running the words he would use in his report over in his mind. How could he phrase it to inform the top brass that this method of patrol – waiting near likely targets in the hope of catching bombers before they struck – was a waste of time and resources?

A tingle of apprehension gave him pause for thought. It might be wiser to state the facts and leave it at that. The carnage night after night was surely all the evidence the top brass needed that their methods weren't working. Was it really worth drawing attention to himself by speaking out? It had been a struggle to earn his commission after starting as a sergeant pilot; he had done it by sheer hard work, not complaining when others with the right old school ties had scaled the ranks faster. Then, just when he felt he had gained enough respect to overcome the handicap of his humble origins, an accident had resulted in the loss of his leg. He had only just regained his wings. He could almost hear the comments to the effect that he had 'lost his nerve' if he made a fuss. Perhaps it would be safer to stay quiet, trust that Fighter Command was already working on a better way of stopping the bombings. He didn't want to risk a transfer to a training squadron.

–

May paced towards Jess, realised she was wringing her hands and clasped them firmly behind her back. 'You had no right to interfere.'

'No, no!' Jess flung her script down upon the table. 'Remember you're not just acting like you own the place. You *do* own the place.' She regarded May with a sigh. 'If you want to look convincing, you have to feel it. Feel your authority, your God-given right to do as you please on your own land.'

May slumped into the schoolroom chair in despair. 'You've picked the wrong person for Prince Charming.' She hurried on when Jess opened her mouth, determined to say her piece before Jess could talk her out of it.

'I'm not saying I won't be in the pantomime, but Prince Charming? You know I'm not cut out to play him.' She was babbling now, pleading for Jess to understand. 'I'll be a... a serving girl or something.' She could be a serving girl. She knew how *that* felt.

'There isn't a part for a serving girl. The only serving girl is Cinderella.'

'Why don't I play Cinderella, then? You play Prince Charming. You'd make a far better Prince Charming than me.' She felt a welling of hysterical laughter bubbling up in her chest. Only a few days ago she had begged to be let out of acting in the pantomime altogether and now she was asking to play the lead. But she had reconciled herself to taking part – it meant she could befriend Peggy. What she wasn't reconciled to was playing someone whose character was the very opposite of hers.

The irritation drained from Jess's expression. She gave a wry smile and sat in the opposite chair. 'You mean you want to play a shrinking violet who sleeps by the hearth until first the fairy godmother then Prince Charming rescue her?'

May looked away, hot shame burning her cheeks. She knew she wasn't as brave as Jess but it still hurt to have it pointed out by one of her closest friends.

'May, look at me.' Jess's voice was gentle. May raised her gaze to Jess's face and saw not the pity she'd expected but an oddly determined expression. 'I know that's how you think of yourself, but it's not how I see you. Ever.' Jess leaned forward, arms folded upon her knees. 'Do you know what I thought the first time I saw you?'

'How did the giraffe escape from the zoo?'

'No!' Jess's brows drew together. 'Stop putting yourself down. I thought why is that beautiful girl trying to hide her looks?'

'I'm not—'

'Yes you are. But that was only my first impression. When I got to know you, I saw how brave and capable you are. You've only shown glimpses of it so far, it's like you're trying to hide who you are most of the time, but every now and again, you show everyone who's really hidden, crushed inside the mouse you try to pretend you are most of the time.'

'Don't be silly.'

'I'm deadly serious. Who took charge in the bomb shelter that time? Not Hellerby.'

'She was unconscious!'

'Yes, but there were others there who were technically senior, yet you're the one who stepped up.'

'I…' May was at a loss for words but felt Jess was reading too much into the bomb shelter incident. She hadn't done anything special; she'd just made sure as many people as possible got out alive.

'And Milan's told me how you tackled Alex when the two of them followed Karol through the hedge into the Waafery.'

'I didn't tackle him. I tripped and got tangled up with him.'

'Don't let Evie hear you say that,' Jess said with a grin. 'But you were out there in the grounds, weren't you, when you must have been scared.'

'I was with Jean Ellerby.'

'Then how about this?' Jess's expression became more serious. 'You've agreed to play a part in the pantomime, even though you're terrified of performing in public, because you want to help a poor girl. If that doesn't make you a heroine, I don't know what does.'

May felt her cheeks burn for an altogether different reason than before. 'That's beside the point,' she said. 'We were talking about the part I play.'

'It's precisely the point,' Jess said. 'You asked for acting lessons, and I wouldn't be helping you if I made you play a role you've already been playing for twenty years. I know you're finding this difficult—' Jess pointed at the pages containing the first scene of the pantomime '—but I know you can do it. I wouldn't have cast you as Prince Charming if I didn't think you would be amazing. This is my pantomime, remember. My idea. I want it to be a success.'

May hadn't thought of it that way. She'd been so intent upon helping Peggy, so wrapped up in her fears of performing in public, that she hadn't thought of Jess's commitment to the play, how her reputation would be on the line. Some of the fears subsided. Jess wouldn't have given her the part if she thought May couldn't manage it. 'You really think I can do it?' she asked.

'Absolutely. You're the best one for the part.' Jess picked up the script. 'Now, how do you think Prince Charming feels when he sees Cinderella in the forest? He's been chasing the stag all day, through the royal forest, he's finally got it cornered, when this slip of a girl, who shouldn't even be there, starts telling him off for trying to harm an innocent creature.'

'Well...' May picked up her copy of the script and stared at the words until they blurred. 'I suppose he would be angry with Cinderella for ruining the hunt.'

'Good. Anything else? Why doesn't he just tell his men to arrest her?'

'Oh. Well, he's attracted to her, isn't he?'

'Exactly. There wouldn't be much of a story if he wasn't. So he's both annoyed with her and attracted. How are you going to act like that?'

'I've no idea.'

'Let's start with the anger. That's how he feels at the start. Say your line: "You had no right to interfere," in an angry voice.'

Feeling more than a little silly, May arranged her face in what she hoped looked like an angry scowl and repeated the line in a gruff voice. 'How was that?' she finished.

'Better. But it's not just your voice that's angry, it's your whole body.' Jess paused, thinking. Then she raised a finger. 'I know. Imagine how you felt when Mrs Evans was being so rude about WAAFs.'

May immediately felt tension run up her spine and clench her jaw.

'Now, remember this is panto, so you can really ham it up and make your actions larger than life. Whilst you've got that anger going inside of you, say your line again and let your actions show your anger as much as your voice.'

Jess had barely finished speaking when May turned on her, hands on hips and spat out, 'You had no right to interfere.' She used her height to her advantage, leaning over Jess and scowling down at her.

Jess looked startled and took a step back. 'Better,' she said. 'Much better. Now say it again, but when you reach the word, "interfere," I want you to notice how beautiful Cinderella is.'

All this effort for just one line? At this rate she would have every line right by Christmas 1950. She tried again but this time got a fit of the giggles halfway through.

Jess's lips twitched. 'That might do if Prince Charming was a ten-year-old girl. He's bold and assured, the best at everything he does and used to getting his own way. Whatever he wants, he just has to snap his fingers and it's done.'

'Like Milan, you mean?' May wouldn't have dared to say that usually. Maybe she was getting the hang of Prince Charming after all.

Jess's grin broadened. 'Milan will have to do more than snap his fingers to get what *he* wants, but come to think of it, there is a certain… *Milan-ness* about Prince Charming. If that helps you with his character then by all means, think about how Milan would deliver that line.'

That was easy. May could picture Milan prowling around Jess or, rather, Cinderella, like a leopard toying with its prey. Jess didn't seem to have any trouble handling him, but he would make minced meat of May if he turned his attentions on her. He was nothing like dear, sweet Peter.

The mere thought of Peter made the breath catch in her throat. Peter wouldn't have been hunting a stag in the first place, but if he had bumped into May in the forest, he would have treated her like a princess. She could picture that scene even more clearly than the scene with Milan. Peter would instantly make sure he hadn't frightened her, would find the most comfortable place in the clearing for her to sit and would share a delicious picnic with her, making his servants wait on her so she didn't have to lift a finger.

'May. *May!*'

May was jolted out of her pleasant daydream to find Jess regarding her, her head tilted and one eyebrow raised.

'You were thinking of Peter, weren't you.' It wasn't a question.

Yet again, May wished she were more like Jess. Jess would be able to laugh off being caught out in a daydream about her sweetheart, not blush like a lovesick schoolgirl.

'At least, I hope you were thinking about Peter,' Jess went on. 'If that dreamy expression was you thinking about Milan, there's going to be trouble.'

'Of course it was Peter. I—'

'Hah! I knew it!' Jess waved her script in May's face in a triumphant gesture. 'You only ever look like that when you're thinking of Peter.'

'How do I look? Can *everyone* tell what I'm thinking?' May was too horrified to be cross with Jess for catching her out.

'Oh, don't worry. I only know what you're thinking because I know you so well. I've learnt to spot the signs. Your eyes go all misty and you glow like you're lit up from the inside. You've got it bad, haven't you?' Although Jess's tone was teasing, there was a wistfulness to her expression that took May by surprise. There was no need for Jess to be jealous of May, not when she had the most handsome pilot in Amberton clearly smitten with her.

'I...' She hesitated but, after all, she had always confided her worries about Peter with Evie and Jess until now. There was no reason to change just because Evie wasn't there at the moment. 'I suppose I have. It's just harder now Peter isn't here any more. Now I can't wait to see him but when I do, it feels too pressured. Like a proper date.'

She'd half expected Jess to wave away her worries, tell her to have fun, so she was surprised and moved when Jess patted her on the arm. 'Has Peter put any pressure on you? If he has, I'll—'

'No. You know he's not like that. He promised to give me all the time I need.'

Jess was shaking her head. For a moment, May thought she was disagreeing and was on the point of defending Peter when Jess spoke first. 'There are times I'd like to wring your father's neck. He's got you so twisted up inside, until you believe you're unlovable and you can't trust yourself.'

'That's not it. Not really.'

'Then what's the problem?'

'I don't want a marriage like my parents'. My mum couldn't stand up to him. I don't want to end up as an unpaid servant. Evie talked about having an equal partnership with Alex and that's what I want with Peter. But I won't have that if I can't stick up for myself.'

Jess didn't argue but gave a sympathetic smile. 'Take all the time you need, May. I can feel it in my bones that Peter is the right man for you, but don't make any promises to him until you feel it for yourself.'

Tears stung May's eyelids at Jess's understanding, but Jess wouldn't allow her to become maudlin. 'Now get your act together, Lidford. Give me that line again, and if it helps you to imagine Milan saying them, be my guest.'

–

May found an unexpected enjoyment in her acting lessons with Jess, and her performance of Prince Charming improved. She still dreaded performing in front of an audience, but she no longer feared making a mess of her part. She also discovered a skill at writing that she'd never guessed at. She and Jess met in the NAAFI as regularly as possible and worked on the script together. May surprised herself by thinking up almost as many funny one-liners as Jess. Although she might never be an eloquent speaker, writing gave her a way of expressing herself that she'd never dreamt of. Sometimes, when Jess was on duty at night, May would take up a pencil and another of Evie's unused exercise books and scribble down a few scenes of a story or new lines for the pantomime. She knew her stories weren't worth showing to anyone else, but she enjoyed creating the characters and the worlds they lived in.

They were well into the second week of November before she got another chance to see Peter. When he asked what she would like to do, she asked to go to the cinema. That way she could be with Peter, reassure herself that he was alive and well, without enduring the awkward silences, heavy with the emotion she didn't feel ready to express.

As before, her heart leapt when she saw Peter waiting on the doorstep. She ran her eyes over him, anxiously looking for any sign of injury.

Her concern was mirrored in his eyes. 'Are you quite well, May? No huddling in ditches with other pilots now I've left Amberton? No sneaky Chelsea buns enjoyed with senior officers?'

She laughed, and some of her anxiety faded. Trust Peter to always know how to put her at ease. He leaned in to kiss her cheek and just for a moment she allowed herself to relax in his arms, remembering how safe it felt. It was how she had felt at the Midsummer dance, as though being in Peter's arms blotted out all her worries. But when he stepped back, the feel of his lips still burning on her cheek, she was able to study his face properly. He looked... haunted. There was no better word for it.

Smudges of blue beneath his eyes and in the hollows of his cheeks told a tale of sleepless nights or illness. Come to think of it, his jokey tone had seemed forced.

'How are you?' she asked him. 'You look pale.'

'I'm fine. Just been doing a lot of night flying recently and I can't seem to get the hang of sleeping during the day.'

'Oh. I thought Hurricanes weren't equipped for night flying.'

He gave a tight smile. 'We manage. But you know I can't talk about it.'

Abashed, May nodded. It was hard sometimes, when they spent so much of their waking hours on duty, not to be able to talk about it.

Peter held out his arm. 'Anyway, I want to forget about the war today and enjoy our day out. Your carriage awaits.'

He led her outside. May looked around for his motor-cycle but could only see an ancient Morris Minor. She craned her neck to see past. When Peter marched straight to the car and opened the passenger door for her, she laughed. This had to be another of his jokes.

'Sorry,' said Peter. 'I know it's a bit tatty, but it gets me around. I bought it from a friend last week.'

He was serious? He was certainly still holding the door, looking at her expectantly. 'How can you drive it?' She caught herself glancing down at his prosthetic leg as though checking to see if his leg had grown back.

Peter's eyes sparkled, and his exhaustion seemed to fall away. 'You never once ask how I manage to fly a high-performance aeroplane, yet you worry if I can drive a car?'

'But the pedals...'

He shrugged. 'Pilots have to use their feet on the rudder bars. It's not much different. I just have to take care not to get my foot stuck under the clutch.' He gestured for her to climb in. 'Unless you're too used to being the driver, of course. You could always drive if you prefer.'

May got into the passenger seat but couldn't help a qualm of nerves when Peter climbed in and set off. He soon proved that he could handle the car with just as much finesse as a Hurricane and May relaxed into the journey. It wasn't often that she could appreciate the scenery when travelling, as she was always the driver, focusing on navigating the maze of lanes when all the sign-posts had been removed. They chatted about their mutual friends at Amberton, and in no time the journey felt like their drives from the summer. All May's awkwardness fell away and she was laughing and chatting just as they had before. Just as it had been when May had known she was falling in love with him.

The newsreel was just starting when May and Peter crept into the cinema and stumbled through the darkness to their seats, guided by the dim light of the usherette's torch. At first May was too busy removing her coat and hat and arranging them on the empty seat beside her to take much notice of the images on the screen or the grim tones of the newsreader. Then she caught the words, 'City in the Midlands,' and her attention snapped to the screen. Street after street of flattened buildings flickered into view. May felt sick. These were streets she knew. The city hadn't been named, but it was undoubtedly Birmingham. Whenever people were shown, she strained her eyes, searching for familiar faces, half expecting to see her father's dark, sneering face gazing out at her from the screen. She found herself sinking down in her seat as though it would hide her from view. But mingled with her irrational fear of discovery was a need to know if her father and brothers had survived.

She became aware of Peter looking at her, his eyes gleaming from the reflected lights on the screen. 'Is this your home?' he murmured.

She nodded before remembering he probably couldn't see her. 'It's Birmingham, yes.'

'Do you want to leave? We can try and find out about any members of your family.'

'No point. There's no one important to me in Birmingham any more.' She had told Peter even less than she'd told Jess and Evie about her family, and she wasn't going to start now. Oh, Jess and Evie knew she'd been treated like a servant and about her mother. But they didn't know the worst of it. Not by a long chalk.

She couldn't drag her attention from the news, from the hideous shells of buildings she had once believed would stand for a hundred years or more. To see such a vibrant, teeming city reduced to its bare bones was an odd experience. She was shocked, of course, saddened over all the lives cut short, but it didn't feel any different to her than seeing the reports on London, Southampton or any other place. Birmingham – and her family – were part of her past. She had escaped and had no intention of returning.

It took a while to realise that all was not well with Peter. The cinema seats were narrow, so their arms were touching even though Peter hadn't made a move to hold her hand. Gradually, through the turmoil of her own thoughts came the realisation that Peter's arm was trembling against hers.

'Are you alright?' she whispered. She'd never known Peter to display any kind of emotional upset. True to his name, he was a rock, dependable and steady, someone she could always lean on.

'Yes, yes I'm fine. Just a bit chilly.' May couldn't believe that. If anything, the cinema was rather too warm. Evie would have been able to use logic to point out the flaw in his statement. Jess would have flat out challenged him. Either that or used it as an excuse to snuggle up close. But May was nothing like her friends and couldn't bring herself to emulate either.

Yet she couldn't allow Peter to suffer. Hesitantly, she placed her hand over his on the armrest and squeezed, pouring out her concern through touch as a substitute for the words she couldn't find. At first she feared Peter would pull his hand away, but after a brief hesitation, when his hand seemed to freeze beneath her touch, he turned it palm up and returned her clasp in his strong, warm grip.

May hardly noticed the remainder of the newsreel. Her thoughts were entirely occupied with Peter. What was wrong with him? He hadn't seemed ill and had been in good spirits on the drive to Chichester. But she couldn't forget his almost haunted expression when he'd arrived at High Chalk House. It had to be something to do with his duties, something he had seen or done while flying. She knew enough pilots to know they all reacted differently to their experiences. Peter, who had only returned to flying when the relentless onslaught of the Battle of Britain was dying down, hadn't had long to adjust to the difference between commanding the Operations Room and being in the air, in the thick of the action. It made her all the more frustrated that they couldn't discuss his duties. All she could do was hold his hand and hope that she could impress upon him that she cared and was there for him.

Chapter Seven

'What should I have done, Jess? I've never known Peter be anything other than rock steady.'

Jess tied off the thread she was working with before replying. The girls both had a free evening so they had collected a pile of costumes from the village hall to see if any would be useful. Jess had already picked out a gauzy tulle frock that would be perfect for the fairy godmother. The seam between bodice and skirt had split, so she was sewing it up while listening to May's description of her trip – May still refused to call it a date – with Peter.

'Sounds to me like you did exactly the right thing. Poor bloke must be suffering, seeing action up close for the first time. I'm sure you helped.' Jess set the fairy godmother's dress to one side and pounced on a white shirt with laces at the throat. 'What do you think of this for Prince Charming?'

May held the shirt up to her front and extended the arms. They barely reached past her elbows. 'Is there anything in there for the giant in Jack and the Beanstalk?' She hurried on before Jess could chide her for talking herself down. 'But seriously, Jess, what would you have done?'

Jess took up the dress again but didn't pick up the needle. Instead she regarded May, shaking her head slightly. 'What I would have done isn't the answer. You and Peter are very different people from me and… well, anyone I might walk out with.'

'I just wish I could do more to help him.' May gazed down at the bright green jacket she was mending. It had gold frogging and would be perfect for Buttons once she'd reattached a couple of gold buttons. 'It's just so hard when I don't even know what he's going through.'

Jess patted her hand. 'You're not alone, May. We've all been through the same thing – me, Evie, any other WAAF who's befriended a pilot. We have to watch them fly into danger every day and there's not a thing we can do to keep them safe. All we can do is be there for them when they're off duty. Help them forget they've got to do it all over again the next day and the day after that.'

And with that, May had to be satisfied. Of course Jess was right. She just wished there was something more she could do to help Peter. Whatever he was facing, it must be serious to have caused his shaking fit in the cinema.

A cry from Jess made her look round to see her friend pulling a large brown bundle from the pile. 'What's that?'

'A pantomime horse! All we have to do is stick a pair of antlers on the head – some twigs will do – and we've got our stag.'

The prospect of Milan and Jiří wearing the costume, and the antics their pantomime stag would perform, helped take May's mind off her worry.

The rumble of Merlin engines rose to a crescendo, and what sounded like two or three Hurricanes roared past, setting the empty cocoa cups rattling on the table. From the sound, May guessed they were coming in to land.

'Goodness,' she said. 'I didn't think our boys did night flights.' She thought of Peter. Was he out there some-where? She hated to think of him flying at the best of times, but on a dark, blustery autumn night it was even worse than usual.

Jess grimaced. 'Group seem to have changed their tactics. Our lads have started making more night flights. Haven't you noticed the pilots looking more tired than usual? It was bad enough over the summer when they were flying missions from dawn to dusk; at least they got the nights off. Now they are being called upon to fly at all hours.'

'Just like Peter, then.' May hugged her arms around her chest and prayed that if he was out tonight he would be safe.

The moment passed when, with a cry of triumph, Jess fished out a blue velvet waistcoat from the pile. 'Now this will be perfect for you, May, and there won't be any problem with sleeves.' She examined the waistcoat more closely, holding it up to the light. It would fit May perfectly if they took in the waist. It was a beautiful shade of teal with large gold buttons and a matching brocade panel across the back. The velvet glowed under the electric light.

'Prince Charming,' Jess said, 'you *shall* go to the ball.' Then she scowled. 'Oh no, there are two buttons missing.'

May looked, and sure enough, there was only a loose thread where the middle button should be and also a button missing on one of the pocket flaps. 'Maybe they came off here and they're loose in the pile.' She started to rummage through. If she had to appear on stage dressed as a man, she wanted to wear that waistcoat. Apart from the Midsummer dance, Peter hadn't seen her in anything other than her uniform. She was proud of her uniform, but she enjoyed the anticipation of Peter's reaction when he saw her in this gorgeous waistcoat. Try as they might, though, the girls couldn't find the missing buttons, or similar ones that they could take from another item of clothing.

'You know what this means, don't you,' Jess said in tones suited to a funeral. 'We have to go back to Evans' Haberdashery.'

'You don't have to come, Jess. I can easily find a moment to pop in tomorrow.' May hated the thought of facing Mrs Evans alone, but the woman seemed to save most of her vitriol for Jess.

Jess shook her head. 'What kind of a friend would I be if I made you face that cow alone? No, we'll go together.'

–

Both girls had a couple of hours free the next day in the early afternoon. 'No putting it off,' Jess said, draining her tea as they finished their lunch in the NAAFI. 'Time to face the dragon.'

May put on her cap and greatcoat with a heavy heart. Peggy would be at school, so there was not even the consolation of trying to see her.

'I hope none of Mrs Evans' cronies will be in the store,' Jess remarked, 'or Gawd only knows how long she'll make us wait.'

They walked outside with dragging feet. The sky was heavy with low clouds, matching their mood, and a light drizzle pricked May's face.

Jess scowled and pulled up her collar. 'Any chance you could borrow a car and take us to Chichester?'

May tried not to imagine her flight officer's face if she explained why she wanted the car. 'I don't think it would be considered a reasonable use of our petrol allowance.'

Jess's scowl deepened. 'Even if you say you want to avoid Mrs Evans? I'm sure Flight Officer Payne must have had a run-in with her. Most of us have at one point or other. I'm surprised she's let Peggy take part in the Panto, to be honest.' They had reached the gate by this time and waited for the guard on duty to let them through.

'Maybe she just wants to get Peggy out the house for a while,' May said.

'I suppose so.'

They were about to take the lane into the village when a hail made them look back. Milan and Alex Kincaith – Milan's squadron leader – were hurrying to catch them up. 'Are you going to the pub?' Alex asked. 'We've been stood down already so we're making the most of our freedom.'

When Jess explained with much dramatic face-pulling that they had to go to the haberdashery first, Milan offered to accompany them while Alex saved them a table in the Horse and Groom and got the drinks in.

As soon as they entered the haberdashery, the shop bell jingling jauntily, May wished they'd brought Alex with them as well. Mrs Evans' entire coterie of gossips seemed to be assembled, but that wasn't what made May's stomach give an unpleasant lurch. Standing to one side of the counter, while his wife dithered between blue and green gingham for a new apron, was Arnold Walker.

He glanced round when May, Jess and Milan entered and scowled. 'You again,' he said, sneering at Milan. 'Bloody foreigners can't even do a decent day's work. Our British pilots are still up in the air, risking their lives to defend the country, but not you. All you foreigners ever seem to do is fill the pub and go out with our girls.'

Milan took a step forward, his neck cords taut, his whole body quivering. Jess put a hand on his shoulder, trying to soothe him. He shook her off. 'Maybe if the British and their allies had not sold us to the Nazis, we would not need to be here.' His accent was far more pronounced than usual.

'We'd be better off without you.'

While Mrs Walker and Mrs Evans seemed too engrossed in their conversation to take in the scene in the back of the shop, the other women were casting them sidelong glances. One woman had shaken her head at Mr Walker's accusation, as though she didn't agree with him, though she didn't speak out. Shaking with anger, May drew breath. She had no idea what to say, but she couldn't stay silent when one of their pilots was being insulted.

Jess got there first. She dropped all attempts at calming Milan and faced up to Arnold Walker. 'If it wasn't for him, those Nazi spies you mentioned before would be undercover in this country, wreaking who knows what damage. Maybe even enough to 'ave lost us the war by now. Where were you when 'e was risking 'is life to stop them? And where were you last night when 'e and all 'is friends were getting their planes shot to bits while saving your skins? In bed, or feeding your fat belly, that's where.'

'Well, really!' Mrs Evans had finished serving her customer and was now looking at Jess over the top of her glasses. 'I won't have you talking to my customers like that.'

'Then you should tell that to Mr Walker.' Jess was shaking with rage.

'I'm sure Mr Walker did nothing of the sort. He's a respected member of the village. I'm going to have to ask you to leave. I won't have my customers upset.'

'Come on May.' Jess ushered both May and Milan towards the door. 'We can get what we need from Chichester. We were going to get everything for the pantomime costumes from here, but we'll have to take our custom elsewhere.'

Milan was already outside, the tinkle of the bell setting May's teeth on edge, and May was about to follow when she saw Mr Walker grab Jess's arm. He leaned in close and hissed in Jess's ear. May was close enough to catch his words. 'And good riddance to you, you little slut.'

May was so shocked she could hardly believe what she had overheard. She could only gape at Mr Walker while Jess hustled her through the door. 'Ignore him,' Jess said once they were outside and the door slammed shut behind them. 'Men like him enjoy lording it over women. He's just threatened by a woman in uniform. Men like him don't react well to women who try to tell him what to do.'

Milan was looking between the pair of them. 'What happened?' His face hardened. 'Did that man threaten you?' He made a move towards the door, coming to a stop when Jess pulled on his arm. 'Forget it. He's full of hot air. Let's go to the pub. At least we know 'e won't be there.'

Milan hesitated, seemingly torn between storming back into the shop to give Mr Walker a piece of his mind and going with Jess. May was relieved when he allowed Jess to pull him away. As they strolled towards the pub, May couldn't help noticing Jess was still shaking, and she didn't know if it was from anger or distress at Mr Walker's remark.

It was only when they were in the pub, sitting with Alex at their usual table in the snug, that she seemed to recover her spirits, although she was still fuming on Milan's behalf. 'What gives 'im the right to talk to you like that?' she demanded. 'If Arnold Walker knew even 'alf what you and the other lads 'ave done for us, 'e'd be begging for *more* Czechs in the RAF.'

Milan shook his head. 'It does not matter, Jess.'

'It does. People like 'im—' Jess stabbed a finger in the general direction of Evans' Haberdashery '—they go on about how marvellous our pilots are, how brave and self-less, but what they really mean is how brave and wonderful our British pilots are. They 'ate to think we can't hold back the Nazis alone.'

Milan was still shaking his head. 'They are afraid, and they are lashing out at anyone who speaks differently.'

'Exactly,' Jess said. 'They are afraid of anyone a bit different because they think only someone who looks like them or sounds like them can be trusted. Anyone a bit different is immediately suspicious.' Then she lowered her voice. 'And I really hate it when they treat you with such disrespect.'

'I can put up with a bit of disrespect as long as the RAF let me continue to fight the Nazis.' Milan covered Jess's hand with his own. 'You respect and trust me. That is enough for me.'

Jess looked uncharacteristically flustered. May felt uncomfortable, as though the pair had forgotten she and Alex were also there. Feeling the need to speak before either of them said things they wouldn't want to be over-heard, she said, 'I think I can go into Chichester the day after tomorrow to get the buttons.'

Jess gave a little start and looked grateful for change of subject. 'Thanks, May. You're a gem.' Then she turned to Alex. 'Have you heard from Evie recently?'

The atmosphere lightened, and soon they were all chatting, laughing over the latest scene May and Jess had written for the pantomime. But the encounter with Mr Walker had left May with a growing unease. She could only pray that Jess was right and seeing Milan and Jiří perform would help break down the hostility felt by the likes of Arnold Walker.

–

Another night patrol, this time in a cloudless sky under a bright full moon. As Peter's Hurricane lifted from the ground, he clung to the hope that there would be enough light to find the enemy. A grim mood had settled upon the squadron; they desperately needed a win. There had been whispers that the Luftwaffe were planning a big show and Peter hated to think what it would do to morale if they failed to stop it.

Sure enough, his flight had been in the air less than a minute when they were directed to intercept a Staffel of bombers that had crossed the coast. Nerves tightening, Peter acknowledged the order. With eyes fixed on his instruments, he adjusted course.

'Keep a lookout,' he told his pilots once his readings told him they had reached the interception point. 'We must be nearly on top of them.' He craned his neck, looking all around, up and down, his mouth dry. A faint gleam far below caught his eye, but he relaxed when he saw it was the moonlight reflecting off water. They were too far inland for it to be the sea, so he guessed it was a lake.

He circled, still looking all around. The Staffel had to be close.

A voice crackled over his headset. 'Red Leader, this is Acorn. What have you got?'

'Acorn, this is Red Leader. Not a sausage.' He was unable to keep the frustration from his voice, but he didn't care. 'Please confirm position.'

'Red Leader, this is Acorn. Position correct. Ground observer reports bombers passing below you to your starboard.'

What the hell? Peter flung a glance across his starboard wing, heart hammering, seeing only inky blackness. He had to trust the report, though. On a cloudless night like this, the scene would be clear to ground observers. They would also be able to hear the arrhythmic throb of bomber engines while Peter was unable to hear anything over the roar of his Hurricane.

Then he caught movement in the corner of his eye. At first he thought it was a cloud passing across the moon but when he turned to look, it was as though he'd been doused with a bucket of icy water. No mere cloud – a swarm of bombers, too many to count. Heinkel He 111s. What he had seen was their reflection in the lake. They must have passed between it and the moon. He had them. He called in the sighting and gave the order to break and engage.

Now he knew where to look, he saw the glint of moonlight on a wingtip. This one was his. Forcing himself not to clench his fingers around the joystick, he dived. Before he was close enough to fire, a flash of tracer off his port wing made him react instinctively. He pulled his Hurricane into a roll, all the while craning his neck to locate the source of the attack. There! He lined up to shoot, then jerked back on the joystick when he saw it wasn't an enemy plane but another Hurricane. In the dark they had both targeted the same bomber and both missed. He managed to restrain himself from abusing the pilot over the radio and took out his feelings by punching the canopy.

For a horrible moment he thought he had lost the bombers. He banked steeply, all the while craning his neck to locate the Heinkels. What he saw, though, was a sight to send his blood cold: three Messerschmitt 110s, silhouetted against the moon as they arced down towards Peter's squadron. If the moon revealed three, there were bound to be more. He only had time to shout a warning to the other pilots before they were in range, spitting fire. Peter reacted instinctively and found by some miracle that his manoeuvres had brought a 110 into his line of fire.

'Wait until it's in range,' he muttered. He resented every moment he was wasting on the 110s while the Heinkels must be closing in on their target. Only when the dim shape was so close he thought they must collide did he press the firing button. The 110's nose jerked up, a sign the pilot had been hit. Shrapnel clattered against Peter's canopy; he banked sharply, secure in the knowledge that he had downed his target. Feeling sick, he scanned the sky for more enemy fighters. He released a shaky breath when he saw a flight of 110s pass across the moon – all leaving the fight, noses down, heading for the coast.

'Red Leader to all pilots. Target the bombers. Leave the 110s. Repeat, target bombers.' He prayed none of his men would take the bait and follow the fighters out to sea. He was praying that the Heinkels hadn't got away when another glimpse of movement revealed them. The Messerschmitts had allowed them to continue on their course, and a significant gap had opened between them. He opened up his throttle and pointed his nose at the departing bombers. A glance at his fuel gauge showed he still had enough fuel to take them on and make it back to Oldbourne.

The gap closed, too slowly for Peter's liking. 'Come on, come on.' Peter nursed the throttle eking out as much speed as possible, knowing that by doing so he was further reducing the range. But he would rather stop the bombers and make a forced landing than turn away from the fight. The gap was closing... closing. Attacking a bomber was different from attacking a fighter. Fighters would break and engage in a dogfight. Bombers would, as much as possible, continue flying towards their target, while their gunners would shoot at you from all angles.

Now! They were close enough. Right below him, a dark shape briefly obscured the silvery line of a river. From its silhouette, he identified a Heinkel He 111. He heard the wind howling around the fuselage as he dived, holding fire until the last moment. Then he let fly a burst of fire. Surely at this range he couldn't miss. Cursing, he realised the bomber didn't seem to have incurred any vital damage, for it carried straight on. Streams of bullets flew past his own fuselage. The Hurricane shook as some struck the wing, but like his own attack, there didn't seem to be any serious damage. Nothing his ground crew couldn't patch up when he got back.

He pulled into a steep climbing turn, ready to come round for a second attack. Streams of tracer fire revealed the other Hurricanes of his flight, darting in and out of the huge formation, but even as Peter prepared for another attack on his chosen Heinkel, a heavy feeling of hopelessness overtook him. It was like watching gnats attacking a stampeding herd of buffalo.

He held until he knew he couldn't miss, and fired again, feeling his whole machine judder from the recoil. For a moment he couldn't see any change and he thought he'd missed again. Then fingers of flame streamed from the Heinkel's engine. Certain he'd stopped at least one bomber, he banked sharply, only to sense another dark shape close alongside, far too large to be a Hurricane. The whole scene slowed down. He seemed to have an age to plan every manoeuvre. Then the Hurricane shuddered as a line of bullets hit somewhere near the tail. Immediately the plane pitched into a dive and became unresponsive. He fought for control, kicking the rudder pedals, but nothing happened.

'Blue Leader, this is Red Leader,' he called as he still struggled for control, 'My crate's taken a hit. Think I've lost my tail. Bailing out.'

'Roger, Red Leader.' A pause, then, 'Good luck.'

He felt sick. The squadron's fuel reserves would be too low to continue their pursuit. He might have downed one bomber, but the rest continued towards the target.

Peter had enough control to flip his machine into an inverted dive. He released the canopy, sliding it right back. Now he was dangling upside down with nothing but his harness holding him in his seat. Icy air battered his face as he fumbled for his harness release. His fingers quickly turned numb from the cold. With a gasp of relief he found the release and he fell, only to be stopped with a jolt when his prosthetic leg caught on some unseen obstacle. Suspended upside down, it was impossible to lever himself into a position where he could see what his foot was caught on. With a howl of frustration he jackknifed his body, struggling to work his foot free, but it was stuck fast. Not this way! He couldn't die like this, trapped in a diving plane.

Again, it was an image of May's face that came to him in this moment of crisis. He pictured her hearing the news, and his heart contracted. He wouldn't leave her. Not now. He flailed his free foot, kicking his prosthetic over and over, not knowing if the action would free his prosthetic or wedge it further in. Then suddenly he was free, falling, tumbling over and over. He was so shocked he almost forgot to pull the ripcord, but then his groping fingers found it, and he tugged. The canopy blossomed above his head and he jolted against his harness. Panting, he grasped the lines and looked around. All he could see was the moon and stars against an inky black sky. No sign of the bombers.

He felt sick. Even though his squadron had done all they could, it hadn't been enough. The bombers had got through, and innocent people were going to suffer.

Chapter Eight

May glanced uneasily at the sky as she and Jess cycled to the village hall the following Friday. She hoped the sirens would stay silent tonight. Last night had been clear with a full moon – a bomber's moon – though there hadn't been any raids nearby, thankfully. She could only pray it would be the same tonight and they wouldn't have to spend another rehearsal huddled in the shelter with frightened children.

'Mind the pothole!'

Jess's shout drew May's attention back to the road just in time for her to dodge the rut.

'Pay attention,' Jess called. 'Prince Charming isn't supposed to be sporting a black eye and a split lip.'

May grinned but couldn't help another glance at the sky. There had been rumours of heavy bombing over the Midlands last night. Had Peter been up there? Was he flying tonight? She hadn't heard from him for a few days, which wasn't unusual, although she wouldn't be easy in her mind until she had news.

The only advantage of the persistent worry was that it had stopped her fretting about performing in the pantomime. She would be rehearsing her part for the first time tonight, and she only felt the faintest twinge of nerves.

One worry drove out another, it seemed, for when she saw Peggy, she was able to push thoughts of Peter to the back of her mind. She arrived with the other children, for they had come straight from school, again standing a little apart from them, eyes downcast.

'Do you reckon Mrs Evans will expect her to walk home alone again?' she murmured to Jess as the children dropped their coats and hats on chairs at the back of the hall.

'We can walk her home if she does,' Jess replied. 'As long as we don't have to speak to the snooty cow it won't be a problem.'

Then Jess raised her voice. 'Gather round, everyone.' May bit back a smile at the way Jess seemed to become a perfect teacher. The children clustered around her, their excited chatter dying down. Milan and Jiří were also present and they joined the back of the group. 'Hands up everyone who's learnt the words of the opening song.'

Every child's hand shot up, even Peggy's, although May doubted she'd had any help from Mrs Evans. She'd overheard Mrs Evans say in church that she didn't approve of 'such common entertainment'. Yet again, May wondered why she'd allowed Peggy to take part at all.

'Very good,' said Jess. 'In that case, please leave your scripts in your bags and we'll focus on the acting more this evening. It will be easier to run around and dance if you're not holding the pages and reading the words.'

Mrs Grey, who had recovered from her cold, was at the piano. At Jess's signal, she struck up the merry tune of the opening song. She wasn't as skilled a pianist as Milan, but he was needed onstage to play the stag this time. Under Jess's tutelage, the children quickly mastered the steps of the dance they would perform with Cinderella as the opening number. May, sitting on the steps at the side of the stage, ready to prompt if needed, watched Peggy. She lost her habitual guarded expression as she sang and was soon throwing herself into the dance with the same energy as the other children, singing about their most hated chores.

At the end of the dance, the children moved to the side of the stage while Jess as Cinderella walked a little apart from the group and rehearsed her soliloquy. She bewailed how her stepmother had forced her into a servant's role when she should be managing the house-hold. May was so transfixed at Jess's transformation into Cinderella, convincing even though she still wore her WAAF uniform, she almost missed her cue. For the actual performance, they were going to play a recording of a hunting horn to proclaim Prince Charming's arrival, preceded by the pantomime stag; for now, Jiří was doing his best imitation of one before disappearing back into the adapted horse costume and prancing on stage with Milan. Although no one else was in costume, Jess had insisted that Jiří and Milan should wear the horse costume to help them become accustomed to working together as the stag.

The stag trotted onto the stage, to the giggles of the children. With a drooping head and limp, it was a picture of dejection, and Cinderella helped it to a hiding place behind some 'bushes' – marked for now by a chair – and got the children to disguise it by weaving ivy around its antlers.

May, her knees weak, feeling nothing like the dashing, brave Prince Charming, leapt up from her perch and hurried onto the stage. Thanks to her lessons from Jess she knew her part well and was able to deliver her lines correctly even if not making a particularly convincing thwarted huntsman. It was harder still when the giggles from the children told her the 'stag' was performing its antics behind her back. But she found her nerves melted away acting with the children and people she knew well. At least there was plenty of time before she'd have to perform in front of an audience.

At the end of the rehearsal, the children departed one by one when their foster parents arrived to collect them. Those that arrived together were speaking in low voices, looking grave, but they gave bright smiles when they saw their foster children. May wondered if anything had happened.

Soon all the children apart from Peggy had left. When it became apparent that Mrs Evans was not going to turn up, Mrs Grey offered to see her safely home. 'Honestly,' she said in an aside to May and Jess while Peggy went to put on her coat and hat, 'for someone who's so keen on keeping up appearances, you'd think she wouldn't want a child in her care to make her way home alone in the dark.'

May nodded. She wanted to ask Mrs Grey's advice on how they might help Peggy, but Jess changed the subject. 'Mrs Grey, I wonder if you could suggest someone who would be able to print some programmes for us. Is there a printer in Amberton? It would be so convenient if we didn't have to go all the way to Chichester.'

'Mr Walker has a printing press. He prints the parish magazine. Actually, that reminds me. I must write a piece about the pantomime for the December issue.'

Jess thanked Mrs Grey and before May could ask the vicar's wife about Peggy, Peggy herself returned, and the pair departed.

Jess turned to May, scowling. 'Of all the people to give business to, it has to be Arnold Walker.'

'You could go to Chichester.'

Jess shook her head. 'I'd rather use an Amberton printer. We don't have the time to go back and forth to Chichester. I'll just have to bite the bullet and ask Mr Walker next time I see him.'

They cheerfully abused Mr Walker and Mrs Evans all the way back to High Chalk House. When they walked into the kitchen, they found a couple of WAAFs making Horlicks. Both spoke in hushed voices as though at a funeral.

'What's the matter?' Jess asked. 'Has something happened?'

'Haven't you heard?' one asked, her eyes wide. 'Coventry was bombed last night. It's terrible.'

—

All anyone wanted to do the next day was talk about Coventry. May felt sick when she heard the details. Wave after wave of bombers – over five hundred – had dropped bombs and incendiaries in an attack that had lasted from Thursday evening until the following dawn.

As people spoke in hushed terms of the numbers killed, the cathedral, the medieval buildings, May's thoughts were with the evacuees, all from Coventry. She thought especially of Peggy. The other children seemed to be with caring families, who would surely break the news gently and do all in their power to find out about the children's families. But what would Mrs Evans do? May dreaded to think.

'I bet she won't tell 'er at all, the evil cow,' Jess said when May spoke of her worries to Jess. Both girls had the morning off and were in the Rose Room, huddled around the wireless with several other WAAFs, listening to reports of the work done by brave volunteers to extinguish the burning buildings and search the rubble for survivors. 'She'll let the poor kid hear it from one of her friends.'

It sounded all too likely. As it was Saturday, Peggy wouldn't even have the comfort of being at school with friends or her teacher. 'We have to find her,' May said and rose from her perch on the arm of a sofa, tugging Jess's arm. 'She shouldn't be alone.'

Jess hung back for a moment. She stood on tiptoe to peer over the heads of the gathered WAAFs and see in the mirror to tidy her hair. 'What?' she said, seeing May's exasperated look. 'You never know who we might run into.'

Jess didn't spend long getting ready; soon they were cycling through puddles on the lane to Amberton. A brisk wind whipped through the hedgerows and May had to shield her eyes with one hand to protect them from flying leaves and rain.

'There goes my hairdo,' Jess wailed as she fought to keep her bike steady against the buffeting wind.

'You don't have to come.'

'I'm coming. I'm worried about Peggy too,' Jess replied. 'Although how we'll speak to her if she's with that old dragon, I've no idea.'

In the event, they found Peggy sitting on the wall outside the village hall, swinging her legs, heedless of the weather, her eyes reddened and swollen.

'I don't know nothing,' she wailed when May and Jess sat either side of her. 'Nobody does. Our teacher has been trying to find out, but all the phone lines are down.'

May quelled the impulse to promise to go there herself. What could she do? She had no idea what Peggy's mother looked like, and even if she did, it would be chaos in Coventry. She didn't know anyone there and all the authorities would be working flat out to rescue survivors and inform next of kin. She would just get in the way and stop people from doing their job. Then an idea occurred to her. 'Where does your mother work? Maybe we can get in contact with her employers.'

Peggy wiped her eyes. 'She works in a shoe shop.' She gave its name and address.

May gave her an encouraging smile. 'I can't promise we'll be able to find out, but we'll do our best.' Although how they were to get any news when Peggy's teacher, who had contacts in Coventry, couldn't, she had no idea. 'Of course, your mother might be trying to contact you,' she said. 'She must know how worried you and Davey will be. She would send word to Mrs Evans, wouldn't she?' May hesitated to suggest Peggy go to Mrs Evans' house. Anyone in their right mind would want to get away from there if they possibly could, but there was no escaping the fact that any news would be sent there.

Peggy gave a grudging nod.

May met Jess's eyes over the top of Peggy's head. 'Do you think we should go round there?' After the unpleasantness of their last visit, May knew the last thing Jess would want to do in her precious free time would be to face Mrs Evans, so her admiration for her friend rose even higher when Jess gave a reluctant nod.

In the end, they were saved the trip. The clip clop of a horse's hooves and the creak and rattle of a cart could be heard as they set off with dragging feet for the haberdashery. Mrs Bowes appeared from around the corner, driving her horse and cart. She brought the cart to a halt when she saw May, Jess and Peggy.

'Well, now, you're exactly the young lady I've been looking for.' Mrs Bowes addressed Peggy after a brief smile at Jess and May.

Peggy's mouth trembled. 'Have you heard anything about my mum?' she asked in a quavering voice.

'Oh dear, no I haven't. I'm sorry if I gave you a fright. But I thought you might like to come and spend the day on the farm with your brother. We'll bring you back in good time tonight. If there's any news, it'll be sent to us as well as Mrs Evans.'

Peggy nodded enthusiastically. 'Yes please. I want to see Davey.'

'Hop aboard, then. We'll stop at the haberdashery on the way to tell Mrs Evans where you're going.'

While Peggy scrambled into the cart and wrapped the tartan blanket that Mrs Bowes handed her around her knees, Mrs Bowes shook her head sadly at May and Jess. 'Terrible business. It's in all the newspapers today. Five hundred bombers! I'd never have thought such a thing possible, even in my worst nightmares. I couldn't bear the thought of this young mite all alone today of all days. It was good of the two of you to look out for her, busy as you are.'

'It's no problem, Mrs Bowes,' Jess said. 'Thank you for coming to fetch her. We have to go back on duty in a couple of hours, and we didn't want to leave her alone.'

Once Peggy was settled in the cart, Mrs Bowes picked up the reins and clicked her tongue to urge the horse forward. May watched Peggy until the cart rolled out of sight, her heart breaking for the poor girl who had no idea if she still had a mother.

She turned to Jess. 'If there's anything I can do to help her, anything at all, I'll do it.'

—

'Lidford, there's a phone call for you.'

May froze. She glanced up from where she was pouring boiling water into the teapot in the kitchen of High Chalk House. A WAAF stood in the doorway, pointing towards the hall, where the telephone was situated.

'Thank you.' She replaced the kettle on the hob, her hands starting to shake. Who would phone her? Telephone calls meant bad news. Both Evie and Peter had arranged always to write in unspoken acknowledgement of the fact, none of them wanting to cause alarm by phoning.

Her feet seemed to take charge of her body without conscious thought. She walked through to the hall, her thoughts coalescing to a single point: Peter. Something had happened to Peter. She picked up the heavy receiver and held it to her ear. 'Hello?' Her voice was so weak she had to clear her voice and try again. 'Hello, who's speaking, please?'

'May? Thank goodness you're there.' It was Peter.

Going limp with relief, May dropped into the chair. 'Peter? What's happened? Are you alright?'

'Yes, I'm fine. Sorry to phone. Hope I didn't give you a fright.'

'No, that's okay.' She hardly knew what she was saying. She pressed her free hand to her chest, waiting for the rapid beating to return to normal. 'Why are you calling?'

'I wanted to hear your voice. Long story. I'll explain when I see you.'

That didn't reassure May, but Peter went on before she could ask more.

'Look, will you be able to get any time off in the next day or two?'

'Time off? I suppose so. I can try.'

'I'd like to see you. The only trouble is I can't drive at the moment so—'

'Can't drive?' She seemed to be reduced to parroting his words. 'Then you *are* hurt. What's happened?'

'I'm not hurt. Honest. I— oh, I was going to wait until I saw you, but I can see I'm going to have to explain. I got shot down yesterday and—'

'Shot down?' There she went again. 'Sorry. Carry on.'

She could hear the smile in his voice as he continued. That, more than anything, assured her that he was unhurt. 'I promise you I'm fine. I had to bail out, though, and my foot – the tin one – got jammed somehow. It's all a bit of a blur, to be honest, but when I landed, I noticed my leg hadn't come with me.'

'Oh, Peter, what are you going to do?'

'I've got a peg leg at the moment. Shame you're not doing Treasure Island for your panto – I'd make a convincing Long John Silver. Anyway, I can't fly until I get a new leg, so I wondered if I could see you. Only trouble is, I can't drive, either, so I'd need you to come and collect me. Not very gallant, I know, making a girl run around the countryside after a chap, but—'

'I'd love to see you.' Then, 'Are you sure you're all right?' The relief was giving way to the realisation that Peter had been in mortal danger. To the point that he'd had to jump out of his plane. This phone call could so easily be his CO telling her Peter had been killed in the crash. She understood Evie better now, why she had initially resisted falling in love with a pilot. But now that May knew how close Peter had come to losing his life, how he might be killed in his next flight, she knew she had to see him while she still could.

'I'm fine. The joke is, I might have been killed if I hadn't had a false leg. Funny how life goes. Anyway, if you can get a 48-hour pass, we could go where you liked, within reason. Just name the place.'

Until this phone call, May would have hesitated going somewhere alone with Peter. It would have felt too much like making a commitment she couldn't live up to. Now, however, all she wanted to do was see him, reassure herself he was truly unhurt. Peter would stick to his word not to pressure her, she knew that. She quickly tried to think of a place she'd like to visit. Brighton might be nice again, or somewhere else on the coast.

Then it hit her. She knew exactly where they could go. 'How about Kenilworth?'

'Kenilworth? Are you sure? It's awfully close to Coventry. It might not be safe.'

'I know. You see...' and she poured out Peggy's story. 'I have to do something,' she concluded. 'This poor girl is staying with the most horrible woman, who doesn't give a jot about what she must be going through. If there's any way I can find out what's happened to her mother, I have to try.'

'It'll be chaos there,' Peter said, though from his tone she knew he wasn't arguing against going but warning her not to pin too much hope on the trip. 'Do you have any idea where to start looking?'

'I can get her home address from Peggy, and where she works.'

'That's as good a place to start as any.'

They finished the call by making arrangements to meet at Chichester – Peter's petrol rations wouldn't get them to Coventry and back, so they would have to take the train. May hung up, her heart thumping with trepidation. Was she mad, going into a bombed-out zone? Regardless, for Peggy's sake, she had to try.

Chapter Nine

'This is as far as I can take you. Roads are all blocked in the centre.'

May and Peter thanked the man who had given them a lift from Kenilworth and climbed out of his van.

Nothing could have prepared May for the devastation of Coventry. The smoke could be seen from miles away, thick and black, hovering over the medieval city like a thundercloud. The stench of burning was overpowering, and May's eyes smarted as she surveyed the scene.

'Where shall we try first?' Peter asked, leaning on his stick. Although he had shrugged off the inconvenience of the peg leg, he needed the stick to help him balance.

'I...' May felt the futility of their search. Whole streets had been pummelled to no more than a pile of rubble. Twisted tramlines writhed from the ground, stabbing the air. Fires still smouldered; dust and ashes formed a gritty layer in the back of May's throat. Men and women wandered through the ruins. Some seemed to be conducting systematic searches, looking for what belongings could be salvaged, but many were clearly in shock, wandering aimlessly with blank expressions.

She squared her shoulders. She had promised Peggy she would do what she could, so she wouldn't turn back now, however hopeless it seemed. 'Let's try their house first.' She unfolded the map she'd brought and found their current location. 'Yes, it's not too far from here. Closer than the shop, anyway.' Peter had insisted that he could walk easily enough, though May was sure his temporary leg must be uncomfortable.

Cold dread clutched May's heart the moment they got to the street and saw nothing but pulverised ruins. Only a few people were milling around here, and none of them could say what had happened to Peggy's mother. 'Sorry, love,' one man said. Tears welled in his eyes. 'I was away when it happened.' May saw he was holding a singed photograph, showing a smiling woman with two children. He turned and shambled away like a sleepwalker.

'Oh, God,' May turned to Peter and didn't hesitate when he opened his arms. She pressed her cheek against his shoulder, blinking away tears. 'I knew it would be bad, but I had no idea.' Peter's coat reeked of burning; she supposed her clothes must do so as well. She doubted she would ever be able to get rid of the smell. 'I feel so helpless,' she murmured against his collar. 'I want to help, but I've got nothing to offer. I didn't even bring food. I should have thought of that.' It was worse even than the time she, Jess and Evie had seen the Dunkirk evacuees. At least then they'd been able to offer chocolate and a shoulder to lean on. But the scale of devastation was too much to take in, and these were civilians. They should have been protected from the worst excesses of war.

'You're here for Peggy, remember,' Peter said. 'You can't help everyone, but you are helping Peggy. Focus on what you can do.'

–

Peter reluctantly relaxed his arms as May leaned back and gave him a watery smile. 'I know you're right, but it's hard

119

to accept in the middle of so much suffering.' A furrow appeared between her brows. 'I suppose that must be how you deal with the impossibility of your job.'

Peter went very still. He didn't want to think about his failure to shoot down more of the bombers. Not when it was now clear the ones he had attacked on Thursday night must have been bound for Coventry.

May went on, 'When I hear about the numbers of bombers coming over, night after night, knowing how few fighters we have in comparison, I know it's impossible to stop them. If you shoot down just one, though, that's one payload that won't land on houses or a factory. You can't save everyone, but you can save some.'

'I... I suppose you're right.' Peter forced a smile, yet he couldn't stop himself from wondering what damage had been caused by the bombers he'd intercepted. Had one of their bombs landed on the Hardys' house? Would Peggy's mother be safe and well if he'd shot down just one more?

He pushed the thought to the back of his mind. He'd drive himself mad if he wasn't careful. 'Anyway, we've drawn a blank at Mrs Hardy's home address, but we could still try where she works.' He resolutely used the present tense when referring to Peggy's mother, despite the increasing evidence to the contrary. 'You said it was a shoe shop?'

'Yes.' May unfolded the map again. 'On Hay Lane.' She grimaced. 'It doesn't look hopeful. It's not far from the cathedral.'

Peter's heart sank. They had seen images of the blackened shell of Coventry Cathedral in the newspapers. 'We'll have to walk. There won't be any buses running to the centre.'

May shot him an anxious glance. 'Can you manage?'

'I'll be fine.' The peg leg chafed his stump and made it ache, but it was a small price to pay if they could find Mrs Hardy.

Miraculously, the little shoe shop had survived the blitz relatively unscathed. Windows had been blown out, and a pile of shoes was scattered on the pavement. Glass crunched underfoot as they tried the door. It was open and they discovered the shop was being used as a temporary centre by a group of volunteers. They found Mrs Hughes, the shop owner, occupied in putting together parcels of necessities for those who had been made homeless.

'Oh, I'm ever so worried about Mrs Hardy,' she said, when May broached the subject. 'I've not seen her since that dreadful night. I did hear that she wasn't in her house when it was hit – I've been trying to find her – but some of the shelters were hit, too, and I don't know which one she was in. I wanted to tell her she was welcome to move in with me. What with my Harry and both our lads away in the army, I'm rattling around like a lost thing, all alone in my house.'

'Have you any idea where she might be? If she survived, I mean.' May asked. 'I'm trying to find out on behalf of her daughter and son. They're terribly worried, as you can imagine.'

'Oh, they're sweet children,' said Mrs Hughes. 'It's a mercy they were sent away in time. Now, let me think.' She crammed a bar of chocolate into an already bulging shoebox. 'Plenty of folk have left Coventry to stay with relatives outside the city. She doesn't have much family. I do seem to remember her mentioning an aunt out at Burton Green, I suppose she might have gone there. Now, what was the name?' She put the lid on the box while she pondered and secured it with string. 'Mrs Eastman. No, Easton. That was it.'

'Thank you,' said May. 'We'll try that.'

'If you find her, send her to me, won't you? I'll look after her.'

'Thank you, Mrs Hughes.' Peter pulled some money from his pocket and handed it to her. 'For more parcels.'

Outside the shop, May consulted her map. 'I don't believe it,' she said after a moment. 'Burton Green is only a couple of miles from Kenilworth.'

Peter squared his shoulders, doing his best to ignore his throbbing leg. 'Let's start walking. We'll try and hitch a lift once we're out of the centre.'

Much to his relief, they soon caught a lift from a teenage lad driving a grocer's van, who dropped them at the junction of the lane leading to Burton Green. As they trudged towards the village, hunched against the chill, light rain, Peter found himself thinking over the words he had spoken earlier. *You can't help everyone... Focus on what you can do.* Good advice. If only he could follow it himself. May had summed it up so well, without even knowing of his inner turmoil. He couldn't save everyone, but he could save some. If he was sensible, he would live by those words. Trying to save everyone was an impossibility; that was the road to a breakdown.

Had May guessed what he was going through? He studied her when she stopped to check her map, brushing raindrops from the page. He felt a hypocrite, suddenly, wishing she would open her heart to him when he had held back his own worries. Perhaps if he was more open, it would give her the confidence to confide and trust in him.

'Thank you for what you said earlier,' he said.

She shot him a glance, frowning. 'Why? What did I say?'

'About not being able to save everyone. I hadn't thought of it that way before. It helps.'

'I'm glad.' She folded the map and tucked it in her pocket. 'Another quarter of a mile, I think.' They walked on for a few paces, then she said, 'I could see you were struggling with something. When you told me I couldn't help everyone, it all clicked into place.'

'It's easier said than done, though, isn't it?'

May nodded. 'Perhaps we can keep an eye on each other. I'll remind you when I think you need it, if you do the same for me.'

'It's a deal.' Then, before Peter could stop himself, he couldn't help adding, 'That sounds suspiciously like a relationship, May Lidford.'

He could have kicked himself. He'd promised he wouldn't badger her. However, May wasn't looking at him. She pointed at a clump of trees. 'Is that smoke? There might be a cottage.'

Peter looked and saw a stream of smoke spiral into the air above the trees. 'I think you're right.'

May quickened her pace. 'Let's go there. We can ask if they know where Mrs Easton lives.'

Leaning on his stick, Peter followed, wincing a little as his chafed stump protested. A curly-haired young woman with a harassed face answered the door. 'Oh, yes, I know who you mean,' she said in answer to May's inquiry. 'She lives this end of the village. The first house on Red Lane. You can't miss it.'

'I don't suppose you know if her niece from Coventry is here – a Mrs Hardy?'

The woman pursed her lips and shook her head. 'There's been a number of Coventry folk arrive, poor devils. My own uncle, for one. I don't know if anyone's staying with the Eastons, though.'

An elderly man with wispy white hair shuffled into view in the hallway. He was wrapped in a tartan dressing gown that was several sizes too large for his skinny frame. 'What's that?' he asked in a reedy voice. 'Someone asking for Mrs Hardy?'

May exchanged glances with Peter. 'Do you know her?' she asked.

'Oh, yes. Kind young girl. I met her on the walk here. She helped me carry my cat.' The man's mouth trembled and his eyes filled with tears. 'The only thing I've got left.'

The woman patted the man's hand. 'There now, uncle. You know I'll take care of you.' She turned to Peter and May. 'I'm sorry. I've got to go.'

They thanked her and hurried on their way. 'Oh, Peter, this is wonderful,' May said, turning shining eyes upon him. 'I couldn't bear it if it turns out she's not here after all.'

The breeze had loosened tendrils of dark hair from her severe bun so they framed her face; raindrops beaded her eyelashes. Hope blazed from her face, and she looked so beautiful that he had to fight the urge to kiss her. He gave her his arm. 'Come on. There's only one way to find out.'

In another ten minutes they had reached the house on Red Lane. Mrs Easton answered the door and led them into a warm parlour. A young woman sat beside the fire, wrapped in a bright orange blanket, gazing vacantly at the flames. Although she couldn't be much older than May, deep lines furrowed her brow and dark circles shadowed her eyes, making her look much older. Like the elderly man in the last house, she wore clothes that were clearly borrowed.

May leaned down and patted her shoulder. 'Mrs Hardy?' she said. 'Are you Mrs Hardy, Peggy and Davey's mother?'

The woman's eyes came into sharp focus and she grasped May's hand. 'Peggy? Davey? Has something happened? Oh, God, what's wrong?'

'No, Mrs Hardy, they're fine.' But Mrs Hardy had started to sob, huge convulsive shudders that shook her slender frame, and it took some time for May to calm her and give reassurance that her children were unhurt.

'Are you sure?' she asked for what felt like the hundredth time. May knelt on the hearth rug and put an arm around her shoulders. Peter, hampered by his peg leg, remained standing and gazed awkwardly down at the woman who was now dabbing at her face with a hand-kerchief. May spoke gently, describing Davey's home with the Bowes and Peggy's involvement with the pantomime, glossing over her home with Mrs Evans.

'I'm sorry,' Mrs Hardy said once she had calmed suffi-ciently. 'It's just that these past few days have been like living in a nightmare. It's hard to believe anything good is happening elsewhere.'

'I know. But Peggy and Davey are both well, if worried about you. We promised to try and find you.'

'Thank you. That's so kind.'

Mrs Easton came in then, carrying a tray with tea and carrot cake.

'You know,' said Mrs Hardy eyeing the cake with a smile, 'I think I could manage to eat something.'

Her colour improved as she ate and she asked what was happening in Coventry. 'I know a few people have returned, but I don't know what there is to go back to.'

'You still have a job, Mrs Hardy. The shop is still standing.'

'It is?' Mrs Hardy pressed a hand to her chest. 'And Mrs Hughes?'

'She's fine,' May replied. She repeated Mrs Hughes' offer to house her.

'Bless my soul. That is good news. I heard everything was gone.'

'It's bad, Mrs Hardy, I can't deny it,' Peter said. 'But parts of Coventry are still standing, and it will be rebuilt.'

Mrs Hardy drained her cup, then looked at her aunt. 'I should go back. I'm needed there. Do you think Charlie can spare the petrol to take me?'

Charlie turned out to be Mrs Easton's son. He not only agreed to drive Mrs Hardy back to Coventry, but also drop May and Peter in Kenilworth on the way. In the half hour before he was ready to drive them, Mrs Hardy wrote letters to Peggy and Davey and gave them to May to deliver.

The first thing May and Peter did once they were in Kenilworth was look for a place that served dinner. They walked in silence. Peter, his leg aching, was reluctant to speak in case through pain and tiredness he blurted out another idiotic comment about their relationship. May seemed lost in thought, but she could just be taking care not to trip in the darkness.

After what felt like an age, May stopped and put a hand on his arm. 'Peter... what you said earlier... I...'

Peter's mouth went dry. 'Forget it. It was stupid.'

'No. You were right.'

She spoke so quietly, he wondered if he had misheard. Suddenly all his awareness was focused on her. Everything else – his aching leg, the cold rain, the rumble of traffic – it all faded into the background. 'What are you saying?' He could hardly force the words through his tight throat.

He heard her draw a shaky breath. 'If being in a relationship means watching out for each other, then that's what I want.' She bit her lip and looked down at her feet. 'I mean, if you still want to.'

–

Peter stopped and May stopped too, barely daring to breathe. Ever since he had remarked that what she wanted sounded like a relationship, those words had replayed non-stop in her mind. At the time she had been unable to answer him; the words had been strangled in her throat. It was fear that held her back. Not just fear of committing to a relationship when all she'd seen of relationships in her family was how marriage was a form of oppression, but fear that her time with Peter could be cut short at any moment. When she'd seen Peter's compassion for the victims of the Coventry bombings and his generosity, she knew that even if she could trust no other man in the world, she could trust Peter. Combined with the shock of hearing of his narrow escape, she knew she had to speak up. After all, this could be the last time she and Peter would have together. She could never forgive herself if he went to his grave not knowing she returned his love.

Even in the darkness she could see the glint in his eyes. 'May, I promised not to push you. Don't feel you have to—'

'I'm not saying it because I feel I have to.' She swallowed. She wasn't eloquent at the best of times and it was vital she expressed herself clearly. She tapped her chest. 'I'm saying it because I want you to know how I feel deep inside.'

'Then…' There was another pause, long enough for May to count ten rapid heartbeats. 'Then we can start courting?'

She gulped but nodded her head. 'Yes. I'd like that.' They were the most difficult words she'd ever said but the feeling of relief once they were out made her giddy.

A huge smile lit Peter's face. 'I'll take good care of you, May. I promise.'

Then, with a look of wonder that made her catch her breath, he reached out and brushed her cheek, tracing a path from temple to the corner of her mouth. It was the lightest of touches but it left her breathless and light-headed. He was going to kiss her, she knew it. Her heart felt like it was trying to escape through her throat, and she thought she might faint from the anticipation. Then his lips met hers. It wasn't the demanding, all-consuming kiss she'd seen in films, no grapple for possession. Instead it was softer, gentler, sealing the promise of his words and a first, tentative exploration of what was to come. Hesitantly, she wrapped her arms around Peter's shoulders, her fingers curving around firm muscle. The blood pounded in her ears, drowning out the sounds around them.

When the kiss ended she felt weak-kneed and dizzy. Peter kept his arms around her, and she leaned her head on his shoulder, revelling in their closeness. Gradually her hearing returned and she became aware of other sounds besides her own heartbeat: a dog barking in the distance; an ARP warden shouting at a householder to cover their window.

'Gosh,' she said. It didn't do justice to her feelings, but it was the best she could come up with at the moment.

'I know,' he replied.

Then they were both laughing, and May reminded herself that although this was the start of a new phase in their relationship, nothing had really changed. She had known for a long time that he loved her and she felt like she had been in love with him for ever. She was finally allowing herself to give in to her feelings, that was all.

'I don't know about you,' Peter said, 'but I feel like I could dance all night.'

'It would be wonderful to dance,' she said. Suddenly she didn't feel hungry. She just wanted to be held in his arms all night. Then, 'Oh, but what about your leg?'

'I'll manage,' he replied. 'If nothing else, I'll be able to pull off the sharpest pivot on the dance floor.'

Chapter Ten

'You did what?' Jess cried.

'We kissed,' May replied, face flaming.

'Attagirl, Lidford!' Jess slapped her on the back. 'I knew you two would get together sooner or later. I'm glad you've finally come to your senses. Now come on – I want to hear all the details.'

'It was lovely.' May sat on her bed and gazed down at her bag, which she had just started to unpack when Jess had arrived and demanded an explanation for May's dreamy expression. May was unable to hold back a huge smile as she remembered her first kiss and all the ones that had followed. She had been unable to stop smiling all day, except when she'd had to say goodbye to Peter.

'Lovely? Is that all?' Jess's voice jolted her back to the present. 'I want to hear everything: what it was like, what you said to each other, most especially I want to know why you look like you've got a light switched on inside you.'

'Do I?' May looked into the mirror but she didn't think she looked any different, apart from the hair slightly messed from the cycle ride back from the station. She tried to come up with words to describe their kisses apart from 'lovely', but how could any words be adequate to describe the delightful jumble of sensations and emotions that accompanied each kiss?

Jess shook her head and gave a crooked smile. 'You're back there again, aren't you? I can see it's going to take a while to get anything sensible from you. At least tell me if you found Peggy's mother.'

'We did, and she's fine. Well, shocked and homeless, but she's got a place to stay now and someone to take care of her.' May glanced at her watch. 'In fact, I need to get to the village, to catch Peggy when she comes out of school.' She'd reluctantly insisted that she and Peter leave Kenilworth early so she could find Peggy as soon as she finished school; she didn't rate her chances of getting past Mrs Evans if she wasn't in time to meet Peggy in the village. 'Hopefully I'll see Mrs Bowes, too. I promised I'd let her know.'

'I'll come with you. I said I'd meet some of the lads at the pub later.' Jess picked up her greatcoat and pulled it on. 'You can try to think of a better description than "lovely" on the way.'

They managed to catch Mrs Bowes making her way to the infants' school, who was delighted to hear that Mrs Hardy was safe. May handed her the letter Mrs Hardy had dashed off for Davey in shaky handwriting. They then headed for the junior school. The children were just starting to emerge when they arrived. There was less of the usual chatter and horseplay usually associated with schoolchildren being released from a day's work; of course, it wasn't just Peggy who was affected by the tragedy of Coventry, but all her fellow evacuees. More than one face had swollen, reddened eyes, and here and there were huddles of children with their arms around a classmate with a tear-streaked face. May had to remind herself of Peter's words again, that she couldn't help everyone.

May soon saw Peggy in the doorway. At least there was one child who would receive good news today. Peggy stopped dead when she saw May, seeming to gather her courage before approaching, eyes wide and haunted. A look that should never be seen on a child.

'I found her. She's fine,' May called as soon as Peggy was in earshot.

Instantly Peggy's face lit up and she pelted across the playground to May's side. 'Where is she? Was she hurt?' Peggy asked the moment she could draw breath.

'She's unhurt.' May pulled Mrs Hardy's other letter from her pocket and handed it over. She and Jess fell into step with her to walk her home, with the unspoken understanding that they would stop short of the haber-dashery. 'She wrote you this. Your house was bombed but she's staying with Mrs Hughes now, so she's got food and shelter.'

Peggy tore open the envelope, her eyes alight, and studied the letter. May turned away when the girl scrubbed her eyes with the back of her hand, thinking that she wouldn't want to be seen crying. However, she turned back when Peggy gave a heaving sob. Peggy had stopped walking and her face had crumpled, tears streaming down her cheeks.

'It's alright,' May said. 'I know you must have lost a lot when your house was bombed, but your mother's safe and that's the main thing.'

Peggy drew a shuddering breath. 'You don't under-stand.' Each word was punctuated with a sob.

May crouched beside Peggy and put an arm around her shoulders. She exchanged a glance with Jess who looked as confused as she felt. 'Then what's the matter?'

'I thought she would come for me when you found her. Bring me back home.'

May's heart sank. She shot a pleading look at Jess, who simply shrugged. 'She can't do that, Peggy. Your home's gone.'

'I don't care. I could stay with Mrs Hughes, too.'

'It's not safe. Your mother told me that however bad things got, however much she misses you, it's a comfort to know you're safely away from the bombings.'

'But I hate it here.' Peggy jerked free from May's arm and stood ramrod straight, her fists clenched at her sides, the letter crumpled in one hand. 'I'd rather be in Coventry with all the bombs than spend one more second with Mrs Evans. I hate her. I...' Her face crumpled. 'I want my Mum.' Her words ended on a wail.

May's heart clenched. From another child it might have been a melodramatic statement, but from Peggy it came out as the simple truth.

'What about Davey?' Jess asked. 'Surely you wouldn't want him to be in danger, and you know going home would mean leaving him.'

That seemed to hit the mark. Peggy's shoulders slumped, then she sagged into May's arms and fresh tears poured down her cheeks, soaking the front of May's coat. May didn't try to stop the crying. This was the pent-up flood of weeks of ill-treatment. Tears pricked May's own eyelids, but she resolutely blinked them back. She held the little body as Peggy convulsed with sobs, wishing she could howl out her own helplessness. She had almost as little power as Peggy to change her lot. How on earth was she supposed to help?

May mentally braced herself. Clearly the first thing to do was get Peggy to tell her exactly what she was going through with Mrs Evans.

When the latest storm of tears had subsided and Peggy's breathing had steadied, May said gently, 'Peggy, what's it like with Mrs Evans? I might be able to help if you tell me how she's treating you.'

She had feared Peggy would clam up again, but the girl drew a deep, shuddering breath and said, 'I hate Mrs Evans. She's horrible.'

Well, that much was apparent, but they would need details if they were going to help. 'In what way?'

Stuttering a little from repressed sobs, Peggy said, 'She makes me do all the cleaning.'

May's heart sank. This was too close to her own experience. She could just imagine Peggy working late into the night, scrubbing the floors, dusting and polishing until the house was gleaming to Mrs Evans' exacting standards. She glanced at Peggy's hands, still clutching the collar of May's coat. She'd not thought to look before – now she saw the cuticles were reddened, speckled here and there with blood. The skin over the knuckles was dry and cracked. May's hands had looked just like that. The trouble was, she knew exactly how Mrs Evans would explain it away, because her father had done the same when she'd plucked up the courage to tell a teacher her father made her do all the work. She could imagine Mrs Evans' self-righteous tones as clearly as though she were standing there. 'A bit of hard work never killed anybody. Every girl needs to be trained to do the cleaning and cooking so she can keep a good house for her husband when she's married. I'm doing her a favour.'

She gave Peggy a hug. 'That's awful.' She could at least give Peggy something her teacher had never offered: sympathy.

Peggy nodded. 'Mrs Evans doesn't do anything herself. Says her maid left to do war work, and if I want food and shelter, I need to work to pay my way.'

'Anything else?' May asked. Although she didn't want to hear Peggy was suffering from other cruelties, it would be next to impossible to get Peggy moved merely on the grounds that she was made to do chores.

'She... she hits me sometimes. The other evening I was so tired and had homework to do. When I asked if I could leave cleaning the hob until the next day, she fetched me a clip around the ear. My ears were ringing for hours after that.'

'I'm so sorry, Peggy.' She gave the girl's arm another squeeze.

Jess's face was grim. 'I'll give that bi— that Mrs Evans a clip round the ear next time I see 'er.'

Peggy gave a shaky laugh. 'I'd like to see you try.' She wiped her face with the hanky, looking a little better for having confided in someone.

But May could see Jess was thinking the same as her. If challenged, Mrs Evans would trot out some trite saying like, 'Spare the rod and ruin the child.' Or, in May's opinion, far worse: 'My parents beat me as a child and it never did me any harm.' Whenever May heard that argument, she always wanted to shout: 'It did. It turned you into a vicious bully.'

'Is there anything else you can tell us?' May asked. As it stood, she would do her best to help, but there was nothing Mrs Evans couldn't pass off as normal behaviour.

Peggy shrugged. 'I don't know. I just wish I wasn't so hungry all the time.'

'Hungry?' While rationing was making things like meat, butter and sweets scarcer, in a country village like Amberton, fruit and vegetables were plentiful. No one should be hungry, even if they were missing certain foods.

'She always has enough to feed her friends, but she says children don't need so much food because they're smaller.'

This was dynamite. If May understood correctly, Mrs Evans was using Peggy's rations to feed herself. And how could she, on just her and Peggy's rations, be able to entertain her friends? This needed investigating, and it was something concrete she could report. 'I tell you what,' May said, 'why don't you come to the tea rooms with us now and have a slice of cake? Then we can talk over what to do next.'

Peggy's face lit up for an instant, but then the light was extinguished. 'I can't. Mrs Evans will be cross if I'm late.'

'Of course. I don't want to get you into trouble,' May said. 'Me and Jess—' she glanced at Jess, sure she would want to help, but not wanting to drop her into something without permission. Jess gave a tiny nod. 'Me and Jess will talk over what to do, and we'll do our best to help, I promise.'

Peggy smiled. 'Thank you.'

Jess asked, 'Why didn't you say anything earlier?'

Peggy hesitated, then said, 'She told me that if I wasn't good, she would tell the school she couldn't look after me any more. Then I would be sent away, maybe hundreds of miles from here. I couldn't have that. I have to be near Davey.'

It was a wrench to let Peggy return to Mrs Evans after hearing her story. May, blood boiling, wished they could march straight there and take Peggy away.

'That Mrs Evans has got some nerve,' Jess said, gazing after the little figure. 'To think she treats us WAAFs as though we're contaminating the village by our very presence, when she's treating a child like a slave.'

May couldn't speak for a moment. She too watched Peggy who, with dragging feet, was turning into the High Street. 'How can we let her go, Jess?' She made a move to go after her, but Jess caught her arm.

'Use your 'ead.' Jess gave a choking laugh. 'Blimey, I never thought I would be the one to say that out of the three of us.' May immediately understood Jess was including Evie in the number. May felt the same way. Even though Evie was elsewhere, she was still an invisible presence in their tight group. 'We can't take 'er with us.'

'But we can't let Mrs Evans get away with it.'

'Did I say that?' Jess squeezed her arm then released her. 'Don't worry – I've no intention of letting Peggy stay with that cow a moment longer than she has to, but we've got to do this the right way. We're not part of the village, remember. Whatever we do, we have to make sure Peggy will still be looked after, even if we get transferred.'

She was right, of course. It was easy to forget they could be moved to another location at short notice. Evie had already moved on, and both May and Jess were being encouraged to apply for officer's training like Evie, which would mean leaving Amberton. May suspected Milan was a factor in making Jess drag her feet over her decision. As for herself, she still wasn't convinced she was officer material. Even if she didn't go for it, she could be transferred to the transport section of another station at a moment's notice.

'I wish the village was run like the WAAF,' May said. 'We'd just have to report Mrs Evans to our immediate superior and leave it to the chain of command.' Some people found the rigid hierarchy stifling; to May it was a comfort. She'd had no one to turn to when she'd been under her father's thumb. The structure provided by the WAAF meant security to May.

'Come on, let's go to the pub,' Jess said. 'It's getting cold out here and I've got to be back on duty in another couple of hours. Let's talk it over in the warm.'

The snug of the Horse and Groom was emptier than usual. None of the pilots were there, it being rather early in the day. The only other occupants were Arnold Walker and three men May didn't recognise, sitting at a table around the corner of the L-shaped room. Mr Walker shot them a glance with narrowed eyes while they stood at the bar, ordering lemonades, but he returned to their muttered conversation without making any comment, much to May's relief. She'd dreaded a jibe about Milan or the other Czech pilots.

The girls took their drinks to a table at the opposite end of the snug to Mr Walker. For a while, they sat in silence. May gazed at the row of gleaming horse brasses suspended from the beam above their table while she sipped her drink, but she wasn't really seeing them. Her head was full of Peggy's tale. Peggy had poured out her woes, trusting May to make it better. She couldn't let Peggy down. Not when she understood all too clearly how it felt to live in a home where no one cared for her. Where she was treated as a being with no feelings or wishes for herself, existing only to serve the other members of the household. The

WAAF had freed May, and she couldn't return to the station until she'd done something to ensure Peggy would soon be free of Mrs Evans.

Of course, even though the village didn't have the same rigid structure as the WAAF, there were still systems in place. 'I'm going to speak to Peggy's headmistress,' May said. She started when she heard how loud her voice sounded. With the snug being so empty, there wasn't the usual hum of chatter to screen their conversation from other listeners. She looked at Mr Walker, but he was deep in earnest conversation with his friends, hunched over his beer glass. He gave no sign of hearing. Even so, she lowered her voice before continuing. 'She's supposed to be responsible for Peggy's well-being too.'

Jess nodded. 'Good idea. I can't believe she hasn't noticed Peggy needs help, to be honest. You don't have to know Mrs Evans well to know she's the last person on earth I'd trust to care for a child.'

May caught a movement from the corner of her eye; she thought she'd seen Arnold Walker turn his head at the mention of Mrs Evans. However, when she looked, he was talking to his friends. She must have imagined it.

'When are you going?' Jess asked. 'I'll come with you.'

May drained her glass. 'Right now.' She hoped Jess couldn't hear the quaver in her voice. The prospect of speaking to the headmistress terrified her, but for Peggy's sake she would do it. No one had spoken up for her when she had needed help; she wasn't going to let Peggy suffer alone. 'I won't sleep tonight unless I've done everything in my power to free Peggy from Mrs Evans.' Again the slight movement in the corner of her eye. It must be a trick of the firelight.

At that moment the door creaked open and Milan strode in. His face was set in grim lines, though it softened when he saw Jess. Jess, who had just risen, glanced between Milan and May.

'Stay with Milan,' May said.

'Are you sure?' There was no mistaking the longing in Jess's expression when she looked at Milan.

May wasn't sure at all. The prospect of speaking to the headmistress filled her with trepidation, even taking Jess for moral support. Going alone was a thousand times worse. However, Jess hadn't seen much of Milan lately, and when she had, it had been in the company of May or the pantomime children. She knew from the two days in Peter's company how precious time alone could be. 'Of course. You've got to go back on duty soon and I've got the rest of the day free.'

She comforted herself with the thought that this was good practice for becoming an officer. Officers wouldn't ask their friends to come with them when they had to face a difficult task.

—

The teachers' entrance to the school was still open when May got there and it was with a mixture of hope and apprehension that she saw a gleam of light escape under the door with the sign proclaiming, 'Miss L. Foster, Headmistress.' Reminding herself that this was for Peggy's benefit, she tapped on the door and pushed it open when Miss Foster's voice called, 'Come in.'

Remembering Jess's lessons, May stood tall, straightened her shoulders, held up her chin and strode in.

'Miss Lidford,' Miss Foster said, looking at May over the top of her reading glasses, 'Do come in and sit down. Is this to do with the pantomime? I hope none of the children have been causing bother.'

'Not at all, they've been very good,' May said, perching on the edge of the chair indicated before deciding that a confident person would settle into their chair more comfortably. She sat further back and crossed her legs, folding her hands in her lap while making a conscious effort not to fidget.

'Then how can I help?' Miss Foster took off her glasses, letting them dangle on the chain around her neck. She gave May a stiff smile, but her gaze was already drifting towards the paper on her desk.

Look her in the eye and speak firmly and without hesitation. May could almost sense Jess standing beside her, reminding her how to comport herself. It gave her the courage to maintain eye contact and say, 'It's about Peggy Hardy.'

'Poor girl. She's been so worried about her mother. Well, all the evacuees are worried about family and friends in Coventry, of course. Such a tragedy.'

'As a matter of fact, I was able to find out that her mother is alive and well, so I gave her the good news after school.' Miss Foster drew a breath but May, amazed at her own daring, hurried on before she could speak. 'She told me something that I found very concerning.' May congratulated herself for thinking of the 'I found very concerning' bit. It sounded like something a responsible adult would say. 'As you're her headmistress, I thought you would be the best person to tell.'

Miss Foster picked up a pen and nodded. 'Go on.'

'Well, she's told me that she's very unhappy with Mrs Evans, the lady she's staying with. She said she's being made to do all the work, and—'

Mrs Foster pointed at May with her pen. 'Let me stop you there. Girls do love to over-dramatise their lives. I'm sure that's all that's happening here. The village children are rather overawed by the city children, and the city children are enjoying being the centre of attention.'

'But Peggy wasn't telling the other children, she was telling me, because she thought I could help.'

'Hasn't it occurred to you that her tale is rather too close to the story of Cinderella? She's taken it into her head to identify with a fairy tale character. I'm sure she is missing home, and the shock of the bombings must have been awful, of course. This is just her way of handling it. A way of getting attention.'

The old May would have meekly agreed and apologised for wasting Miss Foster's time. But May knew she needed to dig deep for Peggy's sake and find the May who had defied her father and secretly joined the WAAF. 'She also said Mrs Evans wasn't feeding her properly. I suspect she's using Peggy's rations for herself.'

Miss Foster raised her eyebrows. 'That's a very serious allegation.'

'I wouldn't make it if I didn't think it was true.' May held Miss Foster's gaze steadily, much as she wanted to look away. She tried to put herself in Miss Foster's shoes, tell herself the headmistress had scores of children to look after, some of whom were prone to flights of fancy. Surely if a child said they were being maltreated it needed to be taken seriously? May felt like she was the one under suspicion here, not Mrs Evans.

May had to remind herself she wasn't a naughty child, she was an adult with serious concerns for a child in Miss Foster's school. She was the responsible one for reporting it. It was Miss Foster who was being irresponsible if she refused to take May seriously. And May was a WAAF, for goodness sake! She had faced far worse things than a stern headmistress. It was time to call on all the skills Jess had taught her and really feel that she was in control. How would her flight officer act in this situation?

Miss Foster put her glasses back on and looked down at the paper she'd been reading when May arrived. 'Well, I'll look into it, of course.'

It was meant as a dismissal, but her CO wouldn't have taken it as such, so May couldn't, either. She stood up and towered over the desk. For the first time in her life she was grateful for her height, because it made Miss Foster crane her neck. 'Miss Foster.' She took care with her pronunciation. Jess had worked with her on her accent when she had first arrived at Amberton and had wanted to work in Operations. She had since decided she enjoyed her work in Motor Transport – persuaded mainly by the fact that her job meant driving Peter around the countryside – but now she rounded her vowels just like Jess had taught her. 'A child in your school is being mistreated by her host. You should make it your first priority to ensure she's given the care every child deserves, the care her mother was assured she would be given.'

Miss Foster gave her a stiff smile. 'I hope you're not suggesting I don't take my pupils' welfare seriously. I give you my word I will investigate the matter and take the appropriate action.'

This time there was no ignoring the dismissal. May couldn't help reflecting that if she'd been an officer, Miss

Foster would have taken her seriously. As it was, she felt she had been consigned to the same ranks of 'girls prone to flights of fancy' as Miss Foster's pupils.

All she could do was leave, promising herself to follow up in a few days.

Chapter Eleven

Jess watched May's departing back, torn between going to help her friend and spending some precious time alone with Milan. But it wasn't as if May was going into danger or, heaven forbid, visiting Mrs Evans. When Milan pointed at her drink then the bar, his dark brows raised in enquiry, she nodded, feeling a flutter of pleasure that the handsome pilot should have singled her out. Not that she had any intention of getting serious with him – she wasn't like Evie or May, she didn't want to get tied down to one man. However, Milan was good company and, she had to admit, he was the best-looking man she had ever met. They were both likely to be moved on to other places before long – that was what happened in the forces – but she could enjoy Milan's company while they were both in the same place.

She pulled out her compact and surreptitiously inspected her appearance. The wind had played havoc with her hair, so she pulled her comb from her gas mask case and tidied it as best as she could, praying Milan hadn't noticed. As she snapped the compact closed, she caught a glimpse of Mr Walker's reflection. It reminded her that she needed to ask him about printing programmes for the pantomime. An unpleasant task, but putting it off wouldn't help. She had sketched out a programme over the weekend and tucked it in her coat pocket. Now she pulled it out and approached Mr Walker's table, doing her best to hide her distaste as she wove past the people in the rapidly filling snug.

Mr Walker turned and looked her up and down, leering. 'Hello, darling. Tired of the Brylcreem boys? Want to spend the evening with a real man?'

Her skin crawled. She wanted to do nothing more than run from the Horse and Groom and not stop until she was safely back at the Waafery. It was only the knowledge that she would never get to Chichester in time to get the programmes printed that enabled her to press on. 'Actually, Mrs Grey told me you were a printer.' She held out the draft programme. 'I was hoping you could print two hundred copies of these in time for Christmas.'

Mr Walker's fingers brushed hers as he took the paper. Jess was sure it had been deliberate. He glanced at the programme. 'Shouldn't be a problem.' He named a price that Jess thought was a little expensive, but she didn't want to prolong the encounter.

'Thank you,' she said. 'Can you have them ready the week before Christmas?'

'I can have them ready by the twentieth.' He grinned at her. 'Now, how about I buy you a drink?'

She looked past Mr Walker's shoulder and to her relief saw Milan approach with drinks. While she didn't want to do anything to cause Mr Walker to change his mind about printing the programmes, she also didn't want to be in his company for a second longer than necessary. 'Thank you, but I'm with a friend.'

She backed away. Mr Walker grabbed her hand, enclosing it in a damp grip. Before she could snatch it out of his grip, he'd raised her hand and planted a wet kiss on her knuckles. 'You don't know what you're missing.'

He indicated an empty seat at his table with a jerk of the head. 'Join us when you're bored of your fancy foreigner.' Then he released her.

Jess stumbled to her table, wishing she could wash her hands and scrub away every trace of Mr Walker's touch. She had to make do with wiping her hand on her skirt while she searched the crowd at the bar, looking for Milan.

Then she saw him, holding the drinks, peering around the crowded room. Their eyes met and a flutter of pleasure drove out all thought of Mr Walker as she smiled into Milan's blue eyes and beckoned him to her table. He crossed the room, but whether by accident or design, Arnold Walker had risen and was approaching the bar. He knocked Milan's shoulder, splashing beer down the front of his tunic.

With an exclamation of annoyance, Milan slammed the glasses on the table and then spun around, fists clenched, gazing across the room to where Arnold Walker now sat, laughing with his friends.

Afraid he was going to start a fight, Jess clutched Milan's sleeve. 'Leave him. He's not worth it.'

Milan stood a moment longer, quivering with tension. 'He owes me an apology.'

'That git will never apologise. He's trying to pick a fight. Don't give him the satisfaction.'

Milan muttered something under his breath – probably a Czech malediction – then sat. He pulled out his hand-kerchief and dabbed at the stain on his tunic. 'He will not get away with it.' He glowered at Arnold Walker. 'Oh, do not worry,' he said, when Jess opened her mouth to protest. 'I will not fight him. I do not wish to be banned from the pub. But he *is* a… what did you call him?'

'A git.'

'A good word. I shall remember it.'

Despite herself, Jess laughed. 'As long as you don't use it on your superior officers.'

'Only if they really annoy me.' He raised his glass to her in a silent toast. 'Anyway, I would rather stay with you than fight that git. I am glad you did not leave with May but wanted to stay here with me.'

Jess flashed him a wide smile. 'It's cold outside. I'd rather spend my last hour of free time in the warm.' Give Milan an inch and he'd take a mile. She wished sometimes that Milan wasn't so… intense. Just because she had danced with him at the Midsummer dance, allowed him to kiss her, he seemed to regard her as his. Although she had to admit the kiss had been spectacular, and she couldn't help feeling flattered at his single-minded pursuit. Despite the ruthlessness with which he had dealt with the spies, he had shown her nothing but kindness and treated her with respect.

Respect. She had to hurriedly block out the memories of a time when a man had treated her with anything but respect. No. She had promised herself never to allow him space in her mind again. He wasn't worth it. Flirting with the pilots at Amberton had proved a good way of pushing away the bad memories.

She had to admit, she had not felt so inclined to flirt with other men since meeting Milan. And not many men would have given up their free time to spend dressed up in a stifling pantomime horse's costume. No, she was happy to spend time exclusively with Milan while she was at Amberton. Just as long as he didn't expect more. She would never give a man her heart again.

–

'How awful. Mr Walker is such a... a...' May flapped her hands vaguely, searching for the right description.

'A loathsome git,' Jess supplied.

'I was going to say slimy toad, but yours is better.'

It was the next evening and the two girls were in the schoolroom. It was the first chance May and Jess had had to talk since May had left Jess at the pub. Jess had returned too late for any conversation that night and they had both been busy with their duties ever since. The moment Jess had arrived back at the Waafery, she'd made cocoa for them both and regaled May with the story of what Arnold Walker had said and done at the pub.

'Well, I'm glad you've arranged to get the programmes printed,' said May. 'You were really brave to speak to him alone.'

'I almost wish I 'adn't. Giving 'im our business really rankles, but it would have been too difficult to find a printer in Chichester.' Jess picked up her mug of cocoa, took a sip, winced and put the mug back down. 'I swear I ain't stopped washing my 'ands since then.'

May shuddered. 'Arnold Walker gives me the creeps.' Then she remembered what she'd seen. 'And I'm sure he was listening in to our conversation yesterday.' She frowned into her mug as though she would find inspiration in the swirling steam. 'It's odd. He seemed to take notice when we mentioned Mrs Evans.'

'Mrs Evans?' Jess gave an incredulous laugh. 'I'd almost forgotten 'er.' She shook her head. 'Never thought there'd be someone in the village I'd dislike more.'

She looked like she was about to say more, but the drone of approaching engines made her break off. She rose and gazed at the window, even though it was impossible to see through the blackout curtains. Then the tension drained from her shoulders. 'Hurricanes,' she said. 'Thank God. Sounds like all three returning. Do you think that's three?'

May concentrated. She guessed that Milan must be on patrol tonight. Jess would have been in Ops when they took off. Jess's cup rattled on the table as the Hurricanes flew right over the house, making their descent to the airfield. 'Sounds like three,' she said, and heard Jess release a shaky breath. Not for the first time, she wondered why Jess wasn't more open about her feelings for Milan when she clearly felt deeply for him. But whenever Evie had asked, Jess had insisted she was just having fun, and May didn't like to pry into what was clearly a closely guarded secret.

'Anyway, talking of Mrs Evans,' Jess said, returning to her chair and kicking off her shoes. 'Did you find Miss Foster?'

Now it was May's turn to get agitated. 'I'd almost forgotten in all the excitement. Yes, I told her all about Mrs Evans, not that she seemed to believe me. Or, rather, she thought Peggy was telling tales to get attention.' She swore she could feel bubbles of rage popping in her veins as she related the whole of the meeting. 'I just feel so helpless, like I've let Peggy down,' she said at the end.

'You're not the one who's let her down,' Jess said, her expression grim. 'Maybe there are kids who'd make up stories to get attention, but if Miss Foster had taken the slightest interest in Peggy, she'd know Peggy's not the type.'

'I can't bear to think what Peggy's going through at the moment,' May said. 'She poured out her heart to me, thinking I would be able to make things better for her.

Right now, she could be sitting on her bed, waiting for someone to come and take her to a happier home.'

'You don't know that won't happen. Miss Foster promised to look into it, didn't she?'

'True, but I don't think she'll expect to find a problem.' May gazed gloomily at the froth on the surface of her cocoa. 'She doesn't believe Peggy, so won't be expecting to discover anything amiss.'

The girls sat in silence for a while. The clock ticked away the empty seconds on the mantelpiece; behind the blackout curtains, the sash windows rattled in their frames as a squally wind picked up. Usually May enjoyed these quiet evenings in the schoolroom, but not tonight. How could she enjoy her own escape from home when she knew Peggy was suffering as she had?

'Well, this is a bright welcome!' said a familiar voice. There, framed in the doorway, was Evie, her greatcoat fastened up to her chin, her red hair untidy. She gave them a beaming smile.

'Evie!' Jess leapt to her feet and greeted their friend with an enthusiastic hug. 'What are you doing here? Don't tell us you've been sent back?' May detected a faint note of hope in Jess's voice.

'No such luck,' Evie laughed. 'Didn't Alex tell you?' Here her face lit with a luminous glow. 'I asked him to let you know I've passed my filterer officer's training.'

'That's wonderful,' May said, finally getting her turn to hug Evie. Then, 'You didn't walk up here on your own, did you?'

Evie shook her head. 'Alex walked me here.'

'That explains why your hair's messed up,' Jess said with a wink.

Evie, her cheeks turning pink, ignored Jess and said, 'He's coming back in an hour, but I wanted to see you both as soon as possible.'

'An hour? Is that all?'

'For tonight. I've got four days before I start my officer training and I'm spending them here. What do you think? I've got a room at the Horse and Groom.'

Jess pulled up another chair. 'That's blinkin' marvellous. Take a pew, if you're not too high and mighty to mix with us lowly ACWs.'

'Never!' Evie peeled off her coat, flung it over the back of a chair and curled up in the offered armchair. 'Anyway, I'm not officially an officer until I've completed the training.'

'That's a foregone conclusion,' May said. 'You're going to make a brilliant officer.' To her consternation, she felt tears prick her eyelids.

Evie's expression changed to one of concern. 'May, what's the matter? Has something happened?'

May shook her head, wiping away the tears from her cheeks. 'I just… I missed you so much.' It was hard to force the words past the lump in her throat. May couldn't understand what was happening to her.

'Cheers, May. You really know how to give a girl a confidence boost.' But Jess was smiling as she spoke to take the sting from her words.

May chuckled and the smarting in her eyes faded. 'You've been a brick, Jess. I'd be crying with happiness if it was you returning after weeks away, too.'

'So, as I haven't got long before I've got to leave, who's going to tell me your news?'

'Go on, May, tell her about Peter.' Then, before May could say anything, Jess turned to Evie. 'She's been beaming bright as a searchlight ever since she got back from Kenilworth. And guess who she went there with?'

Evie gave a squeal of delight. 'Peter?'

May nodded, her face burning.

'That's wonderful. Tell me all about it,' Evie said.

And the hour passed all too quickly in news and laughter.

'Are you free any time tomorrow?' Evie asked as she rose to leave. 'I'm going to be on my own most of the day, with Alex on duty.'

'Not until the evening, and we've got rehearsals for the pantomime,' Jess said.

'A pantomime? What a good idea. Can I come?'

–

They collected Evie from the pub on their way to the rehearsals. Milan and Jiří were with them and Alex accompanied Evie. Even though May was overjoyed to have Evie there, she worried she would get tongue-tied performing in front of an audience for the first time.

However, she forgot her nerves when Peggy arrived, alone as usual. The girl gave her such a reproachful look that May's heart sank.

'Where's Susie?' Jess asked, when the children had gathered around. They were a more sombre group than usual, hardly surprising, considering what had happened to their home town.

'Her mum was killed.' It was one of the boys who answered – Danny. He spoke in such a matter-of-fact way, it took a moment for the meaning to sink in. When it did, May felt sick that young children were being forced to confront such horrors.

Another girl, Lottie, nodded, eyes wide. 'She was crying all day at school.'

Jess looked horrified. 'Poor Susie.' She swept her gaze over the rest of the children, brows drawn together. 'What about the rest of you? Have you heard from your families?' Peggy sat silent but the other three children clamoured to answer.

It turned out that the two boys, Danny and George, had mothers with babies. They had left Coventry at the same time as the other children. Lottie's mother had been hurt but would be fine. However, George was still waiting to learn about his grandparents, and Lottie's auntie had been killed.

'The vicar came to see us,' Lottie said, her eyes brimming with tears. 'He was very kind. He took us to church and let us light candles.'

May's heart ached for these children, remembering the devastation she had witnessed in Coventry. It was awful to think that people dear to them had been among the dead.

Jess appeared to be at a momentary loss for words, then she gathered herself. 'Tell Susie we're thinking of her,' she said, 'and let her know she's welcome to come back any time if she feels up to it.' She was silent again for a while and the children sat with bowed heads. 'I've had an idea,' Jess said after the silence had stretched out for several long seconds. 'We can take a collection when we perform the pantomime. To help your families. What do you think?'

Most of the children agreed, nodding enthusiastically. Peggy sat with bowed head, tracing patterns on the dusty floorboards with her fingers.

'Do you feel up to rehearsals tonight? You've been doing so well, it won't matter if you'd rather wait until next week.' When the children insisted they wanted to stay – even Peggy joined in with this – Jess chivvied them to their feet. 'Then let's get started.'

May sat on the steps at the side of the stage while Jess took the children through their opening song. Her job as prompter was unnecessary now, as the children were word-perfect and moved through the steps of the dance in unison. May kept her eyes on Peggy. At the start of the dance, the children were supposed to be dejected, thinking of all the tasks they would have to return to when they finished their play time. They moved as Jess had shown them, with bowed heads and listless, shuffling steps. However, something told May that Peggy's actions weren't part of her performance. Towards the end of the song, the children were supposed to have forgotten their troubles in play, and were trying to coax a smile from Cinderella, who had been sent to collect berries even though it was winter. The other children seemed to have taken the words of the song to heart and had thrown off their troubles for a time and seemed to be wholly in the moment. Peggy performed the same steps, but there was no smile, none of the sparkle the others displayed. With a sinking heart, May concluded that something else had happened since she had last seen Peggy. She must speak to her before she left.

At the end of the rehearsal Jess praised them for the excellent progress they had made and sent them to the back of the hall to put on their coats. May put a hand on Peggy's arm to keep her back. 'What's happened, Peggy? I told Miss Foster about Mrs Evans. Has she said anything?'

'Yes.'

That seemed to be all she was going to say. The Peggy who had poured out her woes had disappeared, leaving this taciturn, uncooperative version in her place. 'Please tell me what happened, Peggy. I want to help.'

'How?' Some of Peggy's old fire kindled in her eyes. 'Telling Miss Foster has made everything worse.' She pulled away from May and stomped down the steps. 'She came to see Mrs Evans last night, said she was sure there had been a misunderstanding, but she needed to check.'

'Oh.' A leaden weight settled in May's stomach as she followed Peggy down from the stage. 'What did Mrs Evans say?'

Peggy scowled. 'She's such a liar. She said she quite understood – Miss Foster was only doing her job.' Peggy put on an affected air and imitated Mrs Evans' refined tones. 'Said she would expect no less from such an excellent headmistress, and of course the kiddies had to come first.' Peggy's lip curled. 'She actually said "kiddies".'

There was a snort behind May's shoulder. She looked to see Jess standing with Evie and Alex. The other children had all gone. 'She should be an actress,' Jess said. 'Don't tell me Miss Foster believed her?'

Peggy nodded. 'Now Miss Foster thinks I was making it all up.'

'I'm sorry if I made it worse,' May said. 'But I believe you, and so does Jess.'

'Absolutely. I'd believe anything of that old b— old busybody.'

'I'm not giving up,' May said. 'I'll keep trying to get you moved to a better home.'

'Thank you.' But Peggy's voice was so dull and hopeless, May knew she didn't expect things to improve.

Once Peggy had left with Mrs Grey, May, Jess, Evie and Alex set off for the pub. Evie murmured something to Alex then came to May's side. 'What's going on with that girl?' she asked.

May blew out a long sigh. 'I don't want to spoil your stay. There's nothing you can do.'

'Maybe not, but I'm offering you a sympathetic ear.' Evie squeezed May's arm. 'When I was confused about Alex, you were a brilliant listener. I'm just returning the favour.'

And so May poured out all her worries about Peggy. Evie didn't interrupt while May was talking, listening carefully to May's recount of the past few weeks. When May had finished, Evie said, 'Poor girl. She's lucky to have you looking out for her.'

'I'm not so sure. It feels like I've made everything worse.'

'How can you say that? You found her mother, for goodness' sake. How many people would have done even half as much in your place?'

'She's still stuck with Mrs Evans, though.'

'Through no fault of yours. You've done everything you can. Don't be so hard on yourself.'

'Listen to her, May,' Jess called. 'She's an officer now, so you have to do what she says.'

'I'm not one yet,' Evie replied, laughing. 'But I'd make it an order if I could.'

'I wish you would give me an order,' May said. 'You always know the right thing to do.'

Evie snorted. 'That's not true. If I could order you, it would be to carry on exactly as you are. You've got good instincts. You *are* helping.'

While it might not have been the instant solution that May had hoped for, she did feel better. And when they reached the door of the Horse and Groom, Evie held May back. 'You've come such a long way since we first met,' she said. 'I'm so proud of you.'

–

'Lidford, a word, please.' Flight Officer Payne strode into the shed where May was checking the oil of her Hillman Minx.

May hastily replaced the dipstick and wiped her hands on a rag then followed her CO.

Payne led May to her office but didn't invite her to sit down. She sat in her chair, regarding a slip of paper on the desk with a scowl. 'I've had a complaint about you.'

May's heart dropped. 'Sorry, ma'am.' She'd been a driver on the station for months and not one of her passengers had ever complained before. On the contrary, she'd only ever received praise both for her driving and her manner. 'May I ask what about?'

'It's from someone in the village, which makes this rather awkward. The station has always had excellent links with the village, so I was disturbed to receive this complaint concerning a member of my flight.' Payne flourished the paper. 'I have to say, I was very surprised. You've always struck me as a quiet, conscientious girl. Indeed, Flight Officer Ellerby speaks very highly of you and commended you for your actions when the station was bombed, so I can't tell you how disappointed I was to see this report.'

May had a horrible feeling she knew what the complaint was about. She braced herself as she stood to attention, remaining silent.

'The complaint is from a Miss Foster, the headmistress of the primary school.'

'Miss Foster?' May was confused. 'Is it something to do with the pantomime?' If anyone was going to complain, she'd have expected it to be Mrs Evans.

· 'It's nothing to do with the pantomime. In fact, Miss Foster was kind enough to say she thought you and your friend—' Payne frowned at the paper '—Halloway were doing fine work with the evacuee children.'

'Then what is she unhappy about?'

'You've been making false accusations about respectable members of the community.'

May went cold. She would never have believed that Miss Foster would stoop so low to report her for trying to help a child.

Payne referred to the report again. 'Apparently you've accused Mrs Evans, who is an active member of the WRVS and a member of the parish council, of stealing rations.' The groove between Payne's brows deepened. 'Moreover, and I must say I find this hard to believe, Mrs Evans reported to Miss Foster that you made a disturbance in her haberdashery store that upset her customers. Can you explain either of these accusations?'

May hesitated. She could only think of Jess's outburst when she had been defending Milan from Arnold Walker's comments. She didn't think Jess had done anything wrong, but didn't want to get her into trouble, either. However she couldn't let either complaint go undefended. If she was ever going to be approved for officer training, she needed her Flight Officer's recommendation.

'One of the children in the pantomime told me she was being badly treated by Mrs Evans,' she said, choosing her words carefully. 'It would have been irresponsible of me to ignore it, so I reported the matter to her headmistress, thinking she was the right person to deal with it.'

Payne's face was unreadable. 'And the other matter?'

'I think the disturbance—'

'You think? You mean you're not sure? There has been more than one?'

'No, ma'am.' Whatever happened, she mustn't get Jess into trouble. 'I just couldn't think of any disturbance I've made. I was in the haberdashery when another customer insulted one of our Czech pilots, but I kept out of it.' May felt safe mentioning the involvement of a pilot, seeing as pilots were RAF and therefore immune to discipline from a WAAF officer.

Payne's face softened fractionally. 'I've heard there's been some ill feeling in the village since that business with the saboteur.'

'Yes, ma'am.'

'Well, it sounds like there has been a misunderstanding, so I won't be taking any further action.'

'Thank you, ma'am.'

'However.' There was a warning note in Payne's voice that made May tense up again. 'Whether fairly or unfairly, the WAAFs are under constant scrutiny when they step outside the station. If I hear your name linked to any other trouble in the village I'll be forced to put you on a charge.' Payne put down the paper and gave May a stern look. 'I can't blame you for wanting to help a child, though I must remind you that we should not be involving ourselves in village affairs. By all means, continue with the pantomime – it's good for morale and improves our reputation in the village. But if I hear you are causing trouble for an upstanding member of the community, I will come down on you so hard, you'll wish you were still buried in that bomb shelter. Do I make myself clear?'

'Yes, ma'am.'

'Very well. Dismissed.'

May saluted and walked out, fighting the urge to run. She could feel her face burning. She had never been in trouble before, and to be reprimanded for caring for the welfare of a child seemed too cruel. Now she was faced with a dilemma. Did she continue to fight for Peggy and possibly wave goodbye to any chance of promotion or did she obey orders and leave Peggy to suffer?

Chapter Twelve

Later that evening she updated Evie on everything that had happened with Flight Officer Payne. They were sat in the quietest corner of the snug in the Horse and Groom. Thankfully there was no sign of Arnold Walker.

'I'm so glad you're here, Evie,' May said when she had run out of words. 'Even if it's just for a few days. You're so much cleverer than me. I'm sure you'll know what to do.'

Evie's brow wrinkled. 'Don't talk yourself down, May. You *are* intelligent. There's more to intelligence than book learning.' A pause, then, 'Have you decided what to do about Peggy? Are you going to do as Flight Officer Payne tells you?'

May had been thinking about this all day. She glanced around the snug to make sure no one else was listening. 'I can't,' she said keeping her voice low. 'I could never live with myself if I ignored a child who needed help.'

Evie gave a faint smile. 'You see – you do know what to do.' She leaned across the table. 'You've got a resilience and a tenacity that will see you through this, May. I have every faith in you. And I'm sure Flight Officer Payne will come round to your way of thinking.'

'What if she doesn't? What if I get kicked out of the WAAF?'

'They won't kick you out. You're too good.'

'What if they do? I can't go home. I escaped once, I'd never get away again.'

Evie squeezed May's hand. 'It won't happen, but if it does, you could lodge with my mum in Cowley. You've got skills now. I bet you could get a job in the Civilian Repair Unit. My mum's working there now, you know, doing really well.' Evie glowed with pride as she mentioned her mother, and May smiled, remembering how Evie had dreaded her first visit home after she had joined the WAAF against her mother's wishes. They had since mended their relationship when Evie had been sent home on sick leave in the summer, and May was glad to see she seemed to be firm friends with her mother now.

Evie paused looking thoughtful, then asked, 'Has Flight Officer Ellerby spoken to you recently?'

May shook her head, then amended it to: 'Well, she did take me aside to say she approved of me helping out with the pantomime.'

'There you go,' Evie said. 'Ellerby would never let you be kicked out. She believes in you almost as much as me and Jess.'

'Ellerby?' May couldn't conceal her surprise.

'Yes. Ellerby. She's never forgotten how you took charge when your air raid shelter was bombed. I know she's not your CO, but you've got an ally in her. If you ever need an officer to take your side, go to her.'

Some of the tightness left May's chest. 'I wish you could get posted back here,' she said. 'You always have a way of cutting through problems. Things never seem so bad once you've dealt with them.'

'Have faith in yourself, May. You'd already decided what to do, hadn't you?'

May thought about it. In her heart she'd always known she couldn't abandon Peggy. 'I suppose so. I feel better, though, knowing I've got help if I need it. Jess has been brilliant, of course—'

'My ears are burning. What about me?' Jess had arrived, bringing Alex, Milan and several other members of Brimstone squadron with her together with a blast of cold air through the open door that temporarily cleared the smoky atmosphere.

May and Evie shifted to make room for Jess, Alex and Milan. The others drifted to the bar, the noise levels in the snug increasing. Evie and Alex greeted one another with a clasp of their hands and a charged glance that spoke volumes about their feelings for each other. Even when they unclasped their hands and joined in with the general conversation, they emitted a strong sense of together-ness. It made May happy to see that Evie's move from Amberton seemed only to have strengthened their rela-tionship. She couldn't help a fleeting thought of Peter. Ever since they had returned from Coventry, she had felt cocooned in the knowledge of his love. She could only pray it would prove as enduring as Evie and Alex's.

A shout of laughter coming from the bar caught her attention. She looked up to see Jiří attempting to down a yard of ale but pouring most of it down his front. May joined in the laughter, but couldn't avoid a quick glance around to double-check that Arnold Walker and his friends weren't there.

Jess must have interpreted her actions. 'He's not here,' she said in a voice quiet enough not to carry beyond their table. 'But we thought bringing the gang would dissuade him from making trouble if he turns up.'

'I hope he doesn't come at all.'

'If he does, it will not be a problem,' Milan said with a confidence May wished she shared. 'He is a coward.' He gestured around the bar. 'There are too many of us here tonight.'

'I still can't believe there are people in the village who would hate the Czechs,' Evie said, her face creased in distress.

'We don't all think that way, love, not by a long chalk.' The landlady had approached the table and collected the empty glasses. She addressed Milan. 'Most of us in the village know what you and the boys in your squadron have done for us. If it weren't for you, we'd probably have swastikas flying all over the village by now. Your drinks are on the house tonight.'

'Cheers,' Jess said. 'What's your name? Maybe we should name the fairy godmother after you to show our appreciation.'

The landlady grinned. 'Vera. Not the best name for a fairy godmother.'

'I dunno. My aunt is called Vera and she's saved my neck more than once. I wouldn't be 'ere if it wasn't for 'er.'

'Well, whatever the fairy godmother is called, we're all looking forward to the panto. It'll really brighten up our Christmas.'

All in all, May was feeling more cheerful by the time they got up to leave. As May was fastening her coat, Evie leaned over to her and murmured, 'Have you thought any more about how to help Peggy?'

May nodded, pulling up her collar. 'I'm going to talk to Mrs Grey, the vicar's wife. If anyone can help, it's her.'

'Good idea,' Evie said. 'I'll come too, if you like.'

'Better not,' May replied with a grimace. 'I don't want you getting a black mark against your name when you're about to do your officer training.'

'You know I'll help if I can.'

'I know. But this is something I need to do for myself. You've been such a support – right from the moment we shared that carriage down from London. I probably wouldn't have survived the first days here if it weren't for you or Jess. But I'm beginning to realise I might have been leaning on the pair of you too much. I need to know I can stand up for myself.'

Evie gave her a hug. 'You'll be fine,' she said. 'You're stronger than you think.'

May's opportunity to speak to Mrs Grey came the next day. It was the day of the first rehearsal up at High Chalk House. Although Jess had distributed scripts when they'd started rehearsals with the children, she had decided to delay the adults' rehearsals to give them time to learn their words. Now that they were only a month away from Christmas, it was time to begin in earnest.

'We won't practise every scene at each rehearsal,' she told the gathered WAAFs once they had collected, together with Milan and Jiří, in the ballroom. The ballroom was a vast, empty space that was occasionally used for exercise when rain prevented the WAAFs from taking walks, but most days it stood empty, gathering dust. There was a photograph on the wall showing how it had looked in former days. Vast windows ran along the length of one wall and, though the photograph was taken at night, the French windows were open, allowing a glimpse of the terrace beyond. Inside, the ballroom was brightly lit from the intricate crystal chandeliers, illuminating men in evening dress and women in low-waisted gowns, sporting ostrich feathers and other elaborate headdresses. There were no chandeliers now – they had all been removed and replaced with ordinary light bulbs. There was no furniture either, apart from a battered upright piano, so the girls had swept the floors and brought in cushions upon which everyone was now sprawled while Jess explained her plan.

'Your officers have very kindly arranged for us all to be off duty together now, and then again for three full rehearsals down at the village hall in the week running up to Christmas. After today, I'll arrange rehearsals around my own watches and pin a schedule in the Rose Room. Write your name against each rehearsal you can attend, so I can work out which scenes to rehearse in each session.'

Then Jess indicated Mrs Grey, who sat on the piano stool. 'Mrs Grey has kindly agreed to attend as many rehearsals as possible. She's composed the music for the songs and will accompany us on the piano.' There was a polite round of applause, and Mrs Grey smiled and nodded.

The rest of the rehearsal was spent with much laughter, reading through the whole script. Milan and Jiří caused gales of laughter as they read their lines as the ugly sisters. In the scene where the ugly sisters vied for Prince Charming's attention at the ball, May laughed so hard she ended up in a paroxysm of coughing when she attempted to speak her own lines.

'How will I get through the scene on the day?' she wheezed when the fit eased. 'If I can't stop myself laughing when we're just reading it through, I'll never manage when we're acting it for real, them all dressed up in their ball gowns.' For she and Jess had already found the perfect costumes for the ugly sisters, both clearly used for previous pantomime dames. One was a hideous emerald green velvet gown with so many flounces, Jess swore it must have been made from stage curtains. The skirt was enormous and had hoops to make it stand out a good foot on all sides. Jiří was to wear this, and as the skirt would fall a little short of the ground, Jess had created a pair of flounced pantaloons. The other dress was styled like a 1920s flapper dress, with fringes that would swirl with each movement. Instead of being an elegant shade like black, silver or gold, it had a lurid mixture of purple and yellow fringes. There was a matching headband with a huge ostrich feather stuck in the back. May had yet to see Jiří and Milan in these costumes, but she wasn't sure she would survive the experience.

Towards the end of the rehearsal, Mrs Grey played through each song and taught them the closing number, which involved the whole cast. May, who had already rehearsed this with the children and therefore knew it by heart, used the time to plan what to say to Mrs Grey.

She took her opportunity when everyone was leaving. The vicar was supposed to collect her, but he'd sent a message saying he'd been delayed, needing to visit a sick parishioner.

'Come and sit in the Rose Room while we wait,' May invited.

'My dear, I am so grateful to all of you for giving up your free time for the play,' Mrs Grey said once they were seated in the pretty sitting room with its sprigged rosebud wallpaper. 'It will go a long way to helping the children on Christmas Day.'

'I'm happy to help,' May said, 'and I know Jess loves being back on the stage. It's very kind of you to help with the music.'

'Not at all,' Mrs Grey replied. 'I want to make this a Christmas to remember for these poor children, for all the right reasons. I know they can't forget what's happened in Coventry, but I hope we can at least provide a distraction for them.' Then her eyes sparkled. 'Although I think our ugly sisters could do that all alone.'

May giggled. 'It will certainly be a pantomime to remember if Prince Charming spends the entire ballroom scene on the floor in fits of laughter.'

Mrs Grey laughed, then said, 'In all seriousness, do let me know if you need any more help. I'm sure I have more time on my hands than you.'

May hesitated but knew she couldn't pass up this opening. 'Actually, there was something I wanted to ask. Nothing to do with the pantomime, though.'

'What is it?'

'It's about Peggy Hardy.'

Mrs Grey raised her eyebrows. 'The girl with Mrs Evans?'

Despite the overwhelming urge to laugh it off and mutter an excuse, May forced herself to remember Peggy's pale, tear-streaked face. She also took courage from the memory of Mrs Grey's expression when she had seen Mrs Evans at church. 'I think… well, I'm almost certain that Mrs Evans is being unkind to her.'

To her relief, Mrs Grey didn't immediately protest that Mrs Evans was an upstanding member of the community. Instead she sighed. 'I was afraid of that,' she said. 'Between you and me, I was very unhappy when I realised she was taking in an evacuee.'

'You were?'

'Oh, yes. I've had dealings with her at WRVS meetings and with various church events. I know this doesn't sound much, but she always displayed meanness. While she was always a prominent figure at charity events...' Mrs Grey hesitated, then said, 'You won't spread this around, will you? My husband is always warning me against gossip.'

'I promise I won't say anything.'

'Well, last year she ran the cake stall at the village fête. I heard later from several women that they thought she had short-changed them. They didn't like to make a fuss because it was for charity. When I counted the takings, though, there was no extra money. It's only hearsay, of course, but enough people reported it to make me think she must have pocketed it.'

May was dubious. 'It's not something I can report to Peggy's headmistress.'

'It isn't. I have nothing but a hunch to go on. Backed up by the experience my daughter had.'

'I didn't know you had a daughter.'

'She's married now and moved away from Sussex. A few years ago, before she left school, she worked for Mrs Evans on Saturdays at her shop. Even though she was there all day, Mrs Evans never offered her food or drink – she had to dash home for half an hour to grab lunch. And even when it was dark, Mrs Evans didn't see her home, always sending her out alone. Small points, I know, but they all add up.' Mrs Grey shook her head sadly. 'I would take Peggy myself, if we could. We already have two evacuees and simply don't have room for another.'

'Can you advise how to help? I tried telling Miss Foster, but she accused Peggy of making up tales to get attention.' May decided not to mention the complaint to her superior officer. 'It took ages to get Peggy comfortable enough to confide in me, and I promised to help, but I'm at a loss what to try next.'

Mrs Grey drew a breath. 'If Miss Foster won't believe Peggy, it's going to be difficult. Mrs Evans is careful always to appear like a pillar of the community.'

'Except when she insults the WAAFs,' May couldn't help saying. 'She never bothers to be civil to us.'

Mrs Grey looked thoughtful. 'You know, that could be her weakness. Maybe there's a way to get her to show her true colours when she doesn't know anyone else is around to witness it.'

–

May was still pondering Mrs Grey's advice in the days that followed. Two questions loomed large. Firstly, what could she do to get Mrs Evans to reveal her true nature and secondly, however was she to persuade Miss Foster to witness it? If Miss Foster complained about her for doing nothing more than voicing her concerns about the welfare of a child, she dreaded to think what she would do if May casually asked her to help set a trap for one of the most respectable members of the community. Neither Evie nor Jess could come up with a solution either.

The days went by, and the time arrived for Evie to depart for Loughborough and her officer training.

'I'll miss you,' May said to Evie when she hugged her goodbye after their last evening together at the pub.

'I'll miss you, too,' Evie wiped a tear from beneath her eye.

'I wish you could have stayed for the panto,' Jess said.

'I might yet get to see it,' Evie replied. 'It's only a two-week course. If I don't have to report to my new post straight away, I'll get more leave. Maybe I'll be back for Christmas.'

'Won't you spend Christmas with your mum?' May asked.

'Not likely,' Jess laughed. 'Not when she could be cosied up with Alex.'

Evie blushed and said, 'Mum already agreed to work extra shifts over Christmas, thinking she would be alone. I'll make it up to her another time.'

It felt wrong to leave Evie behind and return to High Chalk House without her. For a while it had felt like the old days when it had been Evie, Jess and May, united in serving their country and supporting each other through the joys, sorrows and dangers of life in the WAAF.

Jess slung an arm around her shoulders. 'Chin up, May. We've still got each other.' Then she added in a wistful voice, 'And you've got Peter, you lucky thing.'

—

Her only comfort was finding two letters waiting for her when they got back to the Waafery, one of her fellow drivers having collected her post. The first one was addressed in Peter's firm, slanting hand, and May had a flutter of pleasure when she saw it. She slipped it in her pocket, saving it for when she had enough time to fully savour every word.

She looked at the other letter and was about to slit it open when she froze. It had a Birmingham postmark. No one from Birmingham wrote to her. She hadn't had any school friends. She'd wondered why until one girl, whose family had moved to the area from another town, suddenly stopped spending time with her. 'My mum won't let me talk to you,' the girl had whispered, when May had stopped her outside the classroom one day, fighting back the tears, wanting to know why she no longer wanted to be friends. 'Our neighbour told her we should stay away from the Lidfords.' May had not understood why at the time. It was not until much later, when she left school at fourteen, that she'd discovered her father's delivery business was just a front for criminal activity, and that he acted as a fence for some of Birmingham's most notorious thieves.

'I think this is from my father or brothers,' she whispered, holding the letter away from her, as though it was about to burst into flames.

Jess regarded May with wide eyes. 'Oh my goodness. Are you going to open it?'

May shoved the letter into her coat pocket. 'I don't know. Maybe later.'

She ran upstairs, feeling sick. Why would her family be writing to her now? She took off her coat and flung it over a chair in a shadowy corner of the schoolroom, as though doing so would make her forget the letter in its pocket. Curling up in an armchair, she opened Peter's letter and tried to read it, but her mind kept skipping to the letter in her coat pocket. She reached the closing lines without any recollection of what he had written before.

Sunday would be best for them, he wrote, *but let me know which day you can manage. They're so looking forward to meeting you.*

'What?' she said aloud.

'Is that the letter from your family?' Jess had entered the schoolroom without May noticing. 'What do they say?'

'I haven't opened it yet. This is Peter's letter.'

'Peter? What's 'e said to get you in a tizz?'

'I...' May reread the letter, this time forcing herself to concentrate. 'Oh my gosh. He wants me to meet his parents.'

'That's good, isn't it?'

'I suppose.'

Jess sat opposite and studied May, her head tilted. 'You don't sound so sure.'

'It's just... it's a bit soon.' She could do with more time to get used to the new turn their relationship had taken without the added stress of being judged by his parents.

She read the letter through a third time. 'He says he's told them all about me, and they're dying to meet me. And... oh. He's getting his new leg in another week. He'll be back on active duty after that, so doesn't know when we'll next be able to meet.'

'All the more reason to see his parents while he knows he can.'

All the more reason to spend the day alone together, May thought. But she could see Jess's point. Most people loved their families and wanted to spend what time they could with them.

She glanced at the corner where the letter from Birmingham lurked in her coat pocket. At least when she saw Peter she could ask his advice about that.

She still hadn't decided what to do by the next day, when they had another rehearsal with the children. She hadn't taken the letter out of her pocket and it preyed on her mind all through the rehearsals.

'Hark, are those horsemen approaching?'

Jess's line reached May through a daze. There was an edge to her voice that suggested it wasn't the first time she had recited it. With a start, May glanced up from where she had been pacing at the side of the stage and saw the eyes of Jess and all the children looking in her direction. Even the pantomime stag, replete with its improvised antlers, was looking at her.

'Sorry,' she muttered. She made her entry and stuttered her lines in a most un-regal fashion, then made an effort to get into character for her next line. What was it Jess had told her? The joy of acting was that you could experience being a different person for a while. It would be wonderful if she could experience Prince Charming's life for a while. Prince Charming wouldn't dissolve into a puddle of anxiety over a letter. She thrust back her shoulders, straightened her spine and strutted up to Cinderella. 'You had no right to interfere.'

The rest of the rehearsal went so well, Jess was enthusiastic in her praise. 'Act like that on the day and the whole village will give us a standing ovation.' Then she muttered in an aside to May, 'Except Mrs Evans, but we can't expect miracles.'

They had finished rehearsing a little early so the children could try on the costumes Jess and May had picked out. Susie still hadn't returned, so her costume was set aside.

'She just cries all day,' said seven-year-old Lottie as she pulled on a dress with a sky-blue skirt and white bodice that laced up at the front. The hem dragged on the floor and the sleeves draped over her hands, so Jess made her stand on a chair while she pinned up the hem to be sewn later.

'And how are you?' May glanced at Lottie over her shoulder as she held a green jacket behind George for him to thread his arms through. She remembered that Lottie had lost an aunt.

'I cry for my Auntie Pat, too,' said Lottie, tears welling as she spoke. 'But losing your mum must be worse.'

'My Granny and Grandad are alright, though,' said George, buttoning up the jacket with a bright smile. 'They sent me a letter and I could read it all by myself without any help. Their house got bombed, and they were stuck in the cellar. Their neighbours dug them out.'

'How wonderful,' Jess said. 'About them being alive, I mean, not them being trapped in the cellar.'

However, May could only think of Birmingham. Birmingham had experienced a devastating raid a few days earlier. Was that what the letter was about? Once the children had left, she pulled the envelope from her pocket. It might contain important news. What if one of her family had been killed?

'Are you going to read it?' Jess was eyeing her with concern.

'I...' May moved to tear open the envelope then stopped. What if it was an attempt to trap her into returning? She wouldn't put it past them. She shook her head and thrust the letter back in her pocket. 'I'll think about it.'

Chapter Thirteen

She still hadn't read the letter the following Sunday. It sat like a weight in her coat pocket; each time she changed gear on the drive to Portsmouth, the slight crackle of paper reminded her of its existence. Not that she was likely to forget. It had haunted her all week, worrying her even more than her impending meeting with Peter's parents.

'How do I look?' May checked her appearance in the mirror of Peter's car once she had parked outside the row of terraced houses on the Copnor Road where Peter's parents lived. Not for the first time, she wished she was pretty like Jess or Evie. 'Do you think they'll like me?'

'You look beautiful, as always. And they're going to love you.'

It was too late to object now. Peter had phoned midweek as promised, and May had hesitantly tried to tell him she didn't feel ready to meet his parents, but Peter had brushed aside her fears. 'They'll love you. I've told them so much about you, and they're dying to meet you.'

May couldn't tell him it felt too soon; she hated to disappoint him. She wished she could be more like Jess or Evie. Neither of them would have agreed to do something against their better judgement.

May climbed out of the car, suddenly horribly conscious of her limbs. She was sure Peter's parents must be watching from the window. Had Peter told them how tall she was? She shut the driver's door – she was still driving while Peter had the peg leg – and walked up the path, clinging to Peter's hand like a lifeline. She did her best to look happy and eager instead of terrified.

'Come in, come in.' A man in his late fifties opened the door, his eyes twinkling at May. 'You must be May. Peter's told us so much about you.'

Mr Travis was an older version of his son. His hair must have once been the same dark red shade as Peter's, although it was now mostly grey, and he had the same good-natured air about him that made May feel so comfortable with Peter. Her nerves faded.

A door opened at the far end of the narrow hallway and a woman appeared. She was only a couple of inches shorter than May. She looked to be in her early fifties and had a trim figure and a face creased with laughter lines. There were only a few streaks of grey in her light brown hair. 'Oh, you're here already. I didn't hear you knock.' She pulled Peter into a hug and kissed his cheek then turned to May. 'I'm so pleased to meet you, May, not least because it's a relief to meet a woman I don't have to stoop to talk to.'

All May's misgivings melted away. 'It's so nice to meet you, Mrs Travis.'

'Call me Irene, dear.' And much to May's surprise, Peter's mother enveloped her in a hug as enthusiastic as the one she had bestowed upon Peter and kissed her cheek.

May felt a lump in her throat at this wholehearted welcome. She followed the others through into a small front room. The first things to catch May's eye were the holly and ivy garlands draped over the mantelpiece and the colourful paper chains festooned across the ceiling. She gave an exclamation of delight. A cheerful fire crackled in the grate providing welcome warmth after the chilly drive.

'We thought we would celebrate Christmas early, as this might be the last time we're all together before Christmas day.'

'What a lovely idea,' May said. She was more glad than ever that she'd been able to buy some scented soap for Mrs Travis and had picked up a bottle of home-made cowslip wine for Mr Travis from the landlady of the Horse and Groom. She would have felt very awkward not to have brought a gift when it was clear Peter's parents had gone to so much trouble.

At Mrs Travis's invitation, she sat on the sofa opposite the fire and held out her hands to the flames, grateful for the warmth after the cold drive. Peter sat beside her, and Mr Travis took one of the armchairs.

Mrs Travis took the other, then sprang up almost immediately. 'I've been saving our meat rations and we managed to get a decently sized chicken for lunch. I must go back and see to the gravy.'

May rose as well. 'Please let me help,' she said. It seemed wrong to relax while Mrs Travis was busy in the kitchen, however ill at ease she might feel away from Peter. Besides, she was far too anxious to sit still.

As it turned out, she needn't have worried. May had never known such a welcome, and it kept catching her off guard throughout the day. She had also never had such a pleasant family meal. Meals at home had involved May doing all the work then only receiving a meagre portion because her father and brothers were 'the breadwinners of the family and therefore deserved the lion's share'. Mealtimes were for eating, not for talking. Then, while her father and brothers slept off their full stomachs, May would be forced to return to the kitchen to clean the dishes and prepare for the next meal.

The early Christmas meal with the Travises was an event that would stand out in May's memory for a long time. Everyone helped to get the meal ready. Peter and Mr Travis set the table in the back room and carried the dishes through while May and Mrs Travis finished preparing the vegetables and gravy. Then they sat around the table, mouths watering while Mr Travis carved and placed generous slices of chicken onto each plate, serving May and Peter's mother first. There was much laughter as the Travises related tales of family Christmases before the war.

The Travises were also eager to learn about the work May did in the WAAF. 'Peter tells us you are a driver,' Irene said. 'I was impressed to hear that you can drive and even change wheels and things. I'm so proud of the way our women are stepping up for the war effort. I just wish I could do more myself.'

Peter laughed. 'You already volunteer with the WRVS, grow enough food to feed an army in the back garden and pack parcels for prisoners of war. You'd have to give up sleep entirely if you did more.'

'Nonsense,' Irene said, but she gave her son's hand a squeeze, and May could see she was pleased. She turned back to May. 'Anyway, I remembered you were a driver when I was choosing what presents to get for Christmas, and I found these.'

She rummaged in the pile of parcels beneath the Christmas tree. Being only the first of December, it was too early for cutting a real Christmas tree. Irene had improvised by cutting some evergreen twigs, arranging them in a large jug and decorating them with pretty red and gold baubles. She found a small, flat package wrapped in what was clearly reused wrapping paper and handed it to May. 'Happy Christmas, dear. I hope you like them. Go on, open it.'

May carefully untied the green ribbon then unwrapped the paper, taking pains not to tear it. Inside were a pair of slate-blue leather gloves.

'Oh, thank you,' May said, feeling the soft leather in wonder. She drew one of the gloves onto her hand. It fitted perfectly, moulding to her fingers so that she could bend them unimpeded. 'These are beautiful.'

Irene glowed with pleasure. 'I'm so glad you like them. I thought you could wear them while you were driving. I chose blue to go with your uniform.'

May was overwhelmed by such thoughtfulness from a woman she had only met that day. She reached into the bag she'd hooked over her chair, leaning over it to hide her sudden need to blink away tears. 'I...' She cleared her throat to ease its tightness and tried again. 'My gift looks rather mean compared to yours.'

'Nonsense. We didn't expect you to get us anything at all. We know how busy you must be.'

'I wanted to get you something,' May said. She pulled the scented soap from her bag. She'd found the precious bars in a shop in Kenilworth and had originally bought them for Jess and Evie, but she'd decided there would be time to find them another present. 'I wasn't able to find any proper wrapping paper though,' she said, looking ruefully at the newspaper and string wrappings.

Irene, however, professed herself delighted with the soap, breathing in its lily-of-the-valley scent with her eyes closed in an expression of ecstasy. 'This is a real treat, dear. Thank you.'

Mr Travis was also pleased with the cowslip wine and insisted upon pouring it out there and then. May would only accept a tiny amount, knowing she had to drive back, but she joined the family in a toast at the end of the meal.

When it was time to leave May returned Irene's hug with equal enthusiasm. 'Thank you for the wonderful day,' she said. 'I wasn't expecting such a welcome from people who don't even know me.' Her voice went a little husky, unable to prevent herself from comparing today with the years of neglect she'd received from her own family.

'Oh, but you're part of the family now.' Irene squeezed her and then kissed her cheek before releasing her. 'I'm sure there'll be plenty of opportunities to get to know one another.'

Part of the family. As May sat in the driving seat of Peter's car, coaxing the cold engine into life, the words were a heavy burden on her heart. Peter's parents expected them to marry. She supposed it was a natural conclusion. After all, that was what courting was all about – time to find out if you loved a person enough to marry them. But when she had agreed to start courting, any decision over whether she would spend the rest of her life with Peter had felt reassuringly far off. After all, she, Evie and Jess had vowed to take their work seriously, which meant putting duty before any relationships during the course of the war. And who knew how long that would be? Now the welcome from Peter's parents placed her under a smothering weight of obligation which she couldn't shake off.

Peter, too, was quiet. After a while, he told her to turn right then stop when they reached a park.

'This is Baffins Pond,' he said once she had turned off the engine. 'Let's go for a walk. There's still plenty of time before dark.'

May accepted, glad for this chance to be alone with Peter before returning to the bustle of High Chalk House, where Jess would be sure to demand a full account of her day. They strolled hand in hand along the path, Peter leaning on his cane and taking extra care not to slip on the ice. Their breath formed puffs of mist that sparkled in the sunlight. They hadn't gone far before they found themselves beside a large pond – more a small lake – where they stopped to watch the ducks and swans glide by.

'I hope you enjoyed the day,' Peter said eventually. 'I know you weren't keen to meet my parents.'

'It wasn't that I didn't want to meet them,' May protested. 'It felt rather soon, that's all.' And just because she had enjoyed the day, it didn't lessen the fact that she had given in to Peter's wishes all too readily. 'I did have a wonderful time, though. Your parents are perfect.'

'There. I told you there was nothing to worry about, didn't I.' But May couldn't shake off her unease. Peter had been right this time, but it didn't mean May would never have to stand up to him at times where he might be wrong. Did she have the strength?

'I was worried my mother overpowered you,' Peter said then. 'She made such a big thing about you being part of the family. I want you to know that was all her. I never gave her any expectations. I don't want you to feel under pressure.'

The weight on her heart lightened a little. He was still the same Peter, who understood her just as well as Jess and Evie did. She gave him a small smile. 'Thank you. I did feel rather overwhelmed, but I didn't want to say anything because your mother really is lovely. I just… well, I never knew how it felt to be part of a loving family.'

Peter folded her in his arms, and she rested her cheek against his, feeling the faint scratch of stubble. 'I hope I can meet your father one day, just so I can give him a piece of my mind,' Peter said. 'Any man who makes his daughter feel so unwanted in her own family doesn't deserve the title father.'

They stood there for some minutes. A chill breeze ruffled May's hair, blowing her chestnut locks across her eyes. She brushed them away but didn't try to break the embrace. Until she'd met Evie and Jess, she'd never known what it was like to have a friendship where she was accepted and loved for who she was. Until she'd met Peter, she'd never thought it possible that a man would choose her.

'What are you thinking?' Peter murmured.

She gave a soft laugh. 'Are you sure you want to know?'

'Well now I do.' He sounded so worried, May daringly kissed him on the cheek. She found herself wishing for more kisses but hesitated when there were other people around.

'I was just wondering why you chose me when there are so many WAAFs much prettier than me.'

'Are you joking? Have you no idea how beautiful you are?'

Beautiful. He'd called her that before, which she'd always dismissed as flattery. But his dear, sweet face was so earnest, that for the first time it occurred to her that he meant it. He hadn't said *beautiful to me*, which she would have found easier to believe even if it was a veiled insult. No, he'd called her beautiful with no qualification, no bragging that he saw something in her that others didn't.

Hadn't Jess and Evie both insisted she was beautiful? Jess had even said she envied her looks. Would any of them say it if it wasn't true? She'd always thought they were trying to bolster her confidence, but perhaps it was May who was mistaken.

She was still processing Peter's declaration, trying to work out how to respond, when he continued. 'I don't love you because you're beautiful. I love you for who you are: so loyal, kind and generous. You never showed any pity or horror when you found out I only had one leg. Instead you accepted me as I was. And you're so much stronger than you think you are.'

May frowned and leaned back in Peter's arms to study his face. 'Have you been talking to Evie?'

'No. Why?'

'Because she said the same thing.'

'Have you considered that we're both saying it because it's true? Anyway, you should trust Evie even if you don't believe me. That girl is never wrong.'

'But I'm not strong.' She placed the flat of her hand against his chest as though to push him away. He caught her hand and held it.

'Not strong? Count along with me.' He tweaked her little finger. 'One: you didn't stay in an unhappy home but took the initiative to join the WAAF.'

'I left home because I was too weak to stay.' She was somewhat distracted by his thumb which caressed the back of her finger, sending delightful shivers down her spine.

'It takes strength to strike out alone.' Both Evie and Jess had said the same thing to her at one time or other. Maybe it was time she started believing them.

'Two—' he moved his attentions to the next finger '—you're performing in the pantomime.'

'Which I'm terrified about.'

'Yet you're doing it. Everyone's afraid of something, and you're facing your fears.'

Before she could protest that she hadn't been able to turn Jess down, Peter continued.

'Three: there's that time in the air raid shelter. I've heard from more than one person how you didn't panic but calmed everyone else and kept your head. It's possible the outcome would have been far worse if you hadn't organised everybody.'

May didn't have an answer for that. 'I don't know if I can take all the credit. I think I was in shock as much as anyone else. I had to find something to do to stop myself from panicking.'

'That's all anyone else does.'

May remembered his terrifying tale of getting trapped in the Hurricane that would have dragged him to his death. 'Is that how you felt bailing out of your plane?'

Peter nodded. 'Everything seemed to slow down. I had a choice: give in and die or fight until the last. It was sheer fluke that the fastenings of my leg snapped to free me. Anyway, we were supposed to be talking of you, not me.' He took her index finger. 'Four: you went to Coventry to find Peggy's mother. Not many people would have had the guts to walk into a city that had just been bombed and might well be bombed again. And five—' he took her thumb before she could object '—you endured a meal with my parents because it was important to me, even though I'm sure you'd have rather jumped into a sea full of sharks than spend the day with strangers.'

He pulled her hand to his lips and kissed the palm.

May didn't know why, but she couldn't let Peter go on believing she was something she was not. 'I had a letter from home,' she said, extricating her hand from his grasp, 'and I can't bring myself to read it.'

'You think that means you're weak?'

May thought about it. 'I shouldn't be afraid of mere words. They can't hurt me. Yet the thought of reading the letter terrifies me. How can I ever be free of my family if even a letter has this power over me?' It was only as she spoke that she realised the truth. She had run away without facing up to her family. Unless she went back and told her father face to face that she wanted nothing more to do with him, would she ever truly be free?

'Look.' Peter released his hold from her waist and clasped both her hands in his. 'You shouldn't feel guilty for trying to protect yourself from them. They hurt you and showed no signs of repentance. You did the right thing by leaving, and this letter is very likely an attempt to draw you back.'

'Do you think I should throw it away?'

'Only you can make that decision. But promise me one thing.' His expression was grave. 'If you ever decide to go home, let me come with you. You shouldn't have to face them alone.'

'Go back?' She shook her head. 'I'd never do that.' Although it was more a denial of what she feared she would have to do.

'Maybe. Just promise you'll take me with you if you change your mind.'

'Don't worry. I won't go home.' But she couldn't make the promise. She would hate Peter to meet her father. She doubted he'd ever be able to look at her in the same way if he saw where she had come from. She glanced at her watch. 'We'd better get going. I'd prefer not to drive in the dark.'

They retraced their steps through the park. Thankfully, Peter didn't seem to have noticed she hadn't given her word. 'If you ever doubt yourself again, you should talk to Peggy,' he said. 'I bet she thinks you're a heroine for finding her mother.'

'But less of one for failing to get her moved away from Mrs Evans. The woman is vile. I've no idea what made the authorities decide she was suitable for caring for children.'

Peter frowned. 'I thought the vicar's wife was going to sort it out.'

'She'll try but I don't know what she can realistically achieve.' May realised she'd only given the briefest of details of what had happened in Amberton since she'd returned from Coventry. She filled him in, finishing with, 'Mrs Grey said it would be difficult to get Peggy moved unless the authorities had real evidence of Mrs Evans' character.' She recalled Mrs Grey's cryptic remark at the end of their conversation in the Rose Room. 'I think she wants to set a trap to force her to reveal what she's doing.'

Peter stopped abruptly. 'You're not going to take part in that, are you?'

'I don't know. I will if Mrs Grey thinks it would help.'

'You've already been reprimanded for interfering in village affairs. What is this if not interfering? What would your flight officer say if she found out?'

–

May pulled away from him and hugged her arms across her chest. Peter held her gaze, willing her to understand. He had been in the RAF long before the war; he understood how important it was to fit in if you wanted to get ahead. No one deserved promotion more than May. He believed every word he had said about her strength and ability. Unfortunately, he had seen too many promising recruits denied promotion because they had failed to conform to the behaviour expected of an officer or NCO. He had even heard of a case of a WAAF being transferred to Orkney after complaining about her commanding officer.

'Are you asking me to ignore that poor girl's plight just to keep in my flight officer's good books?'

At any other time he would have been pleased at this evidence of May speaking up for herself, but he wasn't so keen when her displeasure was directed at him. 'Not ignore it. And you haven't. You've done everything you could reasonably be expected to do.'

'I can't have. Not if she's still with that awful woman.'

'You raised the matter with the vicar's wife. She has influence in the village. You don't. You can leave it to her with a clear conscience.'

'My conscience will never be clear while Peggy is unhappy.'

'But what can you do?'

May looked down and didn't answer.

He pressed his argument. 'You've tried. And you've been warned not to interfere. You could go far in the WAAF, but not if you get yourself noticed for the wrong reasons.' He should know. He'd spent his time as a sergeant pilot modifying his language so he spoke like the officers, trying to fit in. Even though the RAF was more egalitarian than the other services, you still didn't get promoted if you caused trouble.

'Would you support me if I found a way to help her?' She must mean Peggy.

Peter prodded at a clump of grass with his walking stick. He would always support her. He loved her.

However he didn't want to encourage her in following a course of action that would harm her career. 'If you found a way of helping her without upsetting the powers that be, then of course I would support you. I honestly believe you have already tried everything you can. I think you should let it lie now. Leave it to the vicar's wife.'

May nodded, her eyes downcast. For a moment Peter thought she would object, but she took his arm when offered and allowed him to walk her back to the car without saying any more on the subject.

They didn't speak much on the drive back to Amberton, only exchanging the occasional comment on the view or the weather. May said she needed to concentrate on the road. Peter wasn't convinced seeing as they had got to know one another while May was behind the wheel of a staff car. He let her be, though. He could see she was upset about Peggy. In time, though, he was sure she would see there was nothing more she could do.

If only there was more *he* could do to help *May*. What with weeks of trying and failing to stop enemy raids and now being unable to solve her dilemmas over her letter and Peggy, he was starting to feel useless on all fronts. She had turned to him for advice, however try as he might, he couldn't think of an easy answer to either problem. He'd never thought it possible, but he was starting to miss the days when Amberton had been the target of Luftwaffe raids. He had been able to help May then – comfort her after she'd been trapped in the bombed shelter and protect her when their car had been strafed. It had been terrifying, but he'd known what to do.

Once they arrived back at High Chalk House, they went to the Rose Room. There was no sign of Peter's friend from Oldbourne who had driven him to the house that morning and was supposed to meet him there to take him back.

'He said he was going to have a walk with Pauline and take her to the pub, but they should be back by now,' Peter said, glancing at his watch. Pauline was his friend's sweetheart, who also happened to be a WAAF at Amberton.

'Wait here. I'll try and find him,' May said. She took off her coat and slung it over her arm. A white flutter caught his eye as a slip of paper dropped from May's coat pocket and landed on the rug at Peter's feet. It was an envelope.

Peter picked it up. He moved to hand it to her but then stopped when he saw the shock on her face. Comprehension dawned. 'This is the letter from home,' he said.

She nodded.

Finally this was something concrete he could help her with. 'Let me read it. I'll tell you what it says.'

Chapter Fourteen

May backed from Peter as though he held an unexploded bomb. *Tear it up*, she wanted to cry.

However, she couldn't forget that earlier he had listed all the reasons he thought she was strong. She didn't want him to see how weak she really was. She also didn't want him to think badly of her for ignoring a letter from her family. Now she had met his parents, seen how loving and caring they were, she knew he could never understand what her family life had been like.

She couldn't say no. Not when he so clearly thought he was helping.

Her throat too tight to speak, she nodded.

'Are you sure?'

Of course not. It was a terrible plan.

She nodded again.

Peter tore open the envelope. It was too late to go back now. He drew out the letter – a rough scrap of grubby paper. She backed farther away until her spine made contact with the door jamb. What was he waiting for?

Time slowed down as Peter unfolded the paper. His brows drew together, a look of concern etched in every line of his face. She could see the imprint of ill-formed letters through the back of the thin sheet. Only a few short lines. He must already know what it said. Why didn't he say anything?

Then he looked up and their eyes locked across the top of the letter. 'This is from someone called Ron. One of your brothers?'

She nodded, still unable to force any words through her tight throat.

'He says your father was badly injured in the latest bombing. He's dying.'

Dying. It made no sense. Her father was an unstoppable force. Nothing could kill him.

'He's asking to see you before he dies,' Peter finished.

She shook her head and finally found her voice. 'No. I can't. You don't know what he's like.'

'He's dying.' His face was wrinkled in genuine confusion. May's heart went out to him. He had no idea what it was like to have a father who belittled and bullied. His parents had nurtured and encouraged him, just as parents should. Oh, he knew May had had an unhappy childhood and commended her for escaping, but he would never truly understand what her life had been like. Would never understand her desire to be free of them for ever.

Again, the unwelcome voice sounded in the back of her mind, asking if she could truly be free unless she stood up to her father face to face. She fought the urge to cover her ears and drown out the voice by shouting. It was a stupid notion. She was already free. There was no reason to go back.

Regaining control of her limbs, she took a step forward and snatched the letter from Peter's hands. 'It's been nearly a year since I got out. A year of freedom. I won't go back. What would it achieve?' Apart from a real danger she would end up trapped there. Unable to extricate herself from the far-reaching net of the Lidfords a second time around.

'I'll go with you. I've already said I will.'

'I know. And it's so kind of you, but…' She didn't want him seeing where she came from. It was a far cry from his home. She didn't want him to associate her with her past. Not that she thought he would stop loving her, but because he would end up loving her in spite of her origins. It would always be there, in the back of his mind.

'You'll regret it if you don't.'

How did he know? He hadn't lived her life. He wasn't the one who feared they would never break free if they went back. She had gone to him for support, instead he had first forced her to read the letter and now was trying to persuade her to do something she desperately didn't want to do. She wished she could tell him, make him understand, wished she could speak her mind like Evie or Jess.

She was saved when Peter's friend made an entrance. 'Sorry I'm late. Time ran away with me,' he said. 'Are you ready to leave?'

Peter glanced at May. She could read his unspoken words: *Will you be all right?* She nodded. 'Go. I'll be fine.'

She fixed a smile to her face and kissed Peter on the cheek to say goodbye, relieved that Peter's friend being there meant it was awkward for a more prolonged goodbye. She thanked him for the day out, then ran up to the schoolroom as soon as the door was closed.

Jess wasn't there, but that was all for the best. May needed peace to think. She went into the nursery – the room she'd shared first with Evie and now with Jess – and sat on her bed. Ron's letter was still crumpled in her fist. She'd almost forgotten she'd been holding it.

Was this what life would be like with Peter if she married him? Him making the decisions and only going along with her ideas if he agreed?

She squeezed her eyes shut in a desperate attempt to block the hundreds of conflicting thoughts whizzing through her brain. She had allowed her love for Peter to overrule her common sense. She had been reluctant to get into a relationship with him because she had known she would always defer to Peter. She had persuaded herself everything would work out, because she had wanted so badly to be with him, but she should have held out. Nothing had changed. The way she reacted to something so small as a letter from her brother proved that.

She fumbled for the writing pad she kept in her bedside drawer. With shaking hands she picked up a pen and began to write.

Dear Peter. Dear and more than dear. Could she really do this? She had to. She put pen to paper again, not caring as she usually did that the censor would also read it. If she'd had the courage to say this to his face she would have done. Still, writing was better than nothing. It might be cowardly, yet she couldn't allow him to believe they had a future together when it was impossible. What to say, though? How did she write the words that she knew would break his heart?

You have just left, she settled on finally, *and I wasn't able to say what I know I should have said. You will hate me for taking the coward's way out and putting it in a letter instead, but maybe it's better if you hate me. I do love you. I'll always love you. I want you to know that. I want you to understand that if things were different, nothing would give me greater happiness than to be your love. This is not your fault. Please don't ask yourself if there's anything you could have done differently. There isn't. This is all to do with me. With how weak I am.*

I haven't told you everything about my father. Although I told you how my father bullied my mother, how he mistreated her. I watched her fade away day by day until she died. A tear rolled down her cheek and splashed onto the page. *What I never told you is how angry I got with her for not taking me and my brothers away from him before it was too late. She must have known his abusive behaviour would kill her. Then I watched my brothers turn into younger versions of my father until there were four men in the house bullying us. I was scared then. So scared I would end up just like my mother – too scared to stand up for myself and too scared to leave.*

Gradually, the act of writing helped her organise her thoughts. It was so much easier to explain how she felt without Peter being there. While she knew he would never make light of her fears, she also knew he would attempt to rationalise them. Try to change her mind. She knew she was too susceptible to persuasion. The only safe way to communicate with him was in a letter.

I know you are nothing like my father, she continued. *I know you are a kind and loving man. As I said, this is not your fault but mine. In every relationship there will be disagreements. It will only be an equal relationship if both parties are able to express their views.* Another tear plopped onto the paper, dissolving the ink on the word 'equal'. She watched blue ink swirl inside the teardrop before forming a blot, blurring the end of the word. *I've tried and failed several times. I tried to explain to you why I think I need to help Peggy, even though I know there are others who should be taking responsibility for her. I tried to explain why I didn't feel ready to meet your parents. I know I had a wonderful day, and you were right in that instance, but you can't always be right, and I need to be able to stand up for myself with you. But I can't.*

She paused, reading over the last three words. She had said she had been angry at her mother, but she was also angry at herself. Angry that she hadn't had the courage to tell Peter to his face what needed to be said. As it did need to be said, she put pen to paper again. *I'm sorry. I love you. But we can't be together. I would lose myself completely. Please respect that and don't try to change my mind.*

The words on the page blurring and shimmering through unshed tears, she hastily signed the letter and shoved it into an envelope before addressing it. There. It was done. She had done the right thing. Maybe one day her heart would know that too.

–

May handed in her letter for posting first thing the next morning. If she delayed she would change her mind, and this was the right thing to do. Her head understood, even if her heart was crushed. As she left the Admin block on dragging feet, a voice called her back.

'Lidford, a word.'

May turned and saw Flight Officer Jean Ellerby, who was in charge of the WAAFs in the Ops Room. Thinking it might be to do with the pantomime, May saluted and stood to attention.

'At ease, Lidford,' Ellerby said. 'I wondered if you'd given any more thought to officer training.'

'Oh,' May said, taken aback. When Ellerby had recommended Evie for officer training, she had also told May and Jess they ought to consider it, but neither had applied yet. 'Well, the MT officers have desk jobs. They don't really appeal.'

'What if I told you there was an opportunity as a clerk SD? There's a course at Cranwell you might be interested in. It wouldn't lead directly to a commission, but there would be more interesting officer roles for you as a result.'

May was intrigued. She knew all the WAAFs like Jess and Evie who were designated 'clerk, special duties', or clerk SD for short, were bound by the Official Secrets Act, so they couldn't reveal what they did. Ellerby wouldn't be allowed to reveal the true nature of the course. May wasn't entirely sure what went on at Cranwell, only that it was something very hush-hush and possibly connected with the mysterious work at Bawdsey, where Evie had done her Filterer Officers' training. When Evie had gone there, Jess had speculated that it was something to do with tracking enemy planes.

That was definitely something she was interested in. After Coventry, she wanted to do all she could to help the RAF track and intercept bombers. And she couldn't deny that a change of scene would be welcome now she had broken it off with Peter.

Peter. Her stomach gave an unpleasant lurch.

Ellerby must have interpreted her expression as reluctance. 'Think about it,' she said. 'I'll need to know within a fortnight. If you want to do it, I'll see to it that your CO recommends you.'

The prospect of the mysterious clerk SD training could only distract her for a short while. By the time she reported for duty and was assigned to ambulances, she could think of little else but Peter and the letter. Peter would hate her when he got it. If only she had more courage, she could at least have told him to his face. On the other hand, if she had more courage, she would be able to speak up for herself and wouldn't have needed to break up with him at all.

The only time she wasn't thinking of the letter, she was wondering what to do about her father. She wished she had been able to talk it through with Jess, but Jess had been on watch all night, and they had only crossed paths briefly that morning. Jess had been too exhausted to do more than slur a greeting before collapsing into bed. There was a chance she would see Jess when May had a break for lunch, though, and she counted down the time until she was released. She was just starting to be hopeful that she would be freed for a break without needing to drive out into the cold when her sergeant marched up to her ambulance.

'Lidford, you're needed. One of our Hurricanes has crash-landed.' She gave May the rough location of the crash, then May and a medical orderly, Ted Taylor, were scrambling into the ambulance. May's stomach was in knots as she drove out of the gates; she never knew what sight would greet her when she was sent to a crash. She could only pray the pilot had escaped and they wouldn't be required to transport a corpse to the mortuary. There was always the fear it would be someone she knew. She would hate to be the one to break the news of Alex or Milan's death to Evie or Jess. The knot in her stomach tightened as she thought of Peter.

'Can you see any smoke?' she asked Ted, who was sitting beside her.

Ted took a moment to examine the horizon, looking left and right. 'Nothing,' he said finally.

May relaxed a little. If the Hurricane was on fire, they should be able to see the smoke from here. She had attended one crashed aircraft that had exploded, and never wanted to repeat the experience. She shuddered, remembering the sickly stench of burning flesh. She took a left turn that led up to the village of Burbridge. Before she had reached the outskirts, she saw a Hurricane, nose down in a ditch at the edge of a field of cows. The cows were all gathered at the other end, lowing to make their displeasure clear. While Ted jumped out to open the gate, May gazed at the Hurricane anxiously, looking for any sign of the pilot. Then she saw him on the ground beneath the wing, with another man bending over him.

Ted climbed back into his seat once he'd closed the gate behind the ambulance. 'Better step on it,' he said as May set off across the field, the springs groaning with every bump and lurch as they crossed the uneven pasture. 'Some bloke's there with the pilot and he doesn't sound too happy.'

May could soon make out the pilot and recognised him as Sergeant Pilot Tomáš Novák, a member of Brimstone squadron. He was sitting up, his face smeared with blood, one arm flung up as though to defend himself from the man. May thought she recognised the attacker as a friend of Arnold Walker. She was sure she'd seen him in the Horse and Groom, casting belligerent glares at the Czechs.

Ted glanced back as she braked. 'No sign of the fire tender. Where have they got to? We could use their help if this turns nasty.' He opened the door. 'You'd better stay in here.'

But May couldn't sit and do nothing while Novák needed help. Leaving the engine running, she jumped down and hurried to catch up with Ted. Now she could hear what Mr Walker's friend was saying.

'How do I know you're not a spy? You don't sound British.'

'That's because he's Czech,' Ted said, stepping between the unfortunate pilot and his accuser. 'You must have seen him around Amberton before now. It's Mr Brown, isn't it?' When the man nodded, Ted went on, 'Well, Mr Brown, I promise you Sergeant Pilot Novák won't be sending reports on your cows to the Nazis today.' Then he glanced over his shoulder at Novák. 'Can you walk?' When Novák nodded, Ted said, 'Go with May to the ambulance.'

Novák clambered to his feet, cradling his right arm. He staggered towards May, who darted to meet him, catching him by his left arm when he stumbled and nearly fell.

'Put your arm around my shoulders,' she told him. 'Lean on me.'

They had only taken a few steps when Mr Brown shoved past Ted and marched up to May and Novák. 'You say he's Czech, but that's what they said about that other fellow, the one who turned out to be a spy.' He meant Karol Simek, the pilot who had been part of a Nazi plot. Mr Brown balled his fists. May could smell alcohol on his breath and she felt a twinge of fear. These bullying tactics reminded her horribly of her father, and he had always become more violent when he had been drinking. She had learnt to hide when her father returned home smelling of beer.

Much as she wished she could hide from Mr Brown, she had Novák to look after. She manoeuvred Novák so she was shielding him as much as possible. 'Leave him alone,' she snapped. 'Look at him – he's been hurt. Hurt defending us, I might add.'

Mr Brown looked shocked. Maybe he wasn't used to being told off by a woman. He took a step back.

Gathering her courage, May said, 'By all accounts, the pilot who turned out to be a spy always managed to leave a fight before he was in any danger. You can see Sergeant Pilot Novák has done no such thing. You should be grateful he and his countrymen are here to defend us, not threaten him.'

At that point the roar of an engine and screech of brakes heralded the arrival of the fire tender.

'Having trouble?' One of the crew had jumped down from the truck and was leaning over the gate.

'Everything's fine,' Ted replied. 'Mr Brown here stopped to help, but he'll be on his way once he's opened the gate for us.' Ted gave Mr Brown a meaningful look. Mr Brown clearly had enough wits remaining to know he was severely outnumbered; he muttered something unintelligible and stomped across the pasture to the gate.

'Better late than never,' Ted said to May as he helped May get Novák into the ambulance. 'You did well to stand up to Mr Brown. You've got guts.'

May hadn't felt brave at the time. She had just acted to protect Novák. But she couldn't get Ted's comment out of her mind throughout the journey to and from the hospital, where Novák was hospitalised for observation and treatment for a broken wrist. Despite Mr Brown reminding her of her father, instead of running, she had acted instinctively to protect Novák. She had stood up to him. Maybe her time in the WAAF had changed her.

If that was true, had her decision to break up with Peter been a terrible mistake?

–

'Are you mad?' At Jess's exclamation, several other diners in the NAAFI craned their necks to look at her.

May squirmed. 'Keep your voice down.'

When May's shift had finally ended, she'd gone straight to the NAAFI. The trouble with being a driver when your duties took you out of camp was the difficulty of finding food. She had been so hungry she had wolfed down the watery stew, scarcely pausing for breath. She had then sat sipping her tea and rereading the letter from her brother. She still hadn't decided what to do when Jess had plonked her tray upon the table and sat on the opposite bench.

'Tell me all about your day out with Peter,' she said. 'I've been stuck down the Hole for hours. I need some nice, romantic gossip.'

After everything that had happened, it was impossible to believe she had only been in Portsmouth with Peter yesterday. And so May had stuffed her brother's letter back in her pocket and blurted out about the break-up.

'You go and take your letter back right away,' Jess said, although she did lower her voice. May was relieved to see everyone else turn back to their own meals or conversation. 'You and Peter belong together. I mean, can you imagine Evie without Alex?'

May shook her head.

'Well, it's the same with you and Peter. You can't break up with him.'

'I have to. I—'

But Jess wasn't finished. 'I knew 'e was the one for you when I saw the pair of you dance together at the Midsummer party.'

May hastily took a sip of tea in an attempt to dispel the sudden lump in her throat. She would never forget the dance. Neither of them knew the steps, but it hadn't mattered. All she had cared about was being in Peter's arms, her cheek pressed to his as they swayed in time to the music. She hadn't even noticed when the band had stopped playing the slow, gentle melody. It was only when another couple dancing a frenetic Jitterbug had barged into them that May had realised the band were now playing a rousing upbeat tune. Judging from Peter's dazed expression, he hadn't noticed either. They had separated and laughed, and May had spent the rest of the evening feeling as giddy and light-headed as though she had drunk the entire contents of the punchbowl.

Even then, however, she had known she was making a mistake, but she had refused to listen to the warning voice in her head. Well, she was paying for it now. She wouldn't be in this pain had she refused to get involved with Peter in the first place.

'Do you hear me, May?'

May gave a start. Jess was giving her a severe look. 'I... Sorry. What?'

'I said you have to take that letter back.'

'It will already be gone. I handed it in hours ago.' It was easier to state this simple fact than try and reason with Jess. Especially when her own heart was in full agreement with her friend.

Jess drew a breath, a determined glint in her eye. May couldn't deal with an argument. She knew she would crumble in the face of Jess's relentless reasoning. So she did the only thing she could think of on the spur of the moment. She pulled the crumpled letter from her pocket. 'Anyway, I have something more important to think about.' She hurried on, before Jess could insist that nothing was more important than putting things right with Peter. 'I read the letter. It's my father. He's dying.' She pushed the letter across the table for Jess to read.

Jess gave her a questioning glance then read it. 'What are you going to do?' she asked, folding the paper and returning it. May studied her expression but could see no clue to Jess's opinion.

'I don't know. What do you think?'

Jess gave a tiny shake of the head. 'It has to be what you want to do, May,' she replied, but there was sympathy in her gaze. 'I know your father made your life a misery. Only you can know if you need to see him.'

May studied the scrawl on the rough paper as though this time she would find something in the brief words that she'd missed the last time. 'I don't want to see him or any of them ever again.'

'So don't go.'

Picking up her fork, Jess prodded an unidentifiable lump on her plate with a wrinkled nose. After giving a tiny shrug, she tucked in, as though the matter was over.

If they had had this conversation a day earlier, May might have agreed with her. However, she couldn't forget the encounter with Mr Brown. She hadn't meekly done as he had demanded. Ted had said she had guts. Both Evie and Peter had said that she was stronger than she knew.

'The thing is,' she said, speaking slowly, thinking through every word before she said it, 'I don't think I'll ever be free of my father unless I say goodbye face to face.'

Chapter Fifteen

She still hadn't decided what to do by the time of the rehearsal that evening. The ballroom was a hive of activity and the bustle couldn't fail to lift May's spirits. A group of WAAFs occupied one corner, dressed in overalls, paint-brushes in hand, painting backdrops on large canvas sheets. Another girl sat at a long table with billowing silk from a torn parachute cast over it and falling in folds upon the floor.

Cinderella's ballgown had been one of the costumes they hadn't been able to scrounge from the box of costumes. It had given Jess a major headache, trying on one costume after another, with May viewing it from a distance and declaring that it didn't stand out. If there was one costume that had to be spectacular, it was Cinderella's ball gown, yet the right kind of cloth to make one was in short supply. 'And I'm not going to Mrs Evans for it, either,' Jess had muttered. Then one of the WAAFs who packed parachutes had been given permission to take a parachute and the problem was solved. She had spent several evenings industriously cutting and sewing, and May knew Jess couldn't wait to try on the result.

The actors gathered around at Jess's summons. Milan and Jiří, who had been unable to attend the last two rehearsals because of flying duties, were there. Alex had come with them and now sat at the side of the room, reading a letter. From the smile on his face, May guessed it was from Evie. After learning of the incident with Mr Brown when Novák had crash-landed in his field, Alex had insisted upon accompanying his squadron members to High Chalk House. There hadn't been any trouble since then, and the Czech pilots had all apparently shrugged it off, but Alex had warned everyone to be cautious.

'Right,' said Jess with a clap of the hands. 'We're rehearsing the ballroom scene tonight. Let's all try to get through it without creasing up over the ugly sisters.'

There was good-natured laughter as everyone drifted to take their places.

May was beginning to see the attraction of acting. There was something freeing about throwing herself into playing a character wholly different from her own. While she strode around the ballroom, giving gracious nods to all the dancers casting her coquettish glances, but searching for the one face that eluded her, she was no longer May, her heart leaden with dread about the letter. No. She was Prince Charming. A man who never had to worry about being trapped into servitude by an unloving father. A man who had the power to free the woman he chose from such servitude.

That thought gave her pause, remembering Peggy. She had been so preoccupied with thoughts of her father that she had completely forgotten Peggy. Mrs Grey had been unable to attend tonight, so she couldn't ask if she'd made any progress, but she promised herself she would go into the village at the earliest opportunity to see if there was news. While Peter had recommended she leave matters to Mrs Grey, she couldn't help herself from taking an interest altogether.

Just then, Milan and Jiří stepped out from behind a cluster of girls. Jiří preened his hair while Milan placed a hand upon his hip and snapped open a fan, pouting. 'Ooh, Prince, you look dashing tonight.'

May managed to keep a straight face this time. She could only pray she'd be able to do so when they were in full costume and make-up. 'And you look…' Remembering Jess's direction, she only briefly glanced at the ugly sisters, then looked over their heads. The dancers towards the back of the stage suddenly parted, and there was Jess as Cinderella, stepping carefully and holding her arms as though supporting a voluminous skirt instead of her uniform. May could almost see the glass slippers (which would just be a pair of high-heeled court shoes painted silver) and the ball gown made from floating parachute silk. 'I must dash,' she said, and pushed past the ugly sisters, making a beeline for Cinderella.

'You did say he was dashing,' was Jiří's parting remark.

Somehow, as they acted out the scene, May was able to push the letter to a tiny corner in the deepest recesses of her mind. The knowledge was there if she chose to examine it, but for now she chose to forget it and throw herself into her performance. Everything seemed to go right. She even managed not to trip or stumble when dancing with Cinderella, despite it being a painful reminder of dancing with Peter at the Midsummer dance. Once the scene ended, and Jess called them all together for a few parting comments, she couldn't block out the knowledge any more. With it came the sinking certainty that she would never be free of her father until she saw him and told him to his face that she was leaving Birmingham for ever.

'Well done, everyone,' said Jess. 'You were all stars. Next rehearsal we'll have the costumes ready and I'd like us to play out this scene again in costume. The ones in this scene are the most elaborate, so we need to find out good and early if anyone's going to be hampered by their clothes. Boys—' she addressed Milan and Jiří, 'I've found the perfect wigs for you, so be prepared.'

There was laughter and chatter as the group drifted out of the ballroom in groups of two and three.

Only when they were back in the schoolroom did May tell Jess what she had decided. 'Jess, I'm going to Birmingham. I need to see him. I need to prove to myself that I can look him in the eye, say goodbye and walk out of his life for ever.'

Jess gave a small nod. 'Thought you might see it that way in the end. Good for you, May.'

May hadn't realised how much Jess's approval meant until then. Relief surged through her. 'You think it's the right thing to do?'

'I do.'

There was a pause while Jess checked the blackout before switching on the lights. Then, 'I'll come with you, May. You did point out I hadn't taken any leave for ages.'

May felt a surge of relief; at the same time knew she had to make something clear. 'I'd love you to come. It would have been wonderful to have the company but… don't take this the wrong way – I don't want you to meet my family. I have to do this myself or they'll never accept it.' And she'd never truly accept it, either. She had to find the strength within herself. She couldn't depend on Jess or anyone else for this. She thought fleetingly of Peter, only that was impossible now. She would never go anywhere with him again. Her heart stuttered as she forced a smile. 'I have to go alone.'

—

By the time May was walking through the corridors of Queen's Hospital in Birmingham, she wished she could summon up the same courage that had sent her here alone. Why had she rejected Jess's offer? There was something about this place that filled May with dread. Whether it was the antiseptic smell or the way the tiled walls made every footstep and every hushed voice echo, or just the glimpses of patients, swathed in bandages, lying still and silent, she didn't know but she found the atmosphere unnerving, as though the ghosts of former patients hovered just out of sight, only to be glimpsed from the corners of her eyes.

Following the directions from the kind nurse at the front desk, she turned right into the next endless corridor. At the very end was a door with 'B' painted above it in a bold blue paint. She stopped, gazing at the double doors. Her father was through there. Nausea swirled in her stomach. She couldn't do it. She couldn't force her shaking legs to take another step.

''Scuse me, love.'

May hastily stepped closer to the wall to allow an orderly to push a man in a wheelchair past. The right side of his face was scarred with scabbed burns and his right eye had a dressing covering it completely. May couldn't drag her gaze away from the man as he was wheeled towards Ward B. She had a horrified certainty that there was no eye beneath the bandages, just an eyelid sewn shut.

May had to take several deep breaths once the doors had swung shut behind them. *No turning back now, May, my girl.* It was as though Jess was standing beside her, coaching her in the same way she'd coached her though each scene in the pantomime. *You can do this. Believe in yourself.*

Chin in the air, forcing herself to act as though she owned the place, she strode into the ward. Her uniform helped. It was the symbol of the new family she belonged to. A Lidford no longer, but a WAAF.

The ward was a long room with beds ranked along both sides. Screens partially obscured the occupants. Most of the beds already had visitors sat beside them and a low hum of chatter bounced off the stark white walls. A nurse in a pristine uniform and starched cap sat at a desk at the head of the ward, so, standing tall, May approached. She couldn't bring herself to look at the patients too closely. She didn't want to see her father until the last possible moment.

'Ah yes,' the nurse said, looking up from her notes at May's enquiry. 'Mr Lidford is in the fourth bed on the right.' May turned away, her eyes seeking the bed the nurse had indicated when the nurse added, 'He's been telling us his daughter would be coming soon. He'll be glad to see you.'

It took all May's strength not to flee the ward. How could he have known? She hadn't written to him or any of her brothers. The ward stretched out in a nightmarish fashion, telescoping ahead until all she could see were endless beds diminishing in size the further away they were. She forced her shaking legs to move; the walls grew to a giddying height, threatening to come crashing down upon her. Any attempt to act like a confident WAAF diminished with every step until by the time she was standing at the end of the fourth bed on the right, she was mousy May, the downtrodden daughter of Jack Lidford.

She looked at the occupant of the bed, visible now she could see past the shielding screens. His head was swathed in even more bandages than the man in the wheelchair. Only the lower portion of his face was visible, and that was so scarred she couldn't recognise it as her father's. The arms resting outside the sheets were also bandaged from hand to elbow. Clear, yellowish fluid seeped from beneath the dressings, staining the sheets. May gagged at the mixture of smells assaulting her: the astringent smells of disinfectant and ointments overlain with the sickly odour of infection.

Despite her revulsion, a wave of relief washed over her. This wasn't her father. Her father was a vigorous bull of a man, quick with his fists and with a vicious tongue. He might be in his early sixties, but he was as fit as a man twenty years younger. He would never become this diminished, shrunken shell of a man. There had been a terrible mistake. She could go back to the WAAF – back home – and be free from him for ever.

Then the man cocked his head as though listening. 'Someone's there. Who is it?' May took an involuntary step back. 'Speak up. I know someone's there.' It was her father's voice.

'It's me. May.' And her voice wasn't the clear, confident voice she'd developed over the months in the WAAF. It was a frightened whisper.

The mouth stretched into a leer, revealing blackened crooked teeth, or gaps where teeth should be. 'Meek, mousy May. I knew you would be back.' While the man had lost his physical strength the power of his voice was, if anything, stronger.

May reeled, overcome by memories that she'd fought for so long to suppress. She clutched the bed rail, her knuckles turning white. She couldn't do this. What a fool she'd been. She should have accepted Jess's offer. She could feel her spine hunching. Jess had taught her to walk tall, accept her height and be proud of who she was. Peter had called her beautiful. Not beautiful despite her height, or beautiful to me. Just beautiful. But her dad had always called her meek, mousy, diminishing her day by day, and years of believing she was unlovely and unlovable couldn't be undone in a few months. Not entirely.

'Come closer,' her father said. 'You can't help your old man hovering at the foot of the bed.'

May took two hesitant steps closer. Her throat had closed. She couldn't have uttered a word had she wanted to.

'Because that's why you've come back, isn't it? To help your poor blind father.'

Blind? Dad was blind? Why hadn't Ron mentioned that in his letter? May swallowed and finally managed to force out a sentence. 'I can't stay. I'm in the WAAF now.'

Jack grunted and one of his bandaged hands made a gesture as though swatting an insignificant fly. 'You can leave. You could be released on compassionate grounds.'

So that was why Ron had made no mention of her father's blindness and implied he was on his deathbed. It was a trap. They needed someone to keep house for them and decided it would be her. The May they had known would have been unable to refuse them anything, let alone caring for her father. The trouble was, even though she had changed, she didn't think she could desert a blind man, no matter how badly he had treated her. The walls were closing in and she could see no escape.

'Now you're here,' Jack said, 'you can rearrange my pillows. Damn nurses never manage to get them right.

Then read me the racing results. One of your brothers left me a paper.'

May turned her face away and blinked back tears as she plumped up the pillows. A moment later she remembered her father couldn't see and relaxed slightly. Even so, she took several calming breaths before she picked up the folded newspaper from the top of the bedside cabinet and turned to the racing results. Thanks to her acting lessons, she managed to keep her voice from wobbling as she read, refusing to let her father sense her anxiety. How on earth was she going to get away? It was no good pointing out she was in the WAAF now. She was sure Ron or one of her other brothers had already used one of their many contacts to discover how to get her out. They wouldn't have asked her to come until the trap was well and truly sprung.

–

Peter read the letter through for the third time, but it was no good; he still couldn't make sense of it. He thought back to the last time they had met, racking his brain for any clue that she had been planning to break off their relationship. It couldn't have been their disagreement over how much help May should give to the evacuee girl – all couples had disagreements. May had said so herself in the letter. It had been nothing to break up over. And, yes, she had been reluctant to meet his parents yet had enjoyed the day in the end, seen that his parents were overjoyed to have her in their son's life.

He shoved back his chair and paced the confines of his small office. If he had been able to drive he would have jumped into his car and driven straight to Amberton to demand that May explain herself. He aimed a kick at the waste paper basket with his wooden leg. Instead of sending it flying against the wall as he would have done with his prosthetic foot, he only succeeded in making the bin wobble slightly. Bloody leg. Perhaps May wouldn't have been in such a hurry to get rid of him if he was whole.

He immediately dismissed that thought. May had never shown either the pity or fascinated horror he'd encountered in some other women. It was as though she had seen into his soul and accepted him for who he was from the start.

He returned to his chair. There was a mountain of paperwork demanding his attention, not least being a letter to the parents of a young pilot officer who had been killed the day before. He had only got as far as writing the address when he found himself picking up May's letter again. This time he noticed a tiny blot on the line that read: *It will only be an equal relationship if both parties are able to express their views.* It was as though a drop of water had fallen upon the page. A tear?

Some of his hurt and anger faded. May hadn't written this letter lightly. She had shed tears over it, yet had still done it. She would only have sent it if she truly believed they weren't right for each other. He read it though again, this time he was able to see past his own wounded feelings to the deep pain behind every word. How she had tried to make him understand her point of view over visiting his parents and helping the evacuee girl, and he had dismissed her feelings. The worst of it was, she had asked him to respect her wishes and not to try to change her mind. Irritation flared at that. It put him in an impossible position. If he accepted her request without argument, he was giving her up too easily; if he tried to win her back, he wasn't respecting her request.

He crumpled the letter and stuffed it in his pocket. Then he picked up his pen and continued the letter to the parents of Pilot Officer Clark. He had work to do, and he couldn't waste any more time on a personal matter. Clark's parents would be suffering far worse than him, and he owed it to them to offer them some words of comfort. However, the usual assurances that it would have been a quick and painless death and that he had died saving his country, rang hollow to Peter this time. Clark had been on patrol over Southampton, sent to intercept more bombers, when he had been hit by anti-aircraft fire from their own gunners. Another casualty of the futile attempt to stop bombers in the dark. Peter could only hope he was telling Clark's parents the truth about his end being quick, and as for him being shot down by their own guns, he would never reveal that. All he could do was say Clark had been brave and died in service to his country. Both of which were true. But while men like Clark were dying needless deaths in the air, civilians were being killed by night after night of bombings. When would the powers that be finally change their strategy to one that stopped the bombings so his pilots weren't getting killed for nothing?

He took up his pen again and wrote another empty platitude, then signed his name. He was blotting the ink dry when there was a knock at the door, and an airman arrived with the latest post. Once the man had gone, Peter snatched up the three envelopes and sifted through them. His heart sped up when he saw an envelope that seemed to have come from Amberton, only for it to lurch in disappointment when he didn't recognise the handwriting. Upon opening it, he was surprised to see it was from Jess. Cold foreboding washed over him. It could only be about May. He hurriedly skimmed it, his gaze settling on one section: *I'm so worried about her. She's gone to Birmingham and wouldn't let me come. She's determined to stand up to her father, but what if she can't? What if her brothers find a way to make her stay?*

He reread the whole letter more slowly then picked up his walking stick and marched out of his office and through the dispersal hut, taking no notice of the greetings some of his men called out to him. He was going to see his CO. May had asked him not to try changing her mind, and he would respect that, but nothing would stop him going to her aid.

Chapter Sixteen

A ringing bell drew May back from her musings. She put down the paper as a nurse called out, 'Visiting hours are now over.'

Chairs scraped as the other visitors rose and kissed their loved ones goodbye. May simply put on her coat and said a stiff, 'Goodbye.' She had no intention of kissing him.

'Fetch me some socks from home when you come tomorrow,' her father said before she could make her escape. 'Most of them are full of holes, but you can darn them, there's a good girl. Oh, and bring another pair of pyjamas. Then you can take these home to wash.' He indicated the stained and rolled-up sleeves of his pyjamas.

A flutter of alarm beat in her chest. 'I... I'm due back in a couple of days.' She should run away again. That would be the sensible thing.

'Rubbish. You're not going back. You'll stay and look after your old dad.' And it was as though she'd never left. Jack had never listened to her.

'That's...' She took an involuntary step back and her heel struck the screen. She grabbed it, more to steady herself than the screen. 'I can't just leave the WAAF.'

'You'll do what you're told.' Jack lowered his voice to a rasping whisper. 'If you try going back, your precious WAAF might be interested to receive an anonymous tip-off. What would they do to someone who used to transport stolen items?'

Nothing good, she was sure. They wouldn't care that she had been too frightened to defy her father. As far as they would be concerned, she had been involved in criminal activity, and that would be the end of her career.

She licked dry lips. 'You wouldn't. Not to your own daughter.'

He gave a nasty chuckle. 'Care to risk it?' Then, raising his voice, 'Oh, and bring a copy of the *Gazette* tomorrow.'

She fled with his laughter ringing in her ears.

She left the hospital and retraced her steps to the poky guest house where she had taken a room. She took a bath in the shared bathroom. No matter how hard she scrubbed, she couldn't rid herself of the smells and memories of Ward B. It was only when a woman banged on the door, complaining that May was taking far too long, that May dragged herself out of the water, her skin smarting. She dried and dressed, fumbling with her shirt buttons.

Another bang on the door set her heart pounding. 'Get a move on,' the woman yelled.

'I... nearly ready.' May's voice came out as barely more than a squeak. She grabbed her toilet bag and towel and opened the door.

'About time.'

'S-sorry.' Head down, May scurried to her room. She slammed the door and locked it then sank onto the bed and picked up her comb. With trembling hands she started to run it through her shoulder-length hair.

After a while she glanced up and caught a glimpse of herself in the dressing table mirror. Frightened eyes peered through a dark curtain of hair, and she sat hunched up as though trying to make herself invisible. Meek, mousy May was indeed back.

May flung aside the comb and buried her face in her hands. Visions of days stretching into months and years at the beck and call of her father passed in front of her eyes. If Jack made it impossible to return to the WAAF, where else could she go? Without thinking, she reached for her writing case, which she'd packed in her kit bag. Then her stomach twisted when she remembered she couldn't write to Peter. She would never again find comfort in writing to him. She hadn't thought it possible for her mood to become any bleaker, but the recollection that she would never see him again made her want to curl up in a corner and howl. Was there anyone in the world as miserable as her?

Then she remembered Peggy and felt a twinge of guilt. May at least had choices, even if none of them were happy ones; Peggy had no option but to rely on May to get her away from Mrs Evans. How would she feel to hear May had left Amberton for Birmingham so soon after promising to help? Well, maybe May couldn't write to Peter, but she could let Peggy know she wasn't forgotten. She took out the writing paper and pen and dashed off what she hoped was a reassuring note, letting Peggy know that although she was in Birmingham, she was thinking of her. She would send it to Mrs Grey with a note asking her to hand it to Peggy. As she wrote, her whirling thoughts calmed. Whatever her father expected, she was needed back at Amberton. Both the WAAF and Peggy needed her. Somehow she must find a way to defy her father and stop him from ruining her career. She had no idea how, but she had to try. Her stomach knotted. It would be so much easier if she hadn't left her courage behind in Amberton. *Stand up straight. Chin up. Look like a confident person if you want to feel like one.* May froze. The memory of Jess's voice had been so vivid May had to look to assure herself Jess wasn't in the room.

Even though she was indeed alone, suddenly she didn't feel so alone any more. No matter that Jess, Evie and even Peter were no longer with her, she would never forget their love and encouragement.

'What should I do?' she whispered, although she knew the answer. She had known it all along. She had to face up to her past. That meant returning to the terraced house in Small Heath. It also meant going back to see her father tomorrow. It wouldn't be easy, yet it was the only way to be free of the terrified, submissive creature she had once been.

She recoiled at the thought of returning to the house where she had been little more than a servant, but with Jess's advice ringing in her ears, she stood tall and pulled on her uniform. Jess would also expect her to look her best, so she pinned up her hair into fashionable victory rolls and applied lipstick. Inside, her heart was leaden with dread, but the reflection in the mirror showed a tall, confident WAAF. She would hold onto that image and pray it was enough to see her through the ordeal.

She caught a bus to the city centre then walked to Moor Street to catch a train to Small Heath. All the way, she mentally coached herself in Jess's voice to stop herself from turning around and running back to the guest house. Walk tall. Look confident to make others believe you are.

She had half expected to see the same devastation as Coventry, and while many buildings had been hit, the destruction was spread across a larger area with the majority of buildings still standing. The people around her were carrying on as normal, despite the piles of rubble they had to pick through in places. Unlike Coventry, Birmingham's heart hadn't been torn out. It was strange to see familiar places destroyed or damaged, though, and when she left the train at Small Heath, she froze in shock when she saw the miasma of dust and smoke hovering over what had once been the Birmingham Small Arms factory. She walked to Wenlock Road, afraid of seeing more destruction, but although windows were blown out and some chimneys cracked, it had mercifully escaped the worst. Some houses even had Christmas wreaths on their doors. Strange to think of people celebrating Christmas when so many people must have been killed just a stone's throw away.

She reached her house – her father's house, she corrected herself – and walked through the narrow side passage to the back yard. It was a sizeable yard, separated from the neighbours by high brick walls, with a long outhouse running the length of one wall. There was another smaller outhouse on the opposite side that held the toilet, and it was there that May found the house key, behind a loose brick, just where it had always been hidden. Jess's voice was fading now, and she found herself trembling as she let herself in. She hoped Ron would be out, pursuing whatever shady deals he did for their father. At least she knew her other brothers would be away – they had joined the army when called up; as far as May knew they hadn't tried to avoid conscription. Maybe they, like her, saw military service as a way of escaping life in Birmingham.

The door creaked open and the stench of stale beer, sweat and odorous shoes washed over her. She wrinkled her nose and walked into the kitchen. Flies buzzed around a stack of filthy crockery in the sink. The congealed sauce on some of the plates was crusted, and mould furred the bottom of one of the mugs that lay on its side on the draining board; the dishes clearly hadn't been washed for some days.

The back room wasn't much better. She automatically went to check the blackout before turning on the light only to find the windows were boarded up; the glass must have been blown out during a bombing raid. Newspapers lay on every surface, all open at the racing pages. A plate and mug stood on the table, both covered in crumbs. The table itself was ringed from drinks being slopped onto the scratched wood. A thick layer of dust coated the mantelpiece and the fireplace was choked with ashes. When May had lived here she had kept the room tidy, polished and dusted the furniture and swept the fireplace every day. In cold weather she had kept a fire alight in the grate. Now an air of damp permeated the room and her breath misted in the air. No wonder they wanted her to move back. It didn't look like anyone had done a spot of work since she had left.

She perched on a chair and gazed around feeling sick. What was she doing here? Closing her eyes, she fought the rising panic.

She had come to say goodbye to the place. Get it out of her system. That was all. She would find some socks for her father and darn them, knowing it was the last task she would ever do for him. Then she would return to the guest house and never come back.

Miraculously, she did find some clean socks in her father's bedroom. They were, as her father had said, more hole than sock, but she picked out two pairs then went to find a darning needle and wool in the front room. She made a bundle of the socks and supplies and was about to make her escape when the kitchen door slammed. Heart pounding, May spun to face the door, fearing against all evidence that it was her father. A moment later the front room door opened.

'Well, well.' It was her brother Ron. Standing at six foot four, he was the tallest of the Lidfords, and his muscular build made him the most intimidating. How he had managed to exempt himself from military service on medical grounds, May didn't know. 'Knew you'd come back. About time. Clear the kitchen and make us a meal.' Even from this distance she could smell the beer on his breath.

Do it yourself. That's what Jess would say. May wished she could say it too; she had always been scared of Ron, and with good reason. Now more than ever she regretted coming to Birmingham alone. She rose, stuffing the socks into her gas mask case, making up her mind. Refusing to help would provoke a fight that she would have no hope of winning. It was one thing to face up to her father in hospital, quite another when she was alone with her brother who was quick with his fists. 'I'll wash the kitchen, but if you want food, you'll have to buy it.'

'Lend us ten bob, then. I'm a bit short. You must get paid well in your fancy job.'

'Fine.' It was nearly a week's pay, but if that's what it took, she was prepared to sacrifice it. She counted out the money and handed it over. No doubt he would spend it on drink. She didn't care as long as it got him out of the house, allowing her to get away.

He jerked his head towards the kitchen. 'Go on, then. Get to work.' He threw himself into a chair, raising a cloud of dust, and picked up a paper.

Her mouth went dry. 'Aren't you going out?'

'Later. When I know you're not planning to do another runner.'

Oh, God. He wasn't going to let her leave. This was going to be even harder than she'd feared. She had no option but to go to the kitchen and set to work. She found clean dishcloths in the cupboard under the sink, under her father's toolbox. They had probably lain there unused since she had left. As she washed dishes and scrubbed the filthy counters, she forced herself to calm her panicky thoughts so she could work out what to do.

Her two best friends and Peter – the people who knew her best – had all told her on separate occasions that she was stronger than she thought. Well, here was her first test. If she could get out of this, she was sure she would be able to say goodbye to her father tomorrow.

You are stronger than you think.

The words comforted her as she scraped the worst of the mould from the cups and dishes and plunged them into hot soapy water. Her friends were right – she had blossomed in the WAAF. She had dealt with life-or-death situations. She should be able to escape Ron.

A heavy footstep sounded behind her, accompanied by the smell of beer and stale cigarette smoke.

'So,' Ron said with a sneer in his voice, 'You're finally back where you belong.'

It struck her that Ron expected her to be weak, to give in without a murmur, because that was how she had always been. If she didn't put up a fight, it might put him off his guard.

She put Jess's acting lessons into practice, only applying her advice in reverse. She allowed her head to droop, her shoulders to stoop. She gave a sniffle. 'Why did Dad have to get caught by a bomb?' It didn't require much acting to inject a quaver into her voice.

'Hah. Well, that was a miscalculation.' Ron paced through the kitchen and leaned against the back door so they were now face to face. 'He went into an empty house to see what he could get, when it was hit by an incendiary.'

It took a moment for May to work out what Ron meant. 'He was stealing?'

Ron gave a negligent wave. 'It's hardly stealing. If people wanted to keep their stuff safe, they should lock their doors.'

May opened her mouth to protest then remembered the old May would never argue. She slouched a bit more and said, 'Well, I wish he hadn't been hit. I was happy in the WAAF.'

'Yeah, well you can forget about all that now. Your place is here.' His stomach rumbled, and he scowled. 'Are you sure there's nothing to eat?'

Have a look for yourself if you don't believe me, she wanted to say. Instead she made a show of looking in all the cupboards. 'Sorry. There's nothing.' As if it was her fault no one had been shopping in weeks.

Ron pushed himself away from the door. 'Right, then. I'm off to the chippy. And I expect to find this place clean when I get back.'

May fought to keep the hope from her expression. With a bit of luck he'd end up in the pub and drink himself into a stupor. By the time he got back, she'd be long gone.

As though he had read her mind he said, 'Don't think you're going anywhere.' He held up the door key with a sneer. 'I'm locking you in.'

He pulled on his coat and with a last taunting wave and slammed the kitchen door behind him. The lock clicked into place.

She waited until she heard the gate slam then sprang into action. First she ran to the front door; locked, and no sign of the key. Icy chills ran down her spine as she dashed back to the kitchen. She turned the handle and rattled it in the desperate hope Ron had failed to lock it properly, but it wouldn't budge. Oh, God, and all the windows were nailed up. She'd never get them open.

Nails. That gave her an idea. She squinted at the door hinges. If she could find a nail or chisel, she could knock out the hinge pins. Then, with a bit of luck, she'd be able to work the door free. A year ago it wouldn't have occurred to her, but her time in the WAAF had taught her to be handy with tools.

She dropped to her knees and rummaged in the cupboard under the sink. She was sure she had seen her father's toolbox there. Bingo! She wrenched it open. On top of the tools was a small bunch of keys. For a wild moment she thought they were spare keys for the doors, but then she saw they looked more like padlock keys. They certainly wouldn't fit either of the doors. She flung them aside and looked in the box again. This time she found what she needed: a long chisel and a hammer.

She placed the chisel against the underside of the bottom hinge and tried to knock the hinge pin up using the hammer. Her hands trembled so violently, she missed and hit her thumb. The pain brought tears to her eyes.

There was no time to nurse her bruise; she had to get out before Ron returned.

She struck again, and this time hit the pin dead centre. It was pushed up far enough for her to prise free with her fingers. The other two pins came out just as easily. Now for the tricky bit: working the tips of her fingers between the door and jamb with one hand, she held the door handle with the other and prised the door back. It worked free from the lock, and she staggered back under the whole weight of the door. Good thing she was tall and strong, or she'd have been flattened.

She propped it against the wall and breathed in the cold, crisp air of freedom.

'That will teach you to mess with a WAAF,' she said out loud. Then she slung her gas mask over her shoulder and ran into the yard. She had nearly made it to the gate when she noticed the padlock on the outhouse door. Part of her was desperate to get away in case Ron came back, yet an idea was forming. If she was right, she need never be afraid of Ron or her father again. She could return to the WAAF secure in the knowledge that no report of her past actions would ever reach the ears of her superiors.

It was worth the risk. She raced back to the kitchen and picked up the keys she'd found. With shaking hands she fitted the first key into the padlock and gave a gasp of relief when it snapped open. She pulled open the door. It was dark, but the moon was bright enough to reveal some of the shed's contents: she saw several wireless sets; a tray full of silver cutlery; pictures in their frames. Everything else was just dark shapes, yet there wasn't a doubt in May's mind that she was looking at the spoils of several burglaries. It seemed her father and Ron had taken advantage of the many air raids to burgle houses and maybe even loot bombed buildings.

Feeling light-headed, she closed and locked the door, then pocketed the keys and ran out of the gate. She was free to return to the guest house, but first she was going to pay a visit to the nearest police station.

–

Even a sleepless night, interrupted by an air raid that had her and other residents cowering beneath the cellar steps, couldn't quash May's sense of triumph. For years she had turned a blind eye to her family's criminal activity – had done her best not to think about it, if she was honest – but the knowledge that her father and Ron had taken advantage of the air raids made her blood boil. Handing the evidence to the police had been the best way of freeing herself from her family's influence. Ron would be in custody now, and as for her father... she was almost looking forward to her final visit.

The time dragged by until visiting hours arrived and she could make her way to the hospital with a spring in her step. This time when she entered Ward B she asked in a quiet voice that wouldn't carry to her father if she could speak to his doctor. The nurse nodded and showed her into a small waiting room.

Ten minutes later, a harassed looking middle-aged man with a balding head and the thickest moustache May had ever seen entered the room. 'I'm Dr Benson,' he said, shaking May's hand. 'I gather you wanted to speak to me about Mr Lidford.'

May nodded. 'I wanted to know what sort of care will be provided to help him adapt to his blindness.'

'Blindness?' Dr Benson stroked his moustache. 'Of course, there's a chance he will never regain the sight in his left eye, but there's every reason to believe his other eye will heal without loss of vision.' He went on to explain about the injuries and treatment; May hardly heard through the ringing in her ears. As soon as Dr Benson finished, she thanked him, then marched down the ward to her father's bed. Although she knew Jack couldn't see her, she still stood tall and kept her chin raised.

'It's me,' she said before he could ask who was there. She pulled out the socks. 'I brought the socks you asked for. I even darned them. You'd better take care not to wear holes into these, because I won't be darning any more.' She flung them on the bed. Her heart was hammering against her ribcage and her palms were damp, but she could hear Jess cheering her on.

'You don't mean that,' Jack said. Was that a slight note of hesitation? After all, she had never spoken to him like that before. 'You can bring me some clean pyjamas tomorrow. New ones. These are too itchy.'

'You'll have to put up with them. I'm going back to the WAAF.'

'You don't mean that. You won't leave your old man without anyone to care for him.'

'Why not? You never cared for me or Mum.'

'You won't go. I know you, May. You never learned to say boo to a goose. You'll do as you're told like a good girl. Now, go to the shops and get me my pyjamas. If you hurry, you'll be able to bring them to me before the end of visiting time.'

The power of his voice was so hard to resist. For years she had cowered from him, doing anything to avoid his displeasure. Now it was like Jess, Evie and Peter were there with her, encouraging her, telling her she had escaped from him once and all she had to do was walk out of the ward and she would be free. 'I can't. I told you. I'm going back to the WAAF. Today.'

'You wouldn't leave your blind father to fend for himself?'

She snorted. 'According to your doctor, you'll be about as blind as a lynx. Perfectly capable of taking care of yourself.' May stepped back to avoid his hand, which flailed in the air, seeking her. 'You were going to trap me, fool me into feeling pity for my poor, blind father so I'd leave the WAAF and return to be your unpaid servant. You didn't reckon on me growing a backbone.'

'You can't abandon your family.'

May rounded on him. 'You treated me and Mum no better than slaves. Think on that when you expect me to give up everything for you. I've found a new life now, no thanks to you. One where I'm valued and... and loved.' She drew a shaky breath. She'd hardly ever dared to say more than 'yes' or 'no' to her father, and it took all her courage to hold her ground and keep going. 'You're right. I can't abandon my family. The thing is, you never treated me like family, but I've found one in the WAAF. I'm not abandoning my family. I'm going back to them.' She paced to the foot of the bed. 'Oh, by the way, you needn't worry about someone to take care of you. The police are very interested to talk to you about the goods they found in your outhouse. I've got a feeling you'll be taken care of at His Majesty's pleasure for some time to come.'

She stalked out of the ward, ignoring his shrieks of fury, feeling giddy with elation. She would never go back. Never be afraid of him or her brothers again.

Chapter Seventeen

'May!'

May halted her march through the hospital entrance hall and looked around, her heart thumping. It had sounded like Peter, but he wouldn't be here, surely. She had asked him to respect her decision. It didn't stop her craning her neck to look, and a treacherous part of her prayed it was him. She was about to resume her walk to the doors when she saw him, standing beside a bench beside the large double doors. 'Peter!' She felt a rush of gratitude mingled with white-hot shame. She wasn't ready to face him. Not yet.

'Jess told me you'd gone to Birmingham.' Peter caught up with her and made a movement as though to take her hand before snatching it back. He searched her face. 'Are you all right? She was worried about you.'

'I'm fine.' Now she understood what Jess meant about feeling two conflicting emotions at once. Part of her was overjoyed to see him and wanted to cling to him, reassure herself he was really there. The other half cringed and wanted to curl up in a shadowy corner where he would never find her. But he had come all this way for her. She couldn't in good conscience run away. 'I...' There were no words to express her tangled feelings.

'You look all in,' Peter said, 'Let's find a cafe.' He gave her a crooked smile that made the breath catch in her throat. 'I might even treat you to a Chelsea bun.'

Why was he being so nice? As they strolled in search of a cafe, she felt dazed, disconnected from her surroundings. The shops and people they passed were no more than a blur as she struggled to make sense of Peter's presence. Then, as she turned to walk through a door Peter held open for her, icy cold dread washed over her. Oh lord, what if he hadn't got the letter?

Awareness returned once she was sat down, and she saw she was at a table with a cheerful red gingham table-cloth. Peter sat facing her, regarding her with an air of expectation, brows raised.

'Sorry. Did you say something?'

'I asked what you wanted to eat.'

With a start May realised a waitress stood beside their table. 'Oh. Sorry.' May took a deep breath and noticed that the cafe was filled with a rich, savoury aroma. Her stomach growled, and it struck her that she hadn't eaten anything that day. 'What's that wonderful smell? I'd like some of that, whatever it is.'

The waitress hesitated. 'It's vegetable and pearly barley soup, but we stopped serving lunch at two.' Then she glanced at Peter, and May could swear she preened. 'Oh, but I'll see what I can do.'

She left with a parting smile at Peter. Sudden rage raked May's chest, and she glared at the waitress's departing back.

'Tell me about your father.' Peter said.

She glanced at Peter, heat flooding her face. She had no right to feel jealous when she had cast Peter off in the cruellest fashion. She still couldn't fathom why he was here and was afraid to ask.

'Is he going to make it?' Peter prompted. 'Jess said he was dying.'

May snorted. 'He's not dying. It was a trap. I was so stupid.' She explained what had happened, words tumbling over themselves as she described her feelings of triumph and exhilaration at finally standing up to her father. She could only dart the occasional glance at him as she spoke, but each time she dared to look there was no sign of the anger he had every right to express. She finished her tale more confused than ever.

Finally she plucked up the courage to ask, 'Why did you come? You... you did get my letter?'

'I did.'

The waitress chose that moment to return with two brimming bowls of soup and two brown rolls. 'And that's real butter with them,' she whispered after a glance round at the other customers. 'But don't let anyone else know, because we don't have much left.'

Hungry as May was, it took all her willpower not to yell at the waitress to leave. The silence stretched out between May and Peter while the waitress fussed around the table, setting down the soup and rolls in front of them and placing a dish containing two tiny pats of butter in the centre of the table.

'Oh, there's no salt and pepper. I can fetch some if you—'

'No. That's fine. Thank you.' May waited until the waitress was out of earshot before lifting her head to meet Peter's gaze. 'And?' It was all she could force through her tight throat.

'I understand.'

That was it? No profession of love? No attempt to win her back?

She swallowed. 'Why did you come?'

'I thought you needed help.' He gave a twisted smile. 'Turns out you didn't need it.'

May didn't know how to answer that. They ate their soup in unbearable silence. The precious butter was totally wasted on May, because she couldn't taste a thing. It was only the knowledge that the waitress had gone out of her way to get it that enabled May to finish the meal.

Once Peter finished, he set down his spoon and brushed the breadcrumbs from around his plate. 'Why didn't you ask me to come?' he asked after he had swept every last crumb onto his plate. 'I hate to think of you going through all that alone. I—' he swallowed 'I would never press you to change your mind. You asked me to respect your decision, so I will.'

The swoop of disappointment told her all she needed to know about her own feelings. It dawned on her that she had engineered an impossible situation. Peter couldn't ask her to change her mind without ignoring her request for him to respect her decision. Although she was elated over her recent triumph, there was no way she could ask Peter to court her again. Anyway, there was no guarantee he would want to after she had trampled his heart into the dust. She doubted even Evie would have been able to tell Alex how she felt without Alex declaring himself first. Maybe Jess would, but no amount of acting lessons would ever turn May into someone of Jess's supreme confidence.

She couldn't meet his eyes. 'It wouldn't have been fair.' She hesitated, stirring her tea while she organised her thoughts. It was hard to explain when she didn't understand fully herself. 'I suppose I had to prove to myself I could do it alone. You, Jess, Evie – you've all told me I'm stronger than I think. I needed to test it out for myself, prove to myself I can do things that frighten me.' Apart from telling Peter she had changed her mind, and could he ever forgive her and take her back.

His hand lay on the table next to the sugar bowl. It would be so easy to reach across, put her hand on his. Put all the words she couldn't say into that gesture. But what if he pulled his hand away? He might have come all the way to Birmingham to find her, yet she mustn't misread his intentions. He was a good, decent man. When he'd learned where she had gone, he would have come after her out of duty and kindness, not necessarily love. Who could continue to love a woman who rejected him by letter?

She kept her hand in her lap; the silence stretched out between them until she couldn't bear it. 'Thank you for coming.' She sounded like a child, dutifully thanking a relative at the end of a visit. The words were stiff and stilted but there was no way she could pour out the words in her heart. 'How did you get here? Train?'

He nodded. 'I get my new leg the day after tomorrow, so I'll be able to drive again then.'

'I'm glad.' She had always found Peter easy to talk to before but now she couldn't think of anything to say. 'Thank you for coming.' Wait. She'd already said that.

He made a sudden gesture, quickly stilled. 'May, you know I—' He stopped, looking down at his hands. 'Well, it's something I would do for any friend.' There was a pause, then, 'I can escort you back to Chichester if you like.'

Her heart swelled with gratitude and she had to blink away tears. Why did he have to be so nice? While she knew she should turn down his offer, she hesitated. Now she had said goodbye to her father once and for all, she didn't want to linger in Birmingham any longer than necessary. 'Thank you,' she said. 'When would you like to leave?'

Jess was in the kitchen of High Chalk House when May arrived. She was stirring milk in a pan, an open tin of cocoa beside her. She gave a whoop of joy. 'You're back! I was so worried you would decide to stay.'

'No way. I dealt with my father.'

'Attagirl!' Then Jess's smile faded. 'Did Peter find you?'

May nodded. 'He came back on the train with me.'

'So you're back together again? I knew you'd see sense.' Jess's smile faded when she saw May's expression. 'Oh.'

A sizzling sound and the smell of burning milk arose from the hob. Jess turned back to the cooker with an exclamation of annoyance. The milk was boiling, cascading over the sides of the pan, hissing and spitting when it met the flames. She wrapped a tea towel around her hand and moved the pan off the gas. 'This is all your fault, you know.' She addressed the pan, but May knew the words were aimed at her. She briskly stirred cocoa into what remained of the milk then decanted it into a mug.

'Here,' Jess handed her the steaming mug. 'You must need this more than me.' She filled the kettle with water and placed it on the hob. 'I'll make do with a cuppa.' She scowled. 'Without milk.'

'I'm sorry.' It was all she seemed able to say. She had apologised to Peter for taking him out of his way. He had waved it away. What she had really wanted to do was thank him for coming for her. No. What she had *really* wanted to do was beg him to forgive her and ask if there was any chance he might still love her. Because she loved him with her whole heart. But escaping from a locked house and standing up to her father was one thing. Pouring her heart out to the man who loved her and would never dream of hurting her was, it seemed, completely impossible.

Jess smiled. 'Nah, I was only teasing. I'd just hoped that by sending Peter after you… Well, you can tell me all about it up in the schoolroom.'

Whilst Jess was making her tea, May cleaned the pan and wiped the spilled milk from the hob. Then they took their drinks upstairs to the schoolroom. As soon as they were seated in their usual chairs, May poured out the story, to the accompaniment of Jess's exclamations when she described her father's deception and the escape from her squalid former home. After bottling up her feelings throughout the long and awkward train journey, it felt good to release them.

'I was so happy to see him, Jess, but I feel terrible. He must have practically traded his leg to get leave for the trip at short notice, and what did I give him in return?'

Jess looked uncharacteristically serious. 'He doesn't expect anything. He'd do anything for you. He loves you.'

May took a mouthful of cocoa, swallowing hard to clear the sudden lump from her throat. 'He can't.' She gazed at the swirl of cocoa powder floating on the top of her drink. Her voice came out as little more than a whisper. 'I was so cruel.'

'He understands. He knows why you did it.'

'I wish he'd explain it to me, then. I've no idea why.'

'Yes you do. You're scared that marriage would turn you into your mother, too terrified to ever express your opinion to your husband.' Jess's eyes were kind. 'You know

Peter is nothing like your father, but you don't want to lose the freedom you've won.'

May gazed at her friend in wonderment. 'How do you know all that?' She'd never had anyone explain herself to her. It was unsettling, to say the least.

'I'm an actress, remember. That's what we do – study characters so we can perform them realistically.' Jess leaned forward, gazing at May intently. 'You could make it up with Peter, you know.'

May shook her head. 'It's too late for that. I really hurt him. It was cowardly of me to end it by letter.' The tears that had never been far away during the whole journey back from Birmingham welled up again. 'He gets his new leg soon, and he'll be back on active duty. What if he – what if that was the last letter he ever had? I wouldn't blame him if he's never able to forgive me. I know *I* never will.'

'He still loves you. I'm sure he'd forgive you. Everyone gets scared and makes mistakes. You know you've made a mistake, so why not try to undo it?'

'Maybe if he was still at Amberton.' May gazed moodily at the dregs of her cocoa. 'But there's no reason for him to come back. I won't see him again.'

She rose, feeling hollow inside. She couldn't bear to talk or even think about it any longer. 'I… I'm tired. I'm going to turn in.' She felt too awful even to take her empty mug downstairs to the kitchen. Leaving it on the table to clear away the next day, she dragged herself into the nursery. The blackout curtains were in place, but she didn't bother to turn on the light. She undressed in the dark and pulled on her pyjamas, leaving her uniform rumpled at the foot of the bed. She had never failed to hang up her uniform before. Tomorrow she would regret it, tonight she felt too bone weary to do anything other than fall into bed.

Tired as she was, sleep failed to come. She would never see Peter again. It felt too huge, too terrible to take in.

–

Peter walked into the Officers' Mess to be greeted by cheers from his fellow officers.

'If you'd kept that peg leg much longer, we were going to get you a parrot,' Squadron Leader Greg Parry said, beckoning Peter to join him.

'I can't tell you how good it feels to get back in the air again,' Peter said as he flung himself into an armchair next to his friend. Even the fact that his patrol had failed to intercept any enemy bombers couldn't take away the satisfaction of being back behind the controls of his Hurricane. He stretched out his legs and couldn't help glancing down at his feet, glad to see two shoes again. He hadn't been so happy to see his shoes since he had been five, proud of his new school shoes that his mother had saved for weeks to buy. They had been his first brand new shoes instead of hand-me-downs, and he had insisted on placing them by his bed so they would be the first thing he saw when he woke up.

'You must have missed it if flying a Hurricane makes you grin like that,' Greg said. 'Now, if you were flying Spitfires like me...'

They were back in the familiar banter, arguing over the relative merits of their aircraft. Peter decided it was best not to confess he hadn't been smiling about being back in his Hurricane, but at the thought of his batman's expression if he insisted upon him placing his shoes beside his bed once they had been polished.

However, nothing could make him forget that he had lost May. Deep down he had cherished hopes of his trip to Birmingham, picturing himself rescuing May from her father's clutches. Instead she had managed without him. She had proved his assertion that she was stronger than she'd given herself credit for, but it had rather denied him the opportunity to save her and have her fall into his arms from gratitude. Now he had nothing but the memory of her. That and flying. And the flying wasn't going well.

'Tell me, Greg,' he said, cutting across whatever line his friend was spinning, 'is your squadron still being sent to intercept night bombers?'

Greg shook his head, looking taken aback at the interruption. 'We're mostly doing Rhubarbs and Rodeos now. Why?'

A week ago he would have stayed silent. But May had shown him the way. She had proved herself to be so much stronger than him. For weeks he had held his tongue when being sent out on futile night patrols, even though it was obvious they were intercepting enemy bombers only by pure chance. He might have lost May but he would learn from her. It was time he stopped trying to fit in. Time he stuck his neck out. 'I'm beginning to think it's time we demanded a change of strategy. I'm fed up of blundering around in the dark, hoping to bump into the Luftwaffe while our cities are being bombed to smithereens.'

'Sounds like you should have stayed in Middle Wallop.'

'What? Why?' He had initially transferred to Middle Wallop from Amberton to requalify for operational flying.

'Haven't you heard? 604 squadron are using Beau-fighters with airborne interception devices.'

'I didn't think they'd had much success.' Despite being aware of the trials while at Middle Wallop, he had been too focused on his flight training to take much interest in the operational squadrons.

'John Cunningham used it to pinpoint a Junkers 88 the other day and shot it out of the sky. I was there last week. They're trialling other aids for night fighters, too. Wait. Where are you going?'

For Peter had leapt to his feet. 'I'm off to pay the group captain a visit.'

If May could do it then so could he. It was time he stood up for what he believed was right. He was going to demand that if his squadron was to continue night flying, it should be supplied with Beaufighters fitted with airborne interception. He would also volunteer to work with Middle Wallop to trial other night flying aids.

As he marched off, he felt a weight fall from his shoulders. He had let his need to fit in govern him for too long. He wouldn't let his squadron suffer any more.

All of a sudden he understood why May had ended their courtship. She had wanted his support in helping Peggy; instead he had urged her to keep her head down. To let Peggy suffer to protect her career. Fool. No wonder she had decided she'd be better off without him.

—

May had loved everything about Amberton until now. She loved sharing High Chalk House with the other WAAFs; it felt like the kind of happy extended family she'd always longed for. Now, however, things had soured. There were reminders of Peter at every turning. Drive an officer to the railway station? She'd been there with Peter. Go to the pub? They'd shared many conversations there, the noise of the other customers effectively screening them from being overheard. Wait for Jess outside the Ops? That was where Peter had once worked. Everywhere she went just served to remind her of the gaping absence in her heart that was Peter. She couldn't even look out for letters or phone him any more. Although she took pride in her work, all the joy had gone out from it.

Even the course at Cranwell, which she'd been determined to apply for, seemed out of her reach now. What was the point of applying? She didn't trust her decision-making, not when it had led her to end her relationship with Peter.

'You have to do it,' Jess told May when she plucked up the courage to confess she wasn't going to apply after all. 'I wish someone had photographed you while you were telling me about it. Your face was all lit up. You looked so eager and excited. Don't deny yourself this chance.'

It was evening, and although there was no rehearsal that night, they were working on the costumes, frantically trying to get all alterations finished before the dress rehearsal in three days' time. Jess was sewing lengths of tinsel – donated by Mrs Grey – onto the hem, sleeves and neckline of the fairy godmother's floaty white dress. It would itch like fury, but without it, Jess said the fairy godmother looked more like a debutante at her first ball. The WAAF playing the fairy godmother had agreed, reluctantly, to suffer for her art. May was adding more ruffles to Milan's ugly sister outfit.

May cut a length of bright green thread to match the underskirt and threaded her needle before replying. 'What if I fail? I know what I'm doing as a driver. I'm good at it.' It was a comfortable role. She could also scarcely admit it to herself, but if she left Amberton, it would break her last tie to Peter. Peter knew how to find her while she was here. No matter how much she told herself she was better off without him, she constantly found herself daydreaming of Peter coming to Amberton to beg her to take him back.

Jess put down the dress and looked at May seriously. 'I can't believe you're saying this. Have you forgotten what we promised that day in Brighton?'

'Of course not.' Jess was referring to the vow Evie, Jess and May had made after seeing the Dunkirk evacuees. The sight of those beaten, injured men had awoken them to the seriousness of the war and they had promised to do everything in their power to help the war effort. May felt a flash of indignation that Jess could imagine May had forgotten. 'I'm helping the war effort where I am.'

Jess arched an eyebrow. 'Tell me why you were interested in the course in the first place.'

'Because it's something to do with tracking enemy bombers.'

Jess nodded, a flash of triumph in her eyes. 'There you go. You've seen the results of bombing. We— you can do something to try and stop it. Would you be satisfied carrying on as you are when something so important to you is available?'

May knew Jess was right, knew she would always regret not trying if she chose not to, but she couldn't help asking, 'What if I fail? What if I can't do it?'

'Then you go back to being a driver, knowing you did your best.' Jess added one final stitch fastening the tinsel to a sleeve and then broke the thread off with her teeth before continuing. 'You seem to have lost confidence in yourself just when you were doing so well. You escaped from a locked house and told your father where to go, for goodness sake. You should be proud of yourself.'

May gave a faint smile, feeling warmth kindle in her chest, grateful to have a friend who always wanted the best for her.

'Do you believe in me, May?'

May looked at Jess, startled. 'Of course I do. I wish I had even an ounce of your confidence. You seem to be able to do anything you set your mind to.'

'Well, I believe in you, and I'll carry on believing for the both of us. I know, without a shadow of doubt, that you have the ability to do this. All you have to do is believe in me, which you seem to find easy.'

May couldn't help laughing at Jess's twisted logic, but there was no doubting the strength of Jess's conviction. These weren't empty words. If Jess believed in her so utterly, wouldn't she be letting Jess down if she didn't even try to do the course? Because Jess was right, it was something she had set her heart on.

Still she hesitated. There was still the fact that leaving Amberton would separate her completely from Peter.

Jess, however, seemed to have read her mind. 'You have the power, right now, to put things right with Peter.' She made a gesture at the costumes piled around their feet. 'This is a WAAF Cinderella, remember? Our Cinderella doesn't sit by the fire, waiting for Prince Charming to rescue her. Our Cinderella has more control over her destiny. Which version would you prefer to be?'

'Our version.' Although it was true, her heart quailed.

'Well, then. You still have plenty of time to put things right before you go on the course.'

May threw up her hands. 'All right. You win. I'll do it.'

Jess leapt up from her chair and pirouetted, clutching the fairy godmother's dress to her chest. 'Yes! You're going to slay 'em!'

'I'll tell Ellerby first thing tomorrow.' Jess's enthusiasm rekindled the fluttering excitement May had felt when she'd first learnt of the course. 'I'll go in early.'

'No need. I already spoke to 'er while you were away.'

'What?' May picked up the first weapon that came to hand – a pillow that was to be sacrificed to pad out Jiří's ugly sister overskirt – and aimed a swipe at Jess's head. She was laughing too much to be angry. 'Why didn't you tell me in the first place?'

'I 'ad to make sure you wanted to do it before I told you. I would 'ave grovelled to Ellerby and got her to remove your name from consideration if you were adamant you didn't want to go. You do believe that, don't you?' Jess dodged another blow.

May dropped the pillow, panting. 'I know you would. I don't understand why you told her at all. I could have done it myself.'

'True, but I was asking 'er if I could go too, so I thought I might as well—'

The rest of Jess's words were muffled when May gave a yell of delight and enveloped Jess in an enthusiastic hug, jumping up and down in joy at the same time.

'Jess, that's wonderful! I didn't know you wanted to do it.'

'Yes, I— ow, pins!' Jess extricated herself from the hug and eased the fairy godmother's dress from her front, wincing. But once she'd dropped the dress onto her chair, she was beaming again. 'I was thinking about it a lot while you were away. I love working in Ops, but I think I've got as far as I can go there. While we were in the middle of the Battle of Britain, I felt my work was vital to our pilots. But things have changed, and doing this course will be the best way I can help us through the next stage.'

'And we'll still be together.'

Jess's smile broadened. 'We'll still be together.'

Then May gave a gasp. 'What about Peggy? If we both leave, there'll be no one to help her.'

Jess's face clouded, then she gave a determined tilt of the chin. 'We'll just have to get her away from that cow before Christmas.' She clapped May on the shoulder. 'You escaped from your family. Helping Peggy will be a piece of cake in comparison.'

May could only hope inspiration struck soon, because right now she was out of ideas.

Chapter Eighteen

Inspiration failed to strike, so the hope that Jess and May would still be together at the start of their next adventure was the only bright light in the days that followed. The knowledge that she was running out of time to help Peggy gave May a growing sense of dread.

She also missed Peter dreadfully and doubted the pain would ever be completely healed. Perhaps it was the fact that she had brought it on herself that made it so bad. She could only hope that the excitement and hard work of the course would provide the distraction she needed.

Because even the rapid approach of the pantomime, and the fear of performing in front of the whole village, couldn't drive Peter from her mind. With only a fortnight left before Christmas, Jess had been excused from evening and night watches so there could be rehearsals every evening. These all took place in the village hall. As the children were now word-perfect with their scene, Jess had declared they should have a break until the dress rehearsal. This was scheduled for three days before Christmas Day. Now the cast had moved to the stage at the village hall, it was a new challenge changing costumes between scenes and getting used to the props and scenery.

'Well done, everyone,' Jess said to the assembled cast at the end of a successful rehearsal. Even May felt she had performed well. If only no one turned up to watch, she felt she might survive the performance. The only mishap had been when Jiří, at the back of the pantomime stag, had misjudged his position and stepped off the stage. Only Milan had saved him from falling, and there had been a comical few seconds when the stag's hind legs had flailed in the air before Jiří had scrambled back to his feet. May glanced at him now and saw him rubbing his ribs.

'If you can perform like that on the day—' Jess shot a glance at Jiří '—and keep your feet on the stage, it'll be a hit. No rehearsal tomorrow being Sunday, so I'll see you all here on Monday at five o'clock prompt. But right now, I need a drink. Who's coming to the pub?'

There was a murmur of assent and the cast moved to collect coats and hats. May was standing beside the door, wondering if anyone would notice if she didn't go to the pub when Jess slipped her arm through May's. 'I could read that frown from the other side of the hall. Don't tell me you were planning to slip back to the Waafery.'

'I'm just not in the mood.'

Jess tilted her head as she regarded May. 'You're thinking of Peter again, aren't you?'

May looked at her shoes.

'And will sitting alone in your room help you forget?'

'I—'

'Course not. Come with us. At least it will be a distraction.'

It was impossible to say no to Jess, and in truth, May knew she would only brood if she was alone. She finished buttoning her coat and said with a sigh, 'Fine. I'm coming.' Putting on her cap, she allowed Jess to pull her out of the hall and into the dark street outside. It was a clear night; stars glinted overhead, and a perfect half-moon could be glimpsed above the rooftops, casting its silvery glow upon the rapidly forming frost. It was hard to stay gloomy beneath such a glorious night sky and with the laughter and chatter of their fellow cast members surrounding her. Christmas was around the corner, and May was going to spend it with the first people she had ever been able to call friends.

She couldn't help thinking of Peter with a pang. Christmas would have been even better if she could have spent it with him.

She could write to him. Invite him to the pantomime.

'If I do get accepted on the Cranwell course, I'm going to miss this place,' May said, deliberately pushing aside thoughts of Peter. After all, she was supposed to be trying to forget him.

'Me too,' Jess replied. 'It's not a patch on London, of course, but I'd miss Amberton, all the same.'

'Miss Amberton?' a deep voice asked from behind them. Milan materialised from the darkness just as Jess slipped on a patch of ice. He caught her arm to steady her. 'Are you leaving?'

'We don't know yet,' Jess said. 'Me and May have applied for a course. If we get in, we'll be leaving.'

Milan walked on in silence for a while then said, 'You will tell me if you are leaving? You would not leave without saying goodbye?' May knew this was directed at Jess alone. She felt rather uncomfortable and would have given them space, but she needed to cling to Jess's arm to stop herself from sliding on the icy ground.

Jess gave a laugh that sounded forced to May. 'I'm sure you'll be stuck with me for the duration. I doubt the powers that be will recommend me for promotion.' By this time they had reached the Horse and Groom. When Milan opened the door for them, the deep rumble of masculine laughter spilled out from the snug. 'Come on,' said Jess as they hurried inside out of the cold, 'I'm parched after all that singing. I'll have a lager and lime, please.' Jess gave Milan a push towards the bar.

Milan turned to May. 'What would you like?' Something in his expression told May that he was more shaken by the possibility of Jess's departure than he was letting on. She asked for a lemonade, resolving that as soon as the pantomime was over, she was going to find out once and for all what Jess felt about Milan. Because while Jess may be just enjoying a mild flirtation, Milan seemed far more serious.

While Milan went to the bar, she and Jess pushed through the crowd to take a seat beside the fire. Christmas decorations had been put up in the snug since May's last visit. Garlands of holly, dotted with glossy red berries, hung upon the ceiling beams and around the mantelpiece in place of the usual horse brasses. A large bunch of mistletoe dangled above the door. The blackout curtain would have hidden it from anyone entering, but it was obvious from this side.

The rest of Brimstone squadron were already present. Alex and the British pilots occupied a corner table while the Czechs clustered around the bar. Milan and Jiří joined them, Milan saying something in rapid Czech that made the others roar with laughter. Judging from his gestures, he was describing how Jiří had fallen off the stage.

The blackout curtain twitched and a rough hand pushed it aside. May's heart sank when she saw Arnold Walker emerge, followed by two of his friends. From his flushed face and reddened nose, she guessed he had started drinking before coming out.

'There better not be any trouble,' Jess murmured, her face turned towards the door.

May felt Jess tense beside her when Mr Walker glanced at the group beside the bar and scowled. Thankfully, Alex chose that moment to stroll to the bar and placed himself conspicuously between Mr Walker and the Czechs. If Mr Walker had entertained any thought of antagonising the Czechs, Alex must have put him off. May released a shaky breath when Mr Walker muttered something to one of his friends and then took a seat at the table closest to the door.

'He doesn't look too happy,' May said to Jess. For Mr Walker was glowering at the Czechs who watched in gales of laughter while Milan imitated Jiří staggering around, clutching his ribs.

'He can be as unhappy as he likes, as long as he stays away from our lads.'

It seemed that Mr Walker was not prepared to cause trouble when he was so greatly outnumbered. He and his friends stayed in their corner while the men and women of RAF Amberton took over the rest of the snug. Gradually May relaxed and was able to join in with the other cast members. She was glad she had come. She'd needed something to lift her spirits, and there was nothing like festive cheer for that.

Festive cheer. 'I've had an idea,' she said to Jess.

Jess drained her glass and shot an uneasy glance at Mr Walker, who by now had two empty beer mugs beside him and was halfway down his third. He and his friends seemed to be sitting under their own personal thunder cloud. 'Fire away. If it involves anything to take the scowl off their faces—' she gave a jerk of the head towards Mr Walker's table '—I'm all for it.'

'Why don't we go carol singing? We could take some of the WAAFs with Jiří, Milan and any of the other lads that want to join in?'

Jess's face lit up. 'That's a brilliant idea. Let's go tomorrow.' She lowered her voice. 'With luck it will persuade certain people that the Czechs are human beings too.'

With an energy typical of Jess, no sooner had the idea been raised than she had rounded up a dozen volunteers, including five of the Czechs, to go out the next evening. 'We'll meet at two for a practice,' she told the group, 'and go out at sunset, so we've still got enough light to see by.' Alex, who was part of the group, promised to organise a room on the base where they could rehearse.

'It will make up for missing Svatý Mikuláš,' Jiří told them when most of the group had dispersed back to their own seats.

'Mikularsh?' May said, stumbling over the unfamiliar word. 'What's that?'

'Not what. Who,' Milan said, as he took a seat beside Jess. 'He is… I think you call him Saint Nicholas. It was his feast day on December the 6th. The evening before, Mikuláš visits all the children in the village with an *anděl* – angel – and a…' He said something that sounded like 'chert', accompanied with a gesture that sketched horns on either side of his head. 'The opposite of an angel.'

'Devil?' Jess suggested.

'Yes!'

'It was my favourite night of the year,' Jiří broke in, his eyes shining. With a pang, May saw for the first time the face of the boy he had been before the Nazis had taken over his world. It wouldn't have been many years ago that he had taken part in the festivities as a child. Only a few short years in which his world had been turned upside down by the ceding of Czechoslovakia to the Nazis. She swallowed a lump in her throat as she listened to Jiří's description. Even if none of the villagers enjoyed their carols, she was glad she had suggested it for Jiří's sake.

'Mikuláš goes from house to house, visiting each child,' he was saying, 'and he decides if each one has been good or bad. To the good children, the *anděl* gives a treat.'

'What if they've been bad?'

'The devil gives them a lump of coal,' Milan supplied.

'And if they have been very bad,' Jiří said, his whole face alight, 'the *čert* threatens to put them in his sack and take them to hell.'

'Good thing we missed it,' Jess said. 'We want to cheer the children, not give them nightmares. Although—' she darted a glance at Mr Walker '—I could name some adults I'd nominate for being carried off by devils.'

–

Soon after the arrangements for the carol singing were made, a group of WAAFs declared their intention to return to the Waafery. May, yawning, said she would go back with them, but Jess found herself lingering. It had struck her while listening to Milan and Jiří that if she was selected for the course, she would not have much more time with them. Jiří had become like a younger brother to her and Milan… No. She wouldn't think about how she would miss Milan. But it suddenly seemed vital to spend every possible moment with them… with him. If she left, she might never see him again.

Even as the thought crossed her mind, the old fear clawed at her throat. This wasn't right. She had promised herself she would never let another man into her heart. She sprang to her feet. 'Actually, I should go, too.'

Milan stood. 'You should not go alone. I will walk you back.'

'No need. I'll catch the others up. They can't have gone far.' She pulled on her greatcoat and cap and headed for the door. The blast of icy air made her pause in the doorway to button up her coat before leaving.

'Well, well. What have we here? A pretty WAAF under the mistletoe.'

Jess's skin crawled at the sound of Arnold Walker's sneering tones. He had placed himself between her and the snug. Reaching past her, he pulled the door closed and kept his hand on the door handle, trapping her. Unable to stop herself, she glanced up and saw she was standing directly beneath the bunch of mistletoe. Why hadn't she accepted Milan's offer? Then she would have been with him under the – no. Definitely a bad idea to let her mind drift in that direction.

Over Mr Walker's shoulder she could see Milan pushing past the crowded bar to get to her. Irritation flared. She didn't need a knight in shining armour. She could deal with the likes of Mr Walker. She hadn't survived four years as an actress without developing armour. She put it on now, plastering on the bright smile and flirtatious sideways glance that made a man feel special while keeping him at arm's length. 'It's not very gentleman-like, trapping a girl like that.'

'You don't strike me as a girl who wants a man to be a gentleman.' He leaned over her, his lips stretched in an unpleasant leer.

So much for flirtation. She might have given him a swift kiss on the cheek in exchange for him letting her go, trusting she could manage to hold on to the contents of her stomach, but she refused to be intimidated. She ducked under his arm, intending to escape to the relative safety of the bar, but before she could get clear he grabbed her arm in a bruising grip.

'Oh no you don't,' he snarled in a voice low enough not to be overheard. 'A tease like you needs to be shown her place.'

He leaned over her when a strong, long-fingered hand grasped his shoulder and pulled him away. Jess wrenched her arm free and staggered back, looking to see who had rescued her. Of course. It was Milan who glowered at Arnold Walker, eyes blazing, a muscle jumping in his cheek. 'The lady would like to leave.'

Jess's heart sank. She couldn't deny she was grateful to Milan's aid, but she didn't want him to give Arnold Walker even more reason to dislike the Czechs. Aware of a hush in the snug, she glanced around to see everyone turning to watch, including Alex and… oh no, there was Jean Ellerby. It wouldn't matter that Jess had done nothing wrong, that the disturbance was all Arnold Walker's doing. If she didn't take control of the situation now and get Milan out of there without further incident, she could wave goodbye to any chance of a place on the course.

Slipping her arm through Milan's she said, 'Mr Walker was just asking what time the pantomime was, so he could get it right on the programmes.' She directed a smile at the scowling Mr Walker. 'It's so kind of him to offer to print them.' She stepped towards the door, pulling Milan with her. Milan glared at Mr Walker with narrowed eyes but much to Jess's relief, offered no resistance. 'Come on,' she said. 'Walk with me until I catch up with the others.'

Now she was grateful for all the eyes upon them, for it meant Mr Walker could hardly make more trouble. Praying he would stay in the pub, she allowed Milan to usher her through the blackout curtain and out of the door. 'He's not following, is he?' she asked, tightening her grip on Milan's arm as her foot slipped on the frosty path.

Milan glanced over his shoulder. 'No. Not yet.' He bit off every word, and Jess could sense his suppressed fury through the tense muscles in his arm. 'Why did you provoke him?'

'Provoke?' Jess's anger flared. 'I just walked past 'im. Or is that a crime now?' She let go of his arm. 'I think I can see the others up ahead. Go back and pick a fight for all I care. Get yourself arrested.'

She strode off, pursuing the distant figures of May and the other WAAFs that she could just make out by the faint moonlight. She soon heard the pounding of running feet and Milan caught up with her.

'Wait,' he said. 'I am sorry. I should not have said you provoked him.'

Jess stopped and rounded on him, hands on her hips. 'Then why did you?'

'I do not know,' He raked his fingers through his hair. 'I think...' He paused for a long moment, gazing searchingly into her face.

Jess swallowed, her irritation fading to be replaced by alarm. She bitterly regretted encouraging his attentions. She enjoyed the company of pilots, loving the glamour that clung to them. And when Milan, with his dark good looks, had turned his attentions on her, she had been delighted. She had thought he understood it was just a bit of fun. A bright spot of light to see them through the dark hours on duty.

'I was angry with Mr Walker. I was angry with you because it looked like you were flirting with him.'

'If you must know, I was only flirting to flatter him and persuade him to let me go.' Then she stopped. 'Anyway, it shouldn't matter to you if I was flirting.'

His brows drew together. 'Is that all you have been doing with me – flirting?'

Jess's heart felt like it had been replaced by a lead weight. With any other man, she'd have switched on the charm and said, 'Course not. You're special.' But she couldn't do that to Milan. She had let him get too close, and now they were both going to pay the price. 'I... I'm sorry. I thought you understood. I can't get serious with anyone.' She turned away slightly, unable to meet his gaze. She had never been tongue-tied with a man before but now she struggled to find the right words.

'Will you stop seeing me if you get a place on this course?'

Milan's question should have made it easier for Jess to make the break; instead it felt a hundred times worse. Her throat ached. Part of her wanted to take her words back, say of course she wanted to stay in touch. The prospect of a final goodbye made her want to dash straight to Jean Ellerby and say she'd changed her mind. But even if she wasn't chosen, it would only be delaying the inevitable. She could have no future with Milan, and for his sake it was best to make it clear. 'What would be the point? We both know this has only been for a bit of fun.' She hated herself. If she was honest, it had been more than flirtation for her as well. Why else had she always sat with him when they were together in the pub? Why else had she let him kiss her at the Midsummer dance?

She dared to glance at Milan then. He was still looking at her as though trying to commit her every feature to memory. She half expected him to plead with her to change her mind. Instead, all he said was, 'I see.'

Why the lurch of disappointment? He had given her what she wanted. This was how mature adults behaved. They would continue to see each other, so it was good that they weren't going to make a scene. Then a horrible thought struck. 'The pantomime. You will still take part, won't you?'

He gave a curt nod. 'I promised. I will not let the children down.' And before she could say anything else, he added, 'I will also come carol singing. Jiří is looking forward to it.'

So that was that. She had freed herself from an impossible relationship. She should be relieved. But as she dashed to catch up with May, she felt as though a hand had reached into her chest and crushed her heart.

Chapter Nineteen

The setting sun had turned the sky into a blaze of gold, rose and indigo when the group of WAAFs and pilots left RAF Amberton and made their way to the village. All the Czechs from Brimstone squadron were present with Alex, and several of the WAAFs vied for their attention. Much to May's surprise, Jess didn't walk with Milan; neither did he attempt to single her out. Instead, Milan ignored all attempts by the other WAAFs to lure him to their side and walked with Jiří. He looked unusually sombre, but then again, anyone would look sombre compared to Jiří's capering enthusiasm.

Jess sparkled even more brightly than the frost clinging to the hedgerows. She began the walk arm in arm with one of the pilots May didn't know so well – she thought his name was Petr. Petr seemed to be struck dumb by his good fortune and did little but gaze at her adoringly while she spoke. Eventually, though, she joined May. 'This was such a good idea,' Jess said. 'If the villagers ain't eating out of the Czech's 'ands by the time we've finished, there's no 'ope for 'em.'

'Let's hope they have a better opinion of us WAAFs, too.'

'You, maybe. I'm a lost cause.' So saying, Jess blew a kiss over her shoulder at Petr, who promptly tripped and stumbled into Jiří.

'Jess?' May hesitated, unsure how to put it.

'That's me.'

'Doesn't Milan... I mean, I thought you and he were—'

'Oh, don't fret about Milan. He knows what we 'ad was nothing more than a bit of fun.'

Had. Was. Jess made it sound as though her relationship with Milan was in the past. May shot her an anxious glance. She'd never been able to work out how serious Jess was about Milan, but even if her pain was only a tiny fraction of May's pain over Peter, she wouldn't wish that on her. She opened her mouth, but Jess cut in before she could say anything. 'Shame we can't use lanterns. Doesn't feel like proper carol singing without 'em. But it would give the ARP warden a fit.'

With the mood Jess was in, May had no doubt she could have persuaded even the strictest warden that several blazing lanterns were well within regulation, so she was glad Jess hadn't thought of them earlier. It was also clear that whatever it was that had happened between Jess and Milan, Jess was determined not to speak of it. May gave up for now. Maybe there would be more chance when they were back at High Chalk House.

The narrow tree-lined lane ran into Amberton High Street. The first houses were a huddle of flint cottages with thatched roofs. The last rays of the setting sun shone upon the criss-crossed tape stuck to the windows and the white paint on the kerbstones. There should have been golden light spilling out of the windows and Christmas trees with twinkling lights, just like a Christmas card scene. But this was carol singing in the blackout, so there were no lights or candles to welcome them. All the residents had done what they could to decorate for Christmas, and every door was hung with pretty wreaths of holly, ivy and mistletoe. The singers arranged themselves outside the middle gate and opened their music books. At church that morning, the vicar had insisted upon loaning May a set of hymn books when he'd learned of their plans. May had been grateful for them during the rehearsal earlier, for although they had chosen hymns familiar to all the singers, few of them could remember the words.

They opened with 'Good King Wenceslas,' the men singing the part of the king and the women singing the page's lines. When the group had decided upon the carols, it seemed the natural choice, with the subject being King Wenceslas, or Saint Václav, as he was known in Czechoslovakia. May couldn't think of a more fitting way to celebrate the season: an English carol written about a Czech man. As they sang, doors opened, and the occupants emerged to stand on the steps, listening to the rousing tune with beaming faces.

The next carol was 'Come, All Ye Shepherds'. When May had seen a note in the hymn book, indicating that it was a traditional Czech tune, she had given a cry of joy. Yet another perfect choice. As they sang the joyful, lilting melody, it suddenly didn't matter that there were no Christmas trees visible, no colourful lights twinkling like stars. She could lose herself in the moment, take pleasure in the smiles of the listeners, see them swaying to the music, some humming along, and knowing they, like her, had forgotten their troubles for this short while. The setting sun gilded the treetops, giving all the light they needed.

The last carol they had chosen was 'Silent Night.' A great hush fell over the assembled listeners as they sang the opening bars. May wondered if their thoughts had strayed in the same direction as hers. She couldn't help thinking of all the men, women and children across Europe who would be singing the same song. Different languages, and on different sides of the conflict, but all singing about the birth of the same baby. How many of those singing this Christmas would still be around next year? Tears pricked May's eyelids, and her voice quavered. She had to break off for a moment and clear her throat before she could join in with the second verse. The scene shimmered through a haze of unshed tears, and she could see others unashamedly wiping their eyes.

As the low note of the last word, peace, hung in the air, May felt it had indeed been a prayer for peace. After a pause, the singers started to turn away to head to the next group of houses, but some children dashed out, carrying handfuls of walnuts, even a few mince pies, which they shyly presented to the singers. They all protested, knowing how few treats there would be for anyone this Christmas, but the children insisted, backed up by the encouragement of the adults, who had also come out to join the children. One middle-aged woman with reddened eyes darted back into her house then returned carrying a package wrapped in newspaper. She thrust it into Jiří's hands, saying, 'I'd like you to have this. It was for my Sam, but now he's…' Her eyes filled with tears, and her mouth worked silently for a moment.

His face uncharacteristically grave, Jiří patted her shoulder. 'You are very kind. Are you sure?'

She pulled a handkerchief from her pocket and dabbed her eyes then gave him a tremulous smile. 'Take it. I insist. You look so much like him.' Then she hurried back to her house, her handkerchief pressed to her eyes.

Jiří called his thanks after her then unwrapped the parcel. He gave an exclamation of pleasure and held up a knitted hat and scarf for the others to see. Both were blue with bands of red and white. 'They are in the colours of the Czechoslovakian flag,' he said, his face beaming, as he folded his cap, put it in his pocket then pulled on the hat and scarf.

They were met with a similar reception in the other locations around the village. May's stomach was pleasantly full of mince pies and blackberry tarts by the time they reached the other side of the village for their final perfor-mance, and she held a bunch of purple heather, tied with a white ribbon, that an elderly lady had handed to all the WAAFs. She was also a little light-headed from two glasses of sherry that she had been unable to turn down.

'This was a marvellous idea, May.' Jess slipped her arm through May's, and May caught the scent of sherry in the crisp air. Her cheeks glowed with a rosy flush and she had tucked her heather into the band of her cap. 'I haven't seen anyone cast so much as a black look at the Czechs. Or us, come to that.' She opened her music book, then added, 'Of course, I expect Mrs Evans was ill-wishing us, but at least she didn't come out to scowl at us.'

'I wish Peggy had come out, though,' May said. 'I hope she's all right.' She couldn't help fretting. With only a few days left before Christmas, they were running out of time to help her, especially if she and Jess would be leaving in the new year.

Jess squeezed her arm. 'We'll see her at the dress rehearsal. And Mrs Grey is looking out for her as well. I have every faith that between us we'll see her in a happy home before we go anywhere.'

May wished she shared Jess's optimism. She opened her book and glanced around, taking in the scene. Some people already stood on their doorsteps, probably having heard the singing from further away. The singers were gathered outside a long, low structure that looked as though it had once been a stable. It adjoined a cottage that stood back from the road. Then May noticed a sign attached to the front of the old stable: Amberton Printers.

May nudged Jess. 'Doesn't Mr Walker run Amberton Printers?' She pointed out the sign.

Jess gave a low groan. 'I'm sure 'e does. That must be 'is 'ouse.' She indicated the cottage with a jerk of the head. Then she held up her book as everyone prepared to start. 'Well, we came out to change folks' minds about us. This will be the ultimate test.'

No one emerged from Mr Walker's cottage while they sang, though all his neighbours came out and applauded with great enthusiasm at the end of each carol. At the end of 'Silent Night' the applause was more muted, mainly because many people were too busy wiping their eyes. As before, several women and children approached holding plates of treats for the singers. May saw to her dismay a very determined woman carrying a tray with a large bottle of sherry. She didn't think she would be able to walk back to the Waafery if she drank any more, and the woman didn't appear to be the type that would take no for an answer. Acting on impulse, May slipped into the yard to avoid her.

Jess followed. 'Where are you going?' Jess hissed. 'We don't want to bump into Mr Walker.'

May hesitated, but Mr Walker seemed the lesser of two evils at present. Then a thought struck. 'Are the programmes ready? It would save a lot of bother if we could collect them now.'

'Are you joking? Why see Arnold Walker when we don't 'ave to?'

'We'll have to come back again if we don't get them now. We might as well get it over with. Anyway, the whole point of coming carol singing was to show him what the Czechs are really like. How's he supposed to know if he doesn't see them?' She pointed back to where the others were gathered, with a cluster of villagers around them. The sun had set by this time, the crimson after-glow providing enough light to show Jiří, still sporting his knitted hat and scarf, breaking a jam tart in half, which he then shared with the boy beside him.

Jess scowled. 'Maybe you're right. Where do you think 'e'll be?' She strolled up to the old stable block and looked at the windows, but now May could see they had been boarded up. Probably to comply with blackout regulations.

She tried the door, rattling it, but it was locked. 'We ought to try the house,' she said.

However, the words were hardly out of her mouth when the cottage door opened with a crash and Arnold Walker stormed down the steps. 'Get away from there. This is private property.' He strode towards them with clenched fists, then slowed when he was close enough to recognise them. 'Oh, it's you,' he said. 'What do you want?'

'Please, Mr Walker,' May began, 'we're sorry to disturb you, but we wondered if we could collect the programmes for our pantomime.' She gestured at the group of carol singers. 'As we're already in the village, we thought it would save time if we could take them now.'

'You did, did you? So you thought you'd drag me from the house on a Sunday afternoon.'

'I'm sorry.' May was on the verge of saying she would return the next day, when she became aware of Jess beside her, curving her lips in an exaggerated pout. She didn't know what had got into Jess this evening; flirting with Mr Walker would only make matters worse, she was sure. On the other hand, a little flattery might go a long way. She stepped in front of Jess and said, 'The vicar's wife was telling me of the wonderful job you'd done on the parish magazine this month, and we were just really excited to see the programmes.'

Mr Walker seemed to stand a little taller. 'Oh, well, now you're here I suppose it will clear space to hand them over now.' He drew a bunch of keys from his pocket and selected a large key then moved to the door. 'I don't want you coming in, mind. There's a lot of… of delicate machinery in here.' He stuck the key in the lock and turned it. To May's surprise he didn't then open the door, but sorted through his keys until he found a second one and inserted it into a keyhole slightly lower down. After turning this lock, he repeated the process a third time.

'Talk about security conscious,' Jess murmured in a voice low enough not to carry to Mr Walker. 'What's 'e printing – money?'

'I know. It's a bit strange.' May watched Mr Walker pull open the door and slip inside, tugging the door closed behind him. It almost looked as though he had something to hide.

Curious, she approached the doorway just as it swung slightly open; Mr Walker must have failed to latch it properly. No light escaped. There was just enough light left in the sky to illuminate the interior, and she saw what must be the printing press in the centre of the room with a few small booklets stacked beside it. Several shelves holding boxes lined the back wall, and she could just make out the dim outline of a desk and chair on the far left-hand side of the long room. At first she couldn't see Mr Walker, then a movement beside the desk caught her eye. Mr Walker was crouched down, shoving a box deeper into the shadows. Then he rose and picked up a much smaller box from a shelf at head height.

May moved away from the door, wondering why he hadn't wanted her and Jess to go inside. His furtive behaviour had made her wonder if she would see stacks of black market goods, but there had been nothing she wouldn't expect to see at a printer's.

'Here you go, girls.' Mr Walker emerged with the box under one arm, tucking something into his pocket with his free hand. He handed the box to May then shut the door and locked it. 'Now, don't come around here again after hours. The missus doesn't like to be disturbed.'

'Thank you, Mr Walker,' May and Jess chanted in unison, like chastened schoolgirls, then they hurried to join the others.

'See anything?' Jess asked when they were out of earshot.

May shook her head. 'Nothing.' She described what she had seen, finishing with, 'Perhaps he really was concerned about the press.'

Jess snorted. 'Delicate machinery, my foot. There's nothing delicate about a press. You mark my words – he was hiding something.'

May laughed until her sides ached. The rehearsal at the village hall that evening didn't involve her, however she had come anyway, hoping to catch a moment to talk to Mrs Grey. Peggy had been very subdued at the last rehearsal with the children. May could tell Peggy felt betrayed, and who could blame her? As a consequence, May decided that unless Mrs Grey could report any real progress, she was going to have to take matters into her own hands and find another way of getting Peggy into a happy home. She had no idea how to do that, but after Birmingham she felt sure she could come up with something.

Right now Mrs Grey was fully occupied, playing the piano as accompaniment to the song the ugly sisters were performing. May pressed her hands to her aching stomach muscles as she watched Milan and Jiří mince around the stage, practising flirtatious gestures, singing a song describing how they planned to catch Prince Charming's attention at the ball. May thought she might fall off her chair when Milan used his fan to dart coquettish glances at the imaginary prince over the top of it, fluttering his eyelashes. Who would have thought the intense, serious Milan could be such a gifted comedian?

May glanced at Jess, who was standing at the edge of the stage, waiting for her cue. She was watching Milan with such an expression of sadness it took May's breath away. She couldn't remember seeing Jess display such raw, unguarded emotion. Jess's usual high spirits were unfeigned, May would have bet her life on it, but now she wondered how much Jess used her natural ebullience as a shield to disguise her deeper emotions.

Then Milan and Jiří burst into the chorus, and that was Jess's cue. She dashed onto the stage as Cinderella, trying to smother her laughter at the ugly sisters' outrageous appearance while helping them on with their capes. The moment was gone, and May wondered whether she should ask Jess about it? The prospect was almost as alarming as tackling Mrs Evans over her treatment of Peggy. Not for the first time, she wished Evie was there. Evie was almost as quiet as May but without May's timidity. Evie had a directness about her that usually enabled her to get people to confide even when they hadn't intended to.

The song drew to a close, and Cinderella, laughing, ushered the ugly sisters and her stepmother, played by a suitably regal Jean Ellerby, out of the door. As soon as the door closed, Cinderella's smile faded, and she sang a song about always being left behind. This was such a melancholy song, it usually left May in tears. Maybe Jess's sadness off-stage had just been her way of getting into Cinderella's state of mind in the upcoming scene.

In the final verse, Cinderella sang about her wish to see Prince Charming one more time. Behind her, the fairy godmother drifted onto the stage. Dorothy Eastman, the WAAF playing her, had taken ballet classes before the war, and had choreographed a dreamy, floating dance to perform while Cinderella sang the final verse and chorus. During the actual performance, someone would be perched upon the lighting rig to cast glitter down upon the stage when she made her entrance. At the end of the song, Cinderella turned and saw the fairy godmother. May saw her chance to speak to Mrs Grey. The scene that followed was dialogue between Cinderella and the fairy godmother, with no music. Whilst Dorothy spoke to Jess on stage, explaining that she was going to reward Cinderella for helping the stag, May edged up to Mrs

Grey. Mrs Grey was rearranging the music on the stand in preparation for the transformation scene. They were far enough from the action to speak in low voices without disturbing the actors.

'Mrs Grey, do you mind me asking if you've made any progress with getting Peggy another home?'

Mrs Grey sighed, looking grave. 'I'm afraid not.' She glanced at the stage and lowered her voice. 'I don't want you to think I've done nothing, but no one in authority seems prepared to accept Mrs Evans is anything but a kind, caring pillar of the community. Unless her mother is able to take her home...'

'Impossible. Her house was destroyed in Coventry and she's living with the lady who owns the shop where she works. Besides, however bad things are for Peggy here, I'd hate to see her go to Coventry. It would be far too dangerous.' There was a pause while May remembered the bombed-out buildings, the dazed faces. And there was no sign that Coventry had ceased to be a target despite the devastation. Another reason to do the course at Cranwell. Assuming she and Jess were selected, of course.

May glanced back to the stage to check there was still time before Mrs Grey's services at the piano would be required again. The action had got to the stage where the fairy godmother was warning Cinderella that the magic would wear out at midnight. After that, Cinderella would need to rely on her own resources. May could use a spot of magic to help Peggy; her own resources didn't feel nearly good enough.

'I think I'm going to have to try and get Mrs Evans caught out. Preferably in front of people who can help Peggy once they see what she's going through.'

'I could help.'

May shook her head. 'You're the vicar's wife. If this goes horribly wrong... well, the chances are I'll be transferred elsewhere so I won't have to face the anger of the village. But this is your home. I won't have you doing anything that will make your life difficult.'

Mrs Grey bristled. 'There's more to being a vicar's wife than being respectable. If I see a child in need, I want to help.'

'You can help. I just don't think it a good idea for the villagers to know you were instrumental in setting a trap. They need to be able to trust you.'

Mrs Grey chewed her lower lip. 'I don't know if this helps, but I've noticed Arnold Walker visiting her shop a lot recently. I'm not convinced he's stocking up on embroidery threads.'

May frowned. 'What business would he have with her?'

Mrs Grey shot another glance at the actors before leaning closer to May and dropping her voice so low May had to strain to hear her. 'There's a rumour they're having an affair.'

May choked. 'Surely not.'

'You'd be surprised,' Mrs Grey said. 'I've long since stopped being shocked at what goes on behind the scenes in an ordinary English village.'

'But those two?' May's mind refused to handle the idea of the harsh, intolerant haberdashery owner in a passionate liaison with the bullying Mr Walker. 'Do *you* believe it?'

With a tiny shrug, Mrs Grey said, 'I admit it seems unlikely. However, he *has* been seen with her.'

'There must be another reason.' There was a pause in which they watched Jess as Cinderella promise to leave the ball before midnight. However she tried, May couldn't concentrate on the action. Incredible though it seemed that Mrs Evans would have an affair with Mr Walker, she couldn't deny that there did seem to be some kind of connection between the two.

'I do wonder why such an upright character as Mrs Evans would be seen with Arnold Walker,' Mrs Grey said after a moment. 'I hate to say it about one of our parishioners, but I don't think he's entirely honest. For someone who runs what is a very small printing business, he does seem to have a lot of money to spend. He and his wife don't appear to make do and mend as much as the rest of us. His wife invited me to tea the other day, and she had made cake with real sugar and butter. She said something about saving her rations, but I don't see how she could have stretched them that far.'

May sat upright so fast she knocked the music from the piano and had to scrabble on the floor to pick it up before the transformation scene started. She returned it to the music stand with shaking hands. She'd remembered the excessive locks on the door of Amberton Printers. Why so many locks for a printing press?

Slowly, pieces of the puzzle were falling into place. Peggy was living with Mrs Evans, and clearly wasn't getting all her rations. What if Mrs Evans wasn't keeping them for herself, but giving them to Arnold Walker in return for black market goods?

Was that why Mr Walker had told May and Jess to stay outside while he fetched the programmes? Because he was storing items he had obtained illegally? Even though May felt tantalisingly close to the answer, it was still all guesswork. Nothing she could present to the authorities. If only there was a way to discover the truth.

She turned to ask Mrs Grey if she knew anything more, only to find it was time for the transformation scene. The vicar's wife put her fingers to the keys, preventing further talk, and began to play an eerie melody.

Dorothy Eastman twirled around the floor, waving the wand that one of the WAAFs had made from a peeled birch twig, a paper star and a lot of glitter and glue. The dance was really a chance for Jess to slip back stage and climb into the parachute silk ballgown. May only watched the action with half her attention. She was finally on to something. Something that could discredit Mrs Evans. Was she supplying Peggy's rations to Arnold Walker? Even if she was, how could she prove it?

Chapter Twenty

Frustratingly, May didn't get another chance to speak to Mrs Grey that evening. She was needed at the piano for the rest of the rehearsals and when they finished, Mr Grey arrived to collect her before May could speak to her again. It wasn't until she and Jess were alone in the schoolroom, drinking tea – they had run out of cocoa – that she poured out the tale, her voice trembling with excitement.

'This has to be it,' she said, gesturing with her right hand, forgetting it held her tea cup, and slopping tea all over her dressing gown.

'Maybe so, but how do we catch 'em out?'

We. May beamed at Jess as she dashed out, holding her dressing gown so it didn't drip tea on the rug. If she got a place on the Cranwell course, she hoped Jess got on it too. She wasn't ready to move away from both her best friends.

She changed into a cardigan then put her dressing gown to soak. All the while, she ran through various wild plans in her head, most involving a night-time raid on Mr Walker's office. But even if they could get all the way out there late at night, how would discovering what was stored inside discredit Mrs Evans?

'Right. Let's go over what we know,' she said when she returned to the schoolroom. She counted the facts off on her fingers. 'One: Peggy isn't getting her rations. Two—'

'Mrs Evans is a spiteful cow,' Jess finished for her.

May gave a snort of laughter. 'True, but I don't think we can use that as evidence.' She held up two fingers. 'Two: Mr Walker is definitely hiding something in his office, and three: I suspect he's dealing in black market goods.'

'Anything else?'

May thought for a moment. 'Yes. Four: Mr Walker has often been seen in the haberdashery.'

Jess chewed her lower lip. 'We saw him there, but he was with his wife,' she said after a moment.

May's heart dropped. It was hardly a crime to accompany his wife to the shops. Was that all it had been? Was she building up a tower of false hopes that would come crashing down the moment she tried to prove any wrongdoing?

'Perhaps we could watch the haberdashery. See if Arnold Walker goes there without his wife.' Although how they would do that without raising suspicion, May hadn't a clue.

'Unless his wife is part of the plot.'

'Maybe. We need to see how often he goes there. That will give us something to start with.'

'I think you're forgetting something.' Jess put down her cup and tucked her legs up onto her chair to sit cross-legged. 'We have duties, remember. We can't keep watch on the haberdashery at all hours when I'm stuck down the Hole for most of the day and you're out driving.'

May's shoulders slumped. She flung herself back in her chair. 'We could be barking up the wrong tree anyway. We're trying to help Peggy, not bring down a local black market operation.' She sighed. 'When's the dress rehearsal?'

'Day after tomorrow.'

'Then we'll start by talking to Peggy. We'll ask her if Mr Walker often comes to the shop. It's not much but we have to start somewhere.'

—

Despite her pessimism May did cycle into the village a couple of times before the dress rehearsal. Although she had vowed not to use the haberdashery again after Mrs Evans' verbal attack on Jess, it was too cold to hang around outside the shop. It was also not easy to keep watch without looking conspicuous. There were no convenient tea rooms opposite to enable her to watch the entrance from a warm vantage point, and there were only so many times she could stand outside tying her shoelaces. She went in to buy a reel of thread, but Mr Walker wasn't there, and Mrs Evans eyed her with purse-lipped disapproval that denied May the opportunity to chat and therefore extend her visit. Although the village schools had now broken up for the Christmas holidays, there was no sign of Peggy. May reluctantly realised that nothing could be done until the dress rehearsal.

When May walked into the village hall on the evening of the dress rehearsal, she forgot her worries for a moment. The hall had been decorated for Christmas and May felt like she had walked onto the set of a Christmas film. A tall tree stood to one side of the stage, each branch festooned with silver tinsel and sparkly baubles. A huge angel graced the topmost branch, its serene face cracked from years of use. Strings of fairy lights lit the tree in points of red, blue, green and yellow.

Jess drew a deep breath and smiled. 'It smells of Christmas now.'

The tree wasn't the only decoration. Strings of colourful paper chains festooned the hall, and someone had pinned children's Christmas pictures onto the boarded windows. There were pictures of heaped presents, holly, candles and many pictures of Father Christmas and his reindeer.

They only allowed themselves a short time to drink in the Christmassy feeling, for all the costumes needed to be sorted out, make-up laid out and the props arranged before the children arrived.

'I'd like everyone in their costumes before the children get here,' Jess said. 'Then the make-up team can get to work on you all while May and I help the children into their costumes. The children shouldn't need make-up.'

May hurried to dress in the hunting costume she wore in the first scene. They had found a costume that looked like it had originally been made for a performance of Robin Hood: a green tunic that laced up at the front over a pair of thick brown woollen tights. There was also a feathered cap, a wide leather belt holding a toy knife and a quiver of arrows that she wore slung across her back. Although she had a much more elaborate costume in the ballroom scene, she would have plenty of time to change. Jess wore the same dress she wore for the kitchen scenes – a patched grey dress with a frayed hem. Over it she wore a woollen shawl. That meant all she had to do was remove the shawl for the next scene.

Once May was in her hunting costume she walked out to the front of the stage to watch for the children. They had been scheduled to arrive an hour later than the others to give the WAAFs in charge of scenery and props a chance to set up the stage before there were children underfoot. Three WAAFs were pinning up the canvas backdrops as May walked out. The forest backdrop was just going up and May gasped at the way it transformed the stage into a forest at wintertime. It depicted bare trees stark and tall against a dark grey sky. Each branch had a layer of snow; here and there, holly bushes, picked out in dark green with shiny red berries lent splashes of colour to the shades of grey on the rest of the backdrop. Pots containing evergreen shrubs were dotted around the stage. These had come from the vicarage garden. There were also other pots containing twigs and branches cut from the woods. These were to serve as the trees that the stag would use to hide behind.

As the stage took shape May felt a thrill of mingled excitement and nerves. After so many rehearsals, she had almost forgotten it was to be played in the village in front of an audience. Rehearsals had become an occupation in themselves and she had become so used to performing in front of the other actors and backstage hands, she had forgotten to be nervous. Now seeing the stage dressed for the performance, she realised with a sick twist of fear that the whole village and a good proportion of the RAF personnel would see her. She glanced down at her tunic that only came to mid-thigh, and the knee-length boots. That still left an awful lot of leg on display. What would everyone think?

Resisting the urge to tug down the hem of her tunic, she wandered to the door when she heard the clear chatter of a group of children. A moment later the door burst open, bringing with it a blast of wintry air to match the scene on the stage. The children's faces were rosy from the cold and their eyes were bright as they gazed around the transformed hall.

'Wow! It looks like Christmas,' little George said.

Even Susie, who had insisted she didn't want to miss the pantomime, managed a smile. May sent up a brief prayer of thanks to the thoughtful people who had taken the effort to decorate and make Christmas special for this group of children who were so far from their families, two of whom had lost loved ones.

The adults looking after the children had been invited to the dress rehearsal, and May was pleased to see all had come, with one notable exception.

'Isn't Mrs Evans coming at all?' May asked Peggy.

Peggy shook her head and stared at the floor. May opened her mouth to ask if she was coming to the Christmas Day performance, but Jess appeared at that point and took the children backstage to get changed.

May was about to follow when the woman who had accompanied Susie put a hand on her arm to stop her. 'Mrs Evans might come later,' she said. 'I saw her earlier and asked if she planned to come along. I think she must have forgotten it was on. She said she might drop in later.'

Hoping Mrs Evans wouldn't turn up – she couldn't bear the thought of that sour face scowling at them from the small audience – May went backstage to the two curtained-off areas that had been set aside for the children to change. The costumes were already hung up on hooks. There were peasant-style tunics and trousers for the boys and plain but colourful long dresses made from thick cotton for the girls. There was red for Susie, green for Lottie and bright blue for Peggy. All the dresses were trimmed with cotton wool, which was supposed to look like fur. It hadn't been possible to provide shoes, so the children wore their school plimsolls. Chattering excitedly, the children changed into their costumes, the girls ooh-ing and ah-ing over their dresses. Although they had tried them on before, they hadn't seen the fake fur trim.

When everyone was dressed, Jess called the group to order. 'We're going to run through the whole panto from start to finish without any interruptions. If anyone has any problems, try to keep going but remember to mention it at the end.' Jess looked around the group, making sure she had everyone's attention. 'You've all made brilliant progress, so I know we're going to make a success of it.' She ran through a list of points she had picked up in the last rehearsal, then ordered everyone to take their places for the opening scene.

May went to stand in the wings, her stomach in knots, while Jess and the children took their places on stage behind the closed curtain. If she was this nervous at the dress rehearsal, how was she going to handle the actual performance?

Then the piano struck up and the curtain rose. Jess and the children started their opening song, and time seemed to speed up. Before she knew it, Cinderella was explaining to the children that no one could help her. Her cruel stepmother had sent her into the forest to gather berries, knowing it was impossible to find any in the middle of winter. Then the pantomime stag trotted on, its head drooping and one of the stage hands played a recording of a hunting horn on an ancient record player. Cinderella and the children tried to disguise the stag and hide it behind the bushes. Jiří and Milan were also in the next scene, so wouldn't have time to change completely between entrances. Under the stag costume they already wore their ugly sister costumes and make-up, although without the skirts. They had a few minutes before they made their entry in the next scene, so would pull on their skirts and wigs in that time.

Then May heard her cue. She ran on stage holding her bow and asked Cinderella if she had seen the stag. Her nerves eased as she spoke the familiar lines. Before she knew it, she was presenting Cinderella with the bottle of blackberry preserves from Prince Charming's picnic and watching Cinderella leave. When she had rehearsed this with Jess, Jess had urged her to show how much Prince Charming regretted seeing Cinderella leave while at the same time being irritated at Cinderella's outspoken nature. May had always struggled with that. Now, however, she thought of Peter. How sad she was that Peter was out of her life, yet how angry she was with him for not making more of an effort to win her back. She was able to pour those feelings into her performance, and knew it was the best version she had played.

Prince Charming exited, and the children danced around the stag, feeding it nuts. May stood in the wings, watching, and was distracted from the performance when the hall door opened then slammed closed. She looked to see who had made such a racket and felt a jolt of surprise to see Mrs Evans at the back of the hall, her eyes riveted on the stage. She had shown no interest in Peggy's activities, so why would she want to watch the rehearsal now? May could only imagine it was so she could report to the village gossips how shameful it was that WAAFs were appearing on stage in skimpy tunics and tights.

Her surprise turned to alarm when, instead of taking a seat with the rest of the little audience, Mrs Evans advanced on the stage, mouth working and eyes bulging. The children on stage looked round when they saw the movement but continued with the song. Peggy stopped stock still with a gasp. The children had been holding hands, dancing in a circle around Cinderella. As soon as Peggy stopped, Danny, who was holding her right hand, bumped into her and tripped, landing in a heap upon the stage. Lottie, the next in line from Danny tripped as well but managed to keep her feet.

'You!' screeched Mrs Evans, pointing at Peggy like a witch invoking a curse. The children who were still singing stopped. Susie, George and Lottie huddled behind Jess; Danny, still on all fours, scuttled, crab-like, behind one of Mrs Grey's potted shrubs. Peggy stood frozen on the spot, her face drained of colour.

Mrs Evans didn't stop in front of the stage but stormed past the Christmas tree, sweeping off a bauble. It bounced on the floor with a nasty crack and splintered. She mounted the steps, still pointing at Peggy, and hissed, 'You little lying harridan.'

A glance at Jess showed May that Jess was too tangled up with the other children to intervene. Mouth dry, she ran onto the stage and placed herself between Mrs Evans and Peggy. She held out her hands in a conciliatory gesture; it only seemed to provoke Mrs Evans to greater fury. The difference in height meant nothing to Mrs Evans. She craned her neck and shook her finger in May's face. 'How dare you defend her. How long as she been taking part in these... revelries?' From the expression on her face, she might have said 'orgies'. She lunged at Peggy, making a grab for her arm, but May blocked her.

'I don't understand, Mrs Evans,' she said. 'Miss Foster wrote to all the children's foster parents to explain.' May glanced at Peggy and got her answer in Peggy's blanched expression. Miss Foster must have given the letter to the children to hand to their hosts. Peggy, guessing Mrs Evans would never allow her to attend, had not passed it on.

'Well I never got the letter. How long has she been coming here?'

May hesitated, not wanting to inadvertently get Peggy into even more trouble. Jess extricated herself from the other children and came to stand beside her. 'We've been rehearsing since the start of November. Do you really take such little interest in your charge that you've not enquired where she's going all this time?'

May felt a surge of admiration for Jess. Why hadn't she thought of that?

'She told me she was studying with a friend,' Mrs Evans said in grim tones. 'As she well knows, I would never have let her associate with—' she looked May up and down, making May acutely conscious of the amount of thigh her short tunic revealed. May gave her hem a surreptitious tug. 'With women of loose morals,' Mrs Evans finished with a curl of the lip. She glanced past May and Jess. 'Come along, girl.'

Peggy took a step forward. May put out a hand to stop her and said, 'Please, Mrs Evans. I'm sorry you didn't know, but Peggy's been doing so well. We're performing the pantomime at Christmas. To cheer up the evacuees who are away from their families.' And staying with nasty, dried-up old prunes like you. 'It's in a good cause.' She was babbling now, unable to let Peggy go without a fight. She would fight for Peggy in the way she'd wished someone had fought for her when she'd been under her father's control. 'We're collecting for Coventry.'

Ignoring May, Mrs Evans reached round her and grabbed Peggy's arm, pulling her towards the steps. 'I don't care if you're collecting for the King of England. She's coming with me. You might have no shame, but I have standards.'

All May could do was watch as Peggy, sniffling with tears running down her face, was dragged down the stage steps. None of the other adults made a move to stop her. There was no point. Mrs Evans was Peggy's guardian. Yet May couldn't watch Peggy being dragged off without making one last attempt to intervene. She dashed down the steps and would have run out of the door after Mrs Evans, except Mrs Grey caught her arm to stop her. 'Leave it for now. You won't get anywhere with her while she's in a temper. She has every right to take Peggy away. Give her a day or two to cool down and we'll see if we can change her mind.'

'But it's Christmas in three days.' She couldn't see Mrs Evans changing her mind in that time. It was awful to think of Peggy being forced to spend Christmas all alone with Mrs Evans rather than celebrating with the others at the pantomime.

Nevertheless, Mrs Grey was right. It would be futile to go after them now. May trudged back up the stage steps.

Jess had managed to calm the children and she now smiled brightly at them. 'Don't worry, I'm sure we'll be able to get Peggy back for Christmas Day. Now, you all sang wonderfully. I'm really pleased with you all. Go and sit in front of the audience like we showed you and we can carry on with the rehearsal.'

May slipped backstage to change into her other costume. When she passed the curtained area the girls had changed in, her eyes fell on Peggy's dress and coat hanging on a hook. In her rush to remove Peggy from this den of iniquity, Mrs Evans had forgotten to collect Peggy's clothes. May bundled them up in one of the bags used to transport the stage costumes. She would take them round to Mrs Evans tomorrow and try and persuade her to let Peggy take part.

–

There was no opportunity to take Peggy's clothes to Mrs Evans the next morning. A pilot from Wagtail squadron had been forced to bail out of his Hurricane ten miles from Amberton and May was dispatched to pick him up. Thankfully he had been unhurt so there was no need for a mercy dash to the hospital, and the pilot – a young sergeant pilot called Greg Malin – had been profuse in his thanks. It had been a cheerful ride back to the hospital, with May, Greg and the medical orderly singing Christmas carols at the top of their voices as the ambulance bounced over the rutted roads, sweeping the hoar frost from the skeletal remains of the cow parsley in the hedgerows. It had meant that she hadn't got a break in the middle of the morning to cycle into the village. Even as they burst into the chorus of 'Ding Dong Merrily on High', May spared a thought for Peggy, hoping that she hadn't been severely punished. She felt selfish, relishing the Christmas celebrations for the first time in her life when Peggy was having such a miserable time.

At lunch there was barely enough time to wolf down a watery vegetable pie before she was summoned to drive another pilot to the hospital. He had been forced to do a pancake landing because his Hurricane's undercarriage mechanism had been shot up. He had escaped with just a broken wrist, so after the MO had strapped it up, the pilot was to be taken to the local hospital to have it set properly.

By the time she returned from that trip, May despaired of getting to the village before Mrs Evans closed her shop.

She had just finished cleaning the ambulance when Flight Officer Payne summoned her. She hastily changed out of her overalls and into her tunic and skirt, then went to Payne's office.

'Good news, Lidford,' Payne said without preamble. 'Your application for the clerk SD training at Cranwell has been approved. I don't mind telling you I had my doubts about recommending you after the complaint I had, but Flight Officer Ellerby was most insistent.'

'Thank you.' May could hardly believe her luck. She had been so worried about Peggy she'd completely forgotten about the course.

'It's Flight Officer Ellerby you need to thank. If it wasn't for her, you wouldn't be going.'

Now Payne had imparted her news, May waited to be dismissed; instead, Payne leaned forward over her desk, her gaze boring into May's. 'The course starts in the new year. I'm warning you, I want you on your best behaviour between now and then. If I hear of any other complaint, I'll strike your name from the list. Do I make myself clear?'

Chapter Twenty-One

May burned at the injustice. If Miss Foster had done her job, May wouldn't have had to interfere. She held her tongue, though. There was less than a fortnight until the course started. Surely nothing could go wrong before then. 'Please, ma'am. Do you know if anyone else from Amberton is doing the training?'

Flight Officer Payne peered at a sheet of paper on her desk. 'ACW Jessica Halloway,' she said.

It was all May could do to contain her excitement and not let out a whoop of joy in the cramped office. Then Payne made her joy complete by dismissing her early for the day, as she had been forced to miss nearly all of her breaks. As it was, she broke into a run as soon as she had been dismissed and was outside. Her annoyance at Miss Foster and Flight Officer Payne disappeared. She and Jess were going to be on the same course! Where was Jess?

The NAAFI. May changed course abruptly, causing a young corporal who had been cycling past to swerve and nearly fall off his bike. May called out an apology but didn't pause until she was in the doorway of the NAAFI. She searched the room until she saw Jess's bright blonde head. She was sitting by the window with three airmen. May recognised them as ground crew to Brimstone squadron.

By the time May had managed to weave her way through the busy canteen the men were rising, collecting their trays and eating irons.

'See you later, lads,' Jess said, waving the men away with a cheery smile. Then she saw May. 'I was going to come looking for you. I've just got off duty, and I'm free until Boxing Day. Ellerby gave me the time off to organise the pantomime. Isn't that wonderful? I thought you might like company to take Peggy's clothes back to Mrs Evans.'

In her delight over the course May had nearly forgotten Peggy's clothes. 'I'd love the company. And just wait until you hear what Flight Officer Payne just told me.'

'That we're going on the course together? I know. Isn't it the most wonderful thing?'

And talking nineteen to the dozen, they dashed out to get their bikes.

—

May had hoped to find Peggy helping in the shop, but only Mrs Evans stood behind the haberdashery counter. Thankfully they had struck a quiet time, so they would be able to talk to Mrs Evans about Peggy alone.

May put the bundle of Peggy's clothes on the counter. 'Peggy forgot to collect these yesterday,' she said.

Mrs Evans gave her a purse-lipped look. 'Thank you,' she said stiffly. She evidently expected May and Jess to leave. Her frown lines deepened when May didn't move away. 'Well? Was there something else?'

May and Jess had tried to work out what to say on the ride into the village but neither had come up with any good ideas. 'We'll just have to play it by ear,' Jess had said finally. 'You'd better do the talking, though. She seems to regard me as just one step up from a lady of the night.'

'I don't think she has a higher opinion of me after seeing me in my Prince Charming get-up.'

Now, as she stood at the counter, eyes on a level with a stand displaying a rainbow of cotton reels, May wished it was Jess doing the talking. 'I... ah... we're very sorry you weren't informed about the pantomime,' she said. Best to take a conciliatory tone. 'But we were hoping you would allow Peggy to take part in the pantomime. She's worked so hard for weeks. It would be a shame for her to miss it.'

'She lied to me. I don't reward liars.'

'I know. And if we had known she hadn't given you the letter, we would have come to tell you ourselves.'

'So she lied to you, too. Why would you want her back?'

'Because she's lonely and misses her home. She's very young. I'm sure she'll apologise if you give her the chance. Didn't you ever make a mistake you wished you could undo?'

May didn't know what had made her say that, but she was sure that just for a moment, Mrs Evans' glance flicked to a paperback novel sitting on a low shelf on her side of the counter. May would never have noticed it if Mrs Evans' glance hadn't given it away. May bit back a smile. Was the straight-laced Mrs Evans ashamed at being caught with something as frivolous as a novel? Pressing her point home, she said, 'You don't have to attend if you don't want to. It's on Christmas Day in the afternoon. Perhaps you would appreciate a few quiet hours.' Another thought struck her. 'We will be providing food for the children afterwards.'

Possibly it was the thought of a day without needing to provide Peggy with a meal that struck a chord, because

Mrs Evans seemed to unbend. 'Let me think about it. Maybe if she apologises—'

The shop bell jangled and Mrs Evans glanced at the door. It seemed to May that her expression shifted to one of alarm, quickly hidden. Curiously, May glanced over her shoulder to see Arnold Walker stroll in.

Nerves tingling, she shot Jess a significant glance. Jess gave an almost imperceptible nod in return. Was this the chance they had hoped for? Were they about to discover the reason behind Mr Walker's frequent visits to the haberdashery?

Mr Walker tipped his hat at Mrs Evans. 'Morning. My wife sent me on an errand, but I can come back later if you're busy.'

'Don't mind us,' May said. 'We've finished here.' She gave Mrs Evans a polite smile. 'Send Peggy to the village hall for two in the afternoon.'

She stepped back from the counter, wondering how they could remain in the shop while Mrs Evans spoke to Mr Walker.

Jess rescued her. 'Oh, look at these gorgeous hankies,' she exclaimed as they passed a shelf by the door stacked with pretty lace-trimmed handkerchiefs. 'I could get one for my Auntie Vera for Christmas. She'd love one embroidered with her initials.' Ignoring the fact that it would almost certainly be too late to embroider and post it before Christmas, Jess picked one up and held it for May to inspect. May admired the soft cotton and the delicate lace while straining her ears to catch what Arnold Walker was saying. His voice had dropped to a low murmur, which immediately aroused May's suspicions. However, she could just make out his words.

'She wants some beeswax and three balls of grey wool.'

May felt a lurch disappointment. She exchanged glances with Jess and read the same disappointment in her face.

'Think I'll get these, anyway,' Jess murmured. She collected three of the handkerchiefs and went to stand behind Mr Arnold.

Mrs Evans had wrapped a lump of beeswax in brown paper and placed the three balls of dark grey wool in a bag for Mr Walker. She was just placing the money in the till when she gave an affected start. 'Oh, I nearly forgot.' She picked up the paperback. 'Do thank your wife for lending me this book. You will tell her how much I enjoyed it?'

Mr Walker reached out to collect his purchases and the book. If May hadn't seen Mrs Evans' guilty glance earlier, she would have thought nothing of this exchange, but now she watched with narrowed eyes as Mr Walker took the book. Was that a sheet of paper between the pages? Probably just a bookmark Mrs Evans had forgotten to remove. She had to be sure, though. The thought that this could be her last chance to help Peggy gave her courage. Pretending to trip, she nudged Mr Walker's arm as he reached for the items. He fumbled them and everything fell to the floor. Balls of wool rolled across the polished floorboards, and the book fluttered to the floor, dislodging the loose paper inside. With an exclamation of annoyance, Mr Walker knelt down and lunged for the book. Not the wool, which was rolling away, May noted. She quickly crouched down to seize a ball of wool and managed to catch a glimpse of the loose paper. A second later, Mr Walker had snatched up the book, tucking it under his arm.

'Watch what you're doing,' he snarled.

'I'm very sorry, Mr Walker.' May gathered up the errant balls of wool and the paper bag still containing the little parcel of beeswax. She handed it to him with an apologetic smile. 'I'm so clumsy. I'm always falling over my feet.'

He glanced down at her feet with a sneer, making May horribly self-conscious of her size nine feet in their unflattering regulation lace-up shoes.

Mr Walker stormed out, leaving Jess to pay for the handkerchiefs. Then the girls also left, with May reminding Mrs Evans that Peggy would be fed if she arrived at the village hall for two in the afternoon on Christmas Day.

After a glance around to be sure no one could overhear, May murmured to Jess, 'Did you see what was inside the book?'

Jess shook her head. 'I was too busy trying not to get kicked when he flung himself after it. Did you manage to get a look?'

May gave a triumphant grin. 'I did. It was ration coupons.'

Jess gave a low whistle. 'You think they were Peggy's?'

'I'd stake my life on it. No wonder the poor girl looks so underfed. Arnold Walker must have some kind of black market racket going on, and Mrs Evans is handing him Peggy's coupons in return for...' But May couldn't think what would make the respectable Mrs Evans risk prosecution.

'I bet he's getting hold of nylons and soap, which he's doling out in return for the coupons,' Jess said. 'Do you think other foster parents are involved?'

'Maybe. I—' By this time the girls had rounded the corner of the haberdashery, where the wrought iron gate leading to the small garden behind the shop stood. May could just make out a child's figure, huddled with her arms wrapped around her knees, sitting on the doorstep leading to the living quarters. 'Wait a moment.'

She darted across to the gate and peered through. 'Peggy,' she said, careful to keep her voice down so it wouldn't carry to Mrs Evans.

Peggy raised her head from her knees to reveal a tear-streaked face. 'M-May?' she sniffled.

'Yes. How are you?'

Peggy's face crumpled. 'I'm sorry I didn't tell her. Now she says I can't even watch the panto. She won't even let me see Davey.' She broke into fresh sobs. 'The only time she lets me out is when she wants me to deliver stupid letters to her friends.'

May wished she could reach through and pat Peggy's shoulder, but the gaps between the ironwork weren't wide enough. 'Listen,' she said. 'I think we've managed to persuade Mrs Evans to let you come.'

Hope blazed in Peggy's eyes. 'You're not having me on?'

May shook her head. 'You're going to have to apologise to her. Do you think you can do that?'

Peggy's face screwed up as though May had just asked her to lick the moss off the walls. At first May was worried the headstrong girl would refuse, but after a moment's reflection, Peggy nodded.

'Good girl.'

–

May's spirits were lighter than they had been for a long time as the girls cycled back to High Chalk House, pedalling slowly so they could avoid the frozen puddles in the twilight. They had persuaded Mrs Evans to let Peggy take part in the pantomime; they finally had an idea of what Mrs Evans was doing with the ration coupons that clearly weren't being used to feed Peggy and, best of all, she and Jess would be going to Cranwell together. Even so, May was conscious of a heavy weight dragging her down. Her lack of backbone had made her push Peter away, and now, even though she was beginning to see that Jess and Evie were right, and she could speak out when necessary, she feared Peter would never want her back. Not when she had broken his heart in the most brutal way possible.

He had said he would respect her decision. That meant it was up to her to make the first move. Did she dare try?

'Jess,' she said when they had put their bikes away and were walking towards the back door of the Waafery, 'If I sent Peter a letter, do you think he'd read it?'

'Absolutely.' Jess, who had been uncharacteristically quiet, brightened. 'Take my word for it, May, he'll have been watching the post every day for word from you.'

May swallowed. 'But what if he says he doesn't want to see me?' Dreams of a reunion had sustained her ever since she'd returned from Birmingham. If Peter refused her, she'd have lost both him and hope.

Jess paused, her hand on the door handle. 'It's a risk, but don't you want to end the uncertainty?'

May thought for a moment then nodded. 'You're right. I need to know, one way or the other.'

Jess squeezed her arm. 'Whatever happens, you'll always have me and Evie.' Then she smiled. 'But I don't think you've got anything to worry about. He's crazy about you.'

May could only pray she was right.

When they had climbed up to the schoolroom, Jess marched straight into their bedroom and returned with pen and paper. 'Go on. Write. Ask if he'll take you back.'

May shook her head. 'I'm going to invite him to the pantomime. I finished with him by letter. I need to apologise to him to his face and... well, I'll see what happens if he comes.'

'He'll come.'

May wished she shared Jess's confidence. She sat at the rickety table to write her letter. With Jess pacing around the room, pausing to fidget with the blackout blinds, plumping the cushions and straightening the curtains, it was hard to concentrate. In the end she kept it short, simply writing a brief but heartfelt apology for being a coward and asking if he would come to the pantomime so they could talk afterwards.

'There,' she said once she'd put the letter in an envelope and addressed it. 'I'll put it in the post first thing tomorrow.'

Jess shook her head, glancing at her watch. 'The girls on night watch in Ops should be leaving soon. I'll ask one of them to hand it in for you.' Without waiting for a reply, Jess took the letter and dashed out.

Jess was gone for longer than expected, so May used the time to think over what they had discovered. If they were right, and Mrs Evans had been giving Arnold Walker Peggy's rations, they had to find a way of proving it. But how could they do that? Her run-in with Miss Foster had already shown that the authorities were unlikely to believe May's word over Mrs Evans' if she just reported that she had glimpsed ration coupons inside Mrs Evans' book. She paced the room, covering the same trail followed by Jess only minutes earlier. As much as she tried to concentrate on the mystery of the coupons, her thoughts would flit to the letter. Would Peter get it in time? Would he come? What would she say to him if he did? And every now and again she would get a stab of happiness when she remembered she and Jess were going to Cranwell together. When she compared her life now with the life she had been leading a year ago, it was almost unbelievable. She had come so far.

The thunder of feet on the stairs broke through her musings, then Jess burst into the room, eyes shining. 'Come down to the Rose Room,' she said. 'You'll never guess who's here.'

'Who?' May gathered up her writing materials, but Jess snatched them and tossed them back onto the desk.

'Leave them.' Jess was bouncing on her toes with excitement. 'Come on!'

Jess refused to explain, so May followed her downstairs and into the cosy sitting room on the ground floor. An inkling of the truth was forming.

Jess opened the door with a flourish. 'Look who's here. It's Evie!'

May gave a yelp of delight and rushed in. A moment later she was engulfed in an enthusiastic hug.

'May! It's so good to see you,' Evie cried.

Then all three girls were hugging and talking at once.

May jumped when a masculine voice with a soft Scottish burr said, 'Don't mind me.'

She released Evie and stepped back, abashed. She had always been rather in awe of Alex Kincaith. But he was smiling, so she relaxed and sat on the sofa next to Evie.

Evie, she noticed, still wore her original uniform, not that of an officer. She eyed it anxiously. 'How was your course?'

'I passed. I'm an officer!' Then she obviously must have noticed May eyeing her uniform. 'I'm on leave until the new year, then I report to RAF Watnall. I've had to order my new uniform from a tailor, so it's not ready yet.'

'She passed with flying colours,' Alex said with a proud smile.

'Congratulations! I knew you would do it.' Then May glanced at Jess. 'Are we supposed to salute?'

'Don't be an idiot. Anyway, I heard from Jess you're both going to Cranwell for training. I'd be very surprised if they don't make you both officers soon. Wouldn't it be wonderful if we ended up at the same station?'

There was an air of celebration about the evening. Evie told them she was staying at the Horse and Groom over Christmas and promised to come to the pantomime. She also agreed to distribute some of the programmes around the village as flyers.

After the initial excitement had died down and they had caught up with Evie's news, Evie asked, 'What about that evacuee girl you were worried about, May? Have you been able to help her?'

May filled her in on everything that had happened. 'Jess and I think she's slipping Peggy's ration coupons to Arnold Walker.'

Evie wrinkled her brow. 'What would she gain by giving them away?'

'We thought Mr Walker could be supplying her with black market goods.'

'How could he use the coupons, though?' Evie asked.

May's eyes fell on the handful of programmes which they had given to Evie, and it was as though something clicked in her mind. 'He has a printing press,' she said slowly, her voice trembling with suppressed excitement.

'What if he's not using the coupons to buy things? What if he's using them as templates?'

Jess's eyes widened. 'You think he's forging coupons?'

The more she thought about it, the more sense it made. 'He could be collecting coupons from Mrs Evans to use as examples, and possibly to sell on as well.' May's heart beat a rapid tattoo. She was certain she was right.

'How do we prove it, though?' Jess put in. 'And how does it help Peggy unless we can prove Mrs Evans is involved?' Evie's eyes glinted. 'In one of your letters, May, you mentioned setting a trap. I think now would be a good time.'

'Yes, but how?' May's elation faded, faced with the difficulty of catching Mrs Evans out.

'You said Mrs Evans passed the coupons to Mr Walker inside a book,' Evie said, looking thoughtful. 'Do you think they use that method every time? If so, perhaps you can intercept it in front of witnesses.'

'Of course.' It dawned on May that she had seen Mrs Evans hand Arnold Walker books more than once. 'I can't believe I'd forgotten, but I saw Mrs Evans give Mr Walker a book in church, too.' She chewed her lip. 'The problem is, how do we discover in advance when they're going to make an exchange?'

'I suppose Mrs Evans must send him a letter,' Jess supplied. 'Telling Mr Walker when to collect the book.'

'Letters!' May thumped the arm of her chair in triumph. 'Peggy said she was only allowed out to deliver messages. I bet Mrs Evans uses her to deliver letters to Mr Walker. If we can get Peggy to let us see one first, we'll know when she's going to hand over the next batch of coupons.'

'You're a genius, May,' said Jess. 'I'd bet anything you're right.'

May could hardly believe they'd finally hit upon a solution. 'Then all we have to do is tell Peggy.'

—

Maybe Jess was sickening for something. May watched her friend as they cycled into the village the next morning, their breath forming puffs of sparkling vapour in the freezing air. The more animated May had become, thrilled that they at last had a plan that might free Peggy from Mrs Evans, the more subdued Jess had appeared. Come to think of it, she had been quieter than usual for the past week. Remembering Jess's forced cheer during the carol singing and her reluctance to talk about Milan, May was convinced she knew the reason. With all that had happened over the past week, May had forgotten to ask Jess about Milan. Now she felt guilty for neglecting her friend when Jess had done so much for her.

It was impossible to talk while they were cycling. Not privately, anyway. But once they had propped their bikes up behind the village hall and were strolling towards the haberdashery, May asked tentatively, 'Is everything all right, Jess? You haven't been yourself recently.'

Jess gave a weak smile. 'I'm fine. Just a little sad to be leaving all this behind. We won't have another billet like High Chalk House.'

A few weeks ago, May would have accepted the explanation, even if she hadn't believed it. But May had extricated herself from her father and had even dared to reach out to Peter. It was clear Jess needed help, and May refused to let her down. 'That's not all, Jess. What are you hiding?' She tugged Jess to a standstill and forced her to return May's gaze. 'It's Milan, isn't it? If he's hurt you, I'll—'

Jess pulled May into a hug. 'You're a brick, May, do you know that?'

Really worried now, May pulled away from the hug and took both of Jess's hands. 'Please tell me what's wrong. You've been so much help to me. You literally saved me, you and Evie. You know I'll do anything for you in return.'

Jess released a breath, a soul-weary sigh. 'Milan didn't hurt me. He's a good, kind man who doesn't deserve me. It's me who hurt him. When I told him I might be leaving, he wanted to keep in contact with me, but I said it was best if we went our separate ways.'

'Why?'

Jess suddenly seemed to notice a loose thread hanging from one of her sleeves. She picked at it while replying. 'It's better this way. I'm not right for him. When he finds out I – well—' Jess put on a smile that was too bright and didn't reach her eyes '—you know me, I like to play the field. Milan is so serious, talks about love and wanting to settle down. I don't want that. It's not fair to keep him dangling when we want completely different things.'

Jess snapped the thread, brushed it from her sleeve then took a step towards the haberdashery. 'Anyway, what's done is done. I'll miss him, but it's not the end of the world. Plenty more pilots where we're going, I'm sure.'

May knew there would be no forcing the truth from her. And she couldn't deny Milan had always seemed the more keen of the pair. Maybe it would have been unfair of Jess if she'd left letting Milan think they still had a chance to be together. However she couldn't forget that look of utter desolation she had seen at the rehearsal.

They approached the gate where they had seen Peggy the day before, taking care to keep out of sight from anyone in the haberdashery. They had no wish to be seen by Mrs Evans.

May peered through the gate and into the yard. There was Peggy, not huddled up on the step this time, but kneeling next to it, scrubbing brush in hand and bucket of soapy water beside her. Her knuckles were cracked and reddened from the cold. She scrubbed the step with listless strokes.

'Peggy!' May hissed.

The scrubbing brush stilled. Peggy's pale face turned. 'Oh, it's you.' Peggy leaned towards the open door as though listening. 'You can't stay. Mrs Evans will be out to check on my work in a minute.'

'This won't take long.'

After another glance through the door, Peggy dropped the brush and approached the gate, wiping her wet hands on her greying apron. 'I've already apologised for not telling her about the pantomime,' she said. 'Mrs Evans told me I can go.'

May, conscious that Mrs Evans could appear any moment, lowered her voice. 'That's wonderful. But we think we can prove Mrs Evans is involved in fraud. If so, we'll be able to get you away from here. Does Mr Walker often come into the shop to collect a book?'

Her brow wrinkled, Peggy said, 'Yes. She and her friends belong to some kind of reading circle. Mrs Walker can't get out much so they lend her books.'

May's heart sped up. 'Does Mrs Evans send a message to Mr Walker when she has a book to collect?'

Peggy nodded. 'She sends me.' She tapped the pocket of her apron. 'I've got a message here. I have to take it round when I've finished the step.'

May could hardly believe her ears. But then she heard something that sent chills down her spine. Footsteps approached from within the house, and Mrs Evans voice called, 'What are you doing, girl? Haven't you finished that step yet?'

Peggy went white; before she could dash back to her task, May hissed, 'Quick. Give us the letter. We'll take it.'

Peggy whipped the envelope from her pocket and thrust it through the gaps in the wrought iron gate and into May's hands. Then she flung herself back upon the scrubbing brush.

May tucked the letter into her pocket then grabbed Jess's arm and pulled her away from the gate. As they walked off, doing their best to look like casual passers-by, May heard Mrs Evans' voice. 'Hurry up, girl. I want you to take that message to the Walkers.'

Once they were clear of the shop, May drew the letter from her pocket. It was just a folded piece of paper with Mr Walker's name on the outside. 'Christmas Eve,' she said to Jess after a quick glance around to make sure no one was within earshot. 'She says she can lend Mrs Walker her copy of *Devil's Cub* by Georgette Heyer if he collects it from the shop at midday on Christmas Eve.'

They made a careful note of the time and the title of the book, then paid a passing lad sixpence to deliver the note to the Walkers' cottage. The last thing they needed was to be seen delivering the note themselves.

That done, they set out to find Evie. They didn't have to go as far as the Horse and Groom; as they walked past the village green, they saw her by the pond, watching the ducks waddling across the ice. May, bursting with excitement at their discovery, poured out their news.

'That's marvellous,' Evie said. 'What are you going to do?'

All sorts of wild scenarios flitted through May's mind. They could set a watch on the shop, waiting for Mrs Evans to hand over the book to Mr Walker, catching them red-handed. And then what? It would still be their word against Mrs Evans'. No, there was only one sensible course of action, much as she wished they could be the ones to catch her and see the look on her face when she realised the game was up. 'We have to take this to the police.'

Chapter Twenty-Two

There was a tiny police station in Amberton. It was really just a single room in the cottage used by the one and only police constable in the village. PC Tully was a portly man with a ruddy face who could be seen walking the streets of Amberton, exchanging jovial greetings with the locals. He didn't inspire May with confidence, who would have rather given the information to a younger, more energetic policeman. The trouble was, most of those were now in the services.

However, she needn't have worried. PC Tully, it appeared, had been aware of a black market trade operating in West Sussex, and was only too pleased to ring through to his superiors to report a lead. May was obliged to repeat the whole report over the phone to a Chief Inspector Franklin of the CID.

'Leave it with us, miss,' Franklin said. 'I'll send a couple of officers to watch the shop and apprehend the perpetrators once they've witnessed the handover.'

'But what about the child, Peggy? She's an evacuee being fostered with Mrs Evans.'

'We'll find her temporary accommodation until a new foster family can be arranged.'

May had to be content with that. However, as she left the station, she went cold, remembering Flight Officer Payne's orders about not interfering with village concerns.

305

She could only pray that the police found proof of Mrs Evans' wrongdoing, otherwise she was going to wind up in deep trouble.

–

The rest of the day passed in a blur, so busy that May managed to forget her worries. Most of it was spent at the village hall, arranging everything for the pantomime. While they weren't doing any more rehearsals with the children, Jess had arranged to go over a few more scenes with the adult cast at different times throughout the day. These were mainly to correct problems with props that they had noticed in the dress rehearsal and to cover the scenes that had been disrupted by Mrs Evans' interruption. May watched Jess and Milan carefully when he arrived to rehearse a kitchen scene between Cinderella and the ugly sisters. Although he seemed to avoid Jess's gaze at times, he appeared his usual self and was polite and calm when he spoke to her. If anything, it was Jess who seemed more embarrassed at being in the same room. Maybe Milan wasn't as heartbroken as May had thought he would be. If so, Jess had probably made the right decision.

The next day was Christmas Eve. There was no rehearsal, Jess having declared that the actors needed a day's break to deliver a fresh performance on Christmas Day. Although Jess was excused from duty, May was on standby all day in case any pilots needed collecting. Thankfully they all returned safely from each patrol, so May had nothing more onerous to do than checking her car's oil and tyres.

Just before lunch, she was summoned to see Flight Officer Payne. She made her way to Payne's office on shaky legs. This had to be about her report to the police.

May felt sick. What if the police had confiscated the book only to find there was nothing hidden in the pages? What if they had complained to Payne about her? She would find herself spending Christmas Day scrubbing the cookhouse floor with a toothbrush, and she could forget about the pantomime. She could forget about Cranwell. She could forget about any chance of promotion ever again.

She had to pause outside Payne's office to compose herself and wipe damp palms on her skirt before knocking. Her ears were buzzing so loudly she nearly missed the call to enter. Feeling giddy and sick, she opened the door and stood to attention in front of Payne's desk and saluted.

'At ease, Lidford.'

May relaxed her stance and fixed her gaze on a point just over Flight Officer Payne's left shoulder, concentrating on keeping her features composed.

Payne was reading something on a sheet of paper. May itched to know what it said, but resolutely kept her chin up and her gaze fixed on a note pinned to the noticeboard behind the desk. There was a silence so profound, May could hear the faint tick of Payne's wristwatch.

'I see you've still been pursuing your vendetta against the owner of Evans' Haberdashery, despite my warning to stay out of village affairs.'

'Not a vendetta, ma'am. A concern.' If it hadn't been for all Jess's help with acting, May would never have been able to answer Payne back, but as she was already in trouble she was going to make sure she was punished for what had actually happened.

'I see.' Payne placed another sheet of paper on top of the one she had been reading. May's heart sank. The complaint covered more than one page? 'You might be interested to hear that the police spent this morning watching the haberdashery, following a report from you and another WAAF about ration fraud.'

'Yes, ma'am.' What had happened? Why did Payne have to drag this out? Couldn't she just tell May she had sent the police on a wild goose chase and dole out her punishment?

'At midday, Mrs Evans handed a Georgette Heyer book to a Mr Arnold Walker.' Another maddening pause. May said nothing, knowing Payne was enjoying dragging this out. She wouldn't give her the pleasure of seeing May's agitation.

'The police apprehended Mr Walker and confiscated the book.' At least May could take comfort from knowing the police had taken her report seriously.

Payne picked up a third sheet of paper. 'When the police examined the book, they found ration coupons from three separate children.'

'Three?' In her surprise, May couldn't keep quiet. 'Who— how— I mean, where from?'

'It appears that Mrs Evans has links with other women around the area who are taking rations from the evacuee children they are hosting. When interviewed by the police she fell over herself to name the other women involved.'

'And she was giving them to Mr Walker?' In her desperate need to know more, May forgot to call Payne 'ma'am', but Payne didn't seem to object.

'The police are searching his house and office as we speak. In the meantime, they wished to pass on their thanks to you and your friend Halloway for uncovering what looks like a major fraud.'

May felt weak with relief. 'Thank you, ma'am.' But there was one other thing she was burning to know. 'Do you know what's going to happen to the evacuee Mrs Evans was hosting – Peggy Hardy?'

Payne's face softened. 'The vicar's wife, Mrs Grey, has offered to take her in for now.'

'Oh, that is good news. Thank you, ma'am.'

Payne gave her a broad smile. 'Thank *you*, Lidford. There are times you have to use your own judgement and follow your instincts. By continuing to follow your suspicions, you showed excellent judgement and, I might add, leadership.'

'I was worried about Peggy, ma'am. That's all.'

'You were prepared to stick your neck out for her. Not many people would do that, especially after being warned by their superior officer not to interfere. In short, you behaved like an officer. I shall be putting in a recommendation that you be fast-tracked to an officer's role if you do well on the course.'

May's first thought when she woke on Christmas morning was of Peter. Would he come to the pantomime? The way she had treated him, she wouldn't blame him for staying away. She didn't have time to brood, however, for Jess bounded out of bed.

'It's today! Happy Christmas, May!' Jess certainly seemed to have recovered her spirits.

May beamed back at her. This was her first Christmas with friends, and she was going to enjoy every minute of it, whether or not she saw Peter. She'd been looking forward to this day for weeks.

'Happy Christmas, Jess.' She rummaged in her bedside locker for Jess's present. Her fingers closed over the little parcel and she handed it to Jess. 'I couldn't get any wrapping paper, so used newspaper. I hope you like it.'

'I know I'll love it,' said Jess. She took the present and put it to her nose, breathing deeply. 'I smell roses,' she said with a smile. 'If this is what I think it is, then thank you. I'm down to my last sliver!' She then handed May a small flat box also wrapped in newspaper. 'This is for you. Happy Christmas.'

There came the sound of ripping paper. Jess gave a crow of delight when she saw a large bar of rose-scented soap. 'Where did you get this? I thought I was going to have to resort to coal tar soap after my bar runs out.'

'Chichester. I had half an hour to spare when I was waiting to collect a group of recruits from the station. I found a chemist that had just got a fresh stock in. I bought some for Evie as well.'

'Go on. Open yours.'

May resumed unwrapping her gift and found a pretty little box of rouge, complete with mirror in the lid. 'Thank you. It's lovely.' She gazed doubtfully at the rouge, wondering if she'd be brave enough to wear it. She already felt very daring whenever she wore the lipstick Jess had persuaded her to buy in Brighton.

Jess must have interpreted her expression. 'I'll show you how to put it on. It's the perfect colour for you.'

Once they were dressed, Jess showed May how to blend a little of the rouge along her cheekbones. May turned her face this way and that as she examined it in the mirror.

'You see how it emphasises your cheekbones? You're a true knock-out. A pity you have to wear your hair tied back to play Prince Charming, but I'll brush it out for you after the performance. Everyone will wonder when Katharine Hepburn joined the WAAF!'

May had to admit she liked the effect. She found herself wondering what Peter would think. No. She wouldn't think of Peter. He probably wouldn't come.

Once they were dressed they dashed into the village to meet Evie and then they went to the village hall to set up for the performance. As soon as they stepped through the doors and May saw the stage with its forest backdrop, all ready for the first scene, she felt the first twinges of nerves. They laid out the make-up and had all the costumes hung up in the appropriate changing rooms arranged in the order they were to be worn. There was less to do than they had thought, so when Mrs Grey breezed in after the morning service and invited May, Jess and Evie to an early Christmas dinner, they accepted with pleasure.

When they walked through the door at the vicarage, there was a cry of joy, and Peggy bounded down the stairs and flung herself into May's arms. May staggered back and then hugged her, laughing.

'Thank you!' Peggy cried. 'I never thought I was going to leave Mrs Evans. I wouldn't have done if it hadn't been for you.'

'I'm so glad.' May felt a sudden tightness in her throat. Whatever happened with Peter, at least she could leave Amberton secure in the knowledge that Peggy was well cared for. 'It's Mrs Grey you have to thank for taking you in.'

'Wait – you haven't heard the best news yet. Davey's going to stay here as well. We'll be together.'

'That's wonderful.'

Mrs Grey patted Peggy's shoulder. 'I was so sad to see the two of you split up. I'm only too happy to have him here.' She looked up at May. 'The mother of the two children who were here before has moved from Coventry to Shropshire. She came to collect them. I was sad to see them go, but it means I can take both Peggy and Davey now.'

Peggy was bouncing up and down. 'Mr and Mrs Bowes are bringing him to the pantomime, then he's coming here to stay for good.'

The meal was served promptly at noon. 'Early for Christmas dinner, but it gives us plenty of time to enjoy it before we have to be at the village hall,' Mrs Grey said. It was the best meal May had ever had. The roast chicken was small, but more than made up for with an abundance of vegetables grown in the vicarage garden. Best of all were the roast parsnips, sweet and crunchy.

All too soon it was time to get ready for the performance. They hurried down the frosty paths to the hall. Peggy was already in her dress, which Mrs Grey had pressed for the occasion. May and Jess hurried into their costumes so they would be able to help the other children dress when they arrived. There was no need for greasepaint, as there wasn't proper stage lighting, but they had scrounged make-up from their sister WAAFs and made up their faces with that. Once May was in her hunting costume, acutely aware of her legs in the close-fitting tights, Jess tied her hair back into a plait that reached down to her shoulder blades. Then she made up May's face. She applied powder and used a pencil to emphasise her eyebrows. When May looked in the mirror she was startled by the Amazon warrioress gazing back at her.

All too soon, the children and other cast members arrived. May forgot her nerves in the flurry of helping children into their costumes and making sure all the props were ready for each scene.

At three o'clock, the whole cast gathered around the wireless set that Mrs Grey had brought across from the vicarage, and they listened to King George's Christmas Address. May felt Jess clasp her hand and squeeze when the king said, 'It is, above all, children's day, and I am sure that we shall all do our best to make it a happy one for them wherever they may be.'

May felt tears well up; she tried to blink them away, knowing Jess would scold her if her make-up needed redoing. When she glanced at Jess, she saw tears in her friend's eyes as well. Jess slung an arm around her shoulders, whispering, 'You certainly have. I'm proud of you, May.'

May couldn't hold back the tears then, dabbing at them with her sleeve as the king went on to praise all the nations and organisations that had rallied around to open their doors to children needing a safe haven. And when he spoke of a new unity among neighbours and comrades, May looked at Jess and Evie, hoping they could tell from her smile how glad she was to have two such true friends.

At the close of his speech, the king spoke of their fighting men, and May's thoughts turned to Peter. Would he come? And if he did, what would she say?

Chapter Twenty-Three

All too soon, May heard the creak of the hall door swinging open followed by the tramp of many feet and the babble of eager voices. May, who was arranging the plants on stage behind the closed curtains, couldn't resist peering through. She was stunned at the number of people filing into their seats, clutching the programmes. The gnawing fear, which had subsided while listening to the king's speech, now returned in full force. She had never imagined so many people would want to watch their little pantomime.

Then she felt a hand on her arm and she turned to see Jess in her Cinderella rags. Her eyes were shining. 'I never imagined so many people would want to come.' It echoed her own thoughts precisely, only with a very different emotion. 'We're going to give them a Christmas they'll never forget.'

Oddly, those words helped calm May a little. She thought of all the hardships the villagers had endured – the bombings; rationing; losing loved ones. They deserved a chance to forget their worries for a while.

As though reading her mind, Jess squeezed May's arm and said, 'You can do this, May. This is nothing compared to what you've already achieved. You can bring a little joy into the village this afternoon.'

May nodded and drew a deep breath. Jess was right. She had done this over and over in rehearsal. Everyone in the audience was here for fun, not to criticise.

'Can you see Evie and Alex?' Jess asked. 'And what about Peter? Is he here yet?'

May looked out through the tiny gap in the heavy red curtains. There was Davey, sitting at the front with Mr and Mrs Bowes and the other boys he'd been staying with. He gazed up at the stage, his face alight with expectation. Many other evacuees were there, and May was determined to do her best to ensure they enjoyed the day. Further back, she could see Evie and Alex. They were holding hands, and Evie rested her head on Alex's shoulder. The sight brought tears of happiness to May's eyes. There was Mrs Grey sat at the piano, waiting for Jess's signal to start playing.

But there was no sign of Peter. No matter how May searched the faces of the audience, she couldn't spot his kind, handsome face.

Jess pulled her away from the curtain. 'He'll be here,' she murmured. 'I know it.' She pulled them to the side of the stage. 'Time to take our places.'

It was for the best that Peter wasn't here. It would distract her, knowing he was watching. This way she could keep a clear head for the performance and help make this a special day for the children and the whole village. As four o'clock approached, an expectant hush fell over the audience. Jess, after checking everyone was in position, turned off the lights in the main hall and switched on the stage lights. This was the signal for Mrs Grey to start playing. She struck up the opening song.

The stage hands drew back the curtains and May felt a thrill when the audience gasped at the beautiful woodland scene. Then Cinderella ran onto the stage accompanied by the children, and the pantomime had begun. May was so lost in the performance that she bounded onto the stage when the hunting horn sounded without a thought. Her nerves melted away as she accused Cinderella of ruining the hunt, and hearing children's laughter over the antics of the stag gave her a thrill of delight. The evacuees' enjoyment more than made up for the weeks of hard work and worry.

Before she knew it, she was delivering her parting shot, and the line she had always found difficult, where her anger became attraction. Her movements had become second nature. She paced to the front of the stage, facing the audience. Thankfully they were in darkness, so she could only see vague outlines. She fixed her eyes on the spot where she knew Evie was sitting, instinctively seeking out a friendly face. 'You dare defy me, when you're...' May's attention was drawn by a flare of orange light in the audience. A man in the row in front of Evie was lighting a cigarette. The glow from his lighter briefly lit the face of the man beside Alex. There was no mistaking the cleft chin or the laughter lines around mouth and eyes. It was a face etched onto May's heart. Peter.

Time seemed to slow down. Her heart full of love and hope, she turned to Jess to deliver the rest of her line. 'You're just a servant girl.' She knew from the fractional widening of Jess's eyes that she had finally got the delivery just right. All it had taken was Peter's presence. She exited the stage, hoping the audience couldn't see her legs tremble.

She changed into the costume she would be wearing for the rest of the play hardly aware of what was going on around her. Then Jess, the children, Milan and Jiří exited and the stage hands dashed on to switch the scene to the kitchen.

Jess grasped her shoulders. 'You were wonderful, May. That last line – perfect!'

'Peter's here.' It was all May could say. It was her only coherent thought.

Jess patted her shoulder. 'Then knock him dead. And don't worry. He'll never be able to say no to you after seeing you in those tights and boots.' Then she cocked her head, looking May up and down. 'And he'll enjoy seeing you in this outfit, too.'

May felt her face burn. This suit was straight out of the costume box and fitted her to perfection. It consisted of a long white shirt with a fitted brocade waistcoat over the top. Jess had taken in the waist, giving May curves she'd never known she possessed. She also wore tight-fitting knee breeches over thick white stockings and satin pumps. Until today, Peter had only seen her in skirts and dresses. Now she was very conscious of her long legs and prayed she didn't trip over them and make a fool of herself.

'Please will one of you help with my hair?' It was Milan, holding the towering wig he was supposed to wear as the Ugly Sister.

'I'll do it,' May said hastily, not wanting to make Jess feel awkward about seeing Milan. 'Anyway, you should be on stage, Jess.'

Jess gave a little yelp and ran onto the stage, grabbed her broomstick and took her place. A moment later, Flight Officer Jean Ellerby swept on stage to take her position by the large fireplace that had been expertly painted on the backdrop. The curtains swung open and Jess started to sweep while Jean Ellerby, playing the stepmother, issued a stream of impossible instructions. Things like making a pigeon pie with no pigeons or pastry, dusting the shelves without making the duster dirty and washing clothes without getting them wet.

May half listened to the dialogue while she turned to Milan to fix his wig.

She had just finished when Buttons made his appearance. Soon after, the ugly sisters, Turpentina and Kerosina, entered. May listened to the laughter of the audience and knew it was going well. She peered out from the side of the curtain, looking for Peter. There he was, sitting next to Evie, laughing and clapping with the rest. Was it her imagination, or was he looking into the wings more than at the action on stage? Then he seemed to look right at her. May dropped the curtain as though it burned and sprang back into the shadows. She had to put him out of her mind for now, or she would never get through to the end of the pantomime.

She went to get Jess's ball gown ready for the transformation scene. There wouldn't be much time to get her into it, so she needed to be prepared. But all the while she ran through her mind what she should say to Peter.

Then time seemed to rush ahead. She was watching the fairy godmother run on stage. Then she was helping Jess into the voluminous ballgown of cream parachute silk. A moment later she was striding on stage as Prince Charming, fighting off the advances of the ugly sisters. What seemed like mere seconds later, she was in the kitchen with Jess as Cinderella trying on the 'glass' slipper and then the whole cast was on stage singing the closing song. The audience clapped and cheered but May could only gaze out at Peter's face as he smiled at her from the audience.

Then the curtain came down, and May dashed off stage. She had a sudden horror that Peter would leave without saying goodbye. She didn't wait to get changed, but flew down the steps, only to run straight into Peter himself. After a whole day spent in agonising anticipation of this moment, it took the solidity of his chest to convince her she wasn't dreaming and he really stood there. He had his greatcoat draped over one arm. Please don't let him be leaving.

'Don't go,' she said.

At the same time, Peter said, 'I was coming to see you.'

There was an awkward pause, then May gave a nervous laugh. Courage. That's what she needed. She could almost hear Jess saying, 'How much more courage do you need? You rescued Peggy from that cow of a woman and just pulled off a magnificent performance, even though you were terrified of the mere prospect a few weeks ago.'

She could do this. Drawing a shaky breath, May said, 'Thank you for coming. I wanted to talk to you.' She looked around the room, seeking a quiet corner where they could talk. But the villagers were still milling around, wishing each other a cheery 'Merry Christmas' and putting money into the collection tin. The children were gathered under the tree, opening presents the village had collected for them and eating the treats that people had pooled their rations to provide. There would be nowhere backstage, as all the cast would be changing out of their costumes, removing make-up and clearing the props.

'Let's go outside,' Peter said.

He didn't make any move to hold her hand as they walked through the hall in silence and through the blackout curtain and out the door. It was now fully dark and a blast of cold air made May gasp, reminding her she still only wore the light shirt and waistcoat she had worn on stage. The chill tore through her stockings and the flimsy breeches. Then something heavy and warm settled over her shoulders – Peter's greatcoat. May hugged it around her, relishing its warmth and breathing in the faint scent that clung to it of coal tar soap and cigarette smoke.

They walked around the side of the hall, away from audience members who were now drifting out in groups.

'What did you want to say?' Peter asked. His tone wasn't unfriendly, but there was a noticeable lack of the warmth she usually heard when he spoke to her.

Her heart sank. He hadn't come to win her back. He had come for an explanation and a goodbye.

But she had come too far to let him go without a fight. 'I wanted to apologise,' she said. And her usually hesitant words came to her with ease. 'I was frightened when I wrote that letter. I love you so much, but I was terrified I would lose myself in us.'

She didn't dare look at him in case she saw nothing but rejection in his expression. Instead she gazed up at the stars, frost-bright in the midnight blue sky, blinking away the tears that threatened to fall.

'It didn't occur to you to talk to me about how you felt?' Peter said. May couldn't see his face, but she imagined it was twisted in a scowl. 'Can you imagine how it felt to get that letter out of the blue? You should have spoken to me.'

'I know. I've hated myself ever since, and I know you must hate me. It was cowardly. I'm sorry.'

'I don't hate you.'

And the words were spoken with such gentleness, May dared to look at him. 'You – you don't?'

He shook his head. 'I could never hate you.'

Hope blossomed. 'Even though I hurt you?'

The thin crescent moon gave just enough light to show his gentle smile. 'As much as it hurt, I understand why you did it.'

'I'm not sure *I* can. I was such a coward, but I couldn't see any other way out.'

Peter frowned. 'You're too hard on yourself. And you're not the only one to blame. I've thought a lot about what you said in your letter, and I'm mortified that I didn't listen to you.'

'I was frightened,' May whispered, hardly daring to believe Peter was being so understanding. Her heart hammered as the words came tumbling out. 'You can't know how it felt to see my mother fade away day by day, unable to make her own wishes heard. I was so afraid of becoming like her, never able to speak up for myself. I should have known you were nothing like my father – I *did* know – but I was terrified I was too weak to ever be an equal partner in a relationship.'

'You're not weak. I've always admired your strength. Your resilience.' Peter took her cold hands between his strong, warm ones, and all she could see was the glitter of his eyes as he gazed at her. 'I know how you've struggled to free yourself from your father's shadow, how hard it's been to find your voice. But you *have* found it, and I love you for it.'

He still loved her? She tried to say she loved him too, but a sob choked off the words.

Peter continued. 'Evie told me all about your efforts to free Peggy from a cruel foster mother. The whole village is talking about how you didn't give up when others tried to make you stop. You've shown more resilience than most people I know. Do you still doubt your ability to speak up for yourself?'

She managed to gasp, 'No. That's why...' She had to be brave. There could be no hesitation. She took Peter's hand then leaned forward and kissed him on the mouth. Oh, how she had missed him, missed the feel of his lips on hers. To her joy, he didn't pull away but reached under the greatcoat and drew her close.

She only broke the kiss when she needed to catch her breath. She leaned her head against his shoulder.

'I love you, May,' Peter murmured.

More tears welled, but this time they were of relief and happiness. 'I love you, too. Does this mean you'll forgive me?'

'On one condition.'

May drew back, frowning. 'What?'

'That you forgive me in return. I've been so concerned with fitting in to the expectation of an RAF officer that I placed my anxieties on you. I discouraged you from speaking up and I'm sorry. In future I promise to respect your concerns.'

May felt a heavy weight lift from her shoulders. 'I know you respect me. I wouldn't love you so much if you didn't.'

There was another lengthy pause while Peter kissed her. After a time, he said, 'Does this mean my visits to High Chalk House are back on?'

May gasped. 'Oh! I forgot you didn't know. I'm leaving.' In a breathless voice she explained about the course.

To her relief, Peter pulled her closer. 'That's wonderful. You deserve this chance. I know you'll do well. It doesn't matter where you end up, I'll be thinking of you always.' He leaned in for another kiss.

When May was quite breathless, Peter rested his brow upon hers. 'It doesn't matter how far apart we are, I'll never stop loving you. And at the end of all this madness, I hope you'll agree to marry me.'

May thought her heart might burst from happiness. Too overwhelmed to speak, she could only nod and beam at Peter through the sudden spill of tears. Then they were kissing again, and the world beyond the circle of Peter's arms faded away.

Several minutes later, May was dimly aware of the sound of running feet. 'I'm sure I saw May leave the hall. She must be out here somewhere.' It was Jess's voice.

Peter drew away with a soft laugh. 'Maybe we should return to our friends before they call the police.'

May leaned in for another kiss. 'Let them wait.'

–

'Ready?'

May glanced at Jess and nodded. She picked up her kit bag and, after a last look around the nursery to make sure they hadn't left anything, she walked through to the schoolroom. 'I'm going to miss this place,' she said, patting the back of her favourite armchair. How many nights had she, Jess and Evie spent there, drinking cocoa, encouraging one another, laughing, crying? This was the room where she had first learnt what it was like to have friends.

'I know.' Jess did a slow turn, taking in the room one last time. As she did so, there came the roar of aero engines outside as two or three Hurricanes skimmed the roof of High Chalk House and glided towards the airfield, making the sash windows rattle. 'I'm even going to miss the sound of the Hurricanes,' she said. 'It's always a comfort to hear our lads come safely home.'

They both watched as the Hurricanes made a perfect landing. 'There will be plenty of aircraft where we're going,' May said.

'I know, but it won't be the same.' She didn't say so, but May knew she was thinking of Milan.

'Do you regret leaving?' she asked.

'No.' Jess was definite. 'This is the right thing for both of us. We'll have a whale of a time, just you wait, May Lidford.'

There was a soft knock on the schoolroom door and a young WAAF stuck her head around the door jamb. May recognised her as one of the new drivers. 'Your transport's here.'

They thanked the girl then, taking a deep breath, May said, 'Come on. Missing the train won't create a good first impression.'

Shouldering their bags, they descended the stairs, walked through the kitchen and out the back door for the last time.

'Goodbye, High Chalk House,' May said. It felt like she was saying goodbye to her first real home.

It was odd to be driven instead of being the driver. May slung her kit bag and gas mask into the back of the truck then scrambled in, Jess following. Then it struck her afresh that if she passed the course, her days as a driver were over.

With a jolt that made May clutch at her seat, the truck took off in a spray of gravel. She looked out of the back as the truck shot down the lanes, and May said goodbye to each tree, each familiar view as they sped by. Then they were passing the gates of the RAF base. Jess leaned out and waved at the guards. 'Goodbye, Amberton!'

May said her own silent goodbye. Then as the airfield dwindled into the distance, she allowed herself to look forward to what lay ahead.

Jess was obviously thinking along the same lines. 'There will be other stations, other Waaferies. And plenty more adventures for you and me, you mark my words.'

May turned her back on Amberton, feeling the first thrill of excitement. There would be new friends, too, although she would always treasure her friendship with Jess and Evie above all. They had befriended the shy, gawky girl May had been and encouraged her to blossom into a more confident young woman. Above all, there was Peter. Wherever she went, their love for each other would be a constant.

She grinned at Jess. 'Here's to new adventures.'